TALES OF MYSTERY & THE SUPERNATURAL

General Editor: David Stuart Davies

CRIME SCENES

*A collection of modern
mystery stories*

Crime Scenes

*A collection of modern
mystery stories*

*Selected and introduced
by David Stuart Davies*

WORDSWORTH EDITIONS

In loving memory of
MICHAEL TRAYLER
the founder of Wordsworth Editions

1

Readers who are interested in other titles from
Wordsworth Editions are invited to visit our website at
www.wordsworth-editions.com

For our latest list and a full mail-order service contact
Bibliophile Books, Unit 5 Datapoint,
South Crescent, London E16 4TL
Tel: +44 020 74 74 24 74
Fax: +44 020 74 74 85 89
orders@bibliophilebooks.com
www.bibliophilebooks.com

This edition published 2008 by
Wordsworth Editions Limited
8B East Street, Ware, Hertfordshire SG12 9HJ

ISBN 978 1 84022 093 3

© Wordsworth Editions Limited 2008

Wordsworth® is a registered trademark of
Wordsworth Editions Limited

Typeset in Great Britain by Roperford Editorial
Printed by Clays Ltd, St Ives plc

CONTENTS

*To friends and colleagues in the
Crime Writers' Association*

INTRODUCTION

In the twenty-first century, crime fiction, or mystery fiction as the Americans refer to the genre, has become a very large umbrella under which shelter all kinds, shades and complexions of crime narratives from the time-honoured whodunit to the psychological chiller to the history mystery to the crime procedural to the noir thriller to the gangster epic . . . and so on. Like Topsy, in *Uncle Tom's Cabin*, the genre has 'just growed'. In simple terms the crime story has developed and matured over the last two hundred years or so.

In fact, there is a case to be made that much of fiction is actually crime fiction. There are mysterious murders and deaths and other nefarious deeds in most novels and plays, but to be fair these crimes are not the focus and the *raison d'être* of the narrative. The crime story propels the reader into turning the page in order to find out how the criminal complications embedded in the plot will be resolved: whether, for example, it be how Hercule Poirot will solve the case in his usual brilliant way, or whether Hannibal Lecter's evil machinations will succeed.

It is difficult to pin down the early history of crime fiction, or more particularly detective fiction. Aspects of the genre can be found in the words of ancient writings. A case has been made that Sophocles' play *Oedipus the King* (circa 430 BC) contains elements of the crime fiction genre in that it deals with an attempt to discover the identity of a murderer, which is raised as a central problem at the beginning of the drama and solved in a most dramatic fashion at the end. Oedipus, determined to discover who killed his wife's first husband, spends a great deal of the play in this inquiry, until a final interrogation of a shepherd reveals the horrible truth: Oedipus himself is the murderer. Dramatic events are further heightened by the fact that unknown to him the murdered man was his father and therefore he has unwittingly married his mother.

Since tales have been written down there have been many instances of mysteries presented to the reader and then solved in an ingenious manner, and so in essence crime fiction in has been with us for centuries. However it was only in the nineteenth century that the genre came to be structured and formalised and given an identity of its own. This was largely due to Edgar Allan Poe, the strange, morbidly obsessed American writer, who is now regarded as the father of the modern detective story. In five tales, published in the first half of the nineteenth century, 'The Murders in the Rue Morgue', 'The Purloined Letter', 'The Mystery of Marie Roget', 'Thou Art the Man' and 'The Gold Bug', Poe laid out and clarified most of the ground rules. The first three stories feature C. Auguste Dupin, a brilliant private detective residing in Paris. His activities are recorded by an unnamed chronicler, an admiring and somewhat slow-witted fellow – a character we now refer to as the Watson figure. Dupin is not only brilliant and disdainful of the official police, he is also eccentric. He shuns daylight and lives behind closed shutters, his room illuminated only by 'a couple of tapers which, strongly perfumed, threw out only the ghastliest and feeblest of rays'. Like a sleuthing vampire, he takes to the streets at night to enjoy the 'infinity of mental excitement.' He is also given to astounding his companion by reading his thought processes. Arthur Conan Doyle, who developed and enhanced the character of the brilliant but idiosyncratic sleuth in the creation of Sherlock Holmes, thought Poe 'the master of all'. In his book *Through the Magic Door*, Conan Doyle was generous and admiring enough to confess:

> To Him must be ascribed the monstrous progeny of writers on the detection of crime . . . But not only is Poe the originator of the detective story; all treasure hunting, cryptogram-solving yarns trace back to his 'Gold Bug' . . .

Perhaps the most famous and certainly the grisliest of the Dupin tales is 'The Murders in the Rue Morgue'. An old woman and her daughter are found murdered in a locked room with no apparent means of entry or exit. The police are baffled. Dupin deduces and solves the mystery. This is a seminal story in crime fiction. Dorothy L. Sayers in her introduction to *The Omnibus of Crime* presented a brilliant analysis of this tale:

> [The story features] a combination of three typical motifs: the wrongly suspected man, to whom all the superficial evidence (motive, access, etc.) points; the hermetically sealed death chamber (still a favourite theme); finally the solution by unexpected

means. In addition we have Dupin drawing deductions which the police have overlooked, from evidence of witnesses (superiority in inference), and discovering clues which the police had not thought of looking for owing to obsession by an *idée fixe* (superiority in observation based on inference). In this story also are enunciated for the first time those two great aphorisms of detective science: first, that when you have eliminated all the possibilities, then whatever remains, however improbable, must be the truth; and secondly that the more *outré* a case may appear, the easier it is to solve. Indeed, take it all round, 'The Murders in the Rue Morgue' constitutes in itself almost a complete manual of detective theory and practice.

A complete manual it may have been, but it was not fully utilised until Conan Doyle created Sherlock Holmes in 1887. In the interim there had been some interesting experiments: Inspector Bucket in Charles Dickens's *Bleak House* (1853) and Sergeant Cuff in Wilkie Collins's *The Moonstone* (1868), which is perhaps the first detective novel.

And then there was Eugène Francois Vidocq (1775–1857). He was a real-life criminal who became the first chief of the French Sureté. His ghosted autobiography not only had a great influence on authors of mystery fiction in his own lifetime, but also on detective writers after his death. Staying with the French for the moment, mention must also be made of Emile Gaboriau (1832–1873), who created the detective *Monsieur Lecoq* (1869). The novel focused attention on Lecoq's gathering and interpreting of evidence in the detection of crime.

Once the success of Holmes was established, other authors were inspired either to copy or to experiment with the ingredients found in the stories. From that time onwards the reading public has been swamped with brilliant, idiosyncratic crime-solvers. At first there was a trend for writers to give their detective one very peculiar trait, a novelty element which made the character unique in some way, like the blind Max Carrados, who could make the most incredible deductions through the senses of smell, touch and hearing. Or the Crime Doctor who treated crime as a disease and approached it from a psychological angle. There were female detectives, too, like Loveday Brooke. And purely scientific ones such as Professor Van Dusen, who became known as 'The Thinking Machine'. And there were those characters who worked on the other side of the law like A. J. Raffles,

Colonel Clay and Simon Carn, the Prince of Swindlers, all in various ways echoing Conan Doyle's criminal mastermind, Professor Moriarty, Sherlock Holmes's arch-enemy.

In the early part of the twentieth century, up to the outbreak of the Second World War it seemed that to be successful and attractive to the reading public, a detective had to be an amateur or a private investigator independent of the police and other authorities. It was the great days of Dorothy L. Sayers's Lord Peter Wimsey, Agatha Christie's Hercule Poirot and Miss Marple, John Dickson Carr's Dr Fell, Margery Allingham's Albert Campion and a whole legion of independent sleuths whose adventures were greedily devoured in those difficult between the war years.

Things changed after the devastation of the 1939–1945 conflict. Gradually, policemen were featured as heroes and central characters in works of crime fiction. Writers such as John Creasey with his Inspector West, and under his pseudonym of J. J. Marric with his Gideon novels, which detail the day-to-day life of a Scotland Yard detective, Michael Innes with his career policeman Appleby and Alan Hunter's Inspector Gently novels are just a few examples of the breed that increased in number larger in the 1950s and '60s. Television helped to develop the trend and increase the public's interest in the way in which the official police force tackled crime in the modern age with programmes like *Dixon of Dock Green*, *Murder Bag*, *No Hiding Place* and later *Z Cars* and *Softly Softly*. In the 1960s, P. D. James brought us a detective who had the charisma and independence of attitude of the old-time amateur while working within the constrictions of police procedures. He was Adam Dalgleish, a poet as well as a sleuth, a wonderful blend of the charismatic investigator and the dedicated policeman. He paved the way for Colin Dexter's Inspector Morse and Ian Rankin's Inspector Rebus, both men who carved their own path and followed their personal hunches and deductions, often upsetting their superiors, and yet remaining determined policemen.

It was in the latter half of the twentieth century that more and more crime writers turned their back on modern crimes and the increasingly sophisticated scientific methods used to solve them, to create historical mysteries which did not rely on forensics, fast cars and modern communications to help catch the criminal. At the forefront of this movement was Ellis Peters, who wrote twenty novels featuring her detective Brother Cadfael, a twelfth-century Benedictine monk. Lindsey Davis created a series about Marcus Didius Falco, who solves mysteries set in ancient Rome. There are many other writers in this mould, not only presenting the reader with an engaging drama but providing a rich glimpse into another historical period.

There are those crime novels, of course, in which the detective, if there is one at all, is a very minor member of the cast list. These books – often stand-alone thrillers (i.e. not part of any series) – are character-driven, and our attention is rarely taken by who committed the crime, but rather by why, how, whether the perpetrator will get away with it and if the central character will survive. These novels engage our hearts and emotions rather than our minds. Ruth Rendell, using the pseudonym of Barbara Vine, has created a fine body of work in this particular dark glade of the genre. Her novels such as *Master of the Moor*, *The Dark-Adapted Eye* and *The Chimney Sweeper's Eye* delve deep into the psychology of individuals who have built barriers around themselves which have been breached suddenly, throwing their lives into upheaval. Minette Walters is another novelist special-ising in this psychological approach to a murder story. Rather as one casts a stone into a placid pool of water and studies the resulting ripples on the surface, she places a murder in an apparently quiet community and examines the effect it has on its inhabitants.

It is not my intention to list every subtle variant of the British crime story here. My purpose is merely to show how the form of the crime story has developed and continues to evolve. Like a brilliant diamond, it has many subtle and attractive facets.

This survey has concentrated on the British scene because the writers in this volume, with one exception, are British and nearly all are members of the Crime Writers' Association of Great Britain.

This volume brings together a fabulous group of modern crime writers, from well-established names to those currently making their reputation as masters and mistresses of their craft, as well as a few young lions whose work is sparkling with promise.

Their stories demonstrate with astounding variety and style the point that this introduction aims to make – that crime fiction comes in many packages but that they are all absorbing, ingenious and, in their own dark way, thoroughly entertaining. Start unwrapping them now.

DAVID STUART DAVIES

CRIME SCENES

*A collection of modern
mystery stories*

Under the cherry tree

NATASHA COOPER

Meg Maguire was boiling the kettle so she could make young Dr Simpson an extra cup of tea after the last of the patients had gone. He'd been looking transparent with exhaustion for days, and Meg was worried about him. The other receptionists laughed at her need to mother him and told her she ought to have more sympathy for his wife than for him. But she could see what he was going through.

Watching his clumsy movements and the sunken eyes that stared unseeingly between thick reddened lids, she could remember the desperation she'd felt in the first few weeks of her own baby's life. She knew the torture of being wrenched out of desperately needed sleep by those insistent cries that couldn't be silenced, cries that grew shriller and more urgent with every failing attempt to satisfy the unknown, unknowable, need that had set them off.

When she opened the door, she saw him slumped over his desk with his head resting on his arms, fast asleep. His tufty red hair was sticking up like a small boy's and what she could see of his face was dead white. She put the cup quietly down on the side table, where it couldn't come to any harm even if he woke with a jerk, turned out the bright overhead light, leaving just the lamp on his desk, and took away the pile of patients' notes for filing.

For the first time since she'd arrived that morning, there was peace in the waiting room. The patients had taken their fears and angers away with them and her departing colleagues had switched off the fluorescent lights that made everyone look so ghastly. Meg enjoyed winding down on her own after the frenzy of the day, getting everything tidy for the morning shift, and cross-checking all the requests for repeat prescriptions and the letters to specialists for patients who were really ill.

'Are you busy, dear?' said a hoarse voice from the shadows at the far end of the waiting room.

It was a heart-sink voice that Meg recognised and would have to acknowledge. She left the pile of filing and walked round the counter. It had been raised to shoulder height only two weeks earlier, after the youngest of the receptionists had been assaulted by a man who blamed her because the doctors had no time to see him for a week.

The old woman was sitting in her favourite chair in the corner. Her clothes were the usual collection of haphazardly mended jumble-sale rejects and her shoes were badly cracked. Her chapped lips mumbled against each other and her eyes were full of fear.

'Mrs Crane,' Meg said, making her voice even kinder than usual, 'you shouldn't be here, you know.' She squatted down so that their eyes were at the same level. 'The doctors have all gone now. Surgery's over.'

Mrs Crane lived on her own in some poverty. Meg knew that she came to the surgery for the warmth and company as much as the doctors. But she was looking more gaunt and nervous than usual.

'Aren't you well, Mrs Crane?'

One of the knotted, painful hands with their terribly swollen joints was laid on Meg's arm.

'I saw a murder done, dear. You see, I've got to tell someone.'

'I know you did,' Meg said, relieved. She patted the old woman's shoulder, and was shocked to feel the fleshlessness of her arm under the bundled clothes. 'You told me before.'

In fact she had told them all, over and over again. All the doctors and all the receptionists had heard the story. The first time it had happened, when Meg had only just started to work for the practice, they'd taken Mrs Crane seriously and called the police.

'I saw the grave dug and the body being put in.'

'I know you did. It was in the garden of the house opposite yours, wasn't it?'

Meg could remember with an almost physical squeezing in her guts the embarrassment everyone had felt in the face of the house-holders' fury when the police had ransacked their garden and found nothing. All their beautiful, carefully tended shrubs had been dug up, and the York stone paving removed, and there had been nothing underneath but the expensively fertilised soil: no body; no bones; no signs that the deep earth had ever been disturbed.

'She's been telling you stories to make herself interesting,' the inspector had told Dr Mattheson, the head of the practice at the time. 'They tend to do that, these lonely old things with no family. They need someone to pay attention to them. Though this is several stages beyond shoplifting, I must say.' He had sounded surprisingly tolerant in the circumstances. 'Humour her, if you can, and get on to Social Services if you can't. There's nothing more we can do.'

'And then the wet earth was poured back on top of the body.' Mrs Crane's tear-filled voice brought Meg back to the present.

'It must have been very frightening,' she said, trying to be as tolerant and patient as the big police officer had been all those years earlier. Any minute now her daughter would be coming to collect her, and she didn't want to hang about. Trish was going to take her out to dinner, and the table was booked for nine.

Mrs Crane was still talking about murder and bodies and the wet earth of the grave when Trish arrived. She was in her early thirties, tall and thin, with short, spiky hair and an intense bony face. Meg adored her.

'This is my daughter, Mrs Crane. I'm going to have to go now,' she said. 'You'll be all right getting home, won't you? It's not far to your flat, and it's nice and light with all the street lamps on. Shall I help you up?'

'She's a lawyer, isn't she?' Mrs Crane's sunken eyes had brightened as they focused on Trish's face. 'That's what they said yesterday. They said I ought to talk to your daughter about it, and that she'd be here tonight.'

Meg sighed and privately cursed the gossip of the other receptionists. A new audience would make it impossible to get Mrs Crane moving unil she'd told the whole mad story yet again.

'Come here, dear,' she said to Trish. 'I've got something to tell you.'

'Could you?' Meg asked. 'It won't take long. I'll file the notes and tidy up, and then we can go and eat.'

'Sure,' said Trish, as easily as though she had not been listening to sad, mad stories all day in court. She put her heavy black pilot case on the floor and pulled a chair forward so that she could sit facing the old woman. 'Now what is it that's happened, Mrs Crane?'

'I saw a muder done, dear. No one believes me. But I saw it.'

'I see,' said Trish, casting a startled glance over her shoulder.

Meg allowed her eyes to roll upwards for a second in an unmistakable signal, at the same time explaining Mrs Crane's lack of lucidity and begging for patience. Trish understood, and leaned over to pull a large, pale-blue legal pad out of her case, and a felt-tipped pen. 'Why don't you tell me all about it? Where is the grave?'

'By the cherry tree in the garden, beyond the roots, where the soil's soft and there's nothing to get in the way of the spade.'

Trish blinked. The precision of the description was surprising. From behind her Meg said patiently, 'But there aren't any cherry trees in the front gardens in Walter Street, Mrs Crane. You know that.'

The expression on the old woman's creased and whiskered face changed as Trish watched, from one of fearful confiding to something sharper, angrier almost. It seemed to Trish in that moment that Mrs Crane could not be quite as confused as she made herself appear.

'Come on, Mrs Crane,' said Meg kindly, trying as they had all tried before to bring some rationality into their dealings with her. 'You *know* there are no cherry trees in Walter Street.'

Mrs Crane's eyes watered and her tormented fingers twisted in and out of each other. Trish put one of her cool hands over them, stilling their restlessness and said quietly: 'Perhaps it wasn't in Walter Street where you saw the body being buried. Is that right?'

For a moment it looked as though Mrs Crane was going to agree, but then her eyes filled with tears and her gaze slid away from Trish's face.

'I don't remember.'

'Trish,' said her mother. 'It's getting late. I've done the filing. I think we ought to wrap this up.'

'Just a minute or two more,' said Trish, looking at her again. 'Why don't you ring the restaurant and tell them we may be late? They'll hang on to the table for us.'

'You mustn't take it too seriously,' Meg said quietly.

'Come here a minute.'

Trish told Mrs Crane that she would be back as soon as possible, which aroused a small smile, and went to join her mother, who opened the door to one of the unoccupied consulting rooms.

'Listen, Trish.' Meg shut the door. 'That poor old thing has been telling this story for ages. We've had Social Services, we've had the police, everything's been checked. There's no substance to it. She's dreamed it, or seen it on the telly.'

'I'm not so sure. I think there's more to it. Le me talk to her for a little longer. Dinner will wait for half an hour, won't it?'

Meg remembered young Doctor Simpson, who needed to be gently woken and persuaded to go home. She shrugged.

'All right. But don't let her think you've swallowed the whole idiotic tale. It'll only encourage her.'

'OK. D'you know how long she's lived in the area?'

'Not for sure,' said Meg. 'Although I vaguely remember one of the social workers saying she'd been a land girl round here in the war and stayed ever since. Could that be right?'

'She looks the right sort of age. She must be in her mid-eighties, don't you think?'

'I'll check her notes.' Meg sounded tired enough to give Trish a tweak of conscience, but parts of the story rang too true to be ignored.

'Yes, she was born in 1921, which would make her nineteen in 1940. I must go and talk to Doctor Simpson. I won't be long. See what you can do to soothe her.'

Trish went back to her chair in front of Mrs Crane. She looked as though she'd fallen asleep, but she raised her head as Trish sat down.

'You do believe me, don't you? None of the others do.'

'I do,' Trish said truthfully. 'But I don't think you saw it in Walter Street, or even in Beaconsfield. Am I right?'

There was no answer.

'Where were you living before you came here?'

Mrs Crane began to bite her lower lip.

'It was somewhere with cherry trees in the gardens, wasn't it?'

'That's right, dear,' she whispered. 'By the cherry tree, beyond the roots, where the ground's soft enough to get the spade in easily.'

'Where did the spade come from?' Trish asked in the same easy tone she had used throughout.

'From the shed.' Mrs Crane frowned as though she was surprised anyone could ask such an obvious question.

'Were you on your own when it happened?'

'Yes. Johnny was away at the war. They said he'd come marching home, but he didn't come in time, and then he was angry and he didn't want me anymore.'

Trish could feel rather than hear Meg standing behind her. But she couldn't look away from Mrs Crane.

'So it happened in the war, did it?'

'That's right, dear. In the Blitz.'

'A lot of people died then,' Trish said.

'Not like this.' Mrs Crane's eyes closed. Tears oozed out from under the lids and trickled down the slack skin of her cheeks.

'When you'd dug the soft ground beyond the roots of the cherry tree, what did you do?' Tirsh's voice was absolutely steady. She knew she could trust Meg not to intervene or do anything to distract old Mrs Crane from her confession.

'I wrapped her in her Christening dress and the blanket her gran had knitted and I put her in.' She reached forwards. Her swollen knuckles looked agonising, but Trish took both her hands and held them as lightly as she could. Mrs Crane let her eyes open.

'You know all about it, don't you, dear?

'Nearly,' said Trish. 'You'll feel better when you've told me the rest. How did it happen?'

'We were in bed. It was so cold that winter that I didn't dare leave her on her own, so I took her into my bed. And I was lonely.'

'That was sensible. Did she sleep?'

The old head shook slowly from side to side. 'Not for months. It was the bombs at first. They stopped us both sleeping. But even when they didn't come, she woke all the time. Always crying. Always hungry, and I couldn't feed her. I tried, but she wouldn't suck. I tried bottles, but she didn't like them either, and she always cried.'

Trish could hear that someone had joined Meg, someone bigger, but whoever it was had the wit to stand as still and silent as she.

'Then that night she did sleep. She'd had nearly a whole bottle and she was lying there in my bed in her flannel nightie, sucking her fists and fast asleep.'

'Didn't she wake up again?' asked Trish.

'Of course. The bombs started at eleven and she woke up and I woke up. And I lay there hating Hitler, and hating Johnny, and hating . . . '

'Your baby?'

Mrs Crane looked at Trish, who was still holding her hands, and she nodded.

'So what did you do?'

'I wouldn't have done anything if it hadn't been for the bombs. But we needed to sleep. Both of us needed it so much. You understand, don't you, dear?'

'Yes,' Trish said, releasing one of Mrs Crane's hands so that she could brush some of the wild unwashed hair away from the creased face and stroke her head. 'Yes, I do understand.'

'And so I put the pillow over her head. I wanted to keep the noise of the bombs off her. That's all. I wanted her to sleep so I could sleep.'

'Did you press too hard?'

There was another slow nod.

'And then she was dead and so you dressed her up and buried her under the cherry tree in the blackout,' Trish suggested. 'Isn't that what happened?'

'Yes. And the neighbours were mostly in the shelter so no one saw me. And next day I said I'd sent her to her gran in the country, and then I moved here to be a land girl. And I've tried to tell people, but no one's believed me. Not till now. Perhaps now I can sleep again.'

She pulled her hand away from Trish's and began the difficult business of getting to her feet.

Trish watched her for a moment, then quietly got up to face her mother and a tall, broad-shouldered man with red hair and a wounded-looking face.

'We must talk,' she said.

Yes and no

EDWARD MARSTON

'Well,' said Desmond Roe, thumping the table with a determined fist, 'that leaves us with only one option. We must get rid of him.'

'How?' asked Malcolm Willard, extending his arms in a gesture of hopelessness. 'We have no legal means of doing so.'

'Then we must adopt illegal means.'

Willard gulped. 'You mean that we disable him in some way?'

'I mean that we kill the bastard.'

'That's unthinkable!' protested Ian Voisey, flushing visibly.

Roe was adamant. 'The time has come to think the unthinkable.'

'I'm not sure about that, Desmond.'

'Do you want to let the tyranny go on as before?'

'No, no,' bleated Voisey, 'of course not.'

'Then we have to take drastic measures.'

'Nothing is more drastic than murder,' said Willard. 'And I can see that it's our last resort. But would it solve our problem? We might get rid of Horace Chesterfield, but think of the consequences.'

'The main consequence is that one of us would take over as managing director and put the company back on an even keel. That way, we'd all benefit. It's the one guarantee of survival for the company. Go on as we are and we'll all face ruin.' Roe turned to the fourth person at the table. 'What's your view, Joanna?'

'Joanna agrees with me, I'm certain,' said Voisey, jumping in before she could open her mouth. 'We'll agree to anything that will get shot of Horace Chesterfield but we draw the line at cold-blooded murder.'

'Speak for yourself, Ian,' chided Roe. 'Joanna can voice her own opinion.'

The three men turned to look at the only female member of the board of directors. Joanna Osborne was a striking woman in her forties, tall, slim, handsome, poised and, as usual, impeccably dressed. Her voice was calm and measured.

'Ordinarily,' she said, 'I would hold up my hands in horror at the mere suggestion of taking someone's life, but not in this case. Let's face it. Our managing director has, after all, effectively been murdering us over the past couple of years. To all intents and purposes, he's been feeding the company, its directors, shareholders and employees a form of slow poison. Desmond is right. We're in a crisis situation. We must kill or be killed.'

'I won't countenance the idea!' insisted Voisey.

'If we don't act now, you won't be around long enough to countenance any idea.'

'What do you mean, Joanna?'

'You're next in line, Ian,' she warned. 'Horace told me so. He's sacked all the non-executive directors and now wants to purge the board itself. You're first to go.'

'Why me?' wailed Voisey. 'Why not Malcolm or Desmond or you?'

'Oh, our time will soon come. No question of that. Horace is weeding us out one by one. Either he goes – or we do.' Joanna glanced around their faces. 'And there's another thing that you ought to know.'

The four of them were holding a secret meeting in a hotel room for an emergency discussion. Horace Chesterfield, managing director of the pharmaceutical firm that his grandfather had founded, seemed to be hell-bent on destroying everything that he had inherited. In defiance of the wishes of his board, he had made a series of business decisions that had resulted in a disastrous slump in the share price and a lowering of company morale. There had been a spate of dismissals and resignations. Complaints came from all quarters but the power-mad Chesterfield ignored them. It was almost as if he were determined to take the firm into bankruptcy. Joanna added new fuel to the fire.

'He's been talking to you-know-who,' she confided.

'Never!' exclaimed Voisey. 'They'd swallow us up and spit us out.'

'It's on the cards, Ian.'

Roe was puce with anger. 'He'd *sell* us to our main rival?'

'Yes,' said Joanna. 'And at a rock-bottom price. We'd not only be kicked off the board, we'd get no golden handshake. How would you feel about that?'

'It's iniquitous!' cried Willard.

'Sadistic!' added Voisey.

Roe wagged a finger. 'Now do you see why we must get rid of him?'

'Yes!' replied the two men in unison.

'Then it only remains to work out the best way to do it.'

'May I make a suggestion, Desmond?' asked Joanna with a polite smile. 'I think that one of us should take responsibility. I know that it would be easier to hire a hit man to do it for us, but the fewer people involved, the better. Let's be honest. We all have motive and means to kill Horace Chesterfield. Ian and I are both trained chemists. One of us could surely come up with a concoction that would make our beloved leader die in agony.' Ian Voisey, a stick insect in a pin-stripe suit, nodded in agreement. 'Malcolm has won endless cups for clay-pigeon shooting. He could pick off Horace with one shot.' Malcolm Willard gritted his teeth. 'As for Desmond,' she went on, turning to the burly figure of Desmond Roe, 'he's a Keep-Fit fanatic, the one person here with the strength to kill with his bare hands.'

'Just give me the chance,' said Roe, miming the act of strangulation.

'I'll do exactly that, Desmond.' Joanna took a sheet of paper from her briefcase and tore it into four pieces. 'We'll draw lots. One of these will have the word 'Yes' on it. Whoever draws that will do the deed. We don't need to know who it is. Those of us with 'No' on our pieces of paper must accept that the person who actually murders Horace is the one who takes over as managing director. What do you say – yes or no?'

'Yes!' affirmed Roe, hoping that he would be the designated assassin.

'Well, all right, I suppose so,' said Willard, fearing that he might draw the 'Yes'.

'Ian?' prompted Joanna.

Voisey hesitated while he weighed up the situation. In the end, he accepted that their dictatorial managing director had to go. He gave a nod of assent. Joanna held the pieces of paper below the table while she wrote on them. After screwing all four into individual balls, she tossed them on the table. The men eyed them warily. One word on a piece of paper would alter their destiny. It would turn them into a killer but it would also elevate them into a position of control in the company. Desmond Roe was the first to reach out.

'Wait!' said Joanna, holding his wrist. 'Don't open it here or your expression will give the game away. It's important that three of us don't know who the killer is until after the event. Choose your piece of paper and open it in private. Go on, Desmond.'

She released his arm so that he could pick first. Holding the paper in the palm of his hand, he waved a farewell then got up to leave. Ian Voisey was the next to choose, snatching a piece of paper before hurrying out of the room. Malcolm Willard licked his dry lips and studied the remaining scraps of paper.

'Ladies first,' he said at length.

'Wouldn't you like the satisfaction of putting a bullet between Horace's eyes?' she asked. 'You'd make a good managing director, Malcolm. Go for it.'

Shedding his reservations, he grabbed one of the pieces of paper. Joanna heaved a sigh and took up the last piece, slipping it into her briefcase. Without a word, she got up and went out of the room. Left alone, Malcolm Willard could not wait to see his fate. Unrolling the piece of paper, he looked at the scribbled word and blanched.

'Oh, my God!' he cried.

Horace Chesterfield did not look like a tyrant. He was a big, fat, jovial man in his fifties with a benign smile on his face. Even when wielding a golf club, he seemed inoffensive, a kind and considerate man who looked as if he might apologise to his ball for having to strike it so hard. Malcolm Willard knew better. Chesterfield was ruthless, a cold-hearted villain who cared for nobody but himself. Golf was his passion and he played a round every day, regardless of the weather. Heavy rain kept most people off the course that morning but Chesterfield was undeterred. He went out alone to play his favourite game.

Willard seized his chance. Concealing himself under a golf umbrella, he stalked his victim until he saw his opportunity. Chesterfield was on the thirteenth green, well short of the hole. He would need at least two shots to sink his putt. Willard moved swiftly. Tucked away among the clubs in his golf bag was a high-powered rifle. Pulling it out, he checked that nobody could see him then crouched beside some bushes to take aim. Chesterfield hovered over his putt, rain splashing off his flat cap. All that Willard had to do was to wait for him to lift his head, then he could shoot him between the eyes and make good his escape. It would be a long time before the body was even discovered.

Chesterfield pondered and his assassin waited. The ball was then tapped firmly in the direction of the hole, stopping a few yards short of it. Chesterfield looked up and shook his head in disappointment. Willard's finger tightened on the trigger. At the critical moment, however, he had a strange feeling that he was being watched and it affected his aim. Instead of eliminating a hated enemy, he sent his bullet whistling past the man's ear to embed itself harmlessly in the trunk of a tree. Chesterfield was too engrossed in his game even to notice the attempt on his life. Willard lost heart and fled.

When he was invited to have lunch with the managing director, Ian Voisey was not sure whether to be flattered or alarmed. He had never been singled out before for such a privilege and could not imagine why Horace Chesterfield had selected him now. Voisey was on his guard, recalling what Joanna Osborne had said about his imminent departure from the board. Chesterfield was not known for his generosity. As a rule, the managing director had a four-course meal alone in his office. On this occasion, however, he and Voisey actually went to a top restaurant. It might be a good omen. Chesterfield was in an expansive mood.

'Things will soon pick up, Ian,' he said through a mouthful of food. 'I know that some of my decisions have met with disapproval but they're starting to bear fruit. I feel certain that Chesterfield Pharmaceuticals has a bright future.'

'I hope so, sir.'

'You have to take chances to stay ahead. That's what I did. I'm very grateful that you supported me at the board meeting. It's one of the reasons you're here.'

'Is it?' said Voisey.

'Yes, Ian. Eat up, man. This is wonderful food. More wine?'

'Er, yes, please.'

Chesterfield snapped his fingers and the waiter darted forward to replenish their glasses with Chablis. Voisey relaxed. He had not, in fact, supported the other man at any board meeting, he had simply been too frightened to oppose him. Ian Voisey was a yes-man who hid his true feelings from his managing director. The strategy seemed to have worked. Chesterfield could not have been nicer to him. For the first time in his life, he had a flicker of affection for his egregious boss. Perhaps they had all been wrong about Horace Chesterfield. Or had they?

'I'm afraid that's why you have to go, old chap,' Chesterfield announced.

'Go!' spluttered Voisey.

'Leave. Resign. Withdraw from the board.'

'But you praised me for giving you my support.'

'That's the reason you're out, Ian,' explained Chesterfield. 'I need directors who can stand up to me, who can question my decisions to make sure that they're in the best interests of the company. You just sit there and nod. I thrive on opposition and you've never given it to me. In short,' he went on with a chortle, indicating the food, 'this is your last hearty meal before execution. No hard feelings, I hope?'

Ian Voisey was speechless. At a stroke, he had lost his job, his self-respect and his future prospects. He was far too old to find such a well-paid directorship elsewhere. Removal from the board would cast him into outer darkness. What hurt him most was the way that Chesterfield had enjoyed slipping the knife between his ribs. His boss was positively beaming. After finishing his dessert, Horace Chesterfield struggled to his feet and slapped him on the shoulder.

'Sorry to tip you the black spot, old chap,' he said cheerily, 'but I have to put the company first. You do see that, don't you?' Voisey could not even manage his customary nod. 'Excuse me. Have to go to the Gents.'

He waddled off in the direction of the toilets and left the hapless Voisey in a state of suppressed rage. Any doubts that the latter may have had about removing Chesterfield from the face of the earth now disappeared. Voisey wanted revenge. Reaching into his pocket, he took out the piece of paper on which Joanna Osborne had written the fatal word. The yes-man was now eager to become the 'Yes' man.

Voisey had come prepared. An outstanding chemist in his day, his doctorate had actually involved research into various toxins. It had not taken him long to mix a poison that would fell Chesterfield an hour after he took it and leave him writhing in agony before he died. Voisey did not hesitate. Glancing round to make sure that nobody was watching, he extracted a small bottle from his briefcase and tipped the contents into Horace Chesterfield's wine. The poison was tasteless. The victim would have no warning of what was to come. Voisey would relish the moment when his managing director drained the glass and set retribution in motion.

Unhappily, it never came. Instead of Chesterfield, it was the waiter who approached the table, bearing something on a silver tray. He leaned over Ian Voisey.

'Excuse me, sir,' said the waiter, 'but I have a message from Mr Chesterfield. He had to leave to attend a meeting so he'd like you to settle the bill.' He put the silver tray down. 'I'll just clear a few things away.'

And before Voisey could stop him, the waiter picked up Chester-field's plate, cutlery and wine glass before padding off to the kitchen. Voisey snatched the bill off the silver tray and gaped at the enormous cost of the lunch. He had not only been given a last hearty meal before execution, he was expected to pay for it himself.

Although he was in his fifties, Desmond Roe still worked out regularly in the gymnasium so that he could keep in trim. As he went through his routine with the heavy weights that evening, he thought about the best way to murder Horace Chesterfield. There would be great satisfaction in throttling the man slowly and watching his eyes bulge with horror. Holding him under water until he drowned was another idea that appealed to Roe. His victim could be stabbed, burned or smothered to death. Hanging also came into consideration. The possibilities were endless. What he finally settled for was a swift and violent end. All that he had to do was to bide his time.

Roe was the captain of Chesterfield Pharmaceuticals cricket team, a formidable opening batsman of immense power. What better way to dispatch a loathsome managing director than by using his trusty bat? As president of the team, Horace Chesterfield always attended the matches and was usually among the last to go home. Desmond Roe decided that, after the next game, Chesterfield would not leave the pavilion alive. When the fixture arrived on Sunday, Roe was so buoyed up by the notion of ridding the world of his boss that he excelled himself on the field, scoring a century that was composed almost entirely of boundaries. When he hit his last towering six, he pretended that he was striking the big bald head of Horace Chesterfield.

Everyone crowded in the bar to celebrate a win for the home team and Roe was showered with congratulations. Delighted with his team's success, Chesterfield was among the first to shake his hand but that did not deter Roe from his avowed intent. He wanted blood. Throughout the evening, people began to disperse until only a handful was left. Joanna Osborne was one of them. She waved to Roe.

'I'm off, Desmond,' she said. 'What about you?'

'No, I'll stay to lock up,' he replied, his eyes never leaving Chesterfield. 'It's my responsibility as captain to make sure that the burglar alarm is switched on.'

'You certainly discharged your responsibilities on the pitch. I've never seen you in such good form. You played like a man inspired.'

'That's exactly what I am, Joanna. Inspired.'

'I hope that someone will look after Horace,' she observed, glancing across at Chesterfield. 'He's been drinking heavily. I don't think he should be allowed behind the wheel of a car in that state. Perhaps I should offer him a lift home.'

'No, no,' he said. 'Don't do that. I'll take care of him, I promise.'

She smiled. 'Then I'll leave him in your capable hands.'

Joanna went out and she was soon followed by two of the other stragglers. Apart from Roe, only the barman and Horace Chesterfield were left. Roe dismissed the barman, saying that he would put the takings in the safe and lower the protective grill over the bar.

'Not before I've had one for the road, Desmond,' said Chesterfield.

'Of course not, sir,' said Roe, stepping behind the counter. 'I'll serve you myself. Off you go, Arthur,' he added to the barman. 'I can manage here.'

'Fair enough, Mr Roe,' decided the man. 'Goodbye to you both.'

The barman went out and Roe poured another double whisky for Chesterfield, who was now very unsteady on his feet. He leaned against the counter for support, raised his glass and downed half the whisky.

'Wonderful innings, old chap!' he said. 'It was vintage Desmond Roe. That hook shot of yours was magnificent. Don't know how you do it.'

'I'll show you,' volunteered Roe, seeing his opportunity. 'Wait here.'

He could not believe his luck. Slipping through into the changing room at the rear of the pavilion, he retrieved his bat and took a few practice swings before going back to his companion. Chesterfield was swaying drunkenly.

'Ah, good man,' he said, moving towards Roe. 'I'll bowl you a bouncer and you hook me for six. Are you ready Desmond?'

'Oh, yes,' replied the other grimly. 'I'm ready.'

Tightening his grip on the handle, he took guard in front of some imaginary wickets. Chesterfield pretended to bowl at him and Roe struck out with murderous force, expecting to send him to his Maker by smashing his head open. But he was thwarted. Losing his balance, Chesterfield ducked under the swishing bat and rolled over until his elbow connected with the switch that controlled the burglar alarm. Pandemonium broke out. A bell clanged insistently and a klaxon sounded. The noise was deafening. Roe was so taken aback that he dropped his bat. Before he could pick it up and take a second swing at his victim, the door burst open and the barman rushed in, closely followed by Joanna Osborne.

'What's wrong?' she said. 'Who set off the burglar alarm?'

Desmond Roe tucked the bat under his arm and went out. His chance had gone.

It was ironic. In their chosen ways, three people had tried to kill Horace Chesterfield and each had failed. A week later, he obliged them by dying of natural means, struck down by a massive heart attack that was brought on by a ruinous diet, an excess of alcohol and the cumulative stress of running a large company. Few tears were shed at the funeral and three of the mourners – Malcolm Willard, Ian Voisey and Desmond Roe – were smiling secret smiles throughout the service. Chance had contrived what they could not. They had achieved their objective without having to resort to violent crime.

Everything had worked out for the best. Or so it seemed until they heard the will being read out. One clause in it stunned the trio. In the event of his death, Chesterfield had decreed, Joanna Osborne would take over as managing director of the company. It was all cut and dried. If one of the would-be assassins had succeeded, he would not, in fact, have taken over the reins. They had already been promised to Joanna. Whatever happened, she was destined to come out on top.

The three losers adjourned to the bar to console themselves. After taking a long sip from his drink, Malcolm Willard was the first to express his outrage.

'Joanna cheated me,' he complained. 'I was the one who tried to bump Horace off and I blew it. Even if I had shot him, I wouldn't have become managing director. Joanna was next in line. The bitch!'

'Wait a minute,' said Voisey with surprise. '*You* tried to kill him? But so did I.'

'But I had the piece of paper with 'Yes' on it.'

'You couldn't have, Malcolm, because I did.'

'And so did I,' explained Roe bitterly. 'Don't you see what Joanna did? She outwitted us. She wrote 'Yes' on all four pieces of paper so that each of us was bound to think that *he* was the executioner. She probably didn't bother to look at her piece of paper because she had no intention of doing the dirty work. That was left to us.'

'We can't let her get away with this,' said Willard. 'I'll never forgive her for the torment she put me through. If I had a gun in my hands, I'd shoot her.'

'I'd poison her!' asserted Voisey.

'And I'd knock her for six with my cricket bat,' added Roe. 'Joanna has led us well and truly up the garden path. She holds all the cards.'

'Not necessarily, Desmond,' said Willard thoughtfully.

'What do you mean?'

'I have an idea to put to the pair of you.'

'I'm all ears,' said Voisey.

They sat over their drinks and conspired.

Joanna Osborne was in the managing director's officer when they arrived. She had already made herself at home, replacing her predecessor's gloomy landscape paintings with colourful framed posters and filling the room with cacti and flowers. There was an unassailable air of triumph about her. She smiled at the three men.

'It looks as if I'm the winner,' she said complacently. 'Hard luck!'

'You rigged everything to your advantage, Joanna,' said Voisey.

'All's fair in love and pharmaceuticals, Ian.'

'You betrayed us,' challenged Willard.

'I simply outmanoeuvred you, Malcolm. I've always been a good tactician.'

'Why did you send all three of us off to kill Horace?' asked Roe.

'Because I hoped that one of you would actually do it,' she said. 'Since you were working independently, so to speak, you had no idea that you were not alone. As it happened, you all let me down. I had to wait for Horace to die of his own accord.'

'And where does that leave us?' demanded Voisey.

Her expression hardened. 'Taking orders from me.'

'You're worse than Horace Chesterfield.'

'I know,' she boasted, 'and you'd better get used to the idea.'

Roe squared up to her. 'And supposing we don't, Joanna?'

'Then I'll have to tell the police what I saw through the window of the cricket pavilion. I could see that you were waiting to get Horace on his own and I guessed why. So I lurked outside and watched as you tried to knock his head off his shoulders. As for you, Malcolm,' she continued, turning to Willard, 'I have your bungled attempt at shooting him on film. I followed you around that golf course in the rain with my camcorder. My evidence could get you sent to prison for attempted murder.'

'That's blackmail!'

'I call it insurance. Against the possibility that you or Desmond tried to get even with me. Nobody would believe that I helped to instigate those attacks on Horace. Why should I want him killed when I was due to inherit his crown by legal means?' She gave a brittle laugh. 'I have the two of you over a barrel.'

'You've nothing on me,' said Voisey.

'Oh, but I have, Ian. When I knew you were having lunch with the dear departed Horace, I was sure you'd tried to spike his drink with poison. I bribed the waiter to let me have Horace's wine glass at the end of the meal.' She gave a nod of congratulation. 'You did well. I analysed the contents of that glass myself. It was a brilliant concoction. A deadly poison that would have no taste.' Joanna sat back in her chair. 'I think you'll find that I've covered all the angles, gentlemen. There was a 'Yes' written on my own piece of paper but I had no need to act on the command. I had three loyal foot-soldiers.'

'We're not loyal any more, Joanna,' warned Roe.

'Then I'll have you replaced on the board at once.'

'You may not be around to do that.'

'Desmond is right,' said Willard. 'You see, we decided that the order we were given on those little pieces of paper was still in force. One of us had to remove the managing director in order to take his – or her – place.'

'That's nonsense!' she snapped. 'Get out before I call security.'

'But you won't be able to do that, Joanna,' said Voisey, pulling out the plug on her telephone. 'Scream as loud as you like. Nobody will hear you.'

'Except us,' said Roe.

'Yes,' agreed Willard, 'and don't expect us to come to your rescue.'

Joanna Osborne shrank back in her seat. It no longer conferred the impregnability that she had coveted. The three men were acting completely out of character. She had expected them to be cowed into obedience by her cunning ruse but they were too angry to accept her as their new boss. As they closed in on her, there was a real sense of menace.

'Wait!' she protested, holding up both arms. 'There's no need to go to extremes. We can work this out between us. If you wish, I'll resign as managing director.'

'We're just about to arrange your resignation,' said Roe. 'Only we're giving you more choice than you allowed Horace Chesterfield.'

'Yes,' explained Voisey, taking three slips of paper from his pocket and setting them down in front of her. 'Each piece bears a different name. Check them, by all means. Unlike you, we don't cheat.'

Willard raised a questioning eyebrow. 'Ian – Desmond – or me? Which one of us is going to be your executioner, Joanna?' He moved the pieces of paper around, keeping them face down so that the names were invisible. 'Take your pick.'

'This is some kind of cruel joke!' she said.

'Not as cruel as the one you played on us.'

'Come on, Joanna,' urged Roe. 'Choose a name and nominate your successor. Whoever has the pleasure of killing our ambitious managing director will take over from her. We've agreed to that and, unlike you, our word is our bond.'

'Look, I'll do anything to get out of this!' she pleaded. 'Anything at all.'

'Then jump out of the window,' advised Voisey. 'We're sixteen floors up. You'll have time to regret what you did to us before you hit the ground.'

'No!'

Joanna tried to get up and run but Desmond Roe held her in her seat. Malcolm Willard moved the three pieces of paper around again. There was no escape. She had been hoist with her own petard. In turning them into potential killers, she had put a strange power into their hands. They had nothing to lose now. One of them, she knew, would assist her through the window. She shuddered with fear.

It was Ian Voisey, the quietest of the three, who sounded her death knell.

'Well?' he said. 'Are you going to choose a name – yes or no?'

Initial impressions

JUDITH CUTLER

'Those cars! All those cars!' Mr Winthrop, the Conference Manager, wailed, bursting into my office and dashing to the window. He pointed with a trembling finger. 'Carly, what are they doing here? They're so – so obtrusive!' He stared wildly over the lenses of his new rimless spectacles. They were his latest concession to the twenty-first century, though he clearly missed his horn-rims, which he used to whip off and wave in a gesture of managerial authority. To do him justice, Mr Winthrop was trying very hard to implement the resolutions passed at the last AGM at the instigation of the Chief Executive himself. He had to update himself and the hotel of which he was Conference Manager, the Mondiale. Despite its international-sounding name, the Mondiale was really just a middle-sized fifties-built country town hotel, retro but definitely not chic.

'I think they're to do with the conference, Mr Winthrop,' I said gently, pushing the crossword under my blotter. *The Times*, today.

'Carly,' he bleated again. 'You're my Personal Assistant. Do something!'

I felt almost sorry for him. He'd never wanted to have a young woman like me foisted on him. In his book the only place for a woman in a hotel was in a short black uniform, decorated by a frilly apron and perched on black-clad legs. Here I was, let loose as assistant conference manager. Very scary. And he had to address me with such informality. He'd much rather have called me 'Miss Shaw' but the owners had decreed that we were all to be on customer-friendly first names. In any case, Mr Winthrop, who preferred us to ignore the management directive in his own case, found it hard to shape his mouth into the shape of 'Ms', unless he was addressing a woman with potentially lucrative business.

Today's conference had been set up by a man, however.

About two months ago, Mr Winthrop had summoned me into his office, flourishing a letter in front of me. I could see part of the letter heading. I had to agree with him that Moral Psychologists and Sociologists sounded just the sort of group that the hotel would want to encourage. Indeed, with the current state of our conference diary, any group was the sort the hotel would want to encourage.

With some notable exceptions. We'd had it up to here with hen nights, the things a mob of women baying that they wanted to accomplish with a single male stripper being technically impossible. And even head office concurred with Mr Winthrop's strongly worded recommendation that stag nights were off the menu, after all the female staff had had to barricade themselves in the cellar. Perhaps it wasn't so much the male vulgarity as the consumption of wine needed to keep our spirits up while we were under siege. In fact, we had forcibly to restrain some of our weaker vessels from surrendering spinelessly – and indeed, leglessly – to the would-be conquerors. The fact that most of the latter were by then snoring loudly was irrelevant.

'Professional men,' Mr Winthrop sighed contentedly. 'People with BAs and PhDs.'

'And women,' I chipped in. 'You get women psychologists and sociologists these days.' As if they hadn't been around any time the last fifty years or so.

'Imagine such distinguished scholars making the Mondiale another little spinney in their groves of Academe,' he enthused. 'Once again our corridors will resound to intellectual banter and intelligent laughter.'

It would certainly be better than drunken baying and tipsy giggles.

'But,' he continued, 'as I recall, such men tend to wear corduroy trousers and have leather patches on the elbows of their jackets.'

Not two years ago when I got the BSc (Soc Sci) which took me on to the hotel's graduate training scheme, but I wouldn't interrupt him. In any case, he was pretty well qualified himself. He might not have an Oxbridge degree, but he'd done almost every professional course going: he already had Higher National Diplomas in Catering Management and Hotel Studies and was an associate member of the Hotel Management Association. When he achieved his lifetime ambition, full membership of the Hotel and Catering Management Institute, he'd have more letters after his name than the average eye chart.

'Do you think I should remind them of our dress-code?' he mused. He jotted and inserted the note into a file he'd already opened. The words PROFESSIONAL INSTITUTE peeped coyly from under his thumb.

The man sent to negotiate terms certainly didn't need to be re-minded of any dress code. His suit was so sharp it could have cut him. I could see Mr Winthrop mentally pricing the fabric even as he was lamenting the style. A lot of pound signs showed in his eyes.

He might have priced the jewellery Mr Plumb sported too, with even more pound signs popping up. Although my image of academics wasn't quite as dated as Mr Winthrop's, I'd no idea they went in for heavy gold rings on both hands, thick-linked gold bracelets and what looked suspiciously like a Rolex. Even to lift his arms to comb his hair, Mr Plumb would have needed weight-training. And I fancy he combed it a lot. He smiled too, a very great deal, with newly whitened teeth, especially at me, though I was simply there to reassure him that we were so awash with management staff that no need could possibly be overlooked. Mr Winthrop didn't point out that I'd no doubt be doubling in one of those black uniforms with a frilly apron when the conference banquet took place.

'What you have to consider,' Mr Winthrop was saying, 'is the Mondiale's communications advantages. We're just off the M20 and thus convenient for drivers. Eurotunnel is just down the road in Folkestone, so we can welcome any continental delegates. And of course, Eurostar stops conveniently at the international station.'

Yes, the place should have screamed with possibilities. We were just outside the former market town of Ashford, in Kent. The spawn-ing of new houses made it much in demand as a meeting-place. People needed large (if not elegant) rooms for wedding receptions. Antiques fairs, doll's house fairs: we should be hosting the lot.

At that moment Mr Plumb was probably trying not to scream with boredom. He was saved by a call on his mobile, which he chose to answer.

'He looks just like a matinée idol,' Mr Winthrop whispered hope-fully while Mr Plumb paced round the room giving monosyllabic barks. He gave a winsome little prink to his hair.

Poor Mr Winthrop: I didn't think Mr Plumb would be making a frenzied assault on his virginity while they discussed bedroom accom-modation.

'And will your colleagues be bringing their partners?' Mr Win-throp prompted once Mr Plumb had terminated the call with a word so profane I didn't think Mr Winthrop recognised it – he was in any case too busy preening himself for managing such a politically correct term.

'Partners?' Plumb repeated.

'Your good ladies.'

'Ladies!' He rolled the term round his mouth. 'Ladies,' he repeated. Somehow it didn't feel as if he was changing the subject when he asked, 'How many suites do you have?'

Mr Winthrop rubbed his hands together. 'Three.'

'All with king-size beds?'

'Queen. Two queen-size in each.'

'We'll take all three. And king-size. Understand?'

At this point I'd have announced that the suites were in fact taken that night – oh, one of those mass Moonie weddings or something – but Mr Winthrop simply grovelled a little lower.

'And how many other bedrooms? Single-beds or double?'

'Forty doubles.'

'Singles? For a big booking we may be able to waive the usual supplement.'

'No singles.' The idea seemed to amuse him. 'I'd better see them first.' He looked at me.

Fortunately Mr Winthrop was much too taken with the idea of a profitable conference – I could already see him 'forgetting' to import those large beds – to delegate the guided tour. I was happy with the arrangement: I didn't fancy the speculative leer in my direction I knew would appear on Plumb's face every time he tested a bed. So I was left to make more coffee and requisition the better class of biscuit. Acting on my own initiative, I booked a table for lunch: he'd no doubt want to see the dining room. Two or three? Two. He and Winthrop would talk money more easily without me. I had a nasty feeling, however, that my presence would be demanded, necessary or not.

It was.

I was back in my office having a little trouble with an anagram when they returned. But I wasn't summoned to eat, just to measure out the stage area.

'At the banquet we shall be making presentations to our most successful colleagues,' Plumb said. 'So – '

'Spotlights and sound system then,' Mr Winthrop wrote furiously.

'And a big table for the prizes. Very big.'

'Are they valuable? I'm sure we can make safe space available.'

He was favoured with no more than an enigmatic grunt.

'Late evening entertainment,' Mr Winthrop prompted. 'And after the banquet?'

'The ballroom,' I suggested. Some of the Mondiale's profits ought to be down to me.

'Strobe lights, music – the usual?'

An absent nod. Mr Plumb appeared to be thinking on his feet.

Encouraged, I asked, 'And do you want a theme? They're very fashionable these days. Many of our guests like us to organise line dancing or a salsa evening.'

Plumb reflected. 'Lots of cushions and lots of those things the Romans used to lie on – '

'Couches? But we don't normally – ' Mr Winthrop objected.

'Couches,' Mr Plumb said firmly. 'And pillars and tables with grapes. Those things with leaves for your head – '

'Laurel wreaths,' I supplied, *sotto voce.*

'Drapery.' He turned to me. 'I'm sure you know the sort of thing I have in mind.'

I hoped my smile was non-committal. I was very much afraid I knew all too well what he had in mind. Diaphanous and short for women, toga-like for men – or would he go for tunics, much more suitable for orgies, I'd have thought?

Mr Winthrop chipped in again. 'And will you be bringing in your own entertainment, or do you want Miss – do you want Carly here, my Assistant Conference Manager, to provide it? Although she's young, she's highly professional and can be utterly relied on to come up with something unusual.'

'I'm dead sure she can.' He almost licked his lips. He looked me up and down, from the top of my demurely combed hair to the tip of my sensible shoes, taking in everything – my unmanicured fingers, the *Guardian* crossword I was failing to hide behind my clipboard and the spot of breakfast porridge on my would-be elegant trousers-suit.

I wanted to poke one of my newly-sharpened pencils where it would make his eyes water. 'Can I return to the conference itself? Will you be having any guest speakers at any point? What will they require? Overhead projectors? Screens?'

'Let me see. There's a seminar on Strategy and Management, but the participants will be bringing their own equipment. I'll make sure of that. In addition we'll be welcoming an all-women delegation from the Therapy and Recreation Training School, but their needs will be amply provided for. Oh, how could I forget?' He snapped his fingers in irritation. 'Blackout and soundproofing material. You'll see to it?'

I obediently jotted down the details. 'And will they be needing accommodation? Your Therapy and Recreation Therapy School women?'

'I factored that in into my original total,' he said.

Mr Winthrop being called away, much against his will, to see to the requirements of a group of Normandy dairy farmers and their wives, it fell to me to see Plumb off the premises. I just knew he'd have to touch my elbow as we passed through doors, but I didn't quite expect him to turn to me and say, 'Carly, you've far too many talents to be tucked away in a place like this.'

'It's kind of you to say so. But I'm on the graduate trainee scheme – I shall be moved on to another hotel within the group very soon.'

'I'm sure I could do very much better than a traineeship.' Was I surprised when he slipped me his card? 'My organisation could use someone like you,' he added, showing all those wonderfully white teeth.

Not so much headhunting, I'm afraid, as body-snatching.

I was used to men making passes, or even suggestive remarks. Even men who strip you mentally. It comes with the hotel territory. But there was something extra about Mr Plumb: the way he seemed to be putting a price on me, not the hotel. I was glad to wave him goodbye.

I could have done without the final appraising sweep of his eyes and an ambiguous lift of his eyebrow as he accelerated from the car park in a spurt of gravel.

So here was poor Mr Winthrop looking as if all the Chief Executives of hell were waving motions of censure at a giant AGM. He'd been harassed all day. Ever since the first of Mr Plumb's colleagues had started arriving.

Car parking was the first problem. We catered for normal family cars, even people carriers. The delegates didn't drive normal family cars, even people carriers. Their vehicles were a bit larger. What weren't stretch limos were tinted-window Beamers, which did at least fit into the designated spaces, but looked remarkably sinister en masse.

'I'd no idea that social workers did so well for themselves,' poor Mr Winthrop said, goggling. 'Just think, Carly, you could have been earning that much money if you'd followed – what do they call it? – another career path.'

I didn't tell him that I had the opportunity but a few weeks ago.

If Mr Plumb's suit had been sharp, many of his colleagues' were positively flashy, their rings and bracelets the size of manacles. You could see why Plumb had hesitated over the words 'ladies' and 'partners' too: no one my mother would have accorded the term 'lady' to would have worn boots that high or skirts that short, or leather or pvc with quite so many studs and eyelets. Nor did they carry whips instead of handbags. No, ladies they were not. And I had a nasty feeling that most of them didn't have Mr Plumb's executive status. Not unless there was a seminar for Modern and Demanding Advisory Methods, for the older women delegates only.

I was almost sorry to make the phone call. I'd have loved to see the cups or whatever they were going to present to their most successful colleagues – and to hear the criteria by which the colleagues were judged. I'd have loved to be a fly on the wall at one of the S and M sessions, never having been to such a thing in my life. But I had a spot of civic duty to do, and even if the arrival of a hundred policemen did interrupt the conference, at least Mr Winthrop had followed company policy and insisted on payment in advance.

'Whatever put you on to them?' he asked, collapsing behind his desk and looking so pale I brought in one of the unopened bottles of champagne that Plumb had demanded for each delegate's bedroom. He laid the file in front of him, opening it and rifling through it as if searching for an answer.

Putting a flute of fizz in his numb fingers, I fished out the original letter of enquiry. 'There,' I said, pointing.

'I don't see anything wrong.'

'Professional Institute of Moral Psychologists and Sociologists. P.I.M.P.S. Pimps, Mr Winthrop.'

'But – '

'Therapy and Recreation Training School – just check the initials.'

His eyes and mouth became Os of amazement. 'So the women would be – ?'

'Tarts. And Strategy and Management – '

He buried his head in his hands. 'No. No, don't spell it out. Oh, Carly! But how did you guess?

Best not to tell him about my addiction to word puzzles. He was the boss, after all, and might not appreciate the amount of the Mondiale's time I spent on them. 'It was just something I picked up at the AGM,' I said gently.

Eternally

MARTIN EDWARDS

Playing for time, I said, 'All that happened long ago.'

'I'd love you to tell me about it,' Alice said, putting down her notes and leaning over my bed.

Her perfume was discreet, the faintest hint of sandalwood. If only I were a few years younger. Well, quite a lot of years. I doubted if she was thirty-five and already she'd carved out separate reputations, first as an investigative journalist with the *Washington Post*, more recently as the author of a couple of best-sellers about Hollywood glitterati. She was shrewd and determined. Unwilling to take no for an answer. Exciting in any woman.

I started to cough. A passing nurse paused, but I nodded her away. Alice bent closer to me and I muttered, 'You don't want to listen to a sick old man, talking about the past.'

'It took me a long time to find you.' Wagging a slim finger. 'Hard work. At least the advance covered my flight to London.'

'Why bother? You can write your book without interviewing me.'

'I don't cut corners.' A sweet grin. 'Besides, I never shopped in Oxford Street before.'

'You haven't missed much.'

'Also, I'd like to hear what you have to say.'

I sucked in air: not as easy as it used to be. 'You said a few minutes ago that you just love a good murder mystery. But you're wrong. Max didn't kill his wife. Is that good enough for you?'

The corners of her mouth curved down. The crestfallen expression made her look about nineteen; a man could easily be taken in by it and tell her more than it was safe to disclose.

'You were his friend, of course you believed in him. But even at the time, there was gossip. Rumours that the accident was too convenient.'

'Lorna was pretty and she died young. It's the stuff that myths are made of.' I made a show of stifling a yawn. 'If she'd been a little more talented, a little brighter, people would still remember her name.'

'Some people still do. That's why I have to mention her in my book.'

'There isn't a story. She had too much to drink one evening, fell down the stairs of their Long Island mansion and broke her pretty little neck.'

Alice touched my hand, grazing the palm with her nails. I felt her warm breath on my cheek. 'There is a story if her husband murdered her.'

'You haven't done your homework. Max was innocent. He spent the evening with us. He'd never have had time to get over to the house and kill Lorna.'

She didn't blink. 'Trust me. I always do my research very thoroughly.'

I burst into a racking cough and within a minute the nurse was pulling the curtains around my bed, shooing Alice away. I shut my eyes. I wasn't ready to step through death's door. I needed a little space, a little time, to decide what to say and do. Alice was so focused on making sure she got what she wanted.

In my mind, I saw Max again. A July afternoon in '68. The first time we had met since Lorna's death. He hadn't attended the funeral. Too sick, too eaten up with grief, so the story went. I sat in the front row at the church, not blinking, just remembering. There was an empty space beside me. Patty was still in shock after what had happened.

Max and I had been keeping our distance. He didn't call me, I didn't call him. When I showed up at his apartment on East 61st Street, unable to stay away any longer, I was shocked by the change in him.

He still dressed like Joe College. Plaid pants, baggy crew-neck sweater, white socks and white US Keds. But his hair was different. Thick as ever, but with patches of grey that hadn't existed six months before. He kept glancing past me, as if any moment he expected Lorna's ghost to slink into the room.

'Thanks for coming,' he said.

A smell of burned toast hung in the air. At least it was better than cigarette smoke. The Colts and Packers were playing, but he switched off the set and started bustling in the kitchen. The refrigerator was packed to overflowing with lemons and Pepperidge Farm bread. He kept his gaze away from me as he threw raw eggs and coffee ice into the blender.

'How have you been?'

'Oh well, you know.'

Silly question. I suppose we both must have felt nervous. Were my hands shaking, or is that just an illusion of memory? I kept quiet while he made the coffee milkshake and fiddled with cheese and chopped liver for a Dagwood sandwich.

A baby Steinway sat in an alcove. On the shelves lay half a dozen score pads scooped together with rubber bands. I hazarded a guess that all of the pages were blank.

'Written anything lately?' I asked.

'Not a note,' he said. 'You?'

'Uh-uh.'

I sipped the milkshake. 'So you and Chrissie aren't writing together at present?'

He stared at me. 'I haven't seen Chrissie since Lorna died.'

'I see.'

'Do you?' His cheeks, pale until that moment, suffused with colour. 'I don't think so. Everyone believes that they see. Truth is, they see what they want to see. Something bad.'

I swallowed hard. 'Hey, I'm sorry I didn't get in touch.'

'Why should you have? I was the one who dumped on you. Found another lyricist.'

'I couldn't blame you. Chrissie's ten years younger and a thousand per cent sexier than me.'

'What you aren't saying is, she never wrote a hit song in her life.'

I shrugged. 'Fashions change. The stuff we wrote, it doesn't make the charts any more. You were right, we needed a break from each other. Needed to freshen up.'

'Lorna hated me for it. She told me you were worth ten of Chrissie. She was right, but what the hell? Sorry, Steve.'

Awkwardly, he stretched out a hand and I shook it.

'People are whispering, aren't they?' he said quietly. Not meeting my eyes. Maybe he feared what he might see there.

'What do you mean?'

'C'mon, Steve. We've known each other a long time. We're old friends.'

'The best,' I said fervently. Despite everything, I meant it.

'Then tell me. Everyone thinks I killed Lorna, pushed her down those stairs. Isn't that the truth?'

'No.' The flat denial startled him, made him catch his breath. 'Okay, okay, there are one or two people who love to think the worst.'

'More than one or two. Chrissie's among them. As usual, she flatters herself.' He paused. 'She's stupid enough to believe I killed Lorna, just to be free for her.'

Next day, with Alice back at my bedside and fiddling with her tape recorder, I said, 'I'm not sure Max and I deserve a chapter in your book. We were never Goffin and King, or Leiber and Stoller.'

'You were different, you were a Brit.'

'Who married a girl from Greenwich Village.'

'She was a folk singer,' Alice said, as if I didn't know. 'How romantic.'

'And I was a lyricist whose sole claim to fame was the words to a Cliff Richard B-side. Patty and I met in a club in Soho at the end of the fifties. I'd never met anyone quite like her. She was so lovely, so intense.'

'You wrote songs with her?'

'At first. Not a good idea, we both realised in the end. You can't work with someone you're passionate about. She was a wannabe Joan Baez, but my heart belonged to Tin Pan Alley. After I followed her to New York, I had a couple of breaks, grabbed a short-term contract with Famous Music. It went from there.'

A dreamy look came into her hazel eyes. 'What was it like in those days, working in the Brill Building?'

'One thing it wasn't, was glamorous. Eleven floors of offices and every one housed a music publisher. Each company had its writers' rooms, stuffy cubicles with just enough room for a beat-up piano and a couple of chairs. The windows didn't open, it was hell working with a guy like Max who smoked non-stop.' I coughed to make the point. 'I ought to sue, don't you think? That place surely killed me.'

'You all kept changing partners.'

'Sure. I'd write with one guy in the morning, another in the afternoon. That's the way it worked. But there was something about Max's melodies. They seemed to make a better fit with the words I wrote. Bobby Vinton liked our songs, Jay and the Americans gave us a Top Thirty hit. It went on from there. Before long the two of us were a team.'

'You met Lorna Key at a recording session, so the story goes.'

'It's a true story,' I said. 'There was an Isley Brothers session and we had a song on the date. She was one of the girls singing in the background. You couldn't help but notice her. Even in pigtails and jeans, she was gorgeous. Her voice was raw, even as a kid she was a chain-smoker. Her lungs must have been in worse shape than Max's, but it wasn't her lungs that he was interested in. He said she had potential. Nice euphemism, huh? He wanted her to start recording our demos. I went along with it, even though I never cared much for her sound. Subtlety was never her strong point.'

Alice glanced at her notebook. 'Soon she signed with Kapp Records.'

'Yeah, Lorna thought she'd become a star, but the truth is, Max pulled strings. They were married the week before her first single came out.'

'*Eternally*.'

Alice smiled and crooned the chorus.

> For as long as there's a deep blue sea,
> For as long as there's a you and me,
> I will love you eternally.

I shifted under the bedclothes. 'I never claimed to be William Shakespeare.'

She glanced over her shoulder, caught the puzzled frown of the nurse walking into the ward. In the bed opposite, old Arthur gave a toothless grin and tried to mime applause with his wasted hands.

'It has a hook,' she said. 'I've been humming the blessed thing all day. Can't seem to get it out of my head.'

'Ah, the potency of cheap music.'

'Lorna's voice was stronger than mine.'

'She belted it out,' I agreed. 'Though that wasn't what it called for. *Eternally* is a tender love song. But Lorna, she didn't do tenderness. You talk about murder. Well, she murdered *Eternally*. It was always a favourite of mine. For once, the words came before the music. I'd written it for Patty, a token of our love.'

'I like the melody,' she said. Not altogether tactfully.

'Max was a smart writer. He'd switch time signatures, come up with ten and a half bar phrases, as if it was the most natural thing in the world. Lorna couldn't handle it. She'd stumble over the tricky bits, we did a dozen takes and then settled for the second. I thought it was lousy, kept asking how you can rasp a love song, but Max said it was wonderful.'

'He was besotted with her.'

'That's what people forget. And you know something? He was proved right. That song went straight into the charts at number twenty-nine. Almost made it to the top ten. Lorna Key never had a bigger record.'

'The publicity must have helped. Her marrying the composer.'

'Sure, the Press lapped it up.'

'Did you resent that? Max was always the one in the public eye, not you. Radio announcers used to talk about Max Heller songs, forget they were written by Heller and Jackson.'

I shook my head. 'He liked the attention more than I did. You know, Sammy Cahn once said that most songwriters look like dentists, but Max was an exception. He was handsome and talented and even if his wife wasn't exactly Barbra Streisand, who cared? They made a good-looking couple. So while Patty and I got on with our lives, Max and Lorna kept the scribes busy and our songs benefited. I guess they got more exposure than they deserved.'

'For a while,' she said gently.

'Nothing is forever,' I admitted. 'Flower power came and went. Then there was heavy rock. All of a sudden it seemed that the songs Max and I were writing belonged to a bygone age. There was talk of a TV series, with Lorna and Rick Nelson, but Rick's career was in a tail-spin and it all came to nothing.'

'And then you and Max split up.'

'It was no-one's fault,' I insisted, propping myself up in the bed. I shouldn't be talking so much, the nurse would scold me for tiring myself out. But what did it matter? 'Except perhaps it was my fault, for going down with pneumonia at the wrong time. Max and I had been asked to write a couple of numbers for a TV special. I got sick and finished up in hospital. The deadline was forty-eight hours away, so the television company asked Max to work with Chrissie Goldmark. They hit it off straight away. The songs they wrote were candyfloss, but by the time I'd recovered, they were talking to Scepter about producing a new album together. Not for Lorna, though.'

'Lorna didn't take that well, did she?'

'Could you blame her? Chrissie fancied Max and like all men, he was susceptible to flattery from a pretty girl.'

Alice leaned close again. I supposed it was a trick of hers, a ploy to use when talking to men. A habit, almost. 'Were Max and Chrissie lovers?'

'What do you think?' Playing for time again.

'Everyone I've spoken to believes the two of them had something going.'

'Maybe they did. So what? It doesn't make Max a murderer.'

'Lorna was an emotional woman.'

'Emotional woman? Tautology, Alice.'

She wouldn't be riled. 'Lorna was tempestuous. Her career was fading and she hated that. She must have realised her looks wouldn't last forever. She was smoking eighty a day, her whole life was burning up. Losing her husband to a second-rate wordsmith would have been the last straw. I bet she wanted revenge. Hell hath no fury, you know. Maybe she threatened him with divorce, bad publicity . . .'

'Max never stopped caring for her. Besides, he wasn't a violent man.' Suddenly I felt very tired. Reaching back into the past was draining the life from me.

'Anyone can snap,' Alice said softly.

How could I deny it? Clearing the phlegm from my throat, I said, 'Max didn't.'

'Your loyalty does you credit,' she said, as I closed my eyes. 'But how can you be sure?'

'You're torturing yourself,' I told Max. 'And for no reason.'

'I don't have an alibi, you know. I was hanging out here on my own while Lorna was in the house on Long Island. We'd had a fight. No point in lying to you, it was over Chrissie.'

I checked my fingernails. 'She accused you of having an affair?'

'Yeah, the morning she died. It wasn't an accusation, just a statement of fact. I didn't try too hard to deny it. She asked if I wanted a divorce. If so, she was willing to agree. She didn't intend to spend the rest of her life with someone who had fallen out of love with her. I said I didn't want to rush things and she made a coarse remark and things kind of went downhill from there. You know how it is.'

'So you came back here, to your old bachelor pad.'

'Lucky I kept it on, huh? I haven't had the heart to spend time on Long Island ever since she tumbled down that staircase. Fact is, I could have gone back and killed her, made it look like an accident after she'd been drinking. Which she'd been doing too much. The house is quiet, no-one would have seen me come and go. Who's to say I'm innocent?'

He leaned back and the kitchen stool wobbled dangerously beneath him. The sink was piled high with dirty dishes, there were coffee cups filled with day-old instant Yuban. Looking out on to the terrace, I could see rumpled beach towels and grubby squeezed-out tubes of Bain de Soleil.

Following my gaze, he said, 'I've not been in the mood for tidying.'

'It won't do, Max.'

'Said like a true Englishman. Sorry for falling short in the stiff upper lip department, but the truth is, I'm pretty pissed about all this. All of a sudden, nobody wants to know me. Not even the woman I'm supposed to have committed murder for.'

'You're right,' I said suddenly. 'If you had an alibi, the tongues would stop wagging. You could start your life over.'

'Pity I screwed up by not having Chrissie round that night.'

'Where was she?'

'Jiving at some nightclub. Not my scene. I suppose I was already realising she was a bad habit, one I ought to break. I was supposed to be working on a song, but I had a couple of beers, then a couple more. Before I knew what was happening, I was fast asleep. And then the next morning came the cops, knocking on my door to break the news.'

'Aren't you forgetting something?'

'Like what?'

'Patty and I called round here that night,' I said calmly. 'It would have been about eight. She'd persuaded me to make an attempt to bury the hatchet.'

He stared at me. 'What are you talking about?'

'Patty thought you and I made a good team. She's always been fond of you.'

'No, she hasn't.'

'It's Lorna she didn't like.' I sighed. 'Trouble was, you and I argued. We'd both had a few beers. I took a swing at you and missed. Patty decided it was time for us to go. Not long after nine o'clock, she checked her watch. By then you weren't in a fit state to go anywhere and anyway, according to what I've heard, the authorities are convinced Lorna was already dead.'

His face was stripped of expression. I guessed he was calculating pros and cons. That was Max: he always played the percentages.

'Are you serious about this?'

'Never more so.'

'We don't have to drag Patty into this.'

I noticed the we. Progress. 'Yes, we do. After all this time, we need to make it look credible. People might think I was simply trying to save my old partner's good name if I was the only one giving him an alibi. Trust me, Patty and I have been tossing it around for a few days now. She agrees it's for the best.'

He rubbed his chin. 'I don't know, Steve.'

'Yes, you do. It's the only way. I'll put the word around that I've only just got wind that people are seriously pointing the finger at you. You and I may not be working together any more, but I'm keen to set the record straight.'

'But . . .'

'No buts. You want to spend the rest of your life like some pariah? Think about it.'

I could imagine his mind working, testing my proposition, checking it for flaws. Of course he would go along with it in the end. He had no choice, if Lorna was not to destroy his life, the way she'd almost destroyed mine.

Lorna, Lorna, Lorna. I can still smell the gin on her breath, the last time we were together. Still hear her striking the match to light yet another Lucky Strike from the crumpled pack. Still see her cupping her hands over the sudden flame. Still see her flicking ash all over the imitation Versailles rug. She was just waiting for me to call her a slut, but I said nothing, let her scorn wash over me like breakers on the shore. Even now I cringe at the memory of the coarse words, all the more shocking because they came from a scarlet mouth as cute as a bow-ribbon on a candy box.

'So how are you today?' asked Alice as she set up the tape recorder.

I made a slight movement with my shoulders. The doctor had talked to me that morning. There wasn't much time left.

'You're flying back home tonight?'

'Uh-huh.' She studied me. 'I just want to say thanks for all your help. It can't be easy for you, re-living the past when you aren't well.'

'Those were the best years of my life,' I said. 'It's no hardship to bring them back to mind. You know, I never had another top thirty hit after the spring of '67. Thank God for Muzak. The royalties never stopped dribbling in, enough to keep Patty and me fed and watered.'

'What happened to her career?'

'Same as happened to mine, I guess.' I sighed, spoke almost to myself. 'Doesn't matter, it's been a good marriage these past forty-odd years.'

'She's coming to see you again this afternoon?'

'Never fails. The arthritis gives her hell, but she fights through the pain.'

'Did you stay in touch with Max?'

'Not really. We bumped into each other now and then. Last time I saw him must have been in the early seventies, just before he was killed in that plane crash.'

'You never wrote another song together after Lorna died?'

'No, things never seemed to gell. Our time had passed.'

'So why did you alibi him for Lorna's death?'

Her voice had never sounded so sharp before. I flinched under her laser stare. 'I told you before,' I said. 'He didn't kill her.'

'Maybe he didn't,' she said. 'Maybe someone else did.'

All of a sudden, I felt very cold. 'What do you mean?'

'I talked to Lorna's best friend. After all these years, she's broken her silence, as the saying goes.'

'And?' My voice was no more than a croak.

'Lorna confided in her. Max's affair pissed her off. So she decided to take revenge by bedding you. Dear, dependable, happily married Steve. It helped prove how irresistible she was.'

'Girls talking,' I said. 'It doesn't mean a thing.'

She bent over me again. 'Did she taunt you? Or threaten your security? Maybe it was that. Perhaps she said she would spill the beans. You couldn't risk having Patty find out the truth. Was that why you shoved her down the stairs?'

'No,' I whispered. 'No, no, no.'

Lorna, Lorna, Lorna. The contempt in her glazed eyes that last time, when I told her life wasn't like writing songs. You can't keep changing partners. Nicotine-stained fingers jabbed into my guts as she told me to get out. No-one ever dumped her, she said, no-one. And certainly not a two-bit rhymester like Steve Jackson.

I could have killed her right then. Oh God, how I wanted to.

Patty arrived an hour later. All the time I've been in this place, she's never missed a day. Her love for me has never skipped a beat. She's been so faithful.

When I'd finished telling her about my conversations with Alice and the doctor, she took my hand. Hers was knobbly, deformed by the disease in her joints. I closed my eyes, recalling the smoothness of her skin when she was twenty one.

'So she has her scoop, something to help sell her book? Lorna Key wasn't killed by her husband but by her lover, Steve Jackson?'

'By the time she publishes, I'll be dead and buried. She's made sure of that by taking a good look at me and having a few words with the doctor. No need for her to worry. A corpse can't sue for libel.'

Patty squeezed my hand tighter. 'I won't let her do it. I won't let you do it.'

'Don't be silly.'

'It doesn't matter now. I may be losing you, but not for long. I still have those pills I told you about. You must tell her the truth.'

'Why me?'

'You're the one who always had a way with words.'

'Lorna deserved to die.'

'No, she didn't,' Patty said. 'I was just a jealous bitch who killed another woman because I was afraid she'd wreck our marriage.'

Funny, she'd never talked about it before. And I'd never asked, there was no need. I'd guessed her secret as soon as she came home that night, the stench of Lorna's Lucky Strikes clinging to her clothes, to her hair, to her skin. She'd never meant it to happen, I always told myself. Lorna was just killed by an unlucky strike.

'She didn't succeed, did she?'

She kissed me lightly on the cheek. 'No, darling. No-one could ever tear us apart.'

So there it is, Alice. How wrong you were. This isn't a murder mystery at all. It's just like one of those trite old lyrics of mine, you see. A tear-jerker, a heartbreaker. A story about love.

Missing

BILL KIRTON

Mum died. That's what started it. Terrible, isn't it? Two syllables, seven letters and it's enough to hollow out the universe. Think I'm exaggerating? Your mum's obviously still alive. One minute you're flipping a peanut in the air and catching it in your mouth as you reach to answer the phone, the next, your sister's voice, quiet, apologetic, just saying, 'Bad news. It's Mum.' And all the comfortable stuff around you – your furniture, the pictures on your walls, your ornaments – suddenly belongs to somebody else. Because the person you were, the person who bought it all, arranged it, lived with it, has been catapulted away out of reach. And this new you is just left there, crying, knowing that crying isn't enough, desperate to go and kneel in one of the churches to weep on the shoulder of a god you stopped believing in years ago. Funnily enough, it's like being born. One minute, you're snug inside your space, the next, you're in a gaping new place, with no values, no sense to it, no structure. And the person who's always been there approving of you, keeping you straight, isn't around.

I don't want to dwell on it but I warn you now, it's never far away from me. She was the most precious lady in the world. I don't say that easily. I'm not a guy who misses people. When my wife, Christine, took off with an English teacher because she'd had enough of the irregular hours I worked, I was jealous for about a week, then realised that I was having a great time leaving my clothes over the backs of chairs, eating in front of the telly, coming and going when I pleased without the worms of guilt turning in my head. I was suddenly grateful to the teacher and knew that I never wanted to live with anyone again. People make demands, even when they don't mean to, and I like the way I live too much to start compromising. So, you see, when I say I don't miss people, it's true.

But I miss mum.

Not that I ever saw much of her. She lived in Edinburgh and I've been in Aberdeen for ages. We phoned one another now and again, but not regularly, not every week even. I used to drive down once in a while but I wasn't what you'd call a dutiful son. I took her for granted, I suppose. She was only wee, not much over five feet, and there was no fat on her, not to speak of, but the vacuum she's left . . .

Anyway, as I said, I'm sure that's what started it. I was working on a missing person enquiry and my sister's phone call and the emptiness of the days after it redefined the whole idea of being missing. It's too easy to treat it as a statistic. Not that I was doing that. I was already semi-obsessed with the case. It was one of those where you know exactly who's guilty but can't find enough evidence to take to the procurator fiscal. Cindy Armstrong hadn't come back from a holiday trip to Cornwall. She'd driven down on her own at the beginning of the month and, when she wasn't back by the fifteenth, her husband, Donald, got in touch with us. This is the same Donald Armstrong who, just over two years ago, walked into headquarters in Queen Street, confessed to killing his first wife and was acquitted by the jury in Aberdeen's High Court. It's also the same Donald Armstrong whose company has ridden out the occasional lows of the oil industry by judicious staff pruning; not so much downsizing as annihilation. He drives a Mercedes CLK430 coupé, which he imported from the States for some reason, and lives in a detached architect's special out at Milltimber, not far off the North Deeside Road. He made his money from designing a plug that operators use to seal off offshore oil and gas pipes while they're working on them. I found out about that when I was investigating the death of wife number one. He may be a complete pillock but he's some engineer. You just slip this plug down the line, hit a couple of buttons and the hydraulics squeeze these seals out against the pipe wall so that not even high pressure gas can get through. It's made him rich enough to be able to treat people like . . . I almost said shit, but I'll settle for commodities.

I'd just been made up to detective inspector and was the duty officer when he arrived that first time. It was six in the morning when they called me in. Right from the start, I disliked him. He's sitting there in the interview room, all Paul Smith suit and Nicole Fahri shirt, calmly telling us he's had a fight with his wife and that he's strangled her. He's quiet, keeps his eyes down, but there's no emotion coming off him. It's as if he's there to report a lost bike. At first, with that sort of thing, you're gentle, you take it easy, trying to help them tell the full story. But with him, sympathy was out. He didn't want it, I couldn't give it. Something was going on. It wasn't a hunch or anything like that; the guy was just emotionally cold. His words, his voice, the actual sounds he was making – none of them fitted the context.

His story was that he and his wife, Elspeth, had been for a meal in Les Amis, then gone on to the Amadeus night-club down at the beach. By two in the morning, they were both very drunk and she started accusing him of chatting up some of the young women there. They got a taxi home, arguing all the way, and, when they got inside, the row became a real fight. Elspeth started screaming all sorts of stuff at him, saying he was a sick bastard, a pervert, slapping and scratching him. (He showed us the evidence – deep parallel gouges down the side of his neck and on his left cheek.) He shouted back but didn't touch her until she started calling him a poof. Yeah, one minute she's accusing him of chatting up women, the next he's a poof. You tell me. Anyway, she went on about that, said that he'd never given her a decent fuck, was pathetic, limp-dicked and that she'd make sure that all his pals knew about it.

He couldn't take much of that. ('Well, could you?' he asked us.) Started slapping her back. That made her worse and, in the end, he found himself kneeling on the bed with his hands round her neck, squeezing to shut her up.

As soon as he realised what he was doing, he got up and went out to cool down.

'Where did you go?' I asked him.

'Just around the garden. Out onto the road. Just walking. Trying to get my head together. Not many places to go in Milltimber that time of night.'

'How long did you stay out?'

He shook his head. 'Don't know. But when I went back, she was still there. On the bed. Where I'd left her.'

'So what did you do?'

'Shouted at her. Tried to wake her up. Checked her pulse. Felt her neck. She was cold. I got a taxi straight here.'

'You didn't phone for an ambulance?'

'No point. I thought you wanted scenes of crime to be undisturbed.'

You see, that was weird, wasn't it? He's sitting there with us, his wife's lying dead at home, and he's more concerned with leaving the clues intact than with trying to save her. Talk about helping the police with their enquiries.

When we'd finished the first run-through, I left him making his statement and went straight out to his place with the scene of crime boys. It was like a film set. The bedroom's all plum-coloured walls and velvet drapes. There's rugs and parquet flooring, table lights on all over the place. And there, on the king-size bed with its black sheets and duvet, is Mrs Armstrong, curled up as if she's just decided to take a nap. There were bruises on her face and neck from the fight but, apart from that, no signs of a struggle. Not one. All the rooms were the same. If they'd had the sort of fight he'd described to us, it should have been chaotic. But there was nothing broken, nothing overturned. Maybe rich folks are genteel when they argue. But whatever had gone on in the house, everything was tidy and spotless. There weren't even any creases in the sheets or the duvet she was lying on. He couldn't possibly have knelt on that bed. He must have hovered above it.

When I asked him about that later, he said I'd made a mistake. He insisted that he'd knelt with his legs either side of her, pushing her head hard into the bed. It had been a real fight and there were bound to be signs of it. He even suggested we should look again.

In the end, the tidiness was one of the things which helped him to get away with it. You see, it wasn't the strangling that killed her, it was booze. That was what the medic said. Alcohol poisoning. Armstrong sat there listening to this, saying nothing. He just shook his head once or twice. Like he couldn't believe what he was hearing. I'm not surprised. The stuff his lawyer spouted was all bloody fiction. He reckoned that, when Armstrong left the house, his wife was semiconscious, from drink more than from the attempt to throttle her. At last, she got up, drank some more and tidied the place up while she was waiting for him to come back.

The jury bought it. There was plenty in his favour – the fact that he'd given himself up right away, the evidence, from several of his friends, that Elspeth had a real drink problem and, most of all, the tidiness of the house, which proved that she was still alive when he left and so he couldn't possibly be responsible for her death. It never seemed to occur to anyone that he could have forced the booze down her, made the strangulation marks after she'd died and tidied the place up himself before coming to us with his fairy tale. No pathologist could pick up the fact that the strangling was post mortem if it more or less coincided with her dying. Confessing was a risky strategy, but in the end it worked for him.

He killed her. There's no doubt in my mind of that. It wasn't the first time we'd had to call him in. He beat up two prostitutes one time, left one of them with a broken thumb and blind in one eye. When it came to it, though, they wouldn't press charges. Combination of being afraid of him and getting a fat backhander to keep quiet. It's part of the way he does things. The world has to be shaped his way. If individuals stray from the paths he's made for them, they become . . . inconvenient, and they disappear, either by dying or, at work, by getting the boot.

And then, of course, wife number two goes AWOL. Surprise, surprise.

I thought it was ironic for him to say she was missing. He doesn't know what a missing person is. To understand that, you have to acknowledge that they have their own personal place in the world, accept their separateness, their independence from you and everyone else. None of the people connected with Armstrong has that. They don't go missing; they just stop being who they were supposed to be in his scheme of things. In my book, anyone with that sort of attitude has got serious problems.

I went out to his place to get the details. Again, there was no emotion in him. The same flat voice, as if he was bored by it all. He didn't even try to pretend to be upset. I think he knew what I thought of him and reckoned I wasn't worth trying to convince.

The interview was short and very frustrating. He didn't know where she'd intended staying. Cornwall, that was all. She'd decided to hire a car but he didn't know where from. He hadn't heard from her at all since she'd left. And so on, and so on. I was getting fed up with the grunting and the monosyllables. Tried to provoke him a bit. Asked him whether they'd had a row before she left. He knew what I meant but he just said no. He poured himself a drink. I noticed it was a fifteen-year-old malt. He didn't offer me one.

When I'd finished and was at the door putting on my coat, he lifted his hand and felt the material briefly.

'Police pay still lousy, I see,' he said.

'Serving the public is its own reward,' I said.

'Just as well,' he replied.

I'd meant to be sarcastic but it was a feeble effort. Still, the alternative was to punch him in the face so it was a small victory.

We did all the usual checks. None of the local or national hire firms had any record of Cindy Armstrong hiring a car. She hadn't used an assumed name either because we contacted all the female customers the companies had listed around the relevant dates and they all checked out. None of her friends knew where she'd intended going or even that she was planning a holiday. In fact, two of them, who claimed to be her closest friends, were surprised to hear that she was driving such a long way in her condition. Apparently, she was pregnant. She'd had a miscarriage just eight months before and they knew she was anxious not to do anything that might trigger another. When I heard that, I went to see the two of them myself. They were receptionists for DEFAB, an engineering company specialising in decommissioning offshore structures. I didn't stay long with them because our conversation was interrupted every minute or so by the switchboard beeping and one of them picking up the phone and reciting 'Good afternoon. DEFAB. How can I help you?' in that grooved, sing-song tone they all use. My trip was worth it, though.

'I don't know why she wanted to have a kid of his in the first place,' said Hayley, a blonde twenty-something with cropped hair and eyes whose green probably came from contact lenses. It was as well that they were so fascinating, otherwise I wouldn't have been able to keep my own away from her incredible breasts.

'You're not a fan of his, then?' I said.

'You met him?' was all she replied.

'What did he think about the baby?'

'Wanted her to get rid of it. They started arguing about it the minute she told him.'

'Did they argue a lot?'

Hayley and her friend, Midge, looked at one another, nodding.

'Even before they got married,' said Midge.

When I heard her speak, I guessed where her name came from. I know midges don't make a noise but if they did, her voice is what they would sound like.

'He's a bastard,' she added.

'In what way?' I asked.

'Every way. Treated her like shit. We've seen her with bruises all over, haven't we, Hayle?'

Hayley nodded.

They were happy to slag Armstrong off as long as I wanted but it started to get repetitive and none of it gave me any evidence to work with. I asked about Cindy again and, the more we talked about her, the less likely it seemed that she would just drive off to Cornwall without telling them and everyone else she knew. In the end, I thanked them and was glad to get away from Midge's voice but sorry to be deprived of Hayley's breasts.

Then, that evening, I got my sister's call.

It cut me adrift. Left me insecure, feeling I was in a wide open, empty, empty space. No walls, no points of reference. Lost.

I was no use to anyone for the best part of two days. I never cry but all the tears I'd kept back over the years came out then. Day and night. Hour after hour. I kept saying 'mum' over and over again. I've never been lower. It wasn't just that there was a hole in my life, there was a hole all around it and through it.

I forced myself back to work on the Thursday. All the guys made the right, quiet noises but I needed not to be reminded. I needed to get back into the Armstrong stuff. While I'd been off, Jim Ross, one of my sergeants, had found out that Armstrong's company had been granted a special landfill licence to dispose of some pipes and equipment at their yard which had been contaminated by LSA scale. That's radioactive stuff that gets precipitated from some downhole fluids. It's low level but still nasty. They'd concreted them into an underground chamber and sealed the lot with tons more concrete. And guess when that had happened. Yeah, that's right. Beginning of the month. It was all so obvious, wasn't it? We'd need cast-iron evidence against him before we could get the go-ahead (and the funds) to dig up the pipes. It would be a massive operation and there was bound to be a risk of exposure to radiation.

I lost the place completely when I heard that. It was anger, but it was misery, too. Another person lost. Another gap. In my head, it was as if Armstrong was connected with mum's death. I know, I know, that's stupid, but it was just the way that, for me, a precious, precious person had disappeared and drained everything out of my life with her, while he'd wiped out somebody he must have loved once, just to keep his life easy. And he'd done it before. It made the investigation personal.

We had no body, but I wanted him. I decided to try to upset him again so asked him to come to the station to answer some questions. He tried telling me he was too busy but I didn't give him any options. He knew he had to come. I told him to bring his solicitor, too. I didn't have any reason to but I wanted him unsettled.

When he arrived, I took him down to interview room two. I started the tape and identified the people in the room – myself, Armstrong, his solicitor Ballater, and Detective Sergeant Ross. I made it clear that no accusations were being made but that it was important for us to have everything on record because the evidence suggested that this could be a serious crime.

'What evidence?' asked Ballater.

I just looked at him. He should have known better.

We went though all the stuff Armstrong had already told us – the hire car, the planning of the trip, the silence and his eventual anxiety.

'Yes, that's something that puzzles me,' I said. 'Were you happy about your wife driving all that way?'

'Sure,' said Armstrong, 'She was a big girl.'

I noticed the tense but didn't pick up on it then.

'And about to get bigger,' I said.

He said nothing but his eyes locked on to mine and he was wary.

'That's what I mean, really,' I went on. 'Driving to Cornwall when she's pregnant. Especially after the miscarriage.'

He still said nothing.

'Didn't that worry you?' I asked.

'No.'

'Why not?'

'She was a big girl,' he repeated.

'But surely you didn't want to risk losing a second baby?'

'The kid was Cindy's idea, not mine. She knew what I thought about it.'

Ballater must have caught the aggression in his tone.

'May I ask the relevance of these questions?' he asked, as much to distract attention from Armstrong as to make a point.

'I don't know yet,' I said, then turned back to Armstrong.

'The pregnancy was a source of friction then, was it?' I asked.

'I don't have time for kids.'

'But Mrs Armstrong does.'

He looked hard at me again.

'Ask her,' he said.

His sneering, his disregard for people really got to me. I can usually handle it, but I nearly reached across and punched him. Vulnerable, see? Because of mum. I waited a bit, looking at the various notes I'd brought with me. One of the sheets of paper was a report on Cindy Armstrong's admission to Aberdeen Royal Infirmary when she'd miscarried.

'Tell me about the miscarriage,' I said.

Ballater started another protest but I shut him up.

'What's to tell?' said Armstrong, sitting back as if he was describing a total non-event. 'She threw up a few times, bled all over the bed and that was that.'

'Any idea what caused it?'

'What am I, a fucking gynaecologist?'

Charmer, eh?

'According to the report,' I said, 'there was a fair bit of bruising around her abdomen. How did that happen?'

I didn't expect to get away with it and Ballater was quick to jump in.

'Inspector, this is very irregular. I'm afraid I'm going to have to ask you to . . .'

I ignored him.

'Somebody else you needed to get out of the way, Mr Armstrong? The baby, I mean? Another bit of rescheduling?'

Armstrong and Ballater both stood up. I felt Jim Ross's hand on my arm but I was launched. It was the equivalent of punching him.

'And then it happens again, so this time you dump the baby and the woman who keeps threatening to produce them. Bit of a habit with you, disposing of people, isn't it?'

'Fuck you,' said Armstrong.

Ballater was calm. There was even a smile on his face.

'I want a transcript of that tape and I want your superiors to hear it,' he said.

Jim said, 'Interview suspended at two-thirty-seven', switched off the machine and took out the tape. Ballater and Armstrong were already out of the room.

'What the hell are you doing, boss?' said Jim and went out after them.

And I just started crying again. I went home. Spent the rest of the day there looking at photos of me as a kid.

But I wasn't about to let him get away with it again. I had an interview with the Chief Constable, of course, and he chewed my balls off and threatened suspension, but I didn't let it get in the way of digging for more information. There was plenty of it. Armstrong and his wife were always rowing in public; there were plenty of people, friends of hers and colleagues of his, who confirmed it. Apparently, after she'd married him, she'd become what the shrinks call a depressive. Did irrational things. Her friends said it was because he was always with other women, his friends said that he only went with the other women to get away from her demands. They said she was obsessional and hysterical.

The thing that really got to me, though, was the transcript of an interview we did with him about the two prostitutes he beat up. He denied any knowledge of them but Danny Ritchie, who was interviewing him, was sharp enough to get him talking about prostitutes in general, not just the two involved.

'I don't see the problem,' said Armstrong. 'They're in it for profit. Same as me with engineering solutions. If I don't deliver, I expect to suffer. It's a market place. Dog eat dog.'

'Nobody beats you up, though,' said Danny.

'I'm in engineering, not flesh,' said Armstrong. 'Occupational hazard for them, isn't it?'

'They should be able to choose, though, shouldn't they?' said Danny. He was clever. Talking to Armstrong as if they were in a pub, just having a quiet chat over a bevy.

'Choose? They've made their fucking choice,' said Armstrong. 'They put their bums and tits up for sale. What do they expect? Know what that makes them? Stock items on the inventory. The sad buggers who go to them are just buying substitutes for their wives, spare parts, replacements. If a spare part's no good, what do you do? Chuck it away. Simple as that.'

There was more of the same. He was so bloody sure of himself, so dismissive of the women, so empty of anything like understanding or compassion. The seventeen-year-old in the hospital with her thumb in a splint and bandages over the empty socket of her left eye was discounted. For him, she had no more significance or value than a restaurant menu.

The next time I questioned him, I'd brought all this together and was determined to stay calm and gradually pile the information up until its weight began to affect him. He'd killed two wives (as well as two babies) and he knew that I knew it. I just wanted to show him that he wasn't going to get away with it. I actually started this time with his first wife. I think it took him by surprise, but I was careful with it and there were no complaints. When I brought up the two prostitutes, he was wary, didn't say much, but just listened. Again, though, I kept it low key, kept my cool and just let the facts come out. I didn't accuse him of anything. I did repeat some of the words he'd used in his interview with Danny, but I didn't really accuse him of anything. In a way, I was giving him the chance to . . . what's the word? . . . redeem himself. Yes, that's it.

'You see, you reported your wife as missing, but I'm not sure what you think that means,' I said.

'It means she's gone. Not here any more. What the hell could it mean?'

'But is she missing in the same way that, say, the people you've made redundant are missing?'

His face showed that he didn't know what I was on about.

'Pieces of jigsaw puzzles, they go missing,' I said. 'You see, it means something . . . well, definite, really. Means something's not complete. Being dead, for instance; that's not really being missing, is it?'

'Who says she's dead?' he asked, wary again.

'No, I mean generally speaking. Dead is natural. It's complete. Missing's sort of different. Means the balance is wrong, something's gone from the equation.'

'What's this got to do with . . . ?'

I didn't let him finish.

'I think it would help you in all sorts of ways to learn what being missing means,' I said. 'Change your values a bit.'

'OK,' he said. 'That's enough fucking me about. I've got a business to run. It's time we . . . '

I hit him. A quick, short swing with my right hand, the one holding the Browning .25. It's only a small gun but it adds beef to a punch. I didn't quite connect with his jaw. The punch was too high and his nose started squirting blood. It didn't matter. I didn't want to knock him out, just stun him, disorientate him, so that I could get on with it.

Course, I didn't tell you, did I? It was a Sunday and I'd fetched him from his house and brought him to his engineering yard. That was what the Browning was for. So that he wouldn't argue. We were in the pipe storage area. We'd had to raise our voices to speak over the din of a generator that ran permanently to supply the site with independent power.

He'd fallen back and was leaning on one elbow, slowly shaking his head. I looped a length of cable over him and pulled him up, locking his arms to his sides then tying his wrists together at the front.

I bent, slung him over my shoulder in a fireman's lift and carried him to a rack of 36-inch diameter pipes at the furthest end of the yard. They were stacked with one end hard against the yard wall. When we got to them, I turned and slid his feet into one at about shoulder height, then pushed until he was lying inside it, with his head just at the opening. I tell you, it was a relief to get him off me. I stretched and straightened a bit.

'You're a heavy bugger,' I said. 'You want to watch what you're eating. Still, I might be able to help you with that.'

He was still too groggy to do anything and, if he tried to wriggle out of the pipe, he'd only fall on his head. He was beginning to take notice, though.

'Now then,' I said, 'you know what I think? I think you got rid of your wife – Cindy, I mean, we know you got rid of the first one – and I think you slipped her into one of the pipes you buried over in your contamination area.'

'I didn't . . . ' he said, his words slurring as if he'd had a few.

'And you reported her as missing, but she's not. She's dead. And we've agreed that that's not the same thing.'

'Honest to God,' he said. 'I'm telling you it's not . . . '

'No, no, listen,' I said. 'This is important. She'd only be missing if she was in the pipe and still alive. Dead doesn't count. Just think about that a minute.'

From the look in his eyes, he'd already started thinking about it and he didn't like what he was imagining. I left him to it while I went across to a stack of his sealing plugs. Beside them was a diesel trolley with blocks and pulleys on it to lift individual plugs onto lorries for transport. I started it up, hooked up a 36-inch diameter plug, hauled on the chains to get it clear of the stack and put the trolley in gear to guide it back to where Armstrong was lying. Even if he hadn't cottoned on before, there wasn't much doubt in him when I switched off the diesel, with the plug swinging just a couple of feet away from his face.

'Now then,' I said. 'About your wife. Cindy. Where is she?'

He shook his head. Little spots of blood dripped from his nose onto the inside wall of the pipe.

'You're not making this very easy,' I said. I put my hands on his shoulders and began to push him further in. The pipes are about twelve metres long so there was plenty of room inside. He started to struggle but there was nothing he could do.

'Last chance,' I said.

He was crying now. And terrified. Well, wouldn't you be?

'OK, OK,' he said. 'Bastard, bastard, bastard. Let me out. I'll tell you.'

'No, no. Tell me first.'

He was quiet apart from the sobs, still not willing to admit to anything. I gave another little push to remind him. His reaction was a shout.

'Yes. I killed her, all right? I killed her. She was trying to . . . '

'No, no,' I said. 'That's all I wanted to hear. I don't need the details. You buried her with the pipes, right?'

'Yes,' he said.

It gave me no satisfaction to be proved right. I just looked at him for a while, then pushed him further into the pipe. As I did it, I was thinking about his wives, the two girls he'd battered and, of course, about mum. She wouldn't have approved of what I was doing, but she'd have understood it.

I had to get inside the pipe myself to make sure that he was well along it. I pushed him almost to the end which was up against the wall. I checked the cable holding him and loosened it so that he'd soon be able to work it free. He watched me, whimpering and crying, not managing any words. He was lying on his side, his knees pulled up to his chest and his hands bent in front of his face. I crawled out and hauled on the chains again to get the plug in position. It had two solid rubber seals set back inside its profile. Before I slid it home, I hacked at them with a Stanley knife. I didn't want the pipe to be airtight. Didn't want him to suffocate.

When I did force it inside the end of the pipe, I could tell right away what a good piece of design it was. He'd been screaming on and off since he'd realised what I was up to. It was bloody loud. Echoed a lot. But the minute the end of the pipe was covered, I couldn't hear a thing. Just the whine of the generator. I rammed the plug further in, crawling behind it, heaving against it with my shoulders. It was polished steel. The surface slid very easily along the pipe wall. I didn't stop until I was just about exhausted. By then, it was far enough inside the pipe to be invisible to anyone in the yard. I reckon the section Armstrong was in was about three metres long.

There was just enough room for me to wriggle into position to operate the buttons which set the seals. I heard them hiss into place, gave a few more shoves against the plug to make sure it was set, crawled back out into the light and drove home.

It wasn't a mature thing to do. It made me no better than Armstrong. But I couldn't help myself. I really needed to do it. It wasn't about the law. It was about justice. People. It was about love. And mum.

Armstrong was reported missing at the end of that week. That was over a month ago.

They still haven't found him.

Showmen

PETER LOVESEY

'Getting rid of the bodies was never a problem for me, sir. Sure, we got rid of so many I lost count.'

'Sixteen, they said.'

The cracked lips parted and curved. Sixteen was a joke. Everyone knew the official count had been too low.

'You got away with it, too.'

'I wouldn't say that.'

'Come now, you're a free man, aren't you? Thirty years later, here you are, drinking whisky in the Proud Peacock.'

'God bless you, yes.'

'A reformed character.'

'Well, I'm not without sin, but I've not croaked a fellow creature since those days. I was wicked then, terrible, terrible.'

'Does it trouble you still?'

'Not at all.'

'Really?'

He roared with laughter. Jesus, if I thought about it, I'd never get a peaceful night's sleep.

Talking of trouble, it had taken no end of trouble to find the fellow. Rumour had it that he was now an Oxford Street beggar – but trying to find a particular beggar in Oxford Street in 1860 was like looking for a pebble on Brighton beach. From Hyde Park to Holborn a parade of derelicts pitched for pennies, pleading with passers-by, displaying scars and crippled limbs, sightless eyes and underfed infants. They harassed the shoppers, the rich and would-be rich, innocents up from the country trying to reach the great drapery shops, Marshall & Snelgrove and Peter Robinson.

It took a long morning and most of an afternoon of enquiries before William Hare was discovered outside Heath's the Hatmakers, a lanky, silver-haired, smiling fellow offering bootlaces for sale and not above accepting charity from those who didn't need laces. A 'spare wretch, gruesome and ghoulish', the court reporters had once called him, but at this stage in his declining years his looks frightened no one. Animated, grinning and quick of tongue in his Irish brogue, he competed eagerly for the money in the shoppers' pockets.

To listen to Hare trading on his notoriety, discussing his series of murders, was supposed to be 'high ton', the latest thing in entertainment, the best outside the music halls. He was a good raconteur, as the Irish so often are, with a marvellous facility for shifting the blame on to others, notably his partner, Burke, and the anatomist, Dr Knox.

Of course, he had to be persuaded to talk. He denied his own identity when first it was put to him. The promise of a drink did the trick.

Now, in the pub, he was getting gabbier by the minute.

'Did y'know I was measured by the well-known bumps-on-the-head expert, Mr Combe, at the time of the trial, or just after? Did y'know that?'

'The phrenologist.'

'You're right, your honour. Phrenologist. There's something called the bump of ideality, and mine is a bump to be marvelled at, prodigious, greater than Wordsworth's or Voltaire's. With a bump like mine I could have done beautiful things if my opportunities had been better.'

'You made your opportunities.'

'Indeed I did.' The mouth widened into the grin that was Hare's blessing and his curse.

'You robbed others of their opportunities.'

'That's a delicate way of putting it, sir.'

'No one murdered so many and lived to tell the tale.'

He almost purred at that. 'A tale I don't tell very often.'

'Unless you're paid.'

That nervy smile again. In court, all those years ago, the incessant twitch of his lips had displeased the judge and drawn hisses of contempt from the public gallery. The people of Edinburgh had hated him. The grin inflamed them.

It seemed Hare didn't feel comfortable with his new patron, despite the whisky in his hand. 'Tell me, sir, is it possible we met before?'

'Why do you ask?'

'The familiar way you talk to me.'

The nerve of the man – as if his crimes had made him one of the elect. 'You're notorious, Hare. I know all about you, if that's what you mean.'

'I bet you don't, sir, not *all*. You know the worst, but no one ever told you the best. People shouldn't believe what they read in the newspapers. The queer thing is, I never planned it, you know. The papers made me out to be a monster, but I was not. It was circumstances, sir, circumstances.' He was into his flow now. 'The first one, the very first, wasn't one of those we turned off. He was an old soldier, a lodger in the house, the lodging house my woman Mag and I had in West Port. He faded away of natural causes.'

This caused some macabre amusement. 'Come now.'

'I swear before God, that's the truth,' Hare insisted, planting a fist on the table, 'Mag and I didn't hasten his leaving at all. We wanted him to live a few days more. His rent was due. Four pounds. And fate cruelly took him to his Maker before his quarterly pension was paid. How can you run a lodging house without the rent coming in?'

'So the circumstance was financial?'

'You have it in a nutshell, sir. He left nothing I could sell. I couldn't go up to the Castle and ask the military for his pension. I was forced to go elsewhere for the arrears.'

'By selling the corpse.'

Hare nodded. 'With the help of another lodger, my fellow countryman, Mr Burke, whose name has since become a byword for infamy. Sure and William Burke was no angel, I have to admit. But I couldn't have managed alone. We removed old Donald from his coffin and weighted it with a sack of wood and gave it a pauper's burial. After dark that evening we carried the body up to the College on the South Bridge, with a view to donating it to science.'

'Selling it, you mean.'

'To recover the rent. All of Edinburgh knew the schools of anatomy couldn't get enough corpses. At the time I speak of, 1827, there were seven anatomists at work in the city, doing dissections to educate the students, and that wasn't enough. The dissecting rooms were like theatres, sir, vast places, crammed to the rafters with students, five hundred at a time. Is it any wonder there was a trade in bodysnatching? Not that Burke and Hare rifled graves. Say what you like about us, we never stooped to that. Ours were all unburied. We had this innocent corpse, as I told you, and we went in search of Professor Monro.'

'Why Monro?'

'You have an item to sell, you're better off going to the top, aren't you? And here's a strange twist of fate. We were standing in the quad with our booty between us in a tea-chest when a student happened to come by. I asked him the way to the School of Anatomy. This is where fate interfered, sir. The student wasn't a pupil of the professor. He was one of Dr Knox's canny little boyos. He sent us down to Cowgate, to 10 Surgeons' Square, the rival establishment.' He drew himself up. 'That, sir, is the truth of how we got drawn into the web of the infamous Dr Knox. If we'd got to the professor first, the story might have ended differently.'

'Why is that?'

'Because of what was said, sir.'

'By Dr Knox?'

'His acolytes, the people at Surgeon's Square. We didn't get to see the old devil that night. We dealt with three of his students. You have to admire his organisation. He had students on duty into the night meeting visitors like ourselves and purchasing bodies, and no questions asked. They paid seven pounds ten. We should have insisted on ten, but we had no experience. The students seemed well pleased with what they got, and so were we, to speak the truth. And then they spoke the words that touched our Irish hearts: 'Sure, we'd be glad to see you again when you have another to dispose of.' Ha – and didn't our ears prick up at that!'

' "*Glad to see you.*" Glad to see the contents of your tea-chest, more like.'

A cackle greeted this. 'And do you know who those students were that night? They became three of the most eminent surgeons in the kingdom. Sir William Fergusson, Thomas Wharton Jones and Alexander Miller. And here am I, who assisted so handsomely in their education, reduced to begging on the streets.'

'Shall I fetch another whisky?'

'I won't say no.'

Left alone at the table, William Hare pondered his chances of extracting something more than drink. He had a suspicion the expenses were being met by a newspaper. There was still plenty of macabre interest in the story of Burke and Hare. It was like old times: the law of supply and demand at work again. A paper with an interest in famous crimes ought to be paying him a decent fee for this interview. He might even negotiate a week in a proper hotel.

'Would you mind telling me who you represent?' he asked his companion when he returned to the table.

'Myself.'

'You wouldn't be from the press?'

'Certainly not. I'm a showman.'

Hare stood up, outraged. 'I'm not going into a freak show.'

'Please calm down. I haven't the slightest intention of offering you employment. This is simply a quiet tête-à-tête over a whisky.'

He remained standing. 'What's the show?'

Dismissively, the showman said, 'It's totally unconnected with this conversation. If you must know, I am employed for my voice, in a circus, acting as interlocutor, lecturer and demonstrator for a travelling party of Ojibbeway Indians from North America.'

If anything could silence Hare, it was a man who spoke for a troupe of Ojibbeway Indians.

He resumed his seat. 'What do you want with me, then?'

'I'm curious about what happened.'

'It's all been told before.'

'I know that. I want to hear it from the lips of the man who did it. Tell me about your method. How was the killing done?'

'For the love of God, lower your voice,' said Hare. 'I don't want the whole of London knowing my history.' He'd suffered enough in the past from being named in public.

More quietly, the showman said, 'You've always insisted that Burke was the prime mover in the business.'

Leaning across the table, Hare responded in a low voice, 'He did the suffocating, and that's the truth. He always held the pillow.'

'But you assisted.'

'Only in a passive manner, sir, by lying on the subject, to discourage the arms and legs from interfering. I did it well, too. There was never a mark of violence. Never. That was what saved me from the hangman.'

'That, and your gift of the gab.'

Hare sniffed. 'You're a fine one to comment, by the sound of things. Say what you like, we were professionals, through and through. We didn't take any Tom, Dick or Harry. They were hand-picked. They were not missed usually, being derelicts, simpletons and women of the unfortunate class. And it didn't matter what sort of scum they were when they were lying on Dr Knox's slab. He called them his subjects.' He laughed. 'Straight, that's the truth. His subjects. You'd think he was the king himself.'

'What did you call them? Your victims?'

'Our shots. Did I say a moment ago that none of them were missed? I'd better correct that. We did have an enquiry from the daughter of one of our shots, a grown woman, a whore. She came looking for her mother.' He paused. His timing was part of the act. 'We got sixteen pounds for the pair.'

'Did you ever sell a corpse to anyone else?'

'No, sir. Only to Dr Knox. I'll say this for him – and I won't say much for that odious sawbones – he knew how to guard his reputation. There was one we took to his rooms known in the city as Daft Jamie, a bit of a character this one had been. Jamie always went barefoot, winter and summer, and they were queer feet, if you understand me, misshapen. Well, when we pulled him out of the tea-chest in the dissecting-room, three or four people, including the janitor, said, 'That's Daft Jamie!' But Dr Knox would have none of it. He said it couldn't be. Burkey and I guarded our tongues and took the money.'

'You believe Dr Knox was pretending?'

'I'm sure of it.'

'Why?'

'Because later there was a bit of a hue and cry about Jamie. His mother and sister went around the town asking questions. And as soon as old Knox heard of that, he ordered the corpse to be dissected and the parts dispersed. Mr Fergusson took the feet away and one of the others had the head, so that if the police came calling, no one would know the rest of the body from Adam's.'

There was a pause in the conversation. The appalling details didn't make the sensation that Hare expected. Surely the story was worth another drink? But no. 'And this lucrative career of yours came to an end after only nine months.'

'You must have been a-checking of your facts,' he said caustically. 'Yes, it was no fault of mine. I was having trouble with Burke. There was a falling-out at one point, you know. In the summer, Burkey went visiting his woman's people in Falkirk, and when they returned, he smelt a rat. Thought I'd done a little work on my own account, taken a shot to Dr Knox and pocketed the reward without telling him. The leery devil trots off to Surgeons' Square to get the truth of it. When he's told they paid me eight pounds for a female, he leaves my lodging-house in a huff. Found new lodgings.'

'That must have put a blight on your arrangements.'

'Not for long, sir. Burkey got short of money and came skulking back with a new proposal. A cousin of his woman's, a young girl he'd met in Falkirk, came to stay. He asked me to take the first steps in the matter, the girl being a relative.'

'You did the smothering on this occasion?'

'As a kindness to his family. A ten-pound shot. But Burke never lodged with us any more.'

'You were back in business, though.'

A twitchy smile. 'We did a few more, and then the fates put a stop to our capers. Burke asked me and my woman Mag to his lodging to celebrate Halloween. What a disaster! If only I'd had the sense to refuse. He'd found another shot, of course, some old beggar woman called Docherty. Sure, she was Irish, like Burkey and myself, and only too willing to join the party. But all he had was the one room to do it in. What's more he had lodgers, a family called Gray, who slept on straw on the floor. To simplify matters, I said the Grays could remove to our place that night, and they did. So it was just Burke and his Nell, me and my Mag, and old Mrs Docherty. Well, we all had a few drinks too many, and the old woman screamed 'Murder!' and one of the neighbours went to look for a policeman.'

'You were arrested?'

'No, sir.' The smirk again. 'You know how it is with the guardians of the law. They're like the bloody omnibuses. You can never find one when you want one. What did for us was Burke's incompetence. When the Gray family came back next morning, the corpse was still in the room, under the straw they slept on. Can you believe that? Like a bat out of hell Gray goes to the police.'

Hare's companion took a thoughtful swig of his drink. He wasn't writing any of this down. 'You don't have to talk about the trial,' he said. 'How you turned King's Evidence to escape the noose.'

'To assist the law, sir. They had no case without me. As I told you a moment ago, there wasn't so much as a scratch on the bodies.'

'You had a few more brains in your head than Burke.'

'He swung, as you know, sir.'

'And his corpse, fittingly enough, was presented to Professor Monro to be dissected.'

'Yes,' said Hare cheerfully. 'And did you hear about the lying-in-state?'

'The *what*?'

Hare laughed. 'Burkey was never so popular as when he was on the slab. The judge in his wisdom decreed that he should be anatomised in public and the public demanded to see the result. Thirty thousand filed through the room. Most of Edinburgh, if you ask me. The line stretched for over a mile.'

'Your companion, flayed, salted and preserved, packed into a barrel – for science, as you would put it. His skin cut into pieces and sold as souvenirs. I believe his skeleton can still be seen at the University.'

This was not part of the script, the audience taking over. Hare didn't care for it. Moreover, he had detected a note of censure. He stated emphatically, 'It was no bed of roses for me, sir. They tried their damnedest to make me go the way of Burke. A private prosecution, followed by a civil action. They failed, but it was mental persecution. And when I finally got my liberty I was in fear of my life from the mob outside. They wanted to lynch me.'

'And no wonder.'

'I had to be smuggled out of the jail, disguised. I was put on the southward mail coach. As bad luck would have it, one of my fellow passengers had featured in the trial as a junior counsel, and he recognised me, and blabbed to the others. The news was out. At Dumfries, I was practically mobbed. It was ugly, sir, uncommon ugly. I holed up in the King's Arms for a time, but it wasn't safe. The authorities removed me to the jail for my own safety, and the jackals outside bayed for my blood all night. It took a hundred specials to disperse them.'

'But you got away.'

'Under armed guard. The militia escorted me across the border.'

'You're a fortunate man, Hare.'

'You think so? A ruin, more like. Look at me. I'll tell you who was a fortunate man, and that's the piece of excrement they called Knox. He was in it up to his ears, as guilty as Burke, and guiltier than me.'

'Why so?'

'Knox was the instigator, wasn't he? He knew everything, everything. He dealt with us in person a dozen times. Oh, he denied it of course. For pity's sake, where did he think the bodies were coming from, freshly dead and regular as clockwork? The people weren't fooled, just because he was a doctor.'

'Surgeon, in fact. You should be careful with your choice of words. The people you just referred to were the same crowd you described as the mob a moment ago.'

Hare laughed. 'Mob they may have been, but they knew all about Knox. I know for a fact that they met on Calton Hill and made an effigy of the bastard, and carried it in procession all the way to his house in Newington Place, where they burned it in his garden and smashed all his windows.'

'So they did.'

'You heard of it, too?'

'Indeed,' said the showman. 'Moreover, they attacked his dissecting-rooms. Like you, he fled. He was thought to have gone into hiding in Portobello, so they made another effigy and hanged it on a gibbet at the top of Tower Street there. You were not alone in being an object of hatred.'

'He got his job back,' Hare pointed out. 'The same year he was back in Surgeons' Square cutting up bodies.'

'Ah, but he was obliged to suffer the indignity of a University committee of inquiry. They found nothing actionable in his past conduct. There's the difference, Hare. You stand condemned – or you should have, if there were any justice. Dr Knox was exonerated of blame in the matter.'

'Absurd,' muttered Hare.

'What do you mean?'

'They would never sack him. He was a god to his students. They adored the bastard. His classes numbered over five hundred.'

'However, his career was blighted. You may not know this, but he twice applied for Chairs of the University, and was twice humiliated. He was compelled to relinquish his career at Edinburgh. He moved to Glasgow.'

'And I'm moved to tears,' said Hare. 'I hope he died spitting blood in the poorest tenement in the Gorbals.'

'You're still a bitter man.'

'I've reason to be bitter. Dr Knox underpaid us for the last one.'

'The last one? I don't understand.'

'The old Irish woman I was telling you about. Mrs Docherty, on Halloween. You see, we delivered her to Knox the day the game was up. We had to get rid of it. He only paid us half. Said we could have the rest on Monday. We never got our second five pounds.'

'And that still irks?'

'No man has treated me with anything but derision . . . until today.'

'Just a couple of drinks so far.'

The 'so far' emboldened Hare to say in the wheedling tone that worked best for him, 'Would you see your way to the price of a bed in return for all the inside information I've given you in confidence, sir?'

'I can do better than that. If I give you money, you'll only blue it on drink. I can offer you accommodation. I have rooms in Hackney. A humble address, but better than the places you inhabit, I'll warrant.'

'Hackney. That's not far.'

'Shall we treat ourselves to a cab-ride?'

Hare beamed. 'Why not, sir? And if you want to introduce me to your friends and neighbours, I won't object.'

'That won't be necessary.'

'I am the only man to be exhibited in the Chamber of Horrors in his lifetime. Baker Street – my other address – ' he joked, 'care of Madame Tussaud.'

'Shall we leave?'

'If you're ready, then so am I.' Hare finished the last of the whisky and stood up. He reached out with his right hand, groping at the space between them. 'It would help me if I took your arm, sir.'

'Of course.' The showman enquired with what sounded like a note of concern, 'How did you come to lose your sight?'

'That was after I came south, sir. I got a job. Labouring – that's my occupation. It was all right for a time. I got on well enough with the others. Then – pure vanity – I confided in one of my mates that I was the smarter half of the old partnership. Smart! You know what? They set upon me. Threw me into a lime-pit. Vicious. Destroyed my eyes. I've been a vagrant ever since. Do you know what I most regret?'

'I've no idea.'

He permitted himself another smile. 'I shall never see myself in the Chamber of Horrors.'

'Careful, there's a step down.'

'Down to what, sir?' quipped Hare. 'A meeting with Old Nick?'

They made their way out of the pub and took the first cab that came along. Heading east, it was soon lost to view in the Oxford Street traffic.

* * *

The encounter just described is a fantasy based on accounts of the case, but the story can end with facts. William Hare, who combined with Burke to commit the West Port Murders of 1828, was said to have been a familiar figure, blind and begging in Oxford Street, until about 1860.

The famous anatomist Dr Robert Knox also ended his days in relative obscurity, as a general practitioner in Hackney, and latterly as 'lecturer, demonstrator, or showman to a travelling party of Ojibbeway Indians'. He died of a stroke in 1862 at the age of 71.

Hare just disappeared.

A certain resolution

MARGARET MURPHY

He watched from the warmth of his car. She was home. The curtains were drawn, but the lights glowed behind them. He felt a confused mixture of desire and rage. When she had first rejected him, he hung around her flat, hurt, hoping she would take him back. For days – *weeks* – he had played Heathcliffe to her Cathy, until she became irritated by his persistence. Then, he felt a dull resentment: wasn't he trying to protect her, to keep her safe?

He couldn't say exactly when he began to enjoy the vigil; the feeling grew slowly, and it was bound up with the change in her, from impatience to anxiety. He had provoked it, he knew, with a telephone warning or two, a letter, telling her just how much she needed him, but once it began, her fear seemed to feed on itself, and he became hungry for it. He no longer wanted her to take him back – he could take what he wanted whenever he wanted it. The look of terror on her face when she saw his car parked outside her flat, the tremor in her voice when she answered the phone, thrilled and sustained him during the long nights of watching.

The night he broke into her flat was the most perfect sex he had ever had. Her pleading – her eagerness to appease – a potent aphrodisiac. But he hadn't frightened her enough, it seemed, because the next day the police had come for him.

A six month stint in prison had changed him: he lost some of his easy self-confidence, his persuasive charm. It was replaced by something much harder, and more dangerous.

All he had now was Emma. He lost his job, and the *Mondeo* that went with it, his flat had been re-let, and his friends were no longer keen for his company, fearing for their potato-faced wives.

All his current difficulties, every miserable failure, were down to Emma. And yet he still wanted her. And he wanted Emma to think about him every waking minute of her day. He wanted to be present in her thoughts, her dreams, her nightmares. He would dictate the detail of her plans, where she lived, who she saw, her job – she had lost three since he resumed his watch.

Orange light from the street lamps reflected in the grimy puddles in the gutters, but the sky was clearing, and the moon shone cold and austere on the slate roofs of the terraced houses. It was eleven o'clock, and families were settling down for the night. She lived in a cul-de-sac. The residents provided the only traffic, and it seemed no one was keen to go out on this cold November night.

He watched for the glow of her bedside lamp. Emma no longer slept in the dark; that was down to him, too – he thought of it as a bond between them. She slept at the front of the house, perhaps thinking that she would be able to raise the alarm more easily from there, but when the time came he wouldn't allow so much as a squeak from her.

He was about to close his eyes and snooze for a short while, when he saw a light go on in the hallway and Emma's front door opened. This was the first time he had seen her since the courtroom when she had given her evidence. She looked thinner – he was always telling her she should lose some weight, and now, finally, she had. A dog bounced around at her feet, a German Shepherd. It was no more than a puppy. No threat.

When Emma turned and closed the door, he saw with a shock that she had cut her hair; chopped it to collar length.

She looks like a bloody dyke.

She locked the door – a Yale deadlock and a heavy-looking mortise – and looked anxiously up and down the street before crossing within ten feet of this car. He slid down in his seat, then swivelled to see where she was going.

She walked with her head down, as if willing herself invisible, her soft-soled shoes barely made a sound on the pavement. She was heading for an area of fenced woodland that started at the end of the close and circled around one side of the estate, though not, he noted, the back of Emma's house. What was she trying to prove, going out on her own, in the dark? This was just the sort of behaviour that got her into trouble the first time around.

She opened a low wooden gate and let the dog through, only allowing it off the leash when she was on the other side herself. He *could* leave her to it: wait for her to get back, and then carry on as he had planned. There again, he could let himself into her house and wait for her. Or he could go after her. Maybe he would, just for a bit – kick up a few leaves, make a bit of noise – remind her why a woman shouldn't go out alone at night.

Hard to resist. He grabbed his rucksack from the well of the passenger seat. It contained everything he needed: syringe, ketamine, knife, rope, gag, condoms – he wasn't going to get caught the same way twice.

He walked incautiously, snapping twigs, scuffing up the sodden mulch of autumnal litter. Once or twice he thought he heard an answering '*crack*!', a rustling in the undergrowth. He kept an eye out for the dog: if it doubled back to investigate him, he might need the knife.

The path twisted and veered right, down a slope between two mounds. Bare except for a few strippy saplings, they resembled giant anthills. Here the leaf litter from the overhanging beech and oak trees was thickly layered and, wet with rainfall, it deadened every sound.

She whistled.

He stood perfectly still, watching for the dog. It gave a bark, as if it had found something in the undergrowth, but Emma whistled again and called its name, and it came running, its tongue lolling, ears flapping.

She hadn't seen him. She patted the dog and turned the bend, descending into a cut behind one of the hillocks.

He followed at a trot, the moonlight bright enough for him to negotiate safely the ruts and dips in the path down into the cut. The wind boomed through the upper branches of the trees. It was darker here, and colder. He walked on, more cautiously now, rounded a bend, and stopped dead.

Emma stood, her hands by her sides, no more than ten or fifteen feet away. Her face shone as grey as the moon. There was no sign of the pup, but he heard a whimper and a tentative bark deeper in the wood.

For a while – it couldn't have been more than half a minute, but it seemed much longer – they did nothing. This wasn't how it was supposed to happen. *He* was supposed to choose the time and place. He had waited long enough, thought about it, planned every detail. There was little else to do in prison; he had refined and rehearsed and perfected every stage of his 'new vigil' as he thought of it, and now she had messed it all up.

Well, he thought, shucking the rucksack from his shoulder. *She asked for it.*

Suddenly Emma was moving. She walked towards him; quick, purposeful strides, her head down, avoiding his eyes. He had taught her never to give him that brazen look, and he was gratified that she hadn't forgotten the lesson.

She's going to ask me to leave her alone. She's going to beg.

'Oh, you'll beg, all right,' he murmured, squeezing the clip on the front flap of his bag.

The dog gave another anxious yelp. He thought he saw a shadow flit from one tree to the next at the periphery of his vision. Emma might not be the only dog-walker dragging their pet out for a toilet break between the rain showers – he would have to be quick. He reached into his rucksack, felt the hilt of the knife.

Then she was on him.

A flash of cold light – the glint of a blade.

He pulled, feeling a rising panic. His knife snagged on the material of the flap. Too late. *Too late!*

He lifted the rucksack, using it as a shield.

She drove forward, tearing through the nylon bag, through the padding of his jacket, barely making contact with his flesh. He felt a popping sensation, a sharp shock. He dropped the rucksack and covered his stomach with his hands.

She pulled back, came at him again. In the slow, choreographed moments that followed, he saw that the blade was dulled with blood – his blood. He looked into her face and saw nothing. No fear, no hatred. No emotion at all. He made a grab for her hand and caught the knife blade instead. It sliced his flesh with a faint wet hiss and he felt a vivid burning pain in his hand.

Emma plunged the knife inwards and upwards.

Brace yourself

RUSSELL JAMES

Patterson lets the gun dangle from his hand. You can see he doesn't know how to carry the thing. He lets it trail beside his leg, the barrel inches from his ankles. Occasionally he uses the gun to move wet undergrowth aside. You wouldn't be surprised if you saw mud on the end of the barrel, because you know that Patterson is the kind of man who has rarely *seen* a gun, let alone carried one.

Look at his clothes: jeans, denim jeans – the last thing to wear when tramping through damp woodland. They absorb water from the bushes and retain moisture. Patterson also wears black galoshes and a brown tweed jacket. Under the jacket he wears a navy wool pullover. A big pullover. His jacket has been forced over it and looks tight across the shoulders. His arms move stiffly.

He shouldn't be here.

* * *

Fenner knew that the moment he saw him. Patterson had crunched his green Ford to a halt behind Fenner's Jag on the gravel in front of the house, had heaved his large body out of the Ford and marched across the path with the engine left running. Obviously he realised he couldn't park it at the foot of the steps. He wanted instructions, like a tradesman who should have driven round to the back. Fenner waited for Leighton to tell him so.

But he didn't. Leighton greeted Patterson by name – he was not effusive about it, but not hostile either. 'Glad you found us, Patterson. Decent journey?'

'Bit of a grind. Roadworks on the motorway.'

Leighton turned to Fenner: 'Michael Patterson,' he said. 'Barry Fenner. Another guest.'

Fenner eyed the man with interest. 'Patterson, eh?'

The man nodded. 'Good to meet yer.'

'How do you do?'

But Fenner made no move to shake hands with Patterson. He and Leighton were at the top of the wide stone steps, Patterson on the gravel below. Fenner – thin, aesthetically drawn, pale blond hair – wore a light grey suit. Patterson – dark-haired, large and awkward – wore shirt and slacks. A vivid tie hung loosely around his neck and his shirt was unbuttoned, too small at the collar. One side had become untucked from his trousers. Squinting up at the two men on the steps, Patterson fumbled in his pocket for a pair of spectacles, and once he'd put them on he said, 'That's better.'

Leighton smiled. 'You can switch the engine off, you know. I'll have someone move your car just as soon as they've brought your luggage in. Leave the key inside.'

'Right.'

As Patterson turned back to his car, Fenner glanced at his host for some sign of his reaction – a conspiratorial wink perhaps – but John Leighton's face retained its customary polite expression. Fenner studied him openly. Leighton's dark hair seemed a little thinner than when they'd last met. Perhaps the afternoon sunlight, glaring onto Leighton's black hair, showed how each strand had been flattened into submission with water, brush and comb. Leighton looked older today. People should age gradually. Fenner had read somewhere that every cell in the human body dies and is replaced within a space of seven years, so that before any decade is out, one has become an entirely different person. If ageing should be gradual, it seemed that Leighton had aged seven years in this last month. Cells were dying on his skin. It was as if he'd reached his fortieth birthday and had turned off the switch.

He seemed thinner too.

* * *

Ahead of the others in the wet undergrowth, John Leighton bites his lip. A flicker of anxiety crosses his face, but he hides it. In his Barbour jacket and plus fours he looks less thin than he did yesterday – he looks wiry, quite tough, in fact. He stands with feet planted firmly apart, legs warmly encased in leather-lined *Le Chameau* boots, neat *Habicht* binoculars slung loose around his neck, and he carries a boxlock Holland and Holland Cavalier shotgun in one hand. Two dogs pant in the dewy air as they stand patiently beside him. Leighton is boss.

* * *

'Here comes another car. Would you like to pop up to your room?'

Leighton's tone told Fenner not to wait with him on the steps. It underlined whose house this was, whose guests, whose weekend, and said that Leighton wished to greet his guests alone.

Fenner shrugged. He had no wish to linger at the top of these cold steps, grinning aimlessly into space while Leighton shook hands and prattled to each new visitor. It was dull enough talking to Leighton, let alone to his wretched guests. He went inside.

Alone, John Leighton blinked against low sunlight. Rattling towards the house along the tree-lined drive came a battered Land Rover. Harriet Henderson. Leighton hoped she had not brought dogs with her. She bred the things – made money from doing so, apparently. He had had to speak to her about it once, when she had tried to sell dogs at his dinner table. Leighton didn't know whether she sold dogs as a pastime or whether she needed the extra money – one did not ask. Harriet always wore the same old clothes, drove the same old Land Rover – not that that meant anything. Families with money did not trouble to flaunt the fact.

The Hendersons and Leightons had been neighbours for two hundred years. By now, most of the Hendersons had moved away – had married badly, died, that sort of thing. Harriet was virtually the only one left. She rode to hounds, of course, appeared at the odd gymkhana, but little else. The Hendersons were part of the countryside around here.

Whereas Fenner . . . Where had he come from? One could not be sure about Barry Fenner's background. A London man: that was written in every vein of him. Smart suits, smart car, smart attitudes. When Fenner came down last time – when was it, three weekends ago? – he had tried to impress Emily with highfalutin talk of negotiable securities, insider deals. Perhaps she *was* impressed. All Leighton knew was that when he brought the conversation round to include a couple of items from his own diminishing portfolio, the chap had grown suddenly evasive – as if he'd been delivering lines from a speech he had rehearsed, and he couldn't leave his script. He had floundered. He couldn't improvise. Surprising, that. You'd have expected a chap like Fenner to be quick-witted.

Mind you, thought Leighton, as Harriet's muddy Land Rover came out from beneath the trees onto his gravel forecourt, if Fenner *had* been a stockbroker he could have done them good. Their shares were languishing, to put it mildly. Withering on the bough. Leighton didn't understand the things; investment was like a card game he didn't play. Not everyone could win.

While Harriet clambered from her driving seat Leighton kept a smile on his face. Then he rested it while, with a brisk wave, she stomped around to the back of her muddy vehicle and began to rummage for her luggage. Leighton's Maltese footman rushed down the steps and dithered around her, but she brushed him away. When the footman glanced to the top of the steps he saw Leighton staring at the sky, apparently unaware.

But Leighton was thinking that 'footman' was a ridiculous word. What did it mean? A man who waited on foot. How else should a servant wait – upon a horse? Leighton wondered whether other people still used the term. Was there a more modern word? No doubt in London, where Fenner came from, they used some foreign name – if people in London kept footmen nowadays. Fenner wouldn't, that was sure. Out here in the Cotswolds there was less need to use the latest word, to do the latest thing. Families maintained the old traditions here.

For half the people coming this weekend that was why they came. Once or twice a year they'd forsake their elegant city residences and plunge briefly into country life. They might rediscover the reality of a rural lifestyle – that fact that the real countryside neither smelt nor felt like the immaculate pages of country life magazines, that the grass was uneven, that fields were muddy, that old houses could be damp and grubby in the corners. Guests would eat the kind of hearty meals they would never order in London restaurants. They'd wear old clothes. They'd get up early on a Sunday morning to tramp the woodlands with a shotgun in their hands.

Harriet clumped up the steps and smiled at her old friend. She had a leather carry-all in her hand. 'I've brought a frock.'

'I'm relieved.'

Leighton kissed her cheek and found that her skin tasted faintly of dog. 'Would you like a room to change in before dinner?'

'Better than changing in the hall,' she boomed. 'But if the rooms are full of grockles I'll use a bathroom.'

'Certainly not. Wouldn't hear of it. You'll need somewhere to sit for a while, Harriet. We don't eat till eight.'

'You know me – just plonk me in the library with a glass of Scotch. Many coming?'

'About thirty, I'm told.'

*   *   *

Most of whom have followed Leighton today to the clearing in the wood. They have a sharp early-morning look about them. Cheeks are red, eyes are bright – but one or two, he notices, seem out of breath. Just from walking. Perhaps last night's dinner disagreed with them.

Leighton is surprised to see Barry Fenner out of breath. The man is lean, fit, in his middle thirties, yet he does look tired. Worrying, that. Perhaps he drank too much with his dinner. Perhaps he ate too much. Leighton clucks his tongue.

While the hunters stumble to a halt among tree stumps and strands of bramble, Fenner stands aloof. His face is paler than usual, and his hair glistens like wet straw. But Fenner isn't tired, nor is he unwell. It is just a little early in the day.

Harriet chats to Michael Patterson. The lady and the peasant, Leighton thinks. What can they talk about? Even in shapeless Barbour and tweeds, Harriet's breeding is unmissable, while Patterson looms beside her in his cheap jacket, out of place. Harriet behaves like royalty – minor royalty, mildly famous, like a duchess in a factory, chatting politely with the workmen; effortlessly, meaninglessly. Afterwards, when the duchess sweeps away to the next stop on her itinerary, the workers will recall how she paused with them to pass the day. No side on *her*, they'll say: she spoke to us like we were all the same. A proper lady.

Harriet is the sort of woman I should have married, Leighton thinks – if she hadn't always been so damned ugly. Face like an Airedale. Body like a pug.

Whereas Emily, when we married, seemed to have everything: fine looks, exquisite body – family and fortune, as the Victorians used to say. Leighton smiles ruefully. Perhaps a *fortune* was overstating the case, but Emily had had money. In their first years together she had spent it generously; had helped rebuild the stable block, had converted a row of cottages; had replenished furniture. Even the crystal glasses they used last night were hers. Soon after their honeymoon Emily had dragged John off to a man in Chipping Camden – a craftsman, an artist, really – and had commissioned a full set of his handmade glasses. Three dozen of everything. – Was it three, or four? Could it really have been four dozen?

Leighton sighs at the memory of their first years together, when Emily had danced through his dusty old house like a Fairy Queen dispensing magic. With the wand of money she had touched old pieces of furniture and had transformed them. They had been stripped and polished, and had gleamed throughout his halls. Some pieces, when she had touched them, disappeared. All those yards of stair carpet, worn thin where they turned a step, fraying at the edge. Disappeared. Replaced. Emily had scattered money like a fairy's silver dust, and it had shimmered in beams of sunlight through the dark interior of his house.

When he had married her, John Leighton was only half in love. Deeper passions had come later, but they had nevertheless seeped into the core of him, so deep they had touched his soul.

* * *

No one would have seen that yesterday. Most of the guests came up the stone steps past Leighton's greeting and were led into the house to meet his wife. They were welcomed and put at ease. Together with her husband, Emily and John Leighton made an elegant couple, good-looking and courteous, perfect hosts. In their grand reception hall Emily stood beside her husband in the only day dress she had bought this year. To their guests they chatted on the woollen carpet she had bought twelve years before. She and the carpet had hardly aged at all.

Each guest was made to feel a special friend, as if Emily was honoured that they had condescended to bestow a visit, although half the people who came were John's business contacts: two estate agents, a garage owner, the bank manager, a supplier of feedstuffs and fertiliser. Emily smiled at each of them, squeezed their hands warmly, touched wives on the arm. John Leighton, meanwhile, seemed distant, as if behind his polite smile he was reworking the seating plan for dinner and calculating the number of plates.

He must have been thinking of something else.

* * *

Barry Fenner unpacked in his usual bedroom. Presumably the Leightons had put him in this room to help him feel at home. It was his fourth visit, and each time he had had this room. Nothing changed between his visits except the flowers in the vase. Fresh flowers every time. Fresh sheets. Fresh flowers.

Despite his familiarity with the room, Fenner felt odd in Leighton's house. He did not belong. In his time Fenner had slept in many bedrooms; he had slept in hotels, flats and houses; he had slept under canvas and on a boat. Once, returning from America, he had tried to sleep on the plane. Although he prided himself on his catlike ability to snatch sleep anywhere, he couldn't do so on a plane. And not, for some reason, in this house.

As Fenner hung up his suit he shrugged. No, he did not sleep easily in Leighton's house. The thought of John Leighton in his bedroom along the corridor put Fenner slightly on edge. As in an aeroplane, he could not relax.

But here he was in the same old bedroom, greeted by host and hostess, accepted by the staff. Here he would spend the night. Here he was in the same room he had occupied before. There might even be guests he had met before. Everyone would be relaxed; they regarded Leighton's house as a fine place for a spot of fun.

Fenner, though, would have to be careful.

*   *   *

These upper-class prats have something to sneer at now, haven't they? My stupid jeans. Soaking. I stand out like a brown ale at a vicar's tea party. All right, so I'm not one of them. No way could I have pretended that I was. Right? I know that. But did I have to dress like Charlie Chaplin?

Patterson pulls the steel-rimmed spectacles off his nose and cleans the lenses with his cuff. The damp woodland air seems attracted to the glass. Every hundred yards his spectacles mist over and obscure his view. Anyone watching will see those spectacles as a symbol of how out of place he is. Perhaps nobody *is* watching him. They're too polite.

Or if they are watching, they hide it well.

*   *   *

Fenner sank into a deep bath of hot water. He stroked himself. On his lean body the blond hairs stood up in the warm water and waved like fronds of delicate seaweed. When he sat up to reach for soap, a small wave rushed to fill the space he'd vacated. When he sank down again the water thrashed and sloshed out over the side of the tub.

But it was only Leighton's carpet. It would easily dry out. To Fenner it seemed provincial to have a carpet in the bathroom; he preferred tiles. Carpet might be warmer to the feet, but that only mattered in cold bathrooms. The sort of people who laid carpets rather than heat their bathrooms were the hard-up middle class. The working class, thought Fenner, couldn't afford carpet in the first place – certainly not in the bathroom, where it might get wet.

Although from what Fenner had seen of working-class families on TV, that might not be true – *that* kind of person seemed more casual with possessions than were the middle class. Fenner sniffed. Such possessions as the working class did have were not *worth* preserving, that was the truth of it. While the rich could afford to be careless, the poor just did not care. Only the middle class worried about possessions.

Fenner changed position in the bath, deliberately clumsy. More water splashed over the side. Did Leighton have middle-class habits? It didn't seem likely; his family went back for centuries. How about the beautiful Emily? She was well-born too. Yet one of the pair had acquired this middle-class liking for carpet beside the bath.

Fenner rocked forward and stood up. A swell of soapy water flung itself at the far end of the tub like a wave against a wall, before it crashed down and swept back along the bath, swirling past his legs to the other end. But now that Fenner was standing, the level of water had subsided and did not spill onto the floor. Fenner stepped out of the bath and stood dripping onto the carpet. He dried slowly, paddling the wet woollen pile into a swampy mess around his feet.

Pointless, really. Leighton would never know. A member of his staff would come in tomorrow to clean and air the room. No one would tell Leighton that he had a damp patch on the floor. The carpet would be dry by then anyway. Fenner regretted he didn't smoke. He could have dropped a lighted cigarette and ground it into the blasted carpet.

Why was he thinking in this way? He could cripple Leighton any time he wanted. If he ever opened his mouth about this weekend – if he told the truth or half of it – it would be the end for Mr Leighton. Literally the end. Leighton had so much to lose: the house and land, passed down for generations, would be sold. He would lose Emily and she would keep the children.

Fenner wiped steam from the bathroom mirror and grinned at his reflection. It didn't bear thinking about, did it?

* * *

The sky is lightening. Weak sunlight filters low between the trees. A brighter light would be too sharp and piercing; it would bleach the sides of tree trunks and dazzle the sportsmen's eyes. This morning's feeble light is best. When a bird rises against this low hazy sun the hunters will not be blinded. They'll stare the weak sun full in the face and not lose their aim.

Patterson does not like early rising. In London, on the few days he does wake early, he lies heavily in bed, blearily aware of cars taking people to work and children to school. Only when the rush hour has faded does Patterson's blotchy face emerge from beneath the bed-clothes; only then does he start to think of breakfast.

But sometimes Patterson must rise early. On such a day he'll grumble, but he can be punctual when it matters. Take this morning, for example: to shoot partridges you get up early, God knows why. The wretched birds will flit around the fields all day; they're not going to fly away. But this is how the hunting class likes to do things, as if *they* must suffer too.

Poor bloody partridges. What did they ever do wrong?

* * *

At least they didn't eat partridge last night for dinner. To eat game in the evening and to then trek out next day for more would be like topping up your larder. Better to set out at dawn with the larder empty, track down your quarry and bring it home. You can't expect to be welcomed home a hero if the larder's already stocked. You'll want to sort out the chosen one, shoot it and bring it home. If all you bring is more of the meat that you ate yesterday, you might as well have gone to a butcher's shop.

Emily had intended that the dinner before the shoot should be Italian. The more obvious Game Pie and Hunter's Broth were scheduled for tomorrow night, after the day's exertions. For the first night, pre-hunt, roast beef would be boring and most French dishes, when bulked up, deteriorated into a kind of canteen casser-ole. Cold buffet was out of the question; pies might sink or turn leathery; some guests object to fish.

There was no fresh pasta, only dried.

How the shop in Cirencester could have run out of pasta was beyond Emily's comprehension. Apparently the machine had broken down. A machine! In Italy, peasant women made pasta using only their fingers and a rolling pin. They didn't use a machine. Fortunately, the butcher at the corner of the marketplace had prime condition lamb. Where fresh lamb was found in autumn she didn't ask.

Crown roast of lamb with paper coronets. End of season mint sauce. Three varieties of potato. Exotic vegetables, of an Italian inclination.

For dinner parties the Leighton house came into its own; the panelled dining room was perfect for large numbers. In the centre stood a huge oak table, around which were hide-backed chairs. Behind the chairs and in front of the long serving tables that lined the walls was a wide corridor for staff. Village girls in Laura Ashley cotton swept along with dishes of food. The butler had ensured that the girls knew what to do.

Patterson admired the large oak table. He gripped its top between thumb and fingers to gauge its thickness, then slipped his hand underneath to feel whether it remained the same thickness or was simply panel board thickened at the rim. He pushed his hand forward as far beneath the table as it would go, until the inside of his elbow came up against the rim. All the way in, the wood remained one solid piece. There were several sections – vast slabs of dark oak bolted together – but each slab, he thought ruefully, would need a house as big as this to let it squeeze through the dining room door.

From time to time he glanced at the horsy looking woman beside him, watching how she ate. Patterson's table manners did not come naturally; he had no social poise. No matter how he tried to hold the heavy silver cutlery in his fists, he could not relax. As he watched other diners ripping into their crown roast of lamb he thought it might be easier if he gave up trying to eat nicely and just ate. That was what the others seemed to do. They didn't manipulate their cutlery – they didn't even keep their mouths shut while they chewed – but bad manners looked all right on them.

Patterson realised that he had been placed at the low end of the table, away from family and friends. Obviously Leighton had not mixed the classes in his seating plan. Guests that John Leighton would not normally dine with had been seated furthest away. But at least everyone shared the same large table. Here at the bottom end Patterson was tucked beside a thin farmer and the horsy woman who hardly spoke. Beyond her was a businessman in a suit. He might have spent a thousand pounds on that suit, but he shouldn't have brought it to a country house weekend.

At the far end sat John Leighton beside his wife. Shouldn't she be *my* end? She wasn't. Host and hostess sat side by side among their friends, laughing and talking, enjoying their meal. Whatever they were saying was drowned in the jabber along the sides of the dark table. John Leighton chatted to a thin, regal matron with swept-back hair. Mrs Leighton shared a joke with that blond prat who Patterson had met on arrival, the man who drove the Jag.

Fenner smiled at Emily's witticism and glanced down along the table. When he saw Patterson watching him, his face froze. Because Fenner did not look away, Patterson stared back.

*   *   *

Beneath a tall plane tree Fenner pauses to wait for stragglers. Several men are out of breath. Their feet catch in low brambles. But Fenner is feeling fitter now, up to the mark.

Among the stragglers he sees Michael Patterson stumbling morosely along, eyes fixed to the ground. The man looks so out of place. He's perspiring. Now that everyone has halted, the stupid great oaf has pulled off those pathetic spectacles and is rubbing them dry on a dirty white handkerchief. Why did he agree to come? He obviously hates it here.

Presumably the thought of a weekend among the wealthy was too good to miss. See how the other half lives. Perhaps Patterson thought that some of our polish would rub off on him. Perhaps he thought he could make new business contacts here. Whatever he thought he'll be badly disappointed, that's for sure.

He must have dreaded it would turn out this way. Did he *want* to come? Leighton must have been extraordinarily persuasive.

*   *   *

A similar thought had occurred, idly, to Harriet Henderson at dinner the previous evening.

'What do you do exactly – back at home I mean?'

'I'm self-employed.'

'May one ask at what?'

'Well, I'm in the removal business.'

'Oh.'

Oh. I've never met a removal man. But as our family hasn't moved house for two hundred years, that's hardly surprising. I doubt the Leightons have met one either, before tonight. So why is he here – they can't be moving, can they?

No, quite impossible. Even if they were, they'd hardly invite the removal man to dinner – so why *is* he here? Perhaps he *paid* for this weekend. But John told me specifically that he would never sink to that: filling the house with *nouveaux* who pay to join a shoot. I can't see the objections, myself: damn good money, quickly made. Just wish I had the land. Six weekends a year, and one hardly has to mix with them. I bet it pays better than breeding dogs.

'Have you known John long?'

'John?'

'John Leighton.'

'No. Not very long.'

I see. Well, I think you *paid* for this, my man. I think John has started introducing selected punters and is testing them on the rest of us. What a cheek. He could at least try not to seat them beside his friends.

I'd better look at the other diners. This man next to me in the pale suit and garish tie: he's middle-class. Two men over there are businessmen. Nothing wrong with that, I suppose; one has to invite *some* commercial people – the bank manager, one's stockbroker, people one owes favours to, people one would like to have in one's debt. That must be the case with Mr Patterson. What exactly might John want with him? Perhaps he is having trouble with a tenant, and wants Patterson to move them out.

Hardly. But he does seem an odd sort of man to invite on a shooting weekend. Perhaps John owes him a favour – I can't imagine what. Might John be in his debt?

*   *   *

Emily was wondering the same. That large person sitting by Harriet seems most unsuitable. But recently John has picked up more than one unsuitable business colleague. Perhaps he's in some kind of sordid mess with this ungainly man – has borrowed money from him or something. It's possible. Anything is possible. These last few months, John has seemed distracted – absent, one might say.

But they both had. They were growing apart.

*   *   *

Outwardly affable and enjoying his meal, John Leighton, from the corner of his eye, couldn't help watching Michael Patterson. The way the man handled his cutlery: it hadn't occurred to Leighton that anyone nowadays could be so clumsily inept. Yet it was not from carelessness; anyone could see that Patterson ate with enormous care, painstaking in his handling of knife and fork. Beside him, Harriet Henderson stabbed at her meat, using only her fork in the American style. Yet she did it elegantly. Five hundred years of breeding. God knows what were Patterson's antecedents.

It had been obvious from the start that this man Patterson was an uncultured type, yet somehow up in London he had had a kind of style. A rough diamond, as it were. When Leighton had asked him down for the weekend he hadn't realised that Patterson would be such a misfit. He didn't want the man to stand out like this; people might comment on it, especially afterwards. Someone might ask why Leighton had invited the man.

He glanced at Barry Fenner, and noticed the half-smile that lingered on Fenner's face – that supercilious confident smile that in repose was becoming his usual expression. Fenner's eyes gave him away. They didn't smile. There was nothing soft behind his charm.

There wouldn't be.

At this moment, not only did Fenner wear that infuriating smile but he was bending his blond head towards Emily, almost flirting with her. Leighton flushed. We'll have none of that. If Fenner thinks I can't do anything he's very much mistaken; I will not stand for that.

He's stopped it now. Just as well. But it wasn't because he saw me watching him. He and Emily had some momentary togetherness over a joke; I over-reacted. Because I'm on edge. I mustn't cause a fuss at my own dinner table. Not with these people here.

All the same, Fenner had better not exchange any more of those glances with Emily.

* * *

I think John saw that look, thought Emily – I saw his colour rise. How quickly he gets angry nowadays. So easily aroused – to anger. Not much else.

For a few seconds she sat with eyes cast down, a wistful expression on her face as plates were cleared away. The slight intrusion of serving girls leaning between the diners allowed everyone to break their earlier conversations and begin anew. Emily turned and leant across to ask Mrs Battheson about her camellias – a dull but un-demanding monologue: Mrs B could ramble on for hours.

'Our camellias,' said Emily, 'are quite hopeless. The soil here is lime, you see.'

'Oh, you can overcome that, my dear. No problem at all. Let me tell you how to do it. Shall I?'

Drone on, you bat. Will this meal never end?

* * *

Dessert had barely been scraped from the bowls when Emily rose suddenly to her feet. 'Shall we retire, ladies? While the men cut their revolting cigars.'

Several women glanced uncertainly at their husbands. Others clambered dutifully to their feet. Harriet Henderson declared that she would stay to take a brandy – it was the best part of the meal.

'Well, of course, Harriet, you must do as you like. If anyone else *must* join Harriet, do please feel free. But I'm afraid the men will fill the room with smoke.'

'So will I,' said Harriet. 'I like a good cigar.'

Patterson watched, amused, as with varying degrees of willingness each of the ladies pushed back their chairs and followed Emily from the room. 'Good for you,' he murmured, leaning towards Harriet. He was glad to see someone flout house rules. That Leighton woman was too used to having things her own way. Several women guests had not expected to leave the table. One had still been eating her dessert. Mrs Leighton had caught them on the hop, and had loved doing so. She behaved as if it were perfectly normal for women to sail out of the room and wait somewhere while the men stayed at table and dug into liqueurs. People did things *her* way at Nob Hall.

I wasn't the only one surprised – a woman up there was goggle-eyed, as if she'd just found out she'd come to the wrong party but it was too late to back out. *She* didn't believe that this was the way the upper class behaved – she thought it had all gone out with World War Two.

I bet these are only local rules – how the Leightons behave. But just because it's how they do things here in Gloucestershire doesn't make it right. Put that woman in a public bar in Catford – then see how she'd cope. She'd be as much a lemon as I am here.

Home is best.

* * *

Their pause among the trees becomes a wait. The dogs lie down while John Leighton confers with his beaters, one of whom wets a finger and holds it in the air. He and Leighton stare irritably at the damp grey sky.

Harriet finds herself close to Mr Patterson, and she asks him how he's finding the day. He smiles at her. She is still the only person who talks to him from choice. 'First time out?' she asks.

'Does it show?'

'Don't worry, you'll soon get the hang. Once you see the birds rise, once you've fired a round or two, it'll all seem different. You won't forget this day, Mr Patterson. Carry home a brace of birds and you'll carry the memory too. At odd times later you'll catch yourself thinking back to this cool damp morning, the smell of wet leaves, the stalk to kill. This is something you'll remember to the end of your days.'

'You could be right.'

'And you won't feel the cold any more once the shooting begins. I'm glad we had that snort of brandy before we left. You like a drop of brandy, don't you, Mr P?'

*　*　*

Last night at dinner after most of the women had left – those, that is, who had submitted to Emily's command – every woman except Harriet and a fishlike old soak enmeshed halfway up the table – after they had left in a flurry of female rising, a rustling of silk and sateen, an invisible unmissable cloud of expensive perfume, after their swanlike parting, John Leighton had told his staff – the permanent retainers and the hired help from the village – to serve port, brandy and a choice of cigars.

Barry Fenner, his smile slipping to a disapproving pucker as he sucked globules of Stilton from cracks between his teeth, watched the decanter of port borne to the table. It twinkled from each of its cut glass facets, shimmering like the chandelier above. Safe in the hands of the family butler, the port floated through the darkened room towards the master of the house. Fenner half hoped – a wish he knew was futile – that the butler would set that decanter down beside Michael Patterson. The man sat there, red-faced and awkward, unused to his dinner jacket, embedded at the foot of the table between a horse-and-hounds countrywoman and a thin farmer with oily hair. The horsy woman was on Patterson's right. Surely Patterson, knowing that she had stayed to partake of it, would have passed the decanter to her, to his *right*. Only Patterson, of all the guests seated around the table, might be unaware of what everybody knew, had known since childhood, that port must always be passed to the left, to port, as sailors say. If only the butler would place the port beside him. If only Patterson could be given the chance to grasp the decanter and pass it to his right. What a wonderful *faux pas*! He might even shake the flask.

But with the same inevitability with which the butler carried the port towards Leighton, that huge crass oaf Patterson would probably have known better than that: before setting out on this 'classy' weekend he would have read a book on etiquette. He would have learned about passing the port.

The butler set the port down beside Leighton, then walked quickly back to the sideboard and picked up the next tray. He waddled serenely back with it behind the diners.

Conversation resumed as the two decanters slowly circulated round the table – port going first. Patterson received it from Harriet, and passed it straight to the farmer. His action was instinctive: the decanter came from his right and he passed it to his left. He *couldn't* get it wrong. Fenner would never now discover whether Patterson knew which way the port should move.

Patterson ignored the port. During the meal he had sipped only lightly at the wines – as if he preferred brown ale. But when the brandy arrived he poured a glass and raised it towards Harriet: 'Happy days.'

'Bottoms up.'

'Want a drop more? You couldn't drown a fly in that.'

'I'm quite all right, thank you, Mr Patterson.'

'Go on, have a taste of it. It's what you stayed for, after all.'

Patterson doubled the small quantity at the base of Harriet's brandy balloon. 'That's better,' he said. 'You only had a dirty glass before.' Then he grinned and passed the decanter to the farmer on his left. Fenner found that he was straining to hear their words. He snorted that he should bother.

Harriet raised her drink. 'We needn't wait till everyone has filled their glass. We're quite informal here.'

'Could have fooled me.'

Patterson lifted his large hairy hand and clinked his glass against hers. 'Here's to yer.'

They both drank. As they returned their glasses to the table, Patterson winked.

'A fine Cognac,' Harriet remarked.

Patterson paused a moment, then leant closer to whisper, 'Very nice, but it's not Cognac.'

'Not Cognac?' She tried to match Patterson's discreetly low tone but her surprise wouldn't let her. Harriet seldom spoke quietly.

'No, it's Armagnac. That's still a brandy, you know – French and all that – but it's not technically Cognac. Armagnac. Different region. Just as good.'

'Armagnac?' Several people were listening to them now.

'Yeah. Made by Salas, I should think.'

The surprise left Harriet's face. In the world of dog breeding she often found expertise to lie in the least likely people. That this unprepossessing hulk of a man could tell Armagnac from Cognac was plainly true. It would be foolish to doubt him.

'Do you collect Armagnacs?'

'I used to run a pub.'

*   *   *

Barry Fenner, rummaging beneath his silk pyjamas in the bottom of his suitcase, took out his flask. Funny thing, Patterson knowing the difference between Cognac and Armagnac. Fenner unscrewed the silver cap and sniffed at the contents. Was this Cognac or Armagnac? Fenner had assumed it to be Cognac, because brandy always was. But Patterson had made him wonder. Which was he drinking?

He'd have to ask Patterson.

Fenner chuckled, replaced the cap on his flask without taking a drink, and turned his attention to his pyjamas. Would he need them tonight? He laid them on the bed. For a moment or two he stood undecided in the centre of the room. At the back of his mouth he could still taste his dinner: charred lamb and mint sauce – God, these country bumpkins! He took off his tie.

Having dropped it like a dead snake on his bed, Fenner closed the almost empty suitcase. He lifted it off the bed and slid it across the carpet to the corner of the room. Waiting in that corner was the other item of his luggage – a fleece-lined, soft leather gun slip with carry handles and shoulder straps. Fenner picked up the bag, un-zipped it and took out his shotgun – an AYA 53 sidelock with 28-inch chopper-lump English ribbed barrels and a walnut stock. The gun was hand-finished with traditional game chokings, a gold-plated interior and an action decorated with foliate scrollwork. It had cost a good deal of money.

On the shoot tomorrow morning there would almost certainly be other AYAs but with luck they'd be Countrymen, not the prestigious 53. Fenner checked the gun over, weighing it in his hands. It was empty and clean. In the soft leather gun slip, snug and protected in a separate compartment, were three dozen cartridges. He also had a full 12-bore cleaning kit – the mop, the brush, the jag and bronze, some oil, a duster and the 3-piece set of rods. Fenner ignored them.

From an inner pocket in the fleece lining he took out his pull-through, a small red and white striped rag, attached to a cord with a small weight at the other end. If a pull-through was good enough for the army it was good enough for him – to hell with jag and bronze:

life was too short. He cocked the hammer on his gun, dropped the smooth little weight into the back of one chamber, and let it slip through to the other end of the barrel. Where the weight emerged he pulled to drag the cleansing rag behind. He repeated this with the other barrel. Then he held the gun with the butt pointed to the electric light in the ceiling and squinted up from the outlet into each barrel. Both were spotlessly clean. He lowered the gun. With the chambers empty, Fenner cocked the gun and fired. He listened to the action, then rested his cheek against the cold metal and sniffed the oil.

That should do it, he thought.

Fenner replaced the gun carefully in its slip and laid it on the floor. Then he went to the bathroom and cleaned his teeth. Vigorously.

* * *

John Leighton's teeth had been worrying him for some time. Two of his crowns had worked loose. He had noticed the slip in the first some weeks ago. While he ate, the crown behaved itself, but when he cleaned his teeth the crown rocked slightly beneath the toothbrush. Now a second one was wobbling. Leighton had the uncomfortable feeling that below the unstable crowns his natural teeth were decomposing. He would have to visit his dentist. With luck he might be able to have both crowns adjusted and refitted; there should be no need for false teeth. He was still young. Fairly young.

He climbed into bed and picked up a book, a finely bound Folio edition of *The Undertones of War* by Edmund Blunden. There were pictures, grey and depressing. The words made no sense.

Leighton tossed the book down beside him on the bed. He knew what was wrong. He was trying not to think about tomorrow, but the more he tried to avoid the thought the more strongly it returned. It could not be suppressed. Leighton was reminded of his recent visit to Lake Orta: he and Emily had been to Milan in an unsuccessful attempt to sell horses, and had spent a further consolatory day on Lake Orta. He had gone for a walk alone, without Emily. While standing at the peaceful lakeside he had wanted to photograph a particular effect of sunlight rippling across the clear waters. For his intended composition a small wooden jetty formed an excellent foreground; it had just the right air of Italian neglect. But every time Leighton prepared to take the photograph, someone would walk in his way. The people interrupting his shot were not tourists, they lived there, but although they lived on the lakeside – there was an old lady, two fishermen, an angular man in a suit – they jarred in Leighton's landscape. He did not want them. They did not belong in the picture he was striving to create. Yet they were indigenous. Leighton wanted to create an idealised landscape, sunlight and nature, peaceful cold water, but these intruders would insist on stepping into his frame. One of the fishermen saw Leighton standing there fiddling with his camera, but instead of withdrawing from view the man had tapped his companion on the arm, pointed at Leighton, and had grinned at him, posing for the snap.

Leighton had abandoned his photograph.

Here in the quiet bedroom the thought of tomorrow stuck in the front of Leighton's mind as solidly as had that fisherman on the lakeside. Leighton picked up his book again, and turned the pages without looking at them. He knew he would not sleep. It was ridiculous. After all, it wasn't as if he were going to do the job himself; he would simply be there to see it done.

Leighton knew that the reason the thought kept returning was that he was worried something might go wrong. It shouldn't. He had paid well enough. But it might. The main thing, should that happen, was to make absolutely certain – by the way he reacted and by where he positioned himself – that nothing could be linked to him. If there was a blunder – some accident in the true sense of the word – he must disassociate himself entirely. That should not be difficult. He had only to behave as the others did, displaying shock or outrage as the occasion merited, and then leave the mess to sort itself out.

Leighton bit his lip at the prospect. There must not be a mistake; the consequences were too appalling to contemplate. There must not, there would not, be a mistake. He had engaged a professional, after all.

*   *   *

Fenner decided to wear his silk pyjamas. He had brought them, they suited him, he liked the feel of silk against his skin. He would wear them now, until the time came to take them off.

*   *   *

Patterson wore old-fashioned striped pyjamas, tied with a cord around his belly. In his own bed at home he preferred to sleep naked, unencumbered by folds of flannel around his crotch. But he had imagined Leighton's country house as being large, cold and draughty, with uncomfortable beds and central heating that did not work. He had brought pyjamas to keep warm. Besides, he couldn't be sure about the toilet arrangements. On the one hand, the house might turn out to be like a posh hotel, where every bedroom had its own bathroom – or a basin, at any rate – or the rooms might share facilities down the hall. Knowing how poorly British hotels compared to foreign ones, Patterson did not expect a private bathroom. And if he was going to have to traipse along the corridor for a last midnight pee, he would need warm pyjamas. A dressing gown as well. But in his neat little suitcase there wasn't room for a dressing gown. He hadn't wanted to bring the big case, the one he took on holiday, because it would look too much for a weekend. The overnight bag should see him through.

Snug and secure in his bulky pyjamas, Patterson felt comfortable in bed – a good-sized one, as it turned out. Private bathroom after all. I bet most of these old houses don't have *en suites*: spoil the character, their owners would have said. None of that nonsense here.

Patterson lay contentedly on his back, reading *The Sporting Life*. Now, here was real sport: horses, dogs and football – not this daft business of popping shotguns at unarmed birds. To shoot game was not a sport to Michael Patterson. Not that he knew much about it. Shooting parties on country estates was not the kind of thing that Patterson was invited to. But there was a first time for everything.

It was funny the things that life threw up.

After a few minutes, Patterson finished his paper and dropped it on the floor beside his bed. He switched off the lamp. Warm in his belly was an afterglow of brandy. Two glasses of wine he'd had, then the large Armagnac. Moderation, that's the key. Just enough to enjoy a restful night.

* * *

John Leighton tossed restlessly beneath his blankets. It might be October, and a fairly miserable one at that, yet the room seemed hot tonight – close and shut in. Emily had told him it was because he would insist on having blankets on his bed. She preferred a duvet. But on those occasions – few enough nowadays – when he did spend a night with his wife beneath her duvet, he found the feather-filled cover more stifling than his blankets. A duvet might appear light and airy, but it trapped the heat.

Perhaps I should pop along and visit Emily? I'd better not. It's after midnight, and she might be asleep. I suspect that at this time of night she won't welcome my advances. It's hardly a month since that night when I tapped at her door at midnight and she wouldn't let me in. She called through the door that I was only there because I couldn't sleep, and that I was only wanted her as a sedative.

What a thing to say! It wasn't true. I love my wife. I've tried to tell her, in my way, but a chap doesn't say such things, not an Englishman. One shows one's feelings in the things one does and in the way one tries to behave. A woman can tell.

Or she could tell once. In our early days – just the two of us without children – Emily could tell then. I loved her and she loved me. Simple, really. We both knew it. No one had to say the words. But that night a month ago, when I stammered like a teenager in a soap opera, bleating through her locked bedroom door that I loved her, she didn't believe me. How could she say that? Have her feelings towards me cooled?

I suppose they have. Of course they have. I can't hide from it. Well, perhaps it is just a phase. Women go through phases, don't they, approaching forty? Or does the menopause come later, when they are older? I'm not sure. It's not the kind of thing I know about – and without Emily, there's no one I can ask.

*   *   *

No, menopause had not troubled Emily. Symptoms were unlikely to creep upon her for another ten years, and she was certainly not going to anticipate them. She sat with her ivory satin negligée draped about her fine shoulders, the matching ivory nightie chaste upon her breast, while she brushed her hair. Softly, she smiled into the mirror. To while away the dragging minutes, Emily had taken a leisurely bath, lying neck-deep in warm scented water, the bathroom shimmering with fragrant steam. Moist warm air lingered in her bedroom. Emily checked her watch.

She sat with a hairbrush in her hand. Perhaps her hair looked too long when she wore it down? At dinner she had worn it elaborately styled. Such pretence. Would it not be better to admit her age and succumb to simpler styles? So much time now was devoted to the way she looked – wearing contact lenses instead of spectacles because glasses might spoil her looks or leave a mark across her nose. Was this necessary? She still had her looks. No need for modesty: her looks were good, her carriage fine. – Ah, there's the rub: her carriage fine. It's what one says of a mature woman. Emily looked mature. She sounded mature. Often, Emily spoke with her voice set little above a murmur, attractively husky, she hoped, and seldom raised. It was so easy to sound strident.

A dozen years ago when she had married John he had seemed dashing, rich, considerate – what more could a girl desire? In truth he had been dashing, as dashing as any real-life husband was likely to be. After the honeymoon she learned that he was less rich than she had thought, but there were assets he could sell, should the need arise. And they had arisen, inevitably – but he had remained considerate.

Throughout their twelve years John hardly changed. But Emily had. Living in the country had made her dull. And increasingly in recent years Emily had caught herself ordering John around – that occasional bossiness in her tone. It made her sound like an actress playing a memsahib in India. Isolated in John's big house in the Gloucestershire hills was perhaps a little like living in one of Britain's old colonies; Emily dreaded that she might become like one of those bored colonial wives in Somerset Maugham or Paul Scott. She had never read Paul Scott, but had seen his Raj Quartet on TV. She thought how terrible Scott's women were. She must *not* end up like that.

As she raised the hairbrush to her tumbling hair she heard the gentle tap of a man's fingernails at the bedroom door. Emily rose from her dressing table, slipped across the room and turned the handle. There was no need: the door had not been locked. Nevertheless she had not wanted to call – not at after midnight.

When Barry Fenner came in, his only words before he kissed her were, 'Hello again, my sweet.'

*　　*　　*

'Any moment now,' whispers Harriet. They are at the edge of the woodlands. Unsuspecting birds prowl the edge of the field: ungainly, with little energy to lift their fat bodies off the ground.

'You go ahead,' Patterson mutters in her ear. 'I'm not used to this. Don't want to distract you.'

Harriet turns to smile. 'You won't. Just follow me.'

Harriet smiles again, then turns to peer out into the field. Among these last thinning trees two beaters have moved forward. This will be the third volley of the morning. It will be the last.

Everyone looks eager, hoping to make this broad green field a cornucopia. Through the rough grass pheasants and partridges strut like chickens in a farmyard – and like chickens they have been reared in hutches. But now they've been released.

A little ahead of the shooting party, where everyone can see him, John Leighton holds position. He moistens his lip. A few yards off, Barry Fenner watches the clumsy Patterson, who is frowning at his shotgun as if he has picked a gun up for the first time in his life. Fenner sees Harriet leave Patterson. He sees her drift forward with the others between the final trees.

Fenner follows.

As the silent hunters raise their shotguns the two beaters rush forward to the edge of the large damp field. Birds rise, squawking, into the sky. But several are so large they can hardly lift themselves off the meadow. They run in panic as if they have forgotten how to use their wings. From a dozen shotguns comes a blast of gunfire. Birds and feathers fall from the sky.

Patterson waits four yards behind the party. Fenner has placed himself a yard apart from his companions, and as the hunters blast a second time into the flock of screaming partridges Patterson empties a single shell into Fenner's back.

No one sees him fall. He does not cry out. Patterson swiftly breaks open his gun, slips a fresh cartridge into the chamber to replace the other, then closes the gun and flicks the safety on. Gliding forward to join the party he lets his face resume the mild perplexed expression her has worn all morning.

'Someone's down!' he hears someone call.

Birds still fly shrieking. Two shots ring out. Then there's no more shooting.

Slowly, the hunters turn and glance around. As they scramble through the undergrowth to the fallen Fenner, Michael Patterson squints down at his gun. Two cartridges lie in the chambers. I haven't fired it yet, he could say – it wouldn't work. Then he'll let someone spot that he has the safety on.

But with any luck it won't come to that. No one will think of Patterson.

'He looks as if he's dead.'

By now most of the party has crowded around Fenner, motionless on his front. In the centre of his back, around a ragged hole in his fine green jacket, spreads a dark red stain.

'Is he really – '

'Of course he's dead,' snaps Harriet.

'That's terrible,' declares John Leighton. 'A tragic accident, I'm afraid.'

He thinks of Emily, and of how he'll break it to her. 'I have bad news,' he will later say. 'Something quite ghastly has happened to one of our weekend guests. You must brace yourself, my dear.

A regular correspondent

JOAN LOCK

It was just ten days before Christmas when the unthinkable happened. George Layforth had an experience which he could not turn into light-hearted copy for his column. For that to occur it had to be something catastrophic – and it was.

George's readers adored his sparkling but intimate style, his occasional, well-timed outspokenness but, most of all, his self-deprecating humour. Many imagined him as the perfect dinner guest, witty, charming, yet always modest. Those who bothered to write told him so in their letters. It was never likely to happen because George made a point of keeping his readers at a distance. 'That way I retain my mystery,' he would chuckle.

Then, a year before that fateful Christmas, George began receiving letters from one Henry Gibson-Felloes. Oddly, this correspondent never mentioned the wit, concentrating instead on the unsung wisdom in George's daily diary. It couldn't have been just empty flattery because particular points were picked out and discussed as to *why* they were so perceptive. George was flattered. Wise was exactly how he saw himself. Henry also made a few tentative suggestions for elaborations on certain subjects. Some of these were usable in the column, which made George's life a little easier.

Then the inevitable happened. Henry asked for a meeting but George, as always, declined. He did it tactfully, saying he was tempted but could not break his golden rule. Henry left it for a while, then, when George was getting some flak for a rather rash joke in his diary, asked again, claiming he had some ideas on how to quench the flames of criticism. George weakened – then acquiesced.

'You know me,' he explained to Sadie, his secretary, 'I'm just insatiably curious about my fellow-men.'

Sadie did indeed know George – and that the only fellow he was in the least interested in was the one he saw in the bathroom mirror each morning. She thought him about as self-deprecating as Vlad the

Impaler but knew that he *was* clever. If self-deprecation was what his readers wanted, self-deprecation was what he gave them.

They could have gone to the pub but George felt he must show off to his erudite new friend with the double-barrelled name so decided to take him to his favourite Italian restaurant, which served delicious Tuscan peasant fare at bloated capitalist prices.

'You'll be sorry,' was Sadie's comment and she fervently hoped he would be. 'What if he's a nerd? You'll be stuck with him for the whole evening.'

She was wrong, thought George as they sat down. The man looked civilised. Dressed a little prissily perhaps but otherwise reasonable enough: tall, solidly built, with dark crinkly hair and heavy black spectacles. Granted his skin was very pale, pasty in fact, but the voice, while it might be a bit booming, was educated and of good timbre.

To start, George ordered the bruschetta, making a little joke that his mum would have called it tomatoes on toast and collapsed at the price. Henry riposted that *he* liked value for money and ordered one of the soups 'for which, at least they had to chop a few vegetables'. George hoped it was a riposte but when Henry added, without a trace of a smile, that he would have thought someone as wise as George would have saved his money, he began to fear it was not.

Things looked up when Henry launched into a hymn of praise about George's writing. To George's relief he didn't seem to expect him to be witty and self-deprecating in response. In fact, it soon became apparent that the wit in George's prose went right over Henry's head and what he most appreciated was the impeccable grammar.

'Unlike that of some journalists I could name!' Henry boomed, banging his fist on the table and cutting his hand on his knife.

George handed him his spare handkerchief to wrap around the cut as, with sinking heart, he recognised that bore of bores – the language fanatic. Never mind what you say as long as you punctuate it correctly. However, as well as ridding the world of the dangling participle, with the assistance of the death penalty if necessary, it seemed that what Henry really wanted to do was persuade George to write more seriously.

'It was awful,' he told Sadie the next day, 'a disaster.'

'You'll never get rid of him now,' was her comforting reply.

'At least he doesn't know my real name or where I live.'

'Hmm,' said Sadie doubtfully.

'He did seem to know an amazing amount about me,' George admitted, 'things even I had forgotten.'

But if Henry knew George's real name or where he lived he never made use of that knowledge. He did keep writing, however, his manner becoming irritatingly proprietorial as he offered more and more advice. With Sadie's help George worked out a strategy whereby he would answer, initially, in a mildly friendly manner – then gradually cool it until they were back on the original footing. But Henry kept asking when they were to meet again 'to expand on our fruitful friendship'. George was tempted to throw the letter in the waste-paper basket but Sadie, who knew more about getting rid of odd, unwanted, male admirers, suggested he make an excuse.

'Tell him you are writing a book. You know, "I have taken your be-more-serious comments to heart, so I know you will bear with me . . . " '

It worked, as far as the demands to meet were concerned, but the flow of imperious advice increased tenfold. George decided enough was enough and ceased answering. The letters continued but were at first hurt then increasingly angry in tone.

One day George said, 'That's it! No more! Ready? – *Dear Sir . . .* ' and went on to dictate an extraordinarily vituperative letter to his number one admirer.

'Are you sure you want to send this?' asked Sadie when he sat back, all bile expended. 'He could turn nasty.'

'What can he do? Send it recorded delivery.'

The reply George received was certainly angry but, oddly, that anger was directed only at George's last column. In this, he had not only made a light-hearted reference to rape – a mistake, his postbag had already revealed – but also split an infinitive.

A week went by, two weeks, three. No more letters. They couldn't believe it. It was strange to sort through the mail and not catch sight of that grey parchment-effect envelope with the address inscribed in perfectly penned italic script – initially immaculate but which had become rather wild of late.

'In a way I miss him,' said George ten days before Christmas when enough time had elapsed for them to presume that the letters had ceased for ever.

'Well I find the silence a bit eerie,' said Sadie. 'He's given up too easily.'

'You read too many thrillers. There isn't bound to be an "outcome", you know, most things just tail off.'

'Hmm,' said Sadie.

It was then that the phone rang. Sadie answered then looked at George speculatively. 'You been speeding again?'

'No.'

'Well, there's a big copper in reception who wants to see you – a matter of some urgency . . .'

What the Detective Inspector wanted to know was when George had last seen his good friend, Henry Gibson-Felloes?

'He's *not* my good friend,' said George tetchily.

'That's not the impression we got,' replied the policeman, then added an abrupt 'sir.'

'From whom?'

'From his diaries.'

George was puzzled.

'Mr Gibson-Felloes is missing.'

'Really?'

'You didn't know?'

'Why should I?'

The DI contemplated George's petulant face. 'You seem very agitated about this, sir. I think you better tell where you were on the evening of Friday, 7 December.'

'What *are* you talking about?'

'I'm talking about this, sir. The walls of his flat were splashed with blood and there were signs of an affray. Angry exchanges were heard on that evening and he has not been seen since. We are merely covering all possibilities by contacting his closest friends – and there aren't many of those.' He stroked his chin. 'In fact, just you really.'

'I'm *not* his closest friend! I only met him *once*.'

'His diary disagrees.'

'The man was unbalanced.'

'We have no evidence of that, sir.'

'Just you read his last letter.' He scrambled through Sadie's immaculate filing system. 'Look – he's deranged!'

The policeman looked. 'He certainly seems to be angry about what you wrote. What was that, sir?'

George told him.

'Seems like an honest reaction to me, sir,' said the DI, managing, without a flicker, to convey contempt. He hesitated, then said, 'I should tell you that we have a letter of yours to him which appears a great deal more heated to me. A falling out, it seems.'

George could think of no suitable answer. How to explain . . .
Sadie would help.

'Is this your handkerchief, sir?' The DI held out a sealed plastic
bag containing a white handkerchief bearing George's real initials,
RGF.

'Yes. Yes it is. I lent it to him when he cut his finger – ages ago. But
the cut wouldn't make all those stains.'

'No. No, they are recent,' the DI admitted. 'From the scene.' He
paused, then said, 'You still haven't answered my question. Where
were you on the evening Mr Gibson-Felloes went missing?'

'I would be on my way to my country cottage. I always am.'

The policeman tapped his breast pocket. 'That's very strange, sir.
According to his diaries, that was the time you two always met. You
have witnesses for this occasion?'

'No, of course not!' George yelled. 'I never stop anywhere. I
just go!'

The policeman looked grave. 'I must inform you that when an
acquaintance rang Mr Gibson-Felloes that evening he said he had a
visitor with him.'

'So?'

'He said it was you – as usual.'

'It's a fit-up! He's done this to spite me!'

The Inspector gazed at him wonderingly. 'That's an extraordinary
suggestion, sir. Why would he want to do that?'

The phone rang. It was for the DI. As he listened his eyes never left
George's face. At one point they widened significantly. 'I have just
learned the terms of the will of Mr Gibson-Felloes,' the Detective
Inspector said gravely as he put the receiver down.

'And?'

'He has left the bulk of his estate, £275, 000, to his good friend and
companion, George Layforth.' The Detective Inspector paused. 'Can
you explain that, sir?'

George tried, and tried.

Written in stone

PAUL FREEMAN

Professor Percival Farrell hadn't said a word since they left Khartoum. Now, after a four-hour, haemorrhoid-torturing, jaunt across the Sudanese desert, John Dixon couldn't shut the old duffer up.

'Behold! The ancient city of Kush. Home to the twenty-fifth dynasty of Egyptian pharaohs.'

The professor made a dramatic sweeping gesture, and in the confined space of the land cruiser's cab almost struck his unwilling companion across the face.

As the archaeologist launched into a monologue on the twenty-fifth dynasty, Dixon rolled his eyes and wished he was back in the cool confines of the *Sunday Star*'s London newsroom. His thoughts were on the top drawer of his news desk, on the bottle of scotch lodged at the back. Crikey, he could do with a tot of the hard stuff. Yet perhaps that was why Dixon's editor had chosen him for this assignment instead of one of the young pretenders. Dixon might be the *Star*'s star reporter, but he was getting old, out of shape, taking too many long lunches. Maybe the editor was sending a message. Prohibition was in force in Sudan. It was a dry country in more senses than one.

Farrell was squinting through the windscreen, the tiny man's beak of a nose up against the glass. 'Well, Dixon! What do you think?'

'I reckon we'd get a better view from outside,' said Dixon, opening the passenger door. He stepped down on to sun-baked gravel, into mid-winter sunshine.

Dixon walked to the ridge overlooking the valley, relieved that the myopic professor hadn't driven them into the abyss. He cursed the penny-pinchers in the *Star*'s accounts department, those miserly gits who had denied him a hire vehicle of his own, forcing him to cadge a lift with the shortsighted academic.

Farrell appeared like a Jack-in-the-box at the reporter's elbow, looking as spare and scrawny as an ill-fed chicken. 'Well?' he persisted. 'Well?'

In spite of a natural cynicism, Dixon had to admit that it was an impressive sight laid out in the bowl-shaped valley below him. To his right was a sprawl of collapsed walls and columns – all that remained of the city of Kush. Scattered within the two-thousand-year-old ruins was an assortment of makeshift pole and canvas tents, housing for the dig's Sudanese workforce.

Dixon put his museum-piece camera to his eye and zoomed in. Two women dressed in brightly coloured saris were attending to cooking fires and steaming cauldrons. There was no trace of the native labourers, though.

He trained the lens to the left, where half a dozen VIP tents were set out in a circle, like pioneers' wagons fending off a Red Indian attack. A young woman with frizzy, unkempt hair was regarding Dixon from the opening of one of the tents. Outside another, a middle-aged man sat at a table, brushing dust and dirt away from an excavated artefact. It was rumoured in Khartoum's British Club that until lately this man and woman had been having an affair, that their dalliance had ended in acrimony.

Further to the left of the VIP accommodation was a double row of short, steep-sided pyramids. Half collapsed with age, these strange structures reminded Dixon of broken teeth in urgent need of dental work.

'I always thought pyramids were found in Egypt?' said Dixon, as Professor Farrell sketched the scene in his pocket notebook.

'You haven't listened to a word I've said all through the journey,' snorted the professor. 'This part of Sudan was known as Upper Egypt during the time of the later pharaohs. Two thousands years ago,' he made another expansive gesture, 'this was the city of Kush, home to Pi-Ankhi, the black pharaoh of the twenty-fifth dynasty. Pi-Ankhi was a great imitator of Lower Egyptian architecture – hence the pyramids.'

Nodding at his own ignorance, Dixon turned his camera lens on the pyramids, or 'funeral monuments' as Professor Farrell was explaining in tedious detail. A handsome young man with an aquiline nose and round-lensed glasses was standing on a rickety wooden scaffolding leaning against one of the pyramids. He was running a metal detector up and down the wall. At the base of the pyramid sat a Toyota pickup with winching equipment in the back, the only other vehicle Dixon had seen in the valley.

'Where were the stone tablets found?' asked the journalist, finally alluding to one of the recent discoveries that had so excited his editor and got Dixon packed off to this backwater.

The professor terminated his lecture and pointed towards a spot beyond the pyramids. 'The email from my client university says the tablets and the skeleton were discovered to the west of the pyramid field.'

Dixon redirected his attention to the place indicated, and zoomed in until the image shimmered in the heat haze. A gang of raggedly dressed Sudanese were digging into a patch of wind-blown sand. They had uncovered a number of rectangular slabs of stone, had half uncovered several more. He couldn't see the mysterious skeleton, however, believed by those in the British Club to be the remains of Aldos Valich, the eighteenth century Russian adventurer who half demolished several of the pyramids in his search for treasure.

When Dixon lowered his camera, he found Professor Farrell crouched over a small mound of rocks he had built up into a cone.

'A cairn,' the professor explained sheepishly. 'For good luck. A safeguard.'

'Who would have expected a man in your field of expertise to be so superstitious?' said Dixon, his mouth a cynical twist.

*   *   *

They located the steep track leading down to the archaeological site, and for Dixon the ensuing drive to the camp was a nightmare. His attention was torn between the professor – whose eyes were scrunched up in an effort to improve his weak vision – and the gravel incline they were skidding and sliding down. Eventually though, the land cruiser reached the safety of the valley floor, and Dixon could sigh his relief. As they pushed their way through patches of soft sand towards the VIP encampment, the reporter smiled slyly to himself. For although he had failed to research the twenty-fifth dynasty and the Kushite pharaoh Pi-Ankhi before coming to Sudan, he had made a point of delving into the backgrounds of the archaeological staff involved in the dig. There was a lot of dirt.

The young woman with the frizzy hair came forward to meet the newcomers as they stepped from the land cruiser. Dixon already knew much about her.

'Matilda Benson,' said the one time arch-feminist and anti-globalisation activist. She had turned conformist once her horrified Mummy and Daddy threatened to stop her monthly allowance. 'I catalogue the finds for Doctor Gatlin,' she explained.

'John Dixon. The *Sunday Star*!'

She turned to Professor Farrell, but the professor kept his arms rigid at his sides. He looked through Matilda as if she were not there, then marched off and introduced himself to Doctor Robert Gatlin. The unsociable dig director was still sitting at his table, brushing grime from a statuette, showing little interest in Farrell's arrival.

'Bloody sexist pig,' said Matilda, glaring at the back of the professor's head. A flush of anger had suffused her plain, unmade-up face.

Dixon shrugged. Professor Farrell might be a world-renowned decipherer of ancient languages, but he was equally well-known for his misogyny. A woman's place was at home, having babies, bringing up children, no backchat – full stop. His Victorian attitude had generated enough enemies in high places to leave him without a job-for-life university professorship. An academic pariah, he was condemned to wander the world as a nomadic consultant on undeciphered languages.

Doctor Gatlin held up his statuette and admired a job well done. It was a bronze piece of a gazelle. Dixon wondered if the stories were true that every year Gatlin sold the occasional artefact to fund the Kush dig for a further season.

'I'll work on the stone tablets now,' said Professor Farrell without commenting on the bronze gazelle. He cast a scornful glance back at Matilda. 'I don't eat with women, so send my meals over to me.'

Matilda's face darkened further. She stared daggers, but the professor once more ignored her as he stalked off in the direction of the pyramid field and the enigmatic tablets. Dixon gave Matilda a second apologetic shrug and set off after Farrell, his camera swinging from side to side as he struggled to catch up.

The route to the newly-discovered tablets took the journalist and Professor Farrell through the two rows of pyramids, past the Toyota, past the point where the young man on the scaffolding had been sweeping the walls of a pyramid with the metal detector. Dixon was puffing with exertion when they arrived at the nearly reconstructed pyramid. Too many pub sessions with the London newspaper fraternity was taking its toll.

Dixon recognised the French archaeologist working on the pyramid at once. Marc Le Feuvre's picture had been splashed across *Le Monde* the previous summer. Infamous for his controversial opinions on race, the Frenchman had been accused – and ostensibly cleared – of illegally selling archaeological treasures on the black market.

The metal detector lay discarded in the sand, and Marc Le Feuvre was now brushing dirt from crevices carved into the pyramid's stonework. The Frenchman smiled at the approaching men. Perhaps knowing Farrell's brusque reputation, he dispensed with the formality of introductions.

'You may be interested in this, Farrell,' said Le Feuvre. He jumped down from the scaffolding and led the professor and Dixon to the opposite face of the pyramid. 'What do you make of this carving of Pi-Ankhi? I finished reconstructing and cleaning it last week.'

Dixon tried to stifle his laughter. He failed, and found the two academics looking at him down their substantial noses – Farrell with disdain, La Feuvre with amusement. Once they had made their point that Dixon was an ill-educated lout, they returned their attention to the picture carved into the side of the pyramid. It showed a squatting pharaoh with a contented expression on his face, using a slave (who was down on all fours) as a seat. However, the oddest aspect of the tableau was that behind the pharaoh was a second slave. He was kneeling, hands slightly open like a fielding cricketer, ready to catch the defecating pharaoh's excrement.

'You've got to be kidding me,' said Dixon, lifting his camera for the shot.

'It was quite common in ancient civilisations,' Professor Farrell explained slowly, as though talking to a retarded child, 'for a trusted servant to bury the ruler's bodily waste, thereby preventing the said waste from being used by an enemy for the purpose of witchcraft or sorcery.'

'The stupid black slave catching the stupid black pharaoh's crap,' said Le Feuvre. 'That's not cultural, professor. The darkies are barbarians.'

A deferential cough came from behind. The three men swivelled round and were face to face with a dark-complexioned Sudanese. He wore a grubby shift, loose cotton pants, and had a V-shaped scar carved into either cheek.

'Meet Abdullah el-Banki,' said Le Feuvre. He gave the man a condescending clap on the back. 'He's the last of the pharaohs, aren't you, el-Banki? He traces his ancestors back to Pharaoh Pi-Ankhi himself.'

The Sudanese gave a slight bow. 'I have the honour of belonging to the illustrious house of Pi-Ankhi,' he said in unaccented English.

' "El-Banki"; "Pi-Ankhi"!' Professor Farrell mulled over the two names and nodded. 'A connection seems feasible,' he concluded.

'Let me take a picture of you next to your great grand-daddy,' Dixon suggested, indicating the squatting, carved figure.

El-Banki politely refused. He had come for the Toyota pickup with the winch. They were going to lift the stone tablets, to move them closer to the centre of operations at the VIP encampment.

'Be careful this time,' warned Le Feuvre. 'I don't want you and your monkeys breaking another cable.'

There was a moment of silence as el-Banki regarded the Frenchman with undisguised loathing. 'We'll be careful,' he said finally, and strode off towards the Toyota.

'He's the natives' camp coordinator,' said Le Feuvre. 'Thinks he's a cut above the rest of us, just because he claims to be directly descended from Pi-Ankhi. Truth is, we keep the surly sod on because he's the only one of these buggers who understands English. Educated abroad, yet he returned to this godforsaken hell-hole. Who can understand these people?'

Dixon was only half listening. He had wandered back to the scaffolding and was examining Le Feuvre's metal detector. 'Why were you using this on the walls of the pyramid?'

The Frenchman seemed reluctant to explain, so Professor Farrell filled the awkward silence. 'Three centuries ago,' said the professor, 'Aldos Valich discovered Kushite gold hidden in a niche inside a wall of one of the pyramids. Perhaps Monsieur Le Feuvre is hoping for similar luck. Or perhaps he's already struck lucky.'

'You're accusing me of looting, old man!' said Le Feuvre. 'I was cleared of any wrongdoing.'

Farrell smiled innocently. 'I'm not accusing you of anything. Maybe you just suffer a guilty conscience.'

Le Feuvre's fists clenched and unclenched at his sides, and his lips became an angry slash. Yet before the verbal confrontation could escalate, Abdullah el-Banki drove up in the Toyota and offered Farrell and Dixon a lift to the dig's most recent finds.

*   *   *

'Doctor Gatlin and Miss Benson discovered the tablets a fortnight ago,' el-Banki explained, pointing to a low-lying sand dune, 'during one of their evening walks.'

Dixon and Farrell exchanged a knowing glance, the reporter fighting to restrain a schoolboy snigger.

The Toyota slewed to a stop in the sand. A gang of half a dozen Sudanese labourers had been sitting around doing as little as possible in el-Banki's absence. At his return they got to their feet and resumed digging around the oblong blocks of stone. Each block, Dixon noted, was inscribed in a script resembling hieroglyphics.

Professor Farrell's eyes glittered excitedly, and he whipped his notebook from his top pocket. In an instant he was out of the Toyota, as sprightly as man half his age, rushing towards the tablets.

'Where's this Aldos Valich geezer?' asked Dixon, struggling out of the cab of the pickup. Without photos of the seventeenth-century Russian's skeleton, he had no human-interest angle to his story. The newspaper's readership weren't the sort to be impressed by dissertations on dynasties and hieroglyphics.

El-Banki jerked his thumb over his shoulder, indicating a rectangle of tarpaulin held in place by rocks. A few seconds later, the covering was being pulled away and Dixon was looking into the hole beneath. The grave was shored up by wooden boards, and at the bottom were the reputed remains of Aldos Valich.

There was no skeleton as such. The harsh desert climate had dried the corpse to a desiccated husk. Skin the colour of saddle leather was stretched tautly over bone, overlaid in places by shreds of tattered clothing. But what held Dixon's journalistic attention and got him clicking merrily away with his camera, was the haft of a knife protruding from the Russian's chest cavity.

Dixon whooped with joy. His story suddenly had the makings of an award-winning piece. 'Valich was murdered!' he said jubilantly. 'Murdered!'

El-Banki shrugged. 'It happened three hundred years ago. Who cares now? Sudan was a dangerous place.'

His enthusiasm undiminished, Dixon took half a dozen more photographs, only stopping when a second excited whoop exploded from the lips of Professor Farrell. The reporter and the Sudanese camp coordinator rushed to the excavation. The professor was crawling about on hands and knees, minutely examining a rectangular tablet that had just been uncovered.

'It's a Rosetta Stone! It's a Rosetta Stone!' Professor Farrell repeated over and over.

'Rosetta Stone?' asked Dixon, while el-Banki looked on as though the professor had gone stark, staring mad.

'The Rosetta Stone was the key to deciphering Egyptian hieroglyphics,' Professor Farrell explained. 'Inscribed on it was a mundane text written in both Classical Greek and Egyptian hieroglyphs. Because scholars understood ancient Greek, they were able to decipher the Egyptian hieroglyphs. However, the Kushites had their own system of writing. Until today Kushite hieroglyphs have defied translation. Look!' he said, pointing to a row of hieroglyphs. 'This is Kushite script. And this,' Farrell continued, indicating a scrawl that appeared as illegible to Dixon as a doctor's handwriting, 'is Greek. There were rumours that Valich had deciphered the Kushite language before he disappeared, but I never believed in my lifetime . . .'

Overcome with emotion, unable to continue speaking, Professor Farrell caressed the tablet and rubbed his cheek covetously against the dual text.

'If it's as unique as you say,' said Dixon, taking half a dozen shots of the famous professor hugging a block of stone, 'it must be worth a pretty penny.'

'It's invaluable.' The professor looked up suspiciously at Dixon and el-Banki, then glanced towards the pyramid field. Le Feuvre was once again searching with his metal detector for caches of gold hidden in the walls of the pyramid. 'We must winch this stone into the back of the pickup,' Professor Farrell continued, 'so I can work on it in the remaining daylight.'

'The cables are not strong enough,' warned el-Banki. 'We've tried lifting the tablets before, but the cables break.'

Dixon, crouching down in the sand, held up a length of frayed and discarded cable he had been examining. 'This looks as though it's been half sawn through.'

Professor Farrell snorted derisively. 'Bloody reporters! Looking for conspiracies everywhere! Next thing you'll be harping on about the curse of the pharaohs.' He turned to el-Banki. 'Let's get you and your men to hoist this tablet onto the bed of the truck.' Opening his notebook at a fresh page, the professor said to Dixon, 'Remind Gatlin to send me my meals – I'll be working here all night.'

Dixon took the hint and cleared off.

*　　*　　*

Two trestle tables had been set up back-to-back inside the circle of VIP tents, and a tablecloth thrown over them. As the sun dipped behind the ridge of the valley and the daylight began fading, el-Banki served dinner.

Sudanese-style, using hands but no cutlery, Matilda dug into a bowl of puréed lima beans. However, not being as skilled as the

Sudanese at eating this way, most of her food ended up on the tablecloth. 'So the great professor won't eat at the same table as a woman,' said Matilda, oblivious to the mess she was making.

'Perhaps he's seen how you eat, my dear,' quipped Doctor Gatlin. 'Can't you use a spoon or something? There are limits to how far one should go native.'

Matilda glared at the excavation director.

Dixon felt obliged to defuse the impending row. 'The professor's quite busy right now, actually. He's discovered a tablet he believes to be as important as the Rosetta Stone. It's inscribed in both Greek and Kushite.'

'Really!' said Le Feuvre, his eyes glinting avariciously in the gloom.

Gatlin exchanged a look of mutual understanding with the Frenchman. 'A precious find indeed. Such a discovery could fund the Kush excavations indefinitely.'

'Then let's hope this tablet the professor's found doesn't go missing,' said Matilda.

Le Feuvre was about to retaliate verbally to Matilda's aspersion when the sound of a vehicle drifted across the valley floor. In the distance a light glimmered.

'Professor Farrell must be running a light off the Toyota's engine,' said Gatlin, as he prodding a piece of nondescript meat with his fork. He turned to el-Banki who was lurking in the shadows like a trusty manservant. 'How about fetching us a bottle of arak, Abdullah?'

El-Banki made a slight bow, then disappeared into the night in the direction of the labourers' squalid encampment.

'He gives me the creeps,' said Matilda. 'Skulking around all day, treating his own people like dirt, behaving like this is his personal fiefdom.'

'Well, he is directly descended from a pharaoh,' said Le Feuvre, stoking the fire of Matilda's anger.

Matilda turned to Dixon for moral support. 'I visited his village up the Nile once. It's a filthy place. El-Banki invited me, wanting to impress the white woman. He lives like a king, has a harem of wives and concubines while his 'subjects' barely get enough to eat. They work in his fields all day for a pittance. Any dissenters to his authority are punished. He excuses his abuse of power by claiming it as his divine right – because he's descended from Pi-Ankhi.'

'It's no different from the hierarchy amongst rock monkeys,' noted the Frenchman.

Matilda said simply, 'You're a racist.'

El-Banki chose that moment to reappear with the bottle of arak – the country's favourite illicit firewater. It was unclear whether he had heard the discourse about him. His face gave nothing away. In his left hand he held four shot glasses, and in his right a mineral water bottle filled with a liquid as clear as water, but that smelled like paint stripper. After pouring a generous tot for each of the diners, el-Banki lit two kerosene lamps. One lamp he planted in the middle of the dining table, the other he used to light his way as he took Professor Farrell his supper.

Evening drinks seemed to be a ritual at the dig, and Dixon soon found to his delight that self-service was the order of the day. The first tot had him spluttering into his glass, but where alcohol was concerned he was nothing if not adaptable.

One by one the reporter's companions drifted away to their tents, retired for the night as the desert air cooled to a chilliness Dixon would hardly have imagined. He had half a bottle of hooch in front of him, and an exclusive story of intrigue and discovery was unfolding about him. Life was good.

Sitting back in his chair, Dixon breathed in deeply, marvelled at the strange constellations above him, wondered at the swinging beam of a flashlight working its way up the side of the valley. He sat up, his arak-addled brain trying to make sense of the flashlight. Why was someone climbing up to the ridge where he and Professor Farrell had entered the valley earlier that day? Perhaps it was the professor, too prudish or too proud to take a dump in the communal latrines. With that thought in mind, Dixon folded his arms over his stomach. He fell into a blissful sleep, disturbed only by the racket of a vehicle driving close by the VIP camp at some ungodly hour.

*   *   *

'Wake up, Mister Dixon! Wake up!'

The voice was urgent, but not as urgent as Dixon's need for a couple of aspirin. The reporter was lying fully dressed on his camp bed in the tent Gatlin had assigned him, his arms hugging the half empty bottle of arak. How he had got from the dinner table to his tent was a blank.

'What is it, Abdullah?' he asked thickly, his eyes focusing on the dark, scarred face of El-Banki.

'Professor Farrell! He's dead, sir. You must come at once. I've already woken the others.'

Dixon blinked away the worst of his hangover, swung his feet off the cot. 'Dead?'

'An accident. One of the tablets fell on him.'

Still trying to comprehend the import of the camp coordinator's words, Dixon instructed him to fetch the Toyota.

El-Banki shook his head. 'The Toyota's gone,' he said. 'And Monsieur Le Feuvre's gone, too.'

'Gone?'

Dixon pushed past the Sudanese, flung open the tent flaps, and found Doctor Gatlin and Matilda Benson waiting for him. Matilda looked pale, and the excavation director was scuffing the ground with his feet, seemingly unwilling to take charge of the situation.

'We could take Farrell's land cruiser out to the site,' Gatlin suggested.

Dixon shrugged. 'The professor had the keys.'

'We'll have to walk,' said Matilda. She started trudging across the sand-and-gravel valley floor, towards the stubby pyramids and the excavation site beyond, Gatlin and El-Banki following close behind.

Florid-faced, cursing his sedentary lifestyle, Dixon struggled to keep up with the others. He stopped briefly to rest at the pyramid decorated with the carving of the slave catching Pharaoh Pi-Ankhi's faeces. By the time he reached the excavation, el-Banki and his gang of labourers were milling about, unsure what they were supposed to do at the scene of Farrell's fatal accident. However, Gatlin soon had suspicions it was no accident.

'The tablet Professor Farrell was working on. The one inscribed in Kushite hieroglyphs and Greek. It's not here!

Dixon didn't seem to hear. He, like Matilda, was staring open-mouthed at the corpse of Professor Farrell. One of the tablets lay across the man's crushed chest, and a stream of gore, abuzz with flies, had burst from his mouth. Yet for Dixon, the most disturbing sight was the professor's bulging, imploring eyes. It appeared he hadn't died quickly, but had been trapped beneath the weight of the slab while it crushed the life out of him. Almost as bad as the staring eyes was a rigor-mortis-stiffened arm, stretched out straight, resting across one of the other tablets. A single finger pointed accusingly upwards, possibly at a long-gone assassin.

'It's that bloody frog, Le Feuvre,' said Gatlin. 'You saw him yourself last night when he heard about the professor's discovery. The bastard's stolen the tablet and scarpered.'

'The stone's not important. There's a dead man to think about,' Dixon reminded the dig director. Secretly he wondered which would be the better story to prop up his career at the *Star* – the professor's 'Rosetta Stone', or the professor's murder?

'Maybe it wasn't Le Feuvre who killed him,' said Matilda. She regarded Gatlin suspiciously. 'The tablet is just as valuable to you as it is to him. Perhaps you've done away with the professor and Le Feuvre. Maybe you want us to think Le Feuvre murdered the professor.'

Gatlin laughed uncertainly, saw the earnestness in Matilda's eyes. 'She's crazy,' he said, appealing to Dixon. 'She hated Le Feuvre, said he was a fascist. And the professor – he snubbed her, refused to shake her hand, refused to eat with her. It's Matilda, I tell you. And if the Frenchman's dead too, she did him in.' The dig director backed away from the excavation site, his eyes flitting between Dixon and Matilda. When he was a safe distance away, he shouted to Dixon and the bemused Sudanese labourers. 'Watch your backs! Miss Benson's a lunatic.'

'I've got a knife,' Matilda yelled back. Dixon was unclear whether she meant the knife was for her protection or for retribution against her ex-lover.

When Doctor Gatlin had disappeared from view, Matilda surveyed the shocked and silent faces around her. She reddened in embarrassment, and with an indignant flick of her hair began the trek back to the VIP encampment.

'Shall we bury Professor Farrell?' said el-Banki. 'Before he . . . er . . . ripens?'

Dixon looked about, hoping someone else would take the decision. Realising there was no one else, he gave his assent.

Before setting off to make sure that Doctor Gatlin and Matilda did each other no harm, Dixon bent down and forced himself to check the dead professor's pockets. Panic increased as the search progressed, and it was all he could do not to cry. The keys to the land cruiser were nowhere to be found. He was trapped in the Sudanese desert with no forms of communication, far from civilisation, with a murderer on the loose.

*　　*　　*

Back at the VIP camp, the atmosphere was surprisingly subdued. Doctor Gatlin, sitting at the table outside his tent, was examining and cleaning another artefact. He was studiously ignoring Matilda. For her part, the dig collator was sat cross-legged in the sand, narrowly watching her erstwhile lover.

Dixon observed them for a while. However, since the two archaeologists paid him no heed, and because neither appeared intent on murdering the other, he retired to the confines of his own tent. After the initial shock of finding Professor Farrell dead, everything seemed suddenly so clear. Le Feuvre had seen his chance of making a small fortune by stealing the tablet with the dual inscription, and had seized the opportunity with both hands. The Frenchman was undoubtedly miles away. All they had to do was sit tight until news from the dig became overdue. Someone would be sent from Khartoum to find out what was wrong.

To avoid having to think more on their predicament, Dixon did what he usually did under stressful circumstances – caved in under the pressure and turned to alcohol. After all, he still had half a bottle of last night's arak left.

*   *   *

Someone was creeping around Dixon's tent; someone dangerous. Unable to move, unable even to open his eyes, he hoped the intruder would ignore him, would not throttle, or stab, or shoot him to death. Then Dixon woke up, wallowing in his sweat-drenched cot. He looked about fearfully, but saw no one.

Cautiously he got out of bed and searched for anything out of place. All appeared as it had when he passed out. He made an inventory of his belongings and swore out loud. His camera was missing. No matter though, thought Dixon. The previous evening, as a precaution against theft, he had rewound the film of Aldos Valich's dried corpse and Farrell's extraordinary discovery, and changed the film for a fresh one. He patted his trouser pocket. The film cartridge was safe.

Dixon smiled to himself. He had outwitted the thief. But his smile didn't last long once he began pondering who might have been rooting around inside the tent. Who could possibly want those photographs but Marc Le Feuvre? Perhaps the Frenchman had not fled the scene with his loot, but was lurking in the shadows, perhaps biding his time to dispose of anyone who knew of his crime.

Paranoia threatening to overwhelm him, Dixon stumbled out of his tent. The mid-afternoon sun shone weakly, but still raised sweat on his brow. Neither the dig director nor the collator was about. At first he considered going to Gatlin's tent, but then he recalled that Gatlin and Le Feuvre could be in league. Matilda had no axe to grind with him, so Dixon went to her tent first. For a moment he stood awkwardly outside the tent flap, wondering how to knock on canvas. Finally he tapped at the tent pole and quietly called out her name. No reply. He tried again. Nothing. He pulled back the canvas flap. The tent was empty.

'It doesn't mean anything,' Dixon told himself. 'Matilda could be anywhere on the dig. It doesn't mean something's happened to her.'

With little choice left to him, Dixon decided he must trust Gatlin. From what he had seen of the dig director, the man didn't have the makings of a cold-blooded killer. So what if he sold off the odd antiquity to finance his excavation for another season? That didn't make him a murderer.

Again Dixon went through the pantomime of tapping on the tent pole, quietly urging the occupant to answer his increasingly impatient calls. As before, there was no answer. Wondering vaguely if the ex-lovers had kissed and made up, Dixon tentatively pulled back the tent flap. A sweet cloying aroma assaulted him, the smell augmented by the sound of flies. Reticently he entered the dig director's tent. Doctor Gatlin was lying on his cot, apparently oblivious to the reporter's presence. Dixon inched forward, more and more certain with every step that something was dreadfully awry. He called out Gatlin's name in a whisper until his voice trailed off into shocked silence. Doctor Robert Gatlin lay face up on his cot, the canvas sodden with the man's blood. From the archaeologist's belly protruded the handle of a knife.

In his haste to flee, Dixon fell out of the tent opening. Sprawled on the gravel, he looked about, wild-eyed, for signs of the insane woman who only hours ago had threatened to stab Gatlin to death. The whole excavation site seemed empty though, as if there was no one but him for miles around.

Farrell's tent! Dixon thought to himself. There was a chance, a small chance, that the professor had come back last night for the tools of his trade and had left the keys to his land cruiser amongst his personal belongings.

Dixon staggered the twenty yards to the Professor's tent, pulled back the flap, and discovered the place had been ransacked. Books, papers, clothing were everywhere. But why? What had the killer been looking for? If Farrell's murderer already had the keys to the land cruiser, why turn the tent upside down? It made no sense.

With options rapidly running out, Dixon resolved to trust his fate to the Sudanese labourers. Forcing the pace, the reporter covered the ground to the ancient city of Kush. Yet when he got there, panting and palpitating, the makeshift encampment was deserted. Cooking fires still smouldered, indicating a sudden evacuation. It seemed as though the Sudanese had chosen to leave the mad Westerners – intent as they were on killing each other – to their own devices.

Dixon fell to his knees amongst the ruined walls and columns of a city more than two millennia old. He cursed the Sudanese labourers for cowards and cried tears into the sand. 'Get a grip, John,' he finally told himself. 'Stay calm. It's the only way you'll get out of this mess.'

Stifling his sobs, forcing composure on himself, Dixon thought back over the past twenty-four hours. From the day's horrors, he eventually figured out a clue that could help him discover what was happening at the Kush excavations. The previous night, while Dixon had been drinking, he had seen someone ascending to the ridge above the valley. He had assumed it was Professor Farrell. And when the professor was found dead, he was pointing in the direction of the ridge, towards the cairn he had built, towards his 'safeguard'. Whatever the person who had ransacked the professor's tent was after, it might well be hidden up on the ridge.

* * *

Labouring for breath, dripping sweat as the evening sun prepared to set, Dixon stopped and rested. Having reached the ridgeline, he feverishly sought out the cairn. His eyes finally alighted on the tidy pile of rocks. Another exertion of effort and he was on his knees beside the professor's monument, digging through the rubble until he found the professor's spiral-bound notebook.

Dixon was about to get to his feet when he remembered the film cartridge in his pocket. The killer had stolen Dixon's camera believing the original film was still inside, that the old film hadn't been changed for a fresh one. This cartridge was his insurance, his own safeguard. Dixon thrust the film cartridge into the dismantled cairn, and rebuilt the rocks around it.

Thunk! Thunk! Thunk!

The methodical thudding came from beyond a rise in the ground. Clutching Professor Farrell's notebook, Dixon scrambled up the incline, stones giving way in mini avalanches beneath his feet. Reaching the top, he glance over the parapet of rock and almost cried out with joy.

'El-Banki!' shouted Dixon, rising to his feet and stumbling into the shallow depression beyond the rise.

Abdullah el-Banki was beside the Toyota pickup, sledge hammering rocks. The Sudanese stopped abruptly at Dixon's appearance.

'Thank God!' said Dixon. 'You've found the Toyota. We can get out of here now.'

A flicker of bemusement crossed el-Banki's face, the first inkling Dixon had of a misread situation.

'The professor's notebook,' el-Banki said. 'I hoped you might know where it had got to.' He reached out a hand for the notebook, but Dixon snatched it from his grasp. The camp coordinator smiled slyly. 'Why don't you read something from it?' he suggested.

Confused, Dixon turned to the first page of writing in Professor Farrell's notebook. The handwriting was cramped, almost illegible, and with difficulty the reporter read, 'Translation of the Greek text from the dually-inscribed tablet discovered near the Kushite pyramid field. On this, the twentieth day, of the sixth month, of the thirteenth year of my reign as Pharaoh of Upper and Lower Egypt, I, Pi-Ankhi, hereby elevate my trusty slave el-Banki to the exalted position of Catcher and Custodian of the Pharaoh's Excrement . . . '

Dixon lowered the notebook and glanced over at the rocks that el-Banki had been cracking apart with the sledge hammer. There was writing on some of the pieces – they were the half obliterated remnants of Professor Farrell's 'Rosetta Stone'.

'Three hundred years ago,' el-Banki said, 'the Russian adventurer, Aldos Valich, began excavations at Kush. My ancestors, proud of their royal lineage, were overjoyed when he unearthed the tablets. They imagined the stones chronicled the glories of Pi-Ankhi, the pharaoh who was the first of the el-Bankis. How disappointed they were to find their humiliation written in stone – and how unfortunate for Valich. Then, centuries after my family believed their shame forever buried, Doctor Gatlin and Miss Benson rediscovered the tablets.'

Dixon was incredulous. 'You killed Gatlin and Professor Farrell so no one would find out that the el-Bankis were not descended from the pharaohs?'

'How could my people honour me if they knew the shameful truth? And as you may recall from last night, Mister Dixon, it was not only Doctor Gatlin and Professor Farrell who held the reputation of my family in their hands – not once you had told everyone at the dinner table about the tablet with the dual inscription.'

El-Banki leaned the sledgehammer against the side of the Toyota pickup, unhitched the tailgate and let it fall open.

The sight was too much for Dixon, and he fell to his knees. On the bed of the pickup, side by side, were Marc Le Feuvre and Matilda Benson. The Frenchman's skull had been caved in by a blow to the head, while Matilda's purple, swollen tongue was testament to her strangulation.

From beside the bodies, el-Banki pulled out a spade designed for digging vehicles out of sand. 'Monsieur Le Feuvre I shall bury right here,' he explained. 'The authorities will believe – as you yourself did – that he stole a valuable artefact and fled.'

He pointed to Matilda. 'Miss Benson gave me a run for my money after I killed Gatlin,' he said ruefully, 'but I finally caught up with her. And when I place her body in Gatlin's tent, it will appear they killed one another during a lovers' tiff.'

His voice tremulous, Dixon asked, 'What will become of me?'

'You're my last loose end.' El-Banki smiled apologetically. 'Alone and desperate, in a vain effort to seek help, *Sunday Star* journalist John Dixon will fall to his death while attempting to climb out of the Kush Valley.'

'But I have pictures of the tablet,' Dixon blubbered.

Again el-Banki reached into the back of the pickup, this time lifting out Dixon's camera. He dropped it to the ground, raised the spade, and smashed the camera to pieces. Then, grinning evilly, he advanced on the reporter, the spade held like a cudgel.

'I took the film out of the camera,' said Dixon desperately. 'I've hidden the pictures of Farrell's "Rosetta Stone".'

El-Banki hesitated, his smile faltering. He turned, looked down, and saw a film cartridge lying amidst the wreckage of Dixon's camera. 'Nice try,' he said, and swung the spade.

Shaping the ends

JUDITH CUTLER

If only Hamlet had been tried for Polonius' death the truth would have come out.

Why was it my destiny ever to be involved? God knows it was not my choice, at any point. I was unprepared for any of it. I had always been content with my lot, a serving woman, waiting on Her Majesty. I would mend her clothes, dress her hair, and sleep on my pallet across the door to her apartment to keep her safe and preserve her reputation. There were times, of course, when I heard the measured gait of His Majesty approaching, and knew to make myself scarce. Those times came less and less often, these days, especially now His Majesty's younger brother Claudius had returned and it seemed to me the whole court spent its time carousing. After our seemly, plain suppers, the rich food and Rhenish disagreed with His Majesty, and he came hardly ever to Her Majesty's chamber. I thought at first it was she who went to his, she came reeling back to her boudoir so late, but I have since had cause to change my mind.

To my astonishment, the celebrations changed the Lord Chancellor. I'd always thought of him as a prosy old fool, given to smutty jokes in the presence of us underlings, as if bestowing largesse. Imagine my amazement when his occasional goosings and squeezings of breasts went further – much further. I found myself having to fight him off in the dark corners on the turns of stairs. When I complained to the Queen that this man old enough to be my father had tried to ravish me, she blushed and with downcast eyes admitted that he was so taken with me that he wished to make me his mistress.

Down in Jutland we don't become mistresses. We marry or we stay maids. And so I told Her Majesty.

She raised an eyebrow. 'But his children? They are both – difficult – Maria.'

I nodded. I could hardly do otherwise. Lacking a mother so long, they had become unruly, wayward. He, the older by some years, was inclined to give himself airs, as if he were the head of the house. He'd been sent to Paris, to acquire a little polish and less learning, as his father was wont to say. He was certainly a hothead who would brook no opposition, and I was glad he spent so much time abroad. His sister missed him grievously, and used to pen long effusive letters in response to his, as if he were her absent betrothed. Then she found other objects for her unruly affections. For a week she swooned for the English Ambassador, and when he was recalled a few weeks later, wept over his miniature painted by Master Hilliard. Then it was for the captain of the guard she sighed, then a player from a group of itinerant actors. I said it was because she was young, with too much time on her hands. My advice was that she should fill her hours with plain sewing and visiting the sick, but her father spoilt her yet. Goodness knows whom she would next turn her lovelorn eyes upon. The more trouble for him, said I.

'It seems to me that even if it's a bedding on the wrong side of the blanket, Madam, I'll offend his children. In a small place like this everyone knows everyone else's business.' There was much of her business I rather more than suspected – recently concerning the lord Claudius. 'Mistress or wife,' I continued, 'I won't please them. And if I can't be his wife, you must make him keep those pickers and stealers to himself. I'll not tolerate the tedious old fool's antics any longer.'

'It's not to be a love match then,' the queen sighed, gusty with emotion as young Ophelia. At her time of life, too. Thank goodness she was past the age to worry whether paddling palms with the king's brother would have dire consequences. Or perhaps – just in case – that was why every so often she'd lure the king back to her boudoir, so he could have no doubts over any love child. 'But it would be sensible, Maria – it's better to be a rich widow than a poor spinster.'

So wed we did, but without the pomp I'd have liked. A very hole in corner affair it was, with the pastor mumbling away to himself and my new lord giving a homily as long as any preacher could wish. Then, for all the pre-marital fumblings, my maidenhead was as intact at the end of our wedding night as at the beginning. Of course, he was not a young man, and there was wine a-plenty: however much it provokes the desire, they say, it always takes away the performance. But not the need for the piss-pot under the bed. Was there ever such a man for a weak bladder? Faugh! And such stinking breath, too.

What I certainly did not expect was my instant despatch to my lord's country estate. There were affairs he wished me to oversee, he told me, going into much precise and tedious detail. Indeed I judiciously applied my spur to my steed, all the while pretending I was trying hard to control it and attend to his instructions.

Lord Chancellor the old man might be, and almost running the country, but he had no more idea of how to run a farm than the crown prince would have of swimming the Skagerrak. It must have taken me six or eight weeks to instil some basic principles of domestic economy into the housekeeper, while my new stepson would have been better employed, despite his French silks and clever words, learning to run the farm.

One day all the church bells tolled, one by one, in every hamlet and village in the district. Were we at war? Giving strict instructions that all our treasures were to be sealed and buried deep in the cellar, I summoned my horse and rode home.

To find chaos.

The King, the good old King Hamlet, had died. There was so much grieving and despair it took me a few hours to discover that he had died, not as befitted a great man like him, heroically on the battlefield, but stung by a bee in his orchard where he was having a nap in the sun. I wept with the others. But there must be a new king. With great gusto I set the staff about spring-cleaning young Hamlet's room. It might have been fit for a prince before: now it was fit for the king he was about to become. Flushed with my endeavours, it took me a few hours to realise that no one else talked of expecting him any moment. No one spoke of his coronation. They spoke of something else. It wasn't one rat I smelt, more a whole cellarful, as I cornered my lord that night.

'The Queen to remarry!' I squeaked. 'Whom, My Lord?'

'The new king,' he said, trying to avoid my eye.

'The Queen can't marry Lord Hamlet! Even the worst heathen wouldn't suggest that!'

'Go to, go to. The Queen marries my lord Claudius – '

'How can he be king? When the old king's son lives? And is,' I added, 'a good man, very like his father – kind to the poor, never giving himself airs.'

'A young man,' my apology for a husband muttered. 'Inexperienced.'

'A man of near thirty! And a student at Wittenberg, no less. What he doesn't know about kingship he'll soon learn. As for that Claudius,' I continued, 'the man's a rider, a lecher, a libertine, the owner of no one good quality – '

'A king. Our king. And not inclined to favour fishwives,' my lord said tartly.

Our marriage was not consummated that night, either.

Within less than no time, as the newly-arrived young Hamlet observed, their majesties were man and wife – such a hugger-mugger affair it was too. Almost as quiet as mine. And no wedding journey to compensate. It seemed that the Norwegians had the measure of King Claudius and were planning an invasion, so he made it his business – oh, no, not to ride out as King Hamlet would have done, and deal swiftly and surely with the matter, but to send a pair of underlings with a message. My husband and his newly returned hothead of a son almost came to blows over the decision. It certainly wasn't how Laertes felt a king should behave.

As for young Hamlet, you'd have thought all his philosophy would have taught him how to deal with the situation. In his place I would have disobeyed the king's wish that he stay at court and forthwith returned to university where he'd have been happy. If I'd stayed, it would have been to slit the usurper's throat in the church. But he merely sat in a corner and moped, making odd utterances no one understood. He managed but one sensible thing. Despite the winter weather, despite what should have been a year of mourning, the entire court was supposed to wear bright summer garb. Only he had the sense to swathe himself in his thickest clothes, complete with scarf and cloak. I would slip into his hands sweetmeats I had about me, just as when he was a boy: he would always favour me with a kind word, and sometimes a smile that lit his whole face. Often he seemed about to confide in me, but on cue up would come my husband, so promptly I'd swear he'd been listening.

At last Hamlet seemed to turn a corner, and became downright coltish. Perhaps it was his new-found love. He and Ophelia seemed well on the way to consoling each other, with some encouragement from both me and his mother, I have to say. But both blew hot and cold: the more he pursued, the more she skittered away, and when she turned up the heat, you couldn't see him for dust. A good box about the ears, that's what they both needed, and so I told Polonius.

'Can't you see it's for the best?' he whispered, looking about all the while as if the very dust motes might spy on him. 'If he can't bed her till he's wed her, the good king and queen, fearing he'll go mad for love, will grant their consent and then I'm made for life, Maria. You and I,' he added, somewhat as an afterthought.

'If you ask me, he's so many cares a silly girl playing fast and loose with his emotions can only be bad for him,' I said. 'His father dies, he comes bustling home expecting a coronation – his own, My Lord –

and what does he find? What he should, his mother in widow's weeds, preparing for a dowager's life in a convent? His uncle on his knees before him, swearing due allegiance to his new liege lord? No! He finds his throne usurped, his mother open-legged for a man not worth the snap of her fingers!' I might have added that King's brother or not, Claudius' behaviour was far from regal: his hands were always trying to find their way into serving maids' plackets or tugging their bodices till their nipples peeped out. Fine manners in a newly-wed.

'Hush. Prithee, wife, hush.'

'And what are you planning, Polonius? You play your cards so close to your chest I sometimes think you can't see them yourself!'

He went off huffing and puffing. I was left to consider a new addition to our court, one of Prince Hamlet's fellow students. Horatio. Such a lovely pair of legs he had on him. Though he said little, what he did was always to the point – and he had the sweetest turn of phrase. I began to regret my overhasty marriage: a woman might expect apter treatment from this young man. But in time I began to suspect that he was not, as one might say, a marrying sort. Certainly he was as tender to the melancholy prince as a lover would be.

Not so the next arrivals at court, as nasty a pair as you'd come across in a week's work. More students. But though they would merrily chip and chop their logic with young Hamlet, they took back his every word to either my lord or King Claudius.

At last I could bear it no longer, and happened to find my way on to the battlements at the same time as Hamlet. At the sound of my footsteps he wheeled round in what looked like terror.

'It's only I. Maria.' I said. 'Come to blow a few cobwebs away.'

We agreed that the weather was cold, the wind coming from the north-west, despite the bright sun, and joked about the shape of the clouds. To my surprise, he scribbled in his tablets when I said one looked like a weasel.

'And talking of weasels,' I pursued, 'there are those about the castle who claim to be your friends but who shouldn't be trusted any more than ferrets in a sack. Not Horatio, My Lord. The other pair. Rosenstern and Guidenthing. Whatever they call themselves.' I leaned closer. God, his doublet and hose stank. Waving my hand before my nose, I said, 'You were once so well-turned out, Your Highness – the pattern card, the very mirror of fashion. And now a beggar would spurn this doublet. As for your hose – !'

He touched his nose too, but with the sort of tap that told me he had a secret. 'There is a reason for all this. And the beard. And the lurking in corners. Trust me,' he said.

'Trust! I don't know anyone else I'd trust in this place. Well, Horatio, I suppose. But no one else. No one at all.'

'No one? Surely Ophelia – !'

' – would – I have to be frank – do anything her father bid her.' Only that morning, as we were breaking our fast, I had heard him whispering to the king something about privately loosing her to Hamlet. *Loosing* – as if she were a mare to be tupped. 'And he seems to be – nay, *is* – like this with Claudius.' I crossed my fingers. 'Beg pardon – *King* Claudius. Why don't you do something, My Lord?'

Then I realised why rumours of his madness were no longer whispered, but spoken openly.

Out of the blue, he asked, 'Do you believe in ghosts?'

Without thinking, I crossed myself.

It was as if I'd answered another question. 'Ah! You think they're come from the devil to torment us!'

Did I? 'Perhaps. Or perhaps they're heaven-sent to warn us. All I know, My Lord, is that I have never yet seen one.'

He gave a short, harsh laugh.

'My Lord, you misjudge me. I know they say only the pure can see one.'

'So they do. So an adulteress would not . . . '

'Adulteress! Not I, My Lord!' Should I make it entirely clear? I blushed for my lord Polonius. Did I owe him any loyalty? Not as much as I owed the late king's son. 'Free with my eyes I may be, Highness, but I'm no loose woman. I'm as pure in body as any lady entering a nunnery.'

Another bark of laughter. 'A nunnery! Next you'll be saying Polonius is a fishmonger keeping a bawdy-house!'

'Not that sort of nunnery, either, my lord. Enough of your jests. As for Polonius, to be wife and no wife is no laughing matter.'

He nodded. 'Better that than to be a whore, Maria. When the old man dies, we'll find you a lusty prince for your bed,' he added kindly, with a courtly kiss of my hand to show he meant no unkindness.

'Dies? Creaky gates always last the longest, my lord. As for a prince – go to! I'd be more likely to fetch up with that court card, Osric. If he could ever frame his mouth round such an ordinary word as marriage. They say that manners make the man – but I'll swear he bowed to his mother's breast before he suckled.'

He threw his head back and laughed. 'My good Maria! Well, there may be a few soldiers visiting our court. Fortinbras, for instance.'

'Fortinbras!' My eyes must have gleamed. I'd seen him when he'd accompanied his father here on a state visit. Then he'd been scarcely bearded. Now he'd be just the young man for Ophelia to have one of her crushes on. Poor Hamlet. I asked more soberly, 'But why should he come here?'

'The esteemed Claudius has given permission for Fortinbras of Norway to lead his army across our soil. He intends to wrest a few acres from Poland.'

'Poland! Such poor farming land it wouldn't yield five ducats an acre. What a waste of young life. Why doesn't war carry off the old?' Polonius, for instance. 'Sweet Prince, take care, I beg you.'

He looked at me with sudden kindness as I clasped his hands. 'We all have to die, Maria.'

'But not before our time, Sir, if I may say so. Now, enough of this chatter. They say the Players are to come again. Imagine being able to remember all those words! And say them in public! As if they really meant them, too. But perhaps it's not such an achievement. My Lord Polonius tells me he was a noted actor in his youth. If he ever was young, that is.' I sighed. 'Well, I must see they are well-lodged and well-fed. The poor lads, spending all their time on the road . . . '

The next thing Polonius and Claudius were plotting fairly turned my stomach. Gertrude was to send for Hamlet and tell him to explain his behaviour. There had certainly been a few moments of oddness during our conversation, but on the whole he was no madder than you'd expect any king to be, with all that inbreeding. But apparently he and Ophelia had had a huge argument, ending in her tears. By some coincidence Polonius had heard it all. Coincidence? I doubted it, especially when I heard his next move. I knew Gertrude was worried about him – were we not all? – but no decent mother would have wanted an extra pair of ears at the interview. Yes, my husband was to secrete himself in the room and spy.

'You cannot do that,' I expostulated as we made our way down to the evening's performance by the players. 'It's a betrayal of trust!'

'My dear Maria, madness in great ones must not go unwatched.'

'But by his mother, not by the Lord Chancellor.'

An unpleasant smirk played about his lips.

'And what if he doesn't confess all? What then?'

'Then he will be sent to England.'

'Why?'

'Because they owe us tribute and will do the King's bidding instantly.'

'And what is his bidding?'

The old man's face closed. 'Only his majesty is privy to that,' he lied, his fluttering left eyelid giving him away.

Hamlet sent to England? The king's bidding? I must slip away from the play and search the king's study.

Hamlet to be beheaded! That was what the document on the king's desk said. Instantly. As soon as he set foot on English soil. Without even time for shriving. Even as I reeled, desperate to warn the good young man, I hear voices and – just as if I were my husband – I hid behind a pillar. Something had truly enraged Claudius: I could hear him in the corridor outside, screaming with fury at Gertrude, who, lacking the backbone of a flea, was yes-sir-no-sirring him like a very drab. But then in he marched, with those two blowflies Rosencrantz and Guildenstern, and he grabbed the letter and pressed it into their hand.

I must warn Prince Hamlet! But how could I do that, when I knew he was closeted with his mother?

I used the secret stair behind the arras, meant to be used for a rapid escape in time of attack. As I ran, I drew from my pocket my scissors. There was just a chance that if Polonius felt their blade at his throat he would believe he was threatened by a man and I could drag him away. Once he was safely bestowed in our chamber, I could run back to Hamlet and get him out of Elsinore via the same staircase. He was king, by every right but anointment. He was my liege lord and he had to be saved, even if I lost my life in the endeavour.

It wasn't I but Polonius who died. As soon as Polonius felt the blade, he screamed. I slit his throat. My Lord must have thought he was threatened by an assassin, and ran his sword through the fabric. Again and again he jabbed, till, fearful for my life, I backed into the secret doorway.

When Hamlet pulled back the arras, he assumed it was his blade that had killed the rash intruding fool. I wanted to step forward and explain, but, one of his fits of madness upon him, he turned from me and berated his mother in such terms that I could not stay to listen. So I turned and ran.

Would staying have made any difference? It seemed at the time that even if I had confessed to the murder, even if I had been hanged for the offence, Hamlet would have been despatched for England. All I could do was slip a hasty letter in his pack, warning him what was planned and telling him to insert on the death warrant their names, not his. For my own protection, I asked him – if he survived – to pretend he had a premonition, and acted of his own accord.

I told myself that this way I could be there to support Ophelia and even Laertes when he returned post haste to find his father dead and his sister in strong hysterics. As usual, they all indulged her every whim. I advised bloodletting and a lowering diet. They allowed her to roam free and to harm herself. All Laertes did was raid my chest of herbs and simples, claiming he could not sleep for grief. Now that he sleeps forever, I know his true motive for the theft. It was to poison the rapier with which he was to stab Hamlet in a fencing match.

Oh, yes. Thanks to my message, Hamlet dealt summarily with the two supposed friends and returned to claim his inheritance. He came back on the worst possible day: that of Ophelia's funeral. Yes, the silly girl, with no one to curb her wantonness now her father was gone, had got herself pregnant by one of the serving men and drowned herself when the pennyroyal I'd given her did no good. No one could tell Laertes: he would have killed every last man in the garrison in revenge.

I spoke long and stern to Gertrude. There was no one else to convince her that Hamlet was a true loyal son to his father and that her husband was a cheap usurper. And I think at the end that she believed me. Did she not, even in the throes of death, accidentally poisoned by a draught Claudius had prepared for Hamlet, try to protect her son? Even though to do so was to betray her husband? At least she died with Hamlet's name on her lips.

My dear sweet prince died nobly, in his beloved Horatio's arms. And then in marched Fortinbras. In the miserable bloodbath that was the court, he silenced all by asserting his rights over the country.

And over me.

'In my country,' he said, in that strange guttural accent of his, 'it is the duty of the conqueror to take to wife the widow of the vanquished. You are the senior lady of the court. I claim you as my prize.'

So I ended with the prince Ophelia would have adored. As marriages go, it was neither bad nor good – a matter of convenience. I never wanted for anything, but have never been truly happy.

There are times when I wander the battlements, hoping to hear the ghost of Prince Hamlet assuring me I am forgiven. I know he's visited Horatio. As he himself pointed out, however, spirits speak only to the pure. So some days I think he judges me as I judge myself. As a failure. But then Horatio will remind me what the prince once said to him:

> There's a divinity doth shape our ends,
> Rough-hew them how we will.

Colour me blood

JERRY SYKES

The side of the building had been painted in a thin coat of white emulsion, but the solid colours of more than a decade's worth of graffiti still showed through the paint like blood vessels under pale Irish skin. In front of the wall, a tall scruff of a man with thick knots of dark hair was making shapes in the emulsion with a piece of charcoal. His name was Rob Blake, a local artist, and he had been commissioned by the local residents' association to create a mural on the side of the Community Centre.

Surrounding him in a loose arc, all ADD head jerks and hot feet, was a group of around ten children aged between twelve and fourteen holding in their hands face masks and cans of spray paint in a rainbow of colours. The idea was that once the artist had laid out the basic outline of the mural on the wall, the kids would then fill in the larger shapes to create the solid cast of the image, leaving the artist to add the final details later.

Across the street from the Community Centre, Detective Sergeant Marnie Stone sat and watched from the open window of her old blue Saab. In the centre of the group surrounding the artist, little more than a short head taller than the children, she could see Kate Phillips, one of the hardier members of Camden's Social Services department and an old friend. After a couple of minutes, Marnie called out her name and stuck her hand in the air, but, like the children, Kate seemed fascinated with the workings of the artist, the fluid motion of his hand, the beats of creation, and appeared not to have heard. Marnie could not see much of what was happening through the forest of shuffling limbs, just the occasional glimpse of the hand leaking sinuous lines of soft carbon, and so she had no choice but to sit back and wait.

Marnie had read about the project in the local paper and was curious to see if it would lead to a reduction in crime on the estate, as had been promised in the tenants' association's pitch to the police and the council. There were a couple of faces that she knew for a fact were responsible for a string of robberies and muggings in the area, she had just not been able to gather sufficient evidence, and so at least a couple of old people would be able to walk home in peace tonight. But she would be fooling herself if she thought it would go further than that.

A few minutes later, the artist stood up to stretch his back and the spell he held over his audience was broken. Kate glanced around and saw Marnie watching them. She stooped and said something to one of the kids nearest her, and then walked over to the Saab. The closer she came, Marnie noticed, the deeper the lines that bracketed her mouth became. But then it had never surprised Marnie that social workers appeared to age faster than the rest of the world, including police officers.

'Hello, Marnie, what are you doing out here?' asked Kate, smiling. 'You're not going to arrest Rob, are you?'

'You mean that vandal trying to make the estate a better place to live?' replied Marnie, reflecting the smile. 'Sure, I just wanted to see who his accomplices were first . . . '

'Ooh, don't be cruel,' replied Kate, resting her hand on the lip of the door.

'What's it going to be, anyway?' asked Marnie, pointing towards the Community Centre.

'A warning about the perils of drink and drugs,' said Kate. 'There's going to be the usual logo, Keep it Clean, and then a street scene with kids and families and stuff like that. I don't know, I think I also heard Rob say something about a large bin with needles and guns sticking out of it or something . . . '

'And here's me thinking Walt Disney was dead,' said Marnie.

'Hey, don't knock it,' Kate chastised her. 'If it gives these kids some stake in the estate then it'll be worth it.'

'Yeah, I know,' agreed Marnie, glancing away. She still had her doubts, but she also knew that she would never be able to win an argument with Kate. She started the engine and put the car in gear. 'Anyway, I better be getting back to the station. I just thought I'd drop by and see how you were getting on . . . '

'Much better than I thought,' said Kate, nodding. 'There are far more kids here than I thought there would be . . . Including one or two I never expected to see in a million years.'

'Yeah, I know who you mean,' said Marnie. 'So just remember to count all the paint cans at the end of the night . . . '

Kate gave her a look of mock admonishment, and then broke into a smile. 'Go and chase some real villains,' she said.

*   *   *

The children had been filling in shapes for a little more than ten minutes when the first argument started. Calum Breen, a short kid with dark hair and a pronounced lower lip that made him look like he was sulking all the time, a mask that suited his character to the ground, had been assigned a couple of letters at the end of the slogan, but what he wanted to do was something a bit more artistic, or something a bit more real, as he put it.

'Why can't I do one of the people, or even some of the background?' he asked, a sneer pushing his lip out further.

'Because that's just the way it worked out,' replied Blake, wishing that Kate was still there with him. Five minutes earlier she had told him that she had to go and see a client on the estate but would be back in an hour. He was not used to dealing with a bunch of kids on his own and, although he was loath to admit it to himself, having her there made him feel safer.

'But I don't want to do the letters,' replied Calum.

'Well how about you just do one of the letters and then we move everyone around,' said Blake. 'That way everyone'll get to do a figure and a letter, or a bit of background, or whatever . . . '

'He's just scared of getting it wrong because he can't read,' called out a kid in the centre of the group.

'There's no need for that,' said Blake.

'Yeah, piss off,' said Calum.

'Come on, let's not fight about it,' said Blake. He could feel the group starting to slip out of his grasp, but he wasn't quite sure what to do about it.

The two kids shuffled around in the pack for a brief moment, alternating between hiding behind their colleagues and stepping out into makeshift clearings, before squaring up to one another. Blake waited until the last moment, fearful of wounding their pride, perhaps, and then stepped between them with his palms raised. And just stood there, still and silent, waiting for them to return to the growing spread of colour on the wall. Long minutes later, egos satisfied, the pair traded final insults and then broke up and returned to the task at hand. Blake folded his arms and waited to make certain that it was indeed all over, and then stepped over to watch Calum work. It did not take him long to realise that behind the brash tongue the kid had a natural talent and that perhaps he should give him a break and let him have a bit more input to the project. Trouble was he would have to do it without looking like he was cutting out the other kids.

But fifteen minutes later, two minutes after the kids had traded shapes, Calum had another complaint.

'How come we're just doing a picture of the estate, anyway? It's pretty boring, don't you think? I mean, we live here all the time. Why can't we do something a bit more interesting?'

Blake sighed. 'I thought we talked about this.'

'What about a beach with horses running through the surf,' suggested Calum. 'I don't know, just something different . . . '

'I thought we agreed to do a mural of what we wanted the estate to look like,' said Blake.

'Calum wants it to look like a building site with sand and shit,' piped up a small kid from the centre of the group.

'I never said that,' replied Calum, looking for the source.

'Clubbers sleeping off their highs from the night before,' said another kid, his idea of a beach.

'No, that's not the kind of beach I mean,' protested Calum, still looking for the source of the first voice.

'Grannies pumping coins into slot machines,' suggested another, stretching the beach connection to breaking point.

'What the hell is wrong with you people,' squealed Calum. 'You've got the chance to bring a bit of colour into your lives and what do you do? Paint a cartoon version of what you've already got. Jesus, give it some imagination, won't you?'

'Imagine this,' said one of the kids, giving him a finger.

'This is for all of us, not just for you,' said another.

'Yeah, sod off and find your own wall,' said yet another.

With faceless jibes coming at him from all directions, Calum felt a sickness rise in his throat. He took a deep breath and tried to shake it loose, dampen the tension, but it just seemed to make things worse. Seconds later, past frustration, he turned and pointed his can at the wall, pressed down on the button and held it there, as if that could relieve the pressure within himself. Dark blue paint bubbled and frothed on the wall and a thin trail soon snaked down through the white emulsion.

'Oh for Christ's sake, Calum,' said Blake.

'I knew he'd turn it all to shit,' said one of the kids.

Calum continued to press down on the button.

'Give me the can,' said Blake, his long fingers beckoning. But Calum just ignored him, and after one more polite request, Blake stepped forward and slammed the can out of his hand.

Calum snarled at him and watched the can as it bounced and rattled on the ground, and then stormed off across the estate.

Blake watched him go, and then ran forward a couple of steps and kicked the can into the wall as hard as he could.

*   *   *

Calum was still feeling a little out of sorts a few hours later. Sitting on the back of a bench in the centre of the estate with a couple of his friends who had not been part of the mural project: Match, like the name suggested – kids are nothing if not literal – tall and thin and with a shock of red hair, and Tusk, a regular looking kid with a left canine tooth that poked out from between his lips even when his mouth was closed. The pair had been messing with his head ever since he had joined them on the bench after supper, word had travelled fast, and he was starting to get dark and pissed off, to believe that there was nowhere left to run. At one point, Match had accused him of losing his balls, and as the night had progressed and the more he had brooded on it, the more he had started to believe that Match might in fact be right. A couple of solutions had passed through his head – for an instant he had considered damaging the mural, but then he knew that he would be the main suspect – but nothing had made itself clear. Approaching midnight, he knew that he had to act soon to distance himself from the project and therefore restore his ego.

Taking a final drag on his cigarette, Calum flicked it out into the air and climbed down from the bench. He set off across the estate, breathing hard through his nose like a minotaur.

'Yo, what's happenin', man,' Match called out, standing up and following him. 'What's going on, Calum.'

'Yo, wait up,' cried Tusk, setting off after them.

Match and Tusk fell into step beside Calum, and the three of them headed up through Kentish Town before cutting a right into Dartmouth Park. Here the streets were quieter, darker, and there were less people about, less traffic. Calum led them through a labyrinth of back streets and alleys, streetlights sending shadows to track them, making no attempt to hide themselves, confident in their solid presence. Fifteen minutes after leaving the comfort of the estate, he led them behind a dark parade of shops that represented another kind of comfort.

The off-licence sat in the middle of the parade between a vet's surgery and a greengrocer's, and was well known to all the kids in the area as a cheap target. Calum himself had broken into it at least three times, three that he could remember, and almost every other kid he knew had burgled it at least once. It was like a training ground for them, a rites of passage kind of place.

Match had been following Calum in glum silence, but as soon as he figured out where Calum was going, a broad grin had spread across his face as he knew his friend was coming back to them. It had been a bad time, with Calum either buried in paint and a social conscience or in despair. Match leaned into Tusk and told him the news, watched the other kid respond in the same manner.

'You going to hit the cashpoint,' said Match, his nickname for the off-licence.

'Time I felt the muscle working again,' replied Calum, clenching a fist in front of his heart.

'Yo, back in the world,' said Tusk.

'All right, let's get it on,' said Calum. He led them down the back of the buildings, their feet creating scuffles and echoes in the trash that carpeted the ground. At the back of the off-licence, he held out his right hand and gestured to Match with his left. Match lifted his jacket aside, pulled out a short-bladed knife from the deep thigh-pocket in his cargo pants, and handed it to Calum. As Calum lifted the knife to jam it into the gap between the door and the frame, he noticed the line of dried blood at the base of the blade and an icicle threaded his spine. The blood was from where Match had stabbed some kid in the hand the week before when he had been too slow in handing over his mobile phone. Calum had seen the attack, and although he had been witness to unprovoked violence before, the cold action of his friend had shaken him more than he cared to admit. It had been an insight too far into the mental state of their situation.

The uncomfortable thought stilled him, and when the door creaked and opened a fraction, he thought for a moment that he must have popped it open himself without realising it and looked at the knife for a second in disbelief. And when it creaked again and opened a little further, a slice of light falling across the ground, he was still none the wiser, even when a look of keen surprise appeared on Match's face and his friend turned on his heel and fled. Understanding what was happening, Tusk too was soon up and off on his jaundiced feet into the darkness.

Stuck in that awkward space between thought and action, it was just when the manager's scared face appeared around the door that the truth of the situation hit Calum. Shaking the indecision from his limbs, he took off after his friends, but not before the manager had caught a clear glimpse of his startled face.

* * *

At nine o'clock the following morning, Rob Blake, the artist, and Kate Phillips, the social worker, were sitting on a threadbare sofa in the living room of the flat Calum Breen shared with his mother. DS Marnie Stone had been on the phone to Kate first thing: the owner of the off-licence had recognised Calum at once but because he had not committed an actual offence she was reluctant to speak to him, could Kate go round there and have a quiet word. 'Sounds like I don't have much choice,' Kate had replied, but here she was with Rob at her side for moral support.

Calum's mother was sitting in a matching chair, a cup of hot coffee in one hand and a cigarette in the other. She looked like she had a hangover; bloodshot pupils and red skin.

'So who else was there last night, Calum?' asked Kate. 'The manager said he saw two other kids running off.'

Calum twisted in his seat and said nothing.

'It was almost midnight,' continued Kate. 'Somehow I just don't think that you'd have been out there on your own at that time of night. Do you want to tell me who you were with, Calum?'

Again Calum said nothing.

'Was it Match and Tusk?'

At the mention of the names Match and Tusk, Blake glanced at Kate, a little surprised, and then turned to Calum.

'I thought you said you'd left those two behind when you signed on for the mural,' said Blake, feeling a little hurt.

'Yeah, well, maybe if I'd been allowed to put something of my own into it . . . '

'Is that what all this is about?' said Kate, pressing her hands between her knees. 'A cry for attention?'

'You mean you jeopardised your freedom just because you didn't get your own way,' interjected Blake, incredulous.

Kate rested her hand on his forearm and tried to ease him back, but he pushed on regardless.

'If it really means that much to you then I'm sure we could work something out,' said Blake, feeling the soft touch of the hand on his arm fade. 'It's one thing being a tortured artist, but there's no need for you to go and get into trouble over it.'

'You've torn yourself away from those bad influences before,' said Kate. 'It'll be easier the second time around.'

'I'll think about it,' muttered Calum, and Kate knew then that that was as much as they were going to get from him for now.

Kate touched Blake on the arm again, and this time he knew that it meant something different.

'It'll be good to see you again,' he said, rising to leave.

*   *   *

Under normal circumstances, stubborn pride would have kept Calum from the mural for at least another afternoon, but knowing that it would take no more than three sessions to complete, he understood he had no choice but to swallow that pride and return to the site that afternoon if he wanted to be a real part of it.

And so four o'clock found him walking across the estate with the other kids, together but apart. Without having to ask, the other kids intuited what had happened. Most of them had been witness to his original strop, and also knew his street reputation, and so knew better than to irritate him further. When the group arrived in front of the mural, Blake also tuned into the common mood and just handed Calum a can of paint with a smile and motioned for him to do as he pleased.

For two hours Calum worked in silent concentration, the shadow of the other kids staining his back like perspiration. And the following night he was there again, Blake impressed with his dedication and the sense of Calumness that he brought to the character of the mural, little touches that added a much needed sense of humour – a man in an open window shaving the hair on the top of his ears, a woman in a tracksuit watching aerobics on TV with a cigarette in her mouth. At the completion, both Blake and the kids were pleased with how it had turned out. Not quite as it had been planned, but perhaps all the better for that.

As the kids were cleaning up, or rather sneaking off and leaving Blake to do the cleaning up, Johnson, a tall black man in a crumpled suit, approached the scene. He stood and stared at the mural, smiling, tilting his head from side to side, and then after a couple of minutes looked across at Blake.

'That's some piece of work,' he said.

'The kids did a great job,' agreed Blake.

'I like the little comic touches the best.'

'You mean the figures in the windows,' said Blake, pointing.

'Yeah, those,' said Johnson.

'Yeah, I like those too,' agreed Blake, stuffing tins of paint into a canvas holdall. 'A touch of original thinking.'

'It wasn't part of the plan, then,' said Johnson.

'That was one of the kids,' admitted Blake, not too proud to give credit where due. 'Nothing to do with me, I'm afraid.'

'I think it was the kid with the fat lip,' said Johnson, smiling and pointing at his own mouth.

'You mean Calum,' replied Blake, reflecting the smile.

'And he lives here on the estate,' said Johnson.

'In one of the blocks near Castle Street,' said Blake.

'You think he'd be interested in a solo project – that's if it's all right with you, I mean,' said Johnson.

'Depends what you have in mind, I suppose.'

'You know Carlo's, the café on Kentish Town Road?'

'I've been there a few times,' said Blake. 'Nice homemade fishcakes if I remember right.'

'The wife makes them,' said Johnson, and then fell silent, regarding the mural once more. 'It could be a nice place, a better place, but the trouble is I have a metal shutter that's forever covered in graffiti. If I clean it, then it's covered again the following night. I think the people who walk past at night and see the graffiti must think it's a bad place and decide never to go and eat there. You must understand what I mean. I've been thinking about what to do about it . . . You think . . . You think Calum would be interested in helping me out?'

Blake thought about Calum and what he had brought to the project. 'He's got some strong ideas of his own.'

'But that's what I'm looking for,' said Johnson. 'I wouldn't know where to start if we had to do it ourselves. As long as I have some idea of what he's going to do beforehand. Perhaps if he had one or two ideas I could choose from . . . '

'And he'd be paid for the work, of course,' said Blake.

'Whatever's the going rate,' replied Johnson.

'All right, I'll ask him,' said Blake.

*　　*　　*

For his shutter on Kentish Town Road, Johnson chose a cartoon version of his café with cartoon customers looking out at the real people passing on the street outside. At the rear of the cartoon café were caricatures of Posh and Becks tucking into large plates of pie and mash, fat bellies pushing at their cheap clothing and raw cigarettes burning in a saucer in the centre of the table. Most of the café's trade was during the week and so Johnson shut the café for the weekend to allow Calum to complete the mural in time for opening the following week.

Just like he had learned from Blake, Calum started with painting the shutter in a coat of white emulsion and then sketching the basic shapes of the characters and the furniture with a piece of charcoal. Working hard he had the outline of the design laid out in full ten minutes short of noon and so decided to have some lunch before starting with the paint. He walked to the newsagent's on the corner and bought a can of Coke and a cheese bagel in clingfilm, but the woman behind the counter rebuffed his offer of coins, telling him that she was pleased that Johnson was at last doing something to brighten up the area and that she was thinking of following his lead. She just wanted to see how it turned out first. Calum thanked her and told her to keep him in mind. Popping the top of the Coke he stepped out onto the street and bumped straight into Match and Tusk.

'We've been wondering where you'd got to,' said Match.

'Thought you might be avoiding us, like,' added Tusk.

Calum ignored them and strolled back to the café. He sat on the step and unwrapped his bagel, started to eat. The other two followed him and stood on the edge of the kerb facing him, holding onto a lamp post and swinging their feet in the gutter.

'You coming out with us tonight,' asked Tusk. 'Finish off what we started the other night.'

Calum presumed he was referring to the humiliating episode at the rear of the off-licence in Dartmouth Park, but he had no desire for a repeat performance and, besides, he had something else to keep him occupied now. He took another bite and continued to ignore them, looking off down the street towards Camden Town.

'What's the matter, can't you hear us or something,' asked Tusk.

'He must think he's too good for us now,' said Match, his head poking out of his dark hood like a poison tortoise.

Still Calum ignored them, drinking from the Coke.

'I reckon the police must've put the frighteners on him or something,' said Tusk.

'Turned him back into a child,' agreed Match.

'Won't be the first time. Still, it's like riding a bike. He wants to get back in the saddle it shouldn't be too hard . . . '

'If he leaves it much longer he's going to need those whatchama-callits, those little wheels on the back . . . '

'Stabilisers,' said Tusk. 'Kiddie wheels.'

'If he leaves it much longer he's going to need stabilisers . . . '

Calum listened to the barrage of jibes in silence. On the one hand it hurt him, his friends attacking him like that, but on the other he just wanted them to leave so that he could get on with the mural. He finished the bagel, drained the Coke, and then put the scrunched-up clingfilm into the open mouth of the can. He stood and walked across to the kerb, and stuffed the can into one of the bulging black bin liners piled there like boulders.

'You coming with us, then,' asked Match. 'Finish what we started the other night . . . You can hold the knife . . . '

'I have to finish the mural,' said Calum, uncomfortable.

'That's all right, we can wait,' said Tusk.

'It might be a while . . . '

'We have to wait until it gets dark, anyway,' said Tusk.

'I don't know . . . Perhaps some other time,' said Calum.

'Come on,' said Tusk, a note of pleading in his voice.

'Oh, forget him,' snapped Match, stamping his foot. 'He's not going to come with us, he's just pissing us about. He's gone over to the other side. Painting, for Christ's sake . . . I bet he's not even getting paid for it . . . '

'That's not the point . . . ' started Calum, frowning.

'Child,' Match shouted him down, rattling his fist at the shutter. 'Messing about with a big fat colouring book . . . '

A smirk creased Tusk's face.

'What do we care,' said Match. 'You know if we get caught we're going to say that you were with us anyway.'

* * *

This time DS Marnie Stone came to the flat herself. She said hello to Calum and his mother, accepted the offer of coffee, and then asked Calum where he had been the night before.

'I was here,' muttered Calum, looking at the floor.

'You were here all night?'

'I finished working on the mural when it started to get dark and then I came straight back here.'

'And what time would that have been?'

'I don't know,' replied Calum, shrugging. 'I suppose it must've been about nine or so. Quarter past . . . I don't know.'

'You're sure about that?'

'Half past, then,' said Calum. 'I don't have a watch but I'm sure it was no later than about half past nine . . . '

'You stop and talk to anyone on the way home . . . '

Calum shook his head.

' . . . or call in at any of the shops?'

Calum shook his head again.

'All right, let's come at it from another direction,' said Marnie, looking out across the estate for a moment. 'You know the old ironmonger's on Kentish Town Road? It's about two or three doors down from the café you've been working on . . . '

'Yeah, I know it,' said Calum.

'You ever been in there?'

'I suppose I must've been at some point. Getting new locks and stuff after we've been broken into . . . '

'So you'll be familiar with the layout of the place?'

'I suppose so,' shrugged Calum.

'Does that include the office in the back?'

'I don't know what you mean.'

'The place was broken into last night, Calum,' said Marnie, leaning forward in her chair. 'A large amount of cash was stolen from the office. Cash and a lot of other stuff.'

Calum kept quiet, averted his eyes.

'You know anything about that?'

Calum shook his head. 'No.'

'You're positive about that?'

'Sure I'm positive,' muttered Calum.

'All right, then, what about Match and Tusk?'

'What about them?'

'They're your friends, Calum, your comrades in arms. You must know if they had anything to do with it . . . '

'I haven't seen them in a couple of days,' said Calum.

'You didn't talk to them last night?'

Calum shook his head again, glanced hard at Marnie in confirmation.

'All right,' said Marnie, sighing. 'Let's look at what we've got, shall we? A known thief starts working on a mural in a café down on Kentish Town Road and just a few hours later an ironmonger's shop a couple of doors down from there gets broken into – so that's just a coincidence, is it, Calum?'

'Suppose it must be,' said Calum, shrugging.

'We like Match and Tusk for this one,' said Marnie. 'You case the place for them, Calum? You tell them how to get in?'

Calum kept silent, his attention focused on the floor.

Marnie shook her head and looked out of the window across the estate. 'All right, I'll leave it there for now,' she said after a short time, getting up to leave. 'But just so you know . . . I don't think you were there last night, Calum, but I do think that your two friends were, and it's just a matter of time before I find the proof. If you don't want to help me then that's your decision. But when we do nail them, don't kid yourself that they'll think we figured it all out by ourselves . . .'

*   *   *

Although he was at first pleased with himself for not telling the police that Match and Tusk had been around earlier the afternoon before, the following morning Calum awoke to find it troubling him like a burgeoning toothache. On the one hand he still felt a little proud that he had not offered up Match and Tusk to DS Stone, a solid feature of his culture, he knew, but on the other he knew that it was just a matter of time before she arrested them and that when she did so it was almost inevitable that he would be lumped into the gang as the third man. And although he did not like to think about what that might mean, at best he knew that he would not be allowed to continue with the murals.

The dilemma continued to trouble him long after he returned to school, but a couple of weeks later he saw his chance to get out of the situation on what he saw as his own terms.

On the strength of his work at the café, word spread and he was soon offered another commission, this time to paint a large mural on the side of a car wash at the foot of Camden Road. The wall faced the traffic coming down the hill, a huge area, and after agreeing the design he set to work on it one weekend.

But just as Calum might have predicted, Match and Tusk turned up late on the third night that he was there. He had just completed the background and was about to start on the figures in the cars he had painted – the mural was on a side wall of the car wash and Calum had created a full-scale cartoon version of it as if the wall were made of glass: in the centre of the wall he had drawn a giant foam and rain machine with a grime-streaked car going in one end and a bright clean car coming out of the other – and the sight of his friends made his heart sink in his chest. But Match and Tusk seemed to have lost some of their fire, poking Calum with sullen and blunt jibes as if taunting him had become a bore, and it did not take him long to get rid of them. Watching them walk across Camden Road, Calum felt a smile touch his face.

But it was a brief success: the following morning Detective Sergeant Stone was on his doorstep once more, the electrical store two doors down from the car wash having been burgled the night before. She went at him harder this time, refusing to believe that he had had nothing to do with it. And the harder she went at him, the more Calum dug in his heels. But even as he did so he felt something stirring deep inside, something far deeper than a cultural mistrust of the police and a refusal to grass. This time he knew that it was nothing less than fight or flight.

Ten minutes after Stone left the flat, Calum returned to the car wash to complete the details in the mural.

*   *   *

A little before two o'clock the following morning, chasing up on a call that had come into the station, DS Marnie Stone pulled up in front of the mural with anger and sadness in her heart. Someone had made a good attempt at defacing it, scratching and rubbing different colours of paint across the artwork, but from what she could still make out, the mural looked to be of a police car chasing another car through the car wash. And after taking in some of the finer details the message was made clear to her: Calum was giving her the people she was looking for. In the front car were two clear characters, their features a little smudged but still recognisable: a match with human features and another face with one huge tusk curling out of its mouth. But Calum had not been clever enough, and after his old friends had seen his latest artistic efforts had meted out their own retribution. Calum had been nailed to the wall where he had painted the chasing police car. His feet were hanging in the air about three feet from the ground and his head rested on his chest in a thick splash of blood. For a moment Marnie had the horrific thought that perhaps his tongue had been cut out, but when she climbed out of the car for a closer look she was relieved to see that he was still breathing and that he had in fact been silenced with a cork rammed in between his bloodied and swollen lips.

A dead language

GILLIAN LINSCOTT

It was a morning in early July, the end of the Trinity term of 1869, when they found Linhope dead among the cows and trampled buttercups in Port Meadow. So it must have been two weeks before that, an afternoon in mid-June, when I noticed the girl in University Parks. She came swinging along the path between beds of flowers, straw hat pushed back to show the dark hair curling over her forehead, blue cotton skirt flapping from the speed of her walking to give glimpses of white-stockinged ankle over dusty black boots. She passed the bench where I was sitting with my book, gave me a glance, went skimming on. Then, amazingly, she stopped and came back towards me, walking slowly this time. A few steps away from me she hesitated, close enough for me to hear her quick breathing, then sat down on the end of my bench. I kept my eyes on the book, puzzled. I was in my mid-twenties then, and though no worse looking than the average of men, didn't flatter myself that my face or figure would make young women spin in their tracks. I might have taken her for one of the ladies of the town, except that they did not, in my limited experience, patrol the decorous pathways of Parks in the early hours of the afternoon. Besides, though there was a boldness about the way she walked and dressed, there wasn't an abandoned air about her. She struck me as poised half-way between respectability and the other thing. And yet she wanted something from me, that was clear from her sidelong looks and the sliding of her narrow boot toe on the grass so that I could just see it from the corner of my eye. I shut my book and prepared to move. A little gasp from her.

'Sir, do you speak Latin?'

Whatever I'd been expecting, it wasn't that. Her voice had the accent of the Oxfordshire countryside, not the city. She was looking at me, lips apart, breath coming quickly as if my answer was important to her, yet in Oxford a man who knew Latin was hardly an uncommon commodity.

'Yes. We can't be quite sure, of course, how Cicero . . . '

She waved centuries of debate aside like so many mosquitoes.

'Things like yes and no and pleased or not pleased?'

'You want to learn Latin?'

'Not all of Latin, just some words.'

I didn't know what to say. Ambitions to better themselves among the working classes were to be encouraged, but the idea of setting up a kind of park-bench poor school in the classics was enough to get me laughed out of my college fellowship. Already I was glancing round to make sure nobody I knew had spotted us. She made a little gesture appealing to me not to go, her hand almost touching my lapel. A small hand, white and gloveless.

'What words?'

'Yes and no.'

'For yes, you'd say "certe". There's no word for no. You have to negate a particular action or condition, like "I am not willing. Nolo." '

I knew, while I was saying it, that the whole thing was ridiculous, but she was staring at me out of big dark eyes in a way that made me feel I was giving food to the famishing. She echoed "certe" and "nolo" carefully, like somebody putting straw around ripe apples, storing them away.

'What does "bus" mean?'

It took me a while to work out, from her accent, what she was saying, then I laughed.

'It's not a word in itself, it's a dative or ablative plural noun ending, like "omnibus". You see, any noun . . . '

I could see from her eyes that I'd lost her and the absurdity of sitting there teaching Latin to a young woman who didn't even know what an ablative was made me feel prickly with embarrassment. Besides, I thought I'd seen through this little mystery. The girl must have come into the company of some young devil of an undergraduate who'd been imposing on her simplicity with his rags of learning. Heaven knows what he'd been saying to her. I stood up.

'If you'd allow me to give you some advice, my dear, remember that a man might utter in a foreign language sentiments which he'd blush to acknowledge in his own.'

Then I raised my hat to her, picked up my book and walked away.

I told nobody about it because there was nobody at college I could tell. Especially not – in what turned out to be the last two weeks of his life – my old tutor and now senior colleague, Linhope. In his day, college fellows didn't marry. Linhope, in his late fifties, was one of the old heroic breed of scholars who devoted themselves almost monkishly to their work. The field of his labours had been, for as long as anybody could remember, an obscure Latin poem in four books dating from the first century AD about the history and care of oxen. If questioned, he'd admit that the work wasn't in the first rank, or even the second, of classical poetry. But he'd add, blinking through his glasses, that it was not without interest, not at all. The anonymous poet had used the humble ox as his starting-point for a journey through history, mythology, philosophy – for an investigation into the place of man in relation to the gods above and the earth below. And Linhope would take a sip of port and repeat, 'Certainly not without interest to the general reader.' He must have known, as everybody else knew, that when the great work was finally published, it would be read by a dozen of his fellow scholars at the outside, most of those in Germany. But it had come to Linhope as his allotted task in life, and to neglect anything he could do to make it perfect would have been a kind of blasphemy against his religion of scholarship. His heart and sight were weakening, we all knew. Still, we hoped they'd hold out long enough for him to drive his slow oxen to the press at last.

'He so nearly managed it too', the Master said. 'Another few weeks is all it needs.'

We were at the burial, standing by the graveside as the bearers carried Linhope's coffin with its single wreath of laurel leaves and flowers in the college colours slowly up the path. I knew it was no accident that the Master had come to stand beside me.

He added: 'Of course, he'd have got there terms ago if it hadn't been for The Fragment.'

A few years before, Linhope had come across ten and a half anonymous lines in a previously overlooked manuscript that might, or might not, have been part of the fourth book of the oxen poem. Coming so near the end of his great work, it obsessed him. Should he include it or shouldn't he? The style, metre, subject-matter all fitted very well. The provenance was by no means out of the question. For a few months, he settled on putting it in as an appendix. But then, might not even an appendix confer on it a too-hasty legitimacy and entrap other scholars? He corresponded with colleagues in Europe, America, even Cambridge, wore out his already feeble eyesight comparing manuscripts. Towards the end, men began to avoid him because however the conversation started it would turn to his latest position on The Fragment.

'A few more weeks' work is really all it needs,' the Master said. 'He left his papers in very good order.'

I could see what was coming towards me, as inexorably as Linhope's coffin to its resting place. I tried to stave it off by changing the subject.

'In spite of dying so unexpectedly.'

A drawing-in of the Master's shoulders under his black coat showed I was touching on something that the college preferred not to raise.

'His heart was weak, after all.'

'But among a herd of cows in Port Meadow, with that great bruise on his forehead?'

'Caused when he fell. Or perhaps one of the animals happened to . . . tread on him.'

In summer the grass in Port Meadow is as soft as the breasts of swans. And cows, gentle beasts, are careful where they put their tentative split hooves. I didn't say that to the Master, but couldn't resist some more trespassing.

'Still, nobody's explained what he was doing in Port Meadow early in the morning. It's a good mile and a half from the college, and he never went further afield than the Bodleian Library.'

It had come up at the inquest, which was no more than a formality, and been brushed aside by the coroner as an eccentricity of an elderly don.

The Master admitted reluctantly, 'It's true that Linhope was never an amateur of aimless perambulation.' Then, more urgently, as the bearers reached the edge of the grave and the clergyman took up position, 'I'm quite sure that Linhope would have wished you to see his work to the press. It's mainly a matter of tidying up, no more.'

Through the rest of July, with the undergraduates down for the long vacation and the quadrangle under Linhope's windows so quiet that you could hear the creeper growing up the walls, I toiled at his orderly ramparts of manuscript. His meticulous handwriting hardly varied from the first footnote on page one – where he'd started his labours some twenty years before – to the last where he'd laid down his pen without a smudge or blot. The decades of relentless neatness made me shudder. That summer I was already coming to understand that I'd taken a wrong turn and a scholar's life wasn't for me, and this business of poor Linhope confirmed it. Still, I owed him and the college this last service and I worked away in his rooms rather than move all the papers to mine. By the last day of the month I turned to the very last pile of paper – the business of The Fragment. Even there in his indecision Linhope had been orderly, with all the correspondence and notes in chronological order, all the evidence for and against. With one exception. That was the last page of all. It was an extra copy, in his own handwriting, of those vexatious ten and a half lines. Right across it, still in his own handwriting, but much bigger than I'd seen it anywhere in the past, ran one flaring, triumphant word – 'Certe'. And across the top of the page, another quite different fragment of poetry, also in his hand, '*horrendaeque procul secreta Sibyllae*'.

'Well, what in the world's that doing there?'

Translated, 'the distant refuge of the terrifying Sibyl'. Nothing whatsoever to do with Linhope's oxen or The Fragment. As any schoolboy would know, it was simply a quotation from the sixth book of Virgil's Aeneid, in which the hero Aeneas goes to consult the prophetess of Apollo, the Sibyl.

'What's that, sir?'

The question came from the college servant, old Danby, quietly going about his business on the other side of the room. He and I had become quite companionable over the past few weeks, with Danby packing up Linhope's personal effects as I sorted out his scholarly affairs.

'Danby, did you think Mr Linhope was behaving at all oddly towards the end?'

I shouldn't have put that sort of question to a servant. It just showed how unsuited I was to college life. He might have snubbed me, but he paused, duster in hand and answered.

'Well, sir, he had taken to going out more in the last week or two.'

'Where?'

'One of the boys thought he'd seen him at the top end of Walton Street, near the canal.'

The top of Walton Street was an area of raw new terraces of houses beside the railway line and canal, inhabited by college servants and the smaller sort of tradesmen. No colleges, no libraries, no antiquities. No reason whatsoever for Linhope to be there. But not far away, between the west bank of the canal and the river, lay the broad and pleasant pastures of Port Meadow where, equally inexplicably, he'd been found among the cattle.

That evening after dinner I walked up Walton Street and strolled at random in the network of little roads around Walton Well. Children playing hopscotch on the hard earth outside the houses looked at me curiously for a while, then went on with their games. There was a smell of smoke and warm metal in the air from the railway, but if you stood on the canal bridge you could catch a whiff of meadow-sweet. I went on across the bridge to Port Meadow and watched the sun setting on the far side of the river and the cows moving slowly in the dusk. The next evening I did it again, and the evening after that. I'd no clear idea what I was looking for, any more than I knew what Linhope had been looking for, and yet somehow an uncertainty about my own life had tied itself up with his. My uneasiness hadn't started with the dark-eyed girl on the bench. It had been there before that, but she was part of it.

So, on that fourth evening when I saw her, it hardly came as a surprise. I turned a corner into a street of narrow houses, and there she was in front of me. Even from the back, I recognised her from the blue skirt, the straw hat, and a kind of swinging way of walking. I found myself walking faster. If I'd caught up with her, goodness knows what I'd have said, but I didn't get the chance. At the far end of the street she turned into a low gateway in a fence of green palings. There was an unkempt rose bush bulging over the fence beside the gate and her shoulder brushed it as she went in, whirling white petals over the path. Some were still falling as I went past, but the black painted door of the house was firmly shut and curtains drawn over the windows. I walked back to college with my mind whirling like the rose petals, not knowing whether to be glad or appalled. I'd guessed at an undergraduate, but could it have been my old tutor, wooing a girl in a dead language? Had there been, over the decades, a succession of young women from the lower classes with whom he'd wandered secretly on summer evenings, murmuring Horace or even Catullus to pink, uncomprehending ears? But if Danby was right, it was only in the last few weeks of his life that Linhope had taken to wandering. When I thought of that and those ramparts of manuscript, such a wave of anger and sadness for Linhope, and for myself in thirty years' time, came over me that I thought I must put the whole business out of my mind for good. As a distraction, the following evening I accepted a colleague's invitation to a musical soirée in a new house on the Banbury Road, safely on the university side of Walton Street.

'An Egyptian priestess, from the Pyramids.'

I was doing my duty as an unattached male, passing round cups of tea after the music. My hostess and her friends were talking to each other in the low tones kept for female affairs, but I caught the Egyptian priestess. I suppose I must have looked questioning, because she included me in the conversation.

'Are you a sceptic? You look like one. I was entirely sceptical when I first went there, but she told me things she couldn't possibly have known any other way.'

I realised, with a sinking heart, that I was in for spiritualism. There was something of an epidemic of it at the time, even among people who should have known better. Obediently, I pulled up a chair beside them and settled to my ordained role as sacrificial sceptic. For a while I let it wash over me: spirit guides, automatic writing, a message from a departed cousin about being sorry for what had happened at Ramsgate. Then some phrases hit me like pebbles.

' . . . an uneducated woman in herself . . . touch of a Gypsy to look at her. When the spirits speak in foreign languages she has no idea what . . . '

'Latin?'

The women stared at me.

'Not when I was there. French. Only a few words and not very accurate, but then if the poor child was burned as a witch when she was only twelve . . . '

'This medium, where does she live?'

They thought, I'm sure, that they'd gained a convert and were almost shocked by my surrender. One of them mentioned a name and a street number that meant nothing to me, until she added, 'Off the top of Walton Street, near the canal.'

I waited until early the following evening. The rosebush had shed some more petals. The curtains were still drawn, the front door shut. It sounded hollow when I knocked on it, like an empty house. I waited, heart thumping, more than half hoping that nobody would answer. After a long time there were footsteps inside, light but slow, then she was standing there in the half-open doorway, hair down and feet bare under her skirt, a paisley shawl round her upper body. Where the shawl crossed in front, a rim of pink chemise showed, none too clean. Her dark eyes were sleepy and she gave no sign of recognising me from the park bench.

'I'm a friend of Mr Linhope,' I said.

Still no recognition, of me or the name.

'Is he coming with you?'

Her voice was as sleepy as her eyes and I guessed she was just out of bed.

'He can't. He's dead.'

She hitched the shawl up wearily, like a navvy settling his belt before work.

'So I suppose you want him to talk to you. You'd better come in.'

I followed her into a room behind the drawn curtains. In the shadows I could make out a round table with chairs round it. There was a sideboard against the wall with a trumpet and some other oddments and, in a corner, a cabinet like a booth for a Punch and Judy show, only not so colourful. She sat down at the table.

'Do you want me to look into my crystal ball for your friend? If you want the cabinet or the glass, you'll have to come back later.'

The room seemed airless. There was a smell of cabbage. All her freshness that I remembered from our meeting in Parks was gone. I sat down, two chairs away from her.

'I want to know about what he wanted to know about.'

'I can't remember who you mean.'

'Bos.'

A little intake of breath. The sleep had gone from her eyes. In the shadowy room I could see the whites of them.

'That day in Parks, I thought you were asking about 'bus'. It was 'bos' he said to you, the word for ox. He came here to ask about a poem.'

Came, like Aeneas, to the distant refuge of the terrifying Sibyl. It must have seemed like that to Linhope, so far from his usual haunts and his fastidious habit of mind. And yet, with his time running out, he'd dare even that if there were the remotest chance that his last question might find an answer. The more I thought of it, the more angry I was with the woman sitting there and sweating. I could smell her sweat, sharp and troubling.

'He was trying to ask in Latin,' I said. What else, after all, would the spirit of his dead poet speak? 'So you had to go out and scavenge enough Latin to con him out of his money. And, of course, it turned out to be easier to give him a yes than a no.'

He'd paid dearly, in several ways, for that 'Certe' blazoned across the page.

'We didn't con the old man. We don't con anybody. We just give them what they want.' She was still scared, but angry too. 'That word "bos", the glass spelled out for him the first time he came here. It didn't mean anything to us, but you could see it did to him. He kept trying to ask things in a foreign language. Jed guessed it was Latin and said he'd better come back and have a private session with the cabinet.'

'At which he put a question to your so-called spirits in Latin, and the spirits answered yes?'

'He wanted a yes. In all the time we've been doing it, I've never known anybody want a yes like he did. It was burning off him. He wanted it.'

She was almost shouting. One of her white hands was up on the table, moving towards mine as if it wanted to close round my wrist. One of my hands had got itself on the table too and was moving towards hers. I dragged it away and held it fast between my knees.

'But he wasn't content with a yes, was he? He came back with more questions. Questions you couldn't answer. That's when you killed him, you and your accomplice.'

'No, we didn't mean to kill him. He wanted to kill us. Raving. Talking about going to the police, wanting to throttle Jed. I wouldn't have thought an old man would be like that.'

Not an old man, I thought. A Roman hero who'd gone all the way to Apollo's priestess and found her a fraud in a sweat-stained chemise.

'So he was angry and you killed him.'

'He had his hands round Jed's throat. He was choking him. So I hit him with the crystal ball to make him let go. Any jury would say it was self-defence.'

'But you weren't going to risk a jury, were you? Wait until dark and bundle him out to the meadow like a sack of rubbish. Was it your idea of a joke, putting him among the cows?'

'Cows? What about cows?'

I stood up.

'What are you going to do?'

'Find a magistrate. Do you think you can defraud and murder with impunity?'

I have a dim memory that as I opened the door into the passage-way, she was asking who impunity was. It is only a dim memory, because at that point the entire universe collided with the back of my skull and threw me into a darkness so total that I was not aware even of falling.

'By the canal,' the Master said, twitching his nose against the sick-room scent of beef-tea and freesias. 'If the children hadn't fallen over you, you'd have been dead of cold by morning.'

'Not in summer.'

If his cold disapproval could kill, I shouldn't last the afternoon.

'Is your memory returning? Have you the slightest idea of how you came to be there?'

'Not the slightest memory.'

Which, literally speaking, was true. I supposed that the girl and her accomplice had carried me there in the dark, much as they'd carried Linhope. Perhaps they'd planned to heave me in the canal and been disturbed by some passer-by. Consciousness had returned painfully as I was being jolted back down St Giles late at night, spread along the seat of a cab. The constable who'd been called by the children had taken it for granted that I'd been felled by some pickpocket, and I was too ill to argue. But weakness had given me back the clarity of mind that anger had taken away. I knew now that there was a choice to make. If I told my story, the girl and her Jed might or might not hang. But my old tutor would hang higher, an object of derision for generations to come, the fine scholar who at the very end had blemished a lifetime of work by his dealings with a shop-soiled Sibyl. In any case, was it likely that the two of them would wait to be arrested? By the time I was conscious, they'd have been far away. The two of them would come, as the poet said, to little good, but to Oxford and their friends no more.

'I wonder what you were doing in that part of town in the first place.'

The Master thought it reflected badly on the college. In the next few days, I'd tell him that I'd decided to give up my fellowship. A scholar's life was not for me. Linhope, at the end of his life, had taught me that last valuable lesson. The Master lingered, waiting for an explanation that wouldn't come.

'Linhope's manuscript – we've packed it up for the printer, all except The Fragment. Tell me, have you been able to come to a conclusion. Do we include it, yes or no?'

I thought of the girl's face in the shadowy room, her voice: 'I've never known anybody want a yes like he did.'

'Yes,' I said.

Unacademic. Unprincipled. Unjustifiable. And yet the fact remains that a year later, when Linhope's work was published and my decision past recalling, a professor at a German university found another manuscript that proved beyond doubt that The Fragment really did belong with the oxen poem. And if that was a gift from Apollo that I didn't deserve, Linhope certainly did.

The postman only rings if he can be bothered

PETER GUTTRIDGE

Mrs Spring was floating face down in the pool when her gardener found her. She hung there, half submerged, tangled in a length of filtration pipe. It was Tuesday, ten thirty am. Each morning in the warm months Mrs Spring came into the garden at seven, disrobed and gingerly lowered herself into the chilly waters. The pool, installed for status not swimming, was circular. For fifteen minutes Mrs Spring laboriously circumnavigated it.

From my study on the first floor of our cottage I occasionally had the misfortune to see this ritual. It was a terrible spectacle. Her body had known better days. At least for her sake I hope it had. If my window was open, I would hear her gargled gasps as she breathed with her head sometimes above, sometimes below the water.

On that Tuesday morning, I didn't know anything was wrong until I heard a commotion around eleven. I was having my ear bent, as usual, by my cleaner Donald about Roger Moore (as usual).

Rural unemployment being what it is round here, you can virtually enslave the yokels and they're poor enough to be grateful. Donald does us twice a week for less than the cost of my daily Scotch bill. And I certainly don't intend to do my own cleaning – I'd given up my job to write, not to take on domestic duties, despite what my lovely wife Ruth might sometimes hope.

'See, Mr Stewart, people don't realise what a range he has,' Donald was saying as he pushed a duster in a desultory way along my book-shelves. 'They think he's just a pair of raised eyebrows. But he's played in a lot of different movies, more than you'd think. He was a German officer in one.'

'Did he do the accent?' I said wearily, scrolling through the text on my computer screen.

'Well, no, but that's not my point. My point is – '

'Leave the desk please, Donald.'

'Sorry, Mr Stewart,' he said, riffling quickly through the papers he'd picked up before putting them back on my desk. 'See you got another letter for the Forge.'

We lived in The Old Forge whilst just down the road the Parkers lived in the Forge. The postman regularly mixed up our mail.

Aside from being an anorak about Roger Moore – a little perverse in the late nineties, wouldn't you say? – Donald was incurably nosy. The drawback to employing him was his habit of rooting through the things on my desk if I wasn't around to stop him.

Donald droned on about how his mate had nearly come a cropper the previous night on Century Lane two or three miles away – notorious as the worst accident black spot in the county. Then he interrupted himself.

'Lummy.' (He has a fondness for fifties Ealing films, too.) 'Come and look at this, Mr Stewart.'

I joined him at the window and looked down at two stocky men standing in Mrs Spring's pool. Stripped to their underwear, they were manhandling her body towards a stretcher at the side of the pool.

Beside the stretcher were two neat piles of clothes, topped by police helmets, truncheons and other crime-busting paraphernalia. There was also a set of false teeth. Mrs Spring wore ill-fitting dentures that whistled when she was agitated. She took them out before swimming since underwater they produced a kind of death rattle. Aptly enough, it now seemed.

I sent Donald away, telling him to finish off the next day, then phoned Ruth with the news. It took five minutes to tell her, given that she put me on hold every couple of syllables.

A heart attack, we supposed, the Westwoods and I, an hour or so later. We had congregated with virtually all the rest of the hamlet on the grassy track that runs from the church between our adjacent gardens and Mrs Spring's. Word spreads quickly in a place like ours, cut off as it is from neighbouring villages.

Murder, Mr Deacon the newspaper man announced the next morning. I met him at the post box just after seven. He saw me crossing the lane from the track and clanked to a halt on his decrepit three-gear bike, the basket of newspapers swaying drunkenly before his handlebars.

A bike with three gears is all you need, Mr Deacon insisted, even though everyone else in the western hemisphere was whizzing past him on multi-gear mountain bikes. Only after many years of nagging had his wife persuaded him some months before to invest in a car, a second-hand Fiat Panda. He bought it, reluctantly, but refused ever to drive it.

The road into Novington from his shop at the base of the Downs was steep; he was as usual red-faced and panting.

'The police phoned last night,' he gasped, 'Whilst I was out at darts. Mrs Deacon took the message. They want a statement from me this morning. Tell them if I saw anything.'

'And did you?'

'Well, I saw you Mr Stewart, with that parcel in your hand. I thought to myself, he'll never get that in the post box.' He looked at me as if I must be mad even to try. 'You didn't, did you?'

I shook my head, hiding my surprise behind a smile. Although Ruth and I had moved down here two years before, I was still unused to the fact that in such a small community it was impossible to do anything unobserved, even at seven in the morning. I had seen Mr Deacon from a distance when I took the parcel to the post but he had given no indication that he had seen me.

I wasn't mad, however. I had discovered by chance that the door to our local post box had a faulty catch. It didn't always lock when the postman closed it after emptying the box. Parcels that wouldn't fit in the narrow slit at the top would easily fit through the door. Inconveniently for me the box had been shut tight the previous day.

Mr Deacon, inhibited by his crossbar, made a token effort to lean conspiratorially towards me. 'And I saw that Edith Macrell loitering by the church. She'll be the *prime suspect*.'

With that Mr Deacon straightened his basket of newspapers and set off down the lane to the houses on the far side of Novington Place. I watched him go. Mrs Spring murdered and I had heard nothing. Nor had I seen Mrs Macrell. I wondered if she'd seen me.

A policeman in a smart suit came to see me on the Thursday. He introduced himself as Sergeant Pratt and watched closely to see my reaction.

'Would you like a glass of champagne?' I said, successfully controlling my smirk and waving the bottle vaguely in his direction.

'Celebrating are we, sir?' he said, frowning.

'Something like that,' I said, sneaking a guilty glance at the huge pile of branches the tree surgeon had left by my garden shed about ten minutes before.

The timing of Pratt's visit was a bit of an embarrassment to me. As we stood on the terrace looking across Mrs Spring's vast, well-tended gardens to the sparkling waters of the English Channel I was uncomfortably aware that until this morning I had not had this view.

I should really capitalise the word 'view'. Novington is famous locally for its unparalleled vistas. The View of the dramatic chalk cliffs and the vast expanse of the foam-flecked sea beyond is a constant subject of conversation with those who have the misfortune not to live here but who come humbly and enviously at weekends to see it.

Novington itself is pretty enough, with its jumble of Tudor cottages and grander Georgian villas, but it is the view that both nourishes the spirit and enhances the house prices.

Mrs Spring had access to The View from every part of her exceedingly large garden. We houseowners in the four cottages on the ridge behind her garden were less fortunate. Mrs Spring, a staunch Christian, passed over the Love Thy Neighbour bit of her religion. She did not wish to be overlooked anywhere in her acreage, even in areas where she never ventured. Some years before, therefore, she had planted fast-growing firs to screen us from her sight. In consequence we lost The View.

The Westwoods and Mrs Macrell had been the most affected. Two years before the Westwoods had resorted to copper nails in the bases of the trees but the killing process was a slow one and the Westwoods were not in the first flush of youth. The day after Mrs Spring's death they sneaked into her garden to lop three feet off the forsythia and rhododendrons that had grown wild and high, then celebrated this partial reappearance of their view with dry martinis on the terrace.

The tree surgeon the Westwoods had ordered came on Thursday morning to lop down the fir trees. I thought he might as well raise the skirts of the huge chestnut tree whose lower branches obliterated the view from our garden as convincingly as its upper obscured the sun.

Cynical? Frankly, nobody cared for Mrs Spring. (It was only in the newspaper report I learned that she had a first name – Dorothy. I'd never met anyone who had the temerity to call her anything other than Mrs Spring). She was cantankerous, vindictive, spiteful, malicious, snobbish and bullying. On a good day.

Sergeant Pratt accepted my offer of champagne, then walked slowly from one end of the terrace to the other. He sniffed the champagne, more suspiciously than appreciatively, as he looked at The View.

'Lovely view of the sea,' he observed, narrowing his eyes and finally taking a drink.

'We like it,' I said nonchalantly. 'Can you tell me how Mrs Spring died?'

'A suspicious pathologist, noticing slight bruising on her neck, found evidence that she had been strangled. We estimate the time of death at between seven and seven thirty on Tuesday morning. Can you tell me anything of interest about that period of time?'

I told him what I knew, which was, in essence, nothing.

'I'm sure Mr Deacon is a better bet,' I said. 'When I spoke to him yesterday he said he was going to make a statement. What has he got to say?'

Sergeant Pratt tilted his wine glass thoughtfully. 'He hasn't got very much to say at all, sir. Unfortunately, Mr Deacon was knocked off his bicycle by a hit and run driver early yesterday morning at the bottom of Novington Lane. Mr Deacon is dead.'

'What time?' I asked weakly.

'Between seven fifteen and seven forty five. Do I understand that you saw him yesterday morning?'

'I spoke to Mr Deacon at the post-box around seven. A hit and run driver? But the road to Novington doesn't go anywhere – we never have any traffic.'

'Precisely, sir,' Pratt gave me another searching look. 'Did you see or hear the noise of any kind of motor vehicle around the time you were talking to Mr Deacon?'

'I think I may have heard something afterwards, when I was having my breakfast in our garden. You know, Mr Deacon told me he had seen Mrs Macrell out and about on the morning of Mrs Spring's death.'

Pratt's eyes widened.

'Did he indeed? Thank you Mr Stewart. Tell me now, do you happen to own a red car?'

I shook my head.

'Not any more. I sold Edith Macrell my Golf last year. That's red. Lots of other red cars in the village. Wing Commander Westwood, Patrick Ferguson at Novington Place. My wife's car is red, too.'

When he had gone I phoned Mrs Deacon to offer my condolences. She was tearful but hard at work. 'Nobody else will do it if I don't. As Wing Commander Westwood made clear. He's the limit he is. He phones me up yesterday to say he hasn't got his newspapers. I say 'I'm ever so sorry Wing Commander but I've just heard that Eric –

Mr Deacon – has been run over. The Wing Commander doesn't speak for a minute then he says: "So who's going to deliver my paper today?" '

Sitting on the terrace I pondered the thought that somebody in the village might be a murderer. Possibly a double murderer. Was Mrs Macrell our killer? Everyone knew she was wacko, but could she be a murderess?

Certainly she had fallen out with Mrs Spring over the fast-growing firs. Four years before she had taken rather more drastic action than the Westwoods, setting about the trees with a chainsaw. The subsequent court action cost her dear and she had vowed to get even one day.

I finished the champagne thinking about the police setting a Pratt to catch a Macrell. I can't help thinking in newspaper headlines. After twenty-five years as a sub-editor, during which time my main functions were making the illiterate scrawlings of our celebrity columnists readable and finding puns for headlines, it's in my blood.

I enjoyed subbing – I've always liked to be thorough about details – but I was happy to throw it in when we came down here in favour of the writing I had always intended to do. I had a commission to write what I assured my publishers would be the late nineties domestic version of *A Year In Provence*.

The parish of Novington, some three miles long and half a mile wide, contains retired racing drivers and jockeys, celebrated chefs, former actresses and a world famous artist. There are also a great many weirdos.

I'd outlined the idea of writing about this peculiar congeries over a boozy Soho lunch to a friend who had recently started an editing job at one of the publishing conglomerates. My pitch was that I, Metropolitan Man *par excellence*, would live among country folk who would be as alien to me as Parisians were to Amazonian Indians. Of course, that was before I discovered just how alien they really were.

I was reminded at Mrs Spring's funeral. For someone who was so unpopular she got a very good turnout. Ruth and I could scarcely find a seat. 'They've all come to make sure she's really dead,' I whispered to Ruth. She looked very fetching in black seamed stockings and a short black linen dress – the only black dress she had. She shushed me, then tugged ineffectually at the skirt when she saw me leering at her thighs.

During the service I looked from one to the other of my neighbours wondering which of them was more likely than Mrs Macrell to have killed Mrs Spring. Not that I could really believe Mrs Macrell had killed her – or killed Mr Deacon for that matter. Not deliberately anyway – she *was* a terrible driver.

The pall-bearers, buckling under the weight of Mrs Spring's coffin, led the way out of the church. Two chubby men I assumed were Mrs Spring's sons comforted a bowed old lady. She shuffled on spindly legs, clutching her handbag. If Mrs Spring had lived to be a shadow of her former self, this is who she would have been. It was Winifred, her sister. I met her at the house later.

'She made herself very unpopular I know,' she confided in me. 'But that was because she was so unhappy herself. Dorothy was never the same after her husband died. She loved Frederick so. They'd been married thirty-five years when she was told he had cancer. He was dead a week later.' She looked me straight in the eye. 'Do you know who killed her?' I shook my head slowly, looking beyond her to Mrs Macrell, flushed with sherry, over by the mantelpiece.

Although she lived just three houses away along the track, I'd only met Mrs Macrell some six months after we moved in. I'd put an ad in my local paper to sell my car and she had phoned me to buy it for her son, Jonathan.

I'd gone round to her house to deliver the car at nine in the morning. Mrs Macrell came to the door in a rumpled night-dress. A thin stick of a woman in her early sixties, she had in one hand a small cigar, in the other a glass of red wine.

'Is this a bad time?' I said.

'Any time's a bad time,' she said, taking a swig of her wine. 'I'm a manic depressive.'

'That's nice,' I said, momentarily nonplussed. She looked at me. I stumbled on: 'Are you having a bad week?'

She sniffed.

'Bad year.'

We stood in her doorway as she haggled about the price because I could only find one set of car keys. I promised I'd bring her the other set when I found it – I'm hopelessly untidy – and made good my escape.

'Would you like a glass of wine?' she called after me. I shouted back my thanks but declined the invitation. It was a bit early in the day, even for me.

Janet, my first wife, always used to say drink would be the death of me. If your cooking doesn't get me first, I used to snarl back. She was a vegetarian, so every meal was pulses or beans, pulses or beans. A dinner party at our house could be a hazardous affair. Our guests were discouraged from going anywhere near a naked flame for at least an hour after the main course.

Our attitude to drink – I drank, she didn't – was one of many areas of disagreement between us. But her death affected me more than I thought it would – I suppose because we had been together fifteen years. The Years of Struggle we used to call them. I used to call them. I was in genuine mourning when I met Ruth. I was fifty and here this beautiful brunette, eighteen years my junior, came into my life.

We got on well, even though we had little in common. She was an MBA and had the work ethic very badly. An ambitious East End girl still trying to earn her father's approval. He was a scrap metal millionaire and very dominant in her life.

There were actually two Ruths. One was a tense driven senior executive, the other was a soft sentimental woman who loved nothing more than cuddling up in bed for hours on end. For years she had been struggling to merge the two.

This second Ruth was hopelessly impractical in other endearing ways. She was a living rebuttal to Pavlov's theory of conditioned response. For instance, no matter that she must have used a seat belt thousands of times, when she sat in the passenger seat of a car she never, ever remembered to put the seat belt on unprompted.

Our first months in Sussex were blissful. Candle-lit dinners on the terrace, Chopin and Satie drifting through the French windows into the night. Walks at dusk through the fields, arm in arm.

It was only later that friction developed because of her gung-ho attitude to work. I have my own simple rules for life. They work for me. I sleep at night. But there was no way I could advise Ruth. She read California-speak self-help manuals about being a complete person and getting in touch with the universe within but she scorned my advice as offering simplistic post-hippy placebos.

She was after all living in the real world. She commuted each day to London from the station at Chiltington and some evenings, fraught from work, she drove home far too quickly in her Renault turbo to find me sitting with a bottle of wine in the garden after a creative day writing in the sunshine. She didn't always conceal her irritation.

We didn't go to Mr Deacon's funeral on the following Wednesday, though we sent a wreath. The day after the funeral Mrs Deacon turned up to deliver the newspapers in a gleaming new car, a shiny blue Japanese job. I tried to remember what colour their old Fiat Panda had been. Surely it had been red?

'Have the police managed to find anything out about the motorist who knocked over poor Mr Deacon?' I said when she came to the door.

'Not a thing,' she sniffed, handing me the newspaper. She didn't seem overly concerned.

'New car?' I said politely. 'Nice colour.'

'Brand new, Mr Stewart, thanks. It's not all that's going to be new either. Mr Deacon was so mean he'd skin a flea and tan its hide. For twenty years he had me believing we were one step away from the bankruptcy court. When he died I found out how much he'd really got saved up in the building society. Now I intend to spend some of it.' She walked over to the car, calling back over her shoulder. 'And if he's watching from wherever he ended up, I hope it drives him mad, the miserable old sod.'

The Westwoods threw a drinks party that Sunday lunchtime to show off the magnificence of their view. Their house was one of those that made me want to take a bin bag and fill it with every junky knick-knack in sight, so Ruth and I stayed out on the terrace watching the the seagulls wheeling above the cliffs.

I did my best to avoid the usual fatuous conversation with Mrs Westwood, who always felt she had to talk to me about literature. From the other end of the terrace she honked, in great excitement: 'Donald, do you think Shakespeare wrote the plays?'

'Frankly, Mrs Westwood, I don't give a toss.' Well, no, I didn't say that, but I wanted to. I was cheesed off because we were stuck with David Parker, a blacksmith with artistic pretensions who lived in The Forge. He was a big man with powerful hands. He had one of those silly beards that don't have moustaches and in his black roll-neck sweater he must have looked just the thing in 1959. Shame it was forty years later.

He was married to Lucy, a sparky woman in her early fifties, who we always thought was so *together*. Yoga, pottery, herbal tea and *The Guardian*. Clearly, however, a panic had set in about an imagined lonely old age and she had married this oik. We saw them casually almost every week because of the regular mix-up over mail.

'We've got a letter for you, Ruth,' Lucy said now, rummaging in her handbag and producing a square brown envelope. 'It came about a week ago but I put it somewhere safe then couldn't find it. Sorry.'

Ruth took it from her outstretched hand, glanced at the handwriting on the envelope and quietly stuffed it into her own bag. I
thought I saw her colour slightly.

As I was trying to extricate us from the Parkers, the Wing Commander bore down. 'Phone,' he said. 'Jonathan Macrell. He and
that woman can't make it. Taken in by the police for questioning.
Deacon's death. Maybe Spring's too. Police have the car. Paint
samples. Looks bad. Allowed one telephone call. Used it to send
apologies about drinks. Ass.'

When we got back to our house Ruth, looking distracted, excused
herself and went up to the bathroom, taking her handbag with her.
When she eventually came back down, she avoided my eyes and went
out into the garden. I found her bag upstairs. There was no sign of
the envelope Mrs Parker had handed to her.

I watched Ruth in the garden from our bedroom window. She
looked like she was settling in for an afternoon's work so I made a
phone call then went over to the local stables for my regular Sunday
hack. It was a hobby I'd taken up when we first moved down here. I
used to do a lot of things then.

When I was made redundant – with the minimum payoff might I
add – I sold the house in London and bought a cheaper one down
here – ours is the smallest in Novington. I lived on the profit from
the house for a while but it didn't go far. I couldn't get an advance
on my book – first-time author – so I borrowed money from Ruth's
father to live on while I wrote it. He thought the loan was for an
extension to the house. He could well afford it, but he set it against
Ruth's eventual massive inheritance.

Ruth was very good about it, but the situation caused strain between us. After all, why do women go for older men if not to be taken
care of, financially and emotionally? She didn't expect to be keeping
me. I think she respected me less.

Maybe that's why she began her affair. I'd become suspicious
about three months before Mrs Spring's death. Ruth was frequently
home late. If I asked, she'd say she'd been working. If I said I'd
phoned her and there had been no answer, she said that her secretary had forgotten to switch the calls through when she left for
the night.

A few times at home the phone rang on the answering machine but
there was no message. I would sometimes catch the abrupt end of
a phone conversation or hear the phone hurriedly put down. She
would claim it had been a wrong number. The phone had rung at

six thirty on the morning of Mrs Spring's death. Ruth had just been going out the door – she usually leaves for work about six but she was late that morning. She said the caller had hung up when she answered it.

I'm not the jealous type. I've lived long enough to know about the way these things happen. A cynical part of me was conscious of my financial dependence. As long as I didn't bring the subject of other men up she was warm and loving.

The police let Jonathan go on Monday, although they still held his mother. The same day, Donald the cleaner delivered some hot news. He had his own key to the house, so as usual I had retreated to my study in advance of his arrival.

First he asked me if he could do the study and the other rooms upstairs the following morning as he was running late.

'Sure,' I said, pleased to postpone the inevitable monologues about Roger Moore. Even then, he wasn't quite ready to go.

'Crikey, Mr Stewart, a woman in Chiltington has died in suspicious circumstances,' he said, hovering in the study doorway. 'That makes three.'

My fingers stopped clacking on the keyboard of my computer. 'I'm sorry to hear that. How did she die?'

'Riding accident. Fell off her horse and broke her neck.'

'How ghastly,' I said, with feeling. Unpleasant memories stirred.

'You might have known her,' he said. 'Valerie James. She used to keep her horse at the stables you go to.'

I said nothing. I was thinking about my first wife, Janet. He sniffed. 'How's your riding coming along?'

'Fine, thanks,' I said absently. Janet had been a keen horsewoman. She used to ride in Richmond Park when we lived in Twickenham. Every Tuesday and Thursday, rain or shine. You could set your clock by her. She too had died in a riding accident. The coroner had concluded that her horse had refused a low jump, she had toppled over his head and broken her neck.

I had begun to learn to ride as a way of exorcising my first wife's death. I'd taken it up when we first moved down here, in what Ruth called my period of second infantilism. But then she didn't know about Janet and I didn't feel I could explain to her.

Ruth had been remarkably incurious about my life before her. She had never even asked how Janet had died. But then, if I'm honest, Ruth was always too self-absorbed to bother much about anyone else. I'd been using the car that day for shopping so I picked Ruth up from the station in the evening. It was close, with black clouds massing and thunder growling ominously. We were going to dinner later with some friends in Chiltington.

Ruth had been acting oddly towards me since the Westwood drinks party, but tonight she seemed particularly subdued. 'Seat belt,' I said, as we waited at a set of lights. She reached for the belt but didn't speak.

We drove home in silence. Ruth went straight upstairs for a bath. When she came out of the bathroom, wearing only a towel, she came into my study, dropped an envelope on the desk without speaking and went to our bedroom.

It was the envelope Lucy Parker had given her at the Westwood's drinks party. I'd been expecting it. I flipped it over, lifted the flap and took out a second envelope. White, good quality. I looked at the familiar handwriting on the front.

I didn't bother to open it. I knew what was in it.

I left it there and went into our bedroom. 'Do you want an explanation?' I said.

'There isn't time,' she said, fiddling with the zip of her dress. 'We've got to be at Tony and Ellen's by eight.' She brushed past me. 'I just want you to know that I know.'

I guessed she wouldn't leave it at that. In the car, sitting stiffly, she said: 'So where did you meet her?'

'Seat belt,' I said, glancing across. 'Look, I sent her a birthday card, I admit that. But that doesn't mean anything. Certainly not what you're thinking.'

'Don't demean us by denying anything,' she snapped at me. 'What about those wrong numbers, those abruptly ended phone calls whenever I came into the room, those guilty looks? I've suspected for a long time. I pressed the redial button on the phone once after you'd been having a whispered conversation. I got through to a woman.'

I didn't say anything. I was thinking furiously.

'What I don't understand is why she sent your card to me,' she went on. 'What did she hope to achieve? Did she think I'd leave you because of her? Or was she being spiteful because you had finished with her?'

She fumbled in her bag for a cigarette. Her occasional cigarettes were a habit that annoyed me, but now didn't seem the time to make a fuss.

'Are you still seeing her?' she said, exhaling smoke.

Okay, okay. Time to come clean. I'd been the one having the affair, not Ruth. It didn't mean I didn't love Ruth. It just meant that I was bored. Bored senseless.

Have you ever tried living in the country? Oh, it sounds wonderful when you're living in the city. And at first it is. Every daybreak is magical as you wake to the birds singing in the trees, the sun burning the mist away over the sea.

You look forward to the long peaceful day stretching ahead of you. But God, do those days *stretch*. They are *interminable*. After a month I was praying for the pitch black nights to fall. Some mornings, at the thought of another slow, empty day ahead I wanted to strangle those bloody birds for being so cheerful.

I was a city person. Always would be. I loved the buzz of city life, loved working on a daily paper, always up against the clock. When those bastards sacked me and I had to move down here, it was as if they passed a life sentence on me. So I started an affair. And just as easily ended it.

'No,' I said truthfully. 'I'm not seeing her.'

The dinner went well, considering Ruth drank too much, laughed too loudly and was too nervously exuberant – but then she was always like that. I drank only mineral water. I observed Ruth distantly. I was sorry that I had hurt her but I was not distraught. I didn't care enough about her.

Don't get me wrong. I loved her – in my way. But my way isn't other people's way. There's always been a coldness in me, a chilly core. I can be gregarious, I can be concerned. But it's all pretence. At a fundamental level, I just don't care.

Tony had a friend who was a policeman. He had the latest news about the murder inquiry. The paint found on Mr Deacon's bike matched samples taken from Mrs Macrell's car. She was going to be charged.

As we were leaving, Ellen said: 'You know we had our own gory death here last Sunday.'

'I heard,' I said, guiding Ruth towards the car.

'A woman broke her neck falling off her horse,' Ellen continued. 'You might have known her, Donald, she used your stables.'

'I heard,' I repeated. I opened the passenger door and helped Ruth get in.

'Valerie James,' Ellen said as I hurried round to the driver's side and opened that door.

'Who – ?' Ruth said, leaning across towards Helen, as I closed the driver's door behind me.

'I heard,' I said as I turned on the engine and the lights, put the car into gear and set it in motion.

Ruth was quiet for the first hundred yards. Then she laughed and said: 'Not the Valerie James who had a birthday recently. Not the Valerie James who was my husband's mistress. The one he said he wasn't seeing any more.'

I automatically glanced down. She hadn't put her seat belt on. I started to say something but she continued talking drunkenly.

'No wonder you're not seeing her.' She stifled a laugh. 'It would be a bit difficult. And probably illegal.'

It remained an oppressive evening. Storm clouds were massed in the sky above us. I had opened the sun roof and now drove slowly through the winding lanes, pleased to feel the breeze on my face.

'Did you love her very much?'

'Don't be absurd,' I said, after a moment.

Ruth leaned her head against the side window and tucked her feet beneath her. Without looking at me she said dully: 'Your first wife rode, didn't she?'

Ever since Ruth dropped the card on my desk, I'd been trying to work out what to do. Ruth was huddled on her seat, gazing blankly at the scenery rushing by. I looked fondly at her. How I loved her, in my way.

And how little that meant. I signalled a left turn.

'That damned birthday card!' I said. 'Everything followed from the fact that the postman doesn't always lock the postbox properly. I thought I was the only one who knew this. But Mrs Spring knew it too. She regularly stole letters from the postbox to discover her neighbour's secrets. She stole my birthday card to Valerie, ten minutes after I'd put it in the box. She eventually sent it to you.'

Ruth stirred in her seat. I could tell she was looking at the side of my face.

'Mrs Spring?' she said cautiously. I glanced at her. Suddenly she looked sober.

'Yes, Mrs Spring, darling. Do keep up. I thought the card had been lost in the post and frankly I was relieved – never put anything in writing if you want to avoid getting caught. Then, at the summer fête, whilst I was on the bookstall selling 20-year-old *Reader's Digests* to an old buffer from Elam, Mrs Spring flourished it in front of me.'

Ruth began to breathe shallowly but said nothing. I took the next right turn. 'She was a nasty old woman, you know. She sent it out of sheer malice. I couldn't have that. I love you. I don't want to lose you.'

A car passed on the other side of the road, its headlights dazzling. I looked away. 'Or your inheritance.'

I took the third exit off a small roundabout onto Century Lane, the worst accident black spot in the county. I slowed down and reached up to close the sun roof. It had started to rain.

'So you . . . ' Ruth's voice trailed off.

I smiled. 'You can say it, darling. I won't be upset. Yes, I killed Mrs Spring.'

Ruth laughed. Rather harshly I thought. 'You won't be upset. Now I've heard anything.'

I smiled again.

'No you haven't. You haven't heard the half of it.'

The rain fell in earnest now, hammering on the roof and wind-screen. 'Valerie phoned me that morning to warn me. Remember the six thirty call? She'd had a call from Mrs Spring the night before. Mrs Spring was gloating. She'd just posted my card to you.

'I went round to the post box to retrieve it before the postman arrived but the post box was locked. So I went to see Mrs Spring as she was about to go for her swim. If I'd known I was going to spend a fruitless week trying to intercept the bloody card maybe I wouldn't have bothered.'

Ruth was looking at the road ahead again. She was wringing her hands. She still hadn't put her seat belt on but now didn't seem the time to say.

'I didn't necessarily mean to do it, darling. But she was so awful to me. I thought she was going to start shouting about it. And then the Westwoods would hear. I tried to stop her shouting. That's all I was trying to do.'

'And on Sunday when you went for a drive – you went to see your mistress?' Ruth whispered. 'Why did you kill her? Had she threat-ened to tell me about your affair?'

'Not exactly, no,' I said. The rain was falling so hard, the wipers could scarcely cope. I slowed down to twenty. 'Some storm, eh? Valerie thought Mrs Spring's death was fishy and she threatened to go to the police unless I left you for her. Well, I ask you, have you met her? Oh, no, of course you haven't. Well she's attractive enough but she's also a crashing bore about horses. Always rambling on about gymkhanas. I swear I usually had sex with her to shut her up.' I glanced at Ruth. 'Sorry darling, that was insensitive of me.'

'But why did Edith Macrell kill Mr Deacon if she hadn't killed Mrs Spring?' Ruth looked at me. I heard her gasp of realisation and felt her shrink against the passenger door. 'You did it. But how? Oh God – you found the other set of keys to the Golf you'd sold Mrs Macrell and drove into Mr Deacon in that.'

'Clever girl,' I said.

We'd reached a straight stretch of road. I steadied myself and put my foot on the accelerator. The windscreen wipers pumped rapidly.

'I regretted Mr Deacon. But when I went down the next day to intercept the postman, get our post and retrieve that damned birthday card, Deacon told me he'd seen me the previous day. I couldn't take the risk, you see. I thought I'd have to pop Mrs Macrell too, just in case, until I had the idea of using her car to kill him.'

'You killed three people so you wouldn't lose the chance to get at my father's money,' Ruth said flatly.

'Well, your father's money is one of your most attractive features,' I said cheerfully. 'But I hear what you're saying. Thing is, it gets easier every time. And the irony is, I'm not going to get the dosh after all.'

It took a few moments for that to sink in, then Ruth grappled with the handle to the passenger door.

'Central locking, love.'

She looked at me fiercely then subsided into her seat. 'How did your first wife die?'

'I know, I know. I've no imagination. Riding accident again. But it's terribly easy to mock up, you see. Much better than other methods. I felt such a fool when the police spotted the clumsy way I killed Mrs Spring. I hoped they'd think she'd got tangled in the filtration pipe.'

The rain showed no sign of slackening. The lane began to wind again. According to Donald, the cleaner, it was extremely hazardous here in winter. Or when the roads were wet. With Ruth dead there was no way to link me with the other deaths because nobody else knew about my affair with Valerie. Nobody alive anyway.

It was going to be dicey for me when we came off the road and hit a tree but for the sake of verisimilitude I was prepared to spend a week or so in hospital. I figured that at thirty miles an hour I would easily survive the impact, given the driver's airbag and my seatbelt. Ruth sadly wouldn't be so lucky.

It was a shame I wouldn't be able to get at Ruth's inheritance. But at least there was the insurance money. I'd test negative for alcohol in my blood so the insurance company would have to pay up. And I'd learned from the meagre pay-off I'd got after my first wife's death not to under-insure my second one.

I slowed, spun the wheel and took the car off the road. I was trying to think of a headline. 'Author Writes Second Wife Off', perhaps. Time moved very slowly. I heard Ruth scream. I think I felt her hand clutch my arm. I braced myself as the thick trunk of a tree rushed towards us. A split second before we hit I thought of Donald. Coming back to do my office in the morning. Nosing around. Reading the birthday card for Valerie James lying open on my desk.

Melusine

MARTIN EDWARDS

On the hillside, bodies were burning. As Jason drove down into the valley, he glanced across and saw the outlines of the bloated carcasses. Their stiffened legs protruded through the flames and pointed to the sky. On a fresh June morning, smoke and fire had turned the sky a strange purple hue that, until the coming of the plague, he had never seen before. A steamy white vapour hung close to the ground. He kept the windows of the van wound up, but the stench from the corpses on the funeral pyre was inescapable. It choked his sinuses and made his gorge rise.

The fields were deserted. Cows and sheep should be everywhere, but only their ghosts remained. All the footpaths were barred with tape and official notices; ramblers had been asked to stay at home. The winding route to Sidebottom's Farm was closed, a red sign blocking the middle of the lane. KEEP OUT — FOOT AND MOUTH DISEASE.

The grey stone cottages where a couple of the farm workers and their families had lived were shuttered and silent. When blisters were found on the tongue of one of Mick Sidebottom's bullocks, the men had been given forty-eight hours to pack their bags and leave. Folk said it was worse than going on evacuation, during the last war. This time the enemy drifted through the air, silent, ruthless and invisible.

His head was pounding and he kept taking the bends in the road too fast. At least there was no other traffic around; the Ministry kept warning against 'non-essential movement'. As he had driven through the smoke and vapour up top, a couple of tiny patches of unburned flesh had landed on the bonnet of his van. He clipped a hedge as he skimmed round a tight bend, but only when he struck a pothole did the bits fall off. At last he slowed as he reached the disinfected matting stretched over a cattle grid. In the distance he could see Gordon Clegg power-washing his tractor for the umpteenth time. Anything to keep the plague at bay.

Five minutes later, the squat church tower came into view. He glanced at his watch. Twelve o'clock. Time for a quick drink at the Wheatsheaf before he called home for half an hour. He had done enough killing and maybe he'd done enough drinking, too, but alcohol helped in a way nothing else did.

Dave Sharpe's rusty Vauxhall was the only other vehicle in the pub car park. He hesitated and thought about going straight to the house. Part of him wanted not to see Dave, not to speak to him, not to have to think about him ever again. But at least if he was swilling beer, he wasn't doing anything more dangerous. Jason took a breath and headed for the saloon.

Sally Binks was behind the bar, wearing a low-cut pink top and flirting with Dave. Apart from a couple of old men in the corner, no-one else was in.

'Usual, love?'

He nodded. 'And one for him.'

'Cheers, mate,' Dave said.

Funny, that. They had disliked each other for years, and still they called themselves mates. They had met on the first day of school at the age of five and on that very morning, Dave had pulled his hair and made him cry, then pretended it was all some kind of joke. As they grew up together, anyone listening to their lazy banter would never have a clue about what went on inside their heads. Jason wondered if he actually hated Dave. He never cared to analyse his feelings, but he thought probably he did hate him. For many reasons, not least because Melanie had said last week that he looked like Kurt Cobain.

'All right?' he asked.

As Sally moved to pick up the tankards, Dave reluctantly shifted his gaze from her cleavage and gave a shrug. 'Feller from Padgett's was in here a few minutes ago. He said that when the rain came after they buried the sheep out Settle way, the bodies exploded. They exploded, literally exploded. He said, if you watched the ground, it looked as though the earth was sweating blood.'

'Wicked,' Sally said as she pulled the levers. Her breasts wobbled, hypnotising Dave again. 'Wicked.'

In the corner of the bar, the television was murmuring. The mid-day news. A government spokesman, carefully compassionate in a Paul Smith suit, was promising that everything was getting better. The detail of his explanation was lost as the old men in the corner hooted with scorn.

' "Back under control?" ' one of them said. 'Tell that to Jack Wilson's widow. No wonder the poor bastard hung himself. Took him and his dad forty years to build that herd.'

'Aye,' his toothless companion said.

'Nothing even wrong with the animals. Slaughter on suspicion, that's what it was.'

The other man supped his pint. 'Aye.'

'See that bugger?' the old man said, jerking a thumb at the screen. 'Pity he's never had blood and brains splashed all over him.'

'Aye.'

Dave winced. He was a postman and his work was already finished for the day. He'd never worked on the land and was one of the few people Jason knew whose life had not been touched by the coming of the plague.

When Jason said nothing, Dave nudged him in the ribs. 'So how are you, mate? And how's the missus?'

His wolfish features gave nothing away, but was there a touch of mockery in his tone? Jason thought so. It wasn't just his imagination.

'I'm all right. So's Melanie.'

'Great. Glad to hear you're looking after Mel. Did I ever tell you how I used to fancy her when she was a kid?'

Dave would have fancied Godzilla if it had worn a skirt. His late mother had fondly described him as *incorrigible*, a favourite word. He'd finished up getting Cheryl Stringer pregnant and marrying her before the baby was born. It wasn't in his nature to do the decent thing, so everyone assumed that it was because he'd never found anyone with a sexual appetite to match Cheryl's. Jason had never cared for Cheryl – she was so in-your-face – but these days she was proving impossible to avoid. In January she had started working as a classroom assistant at Melanie's school and the two couples had fallen into a habit seeing each other regularly. Melanie said that Cheryl was fun, but Jason couldn't help wondering if it was an excuse, an opportunity for his wife to spend more time with Dave. She said that he made her laugh.

'Yeah, you told me.'

'Course, she was too posh for me. For all of us. No offence, mate, but I never figured out how you managed to catch her eye.'

He'd often asked himself that very question, never quite worked out the answer.

Dave drained his glass. 'Same again?'

Jason hadn't finished his drink, but his headache was no better and he decided he'd had enough. Especially of Dave. He pushed the tankard across the counter to Sally and shook his head. 'Another time.'

'Off to kill a few more?' Dave mimicked the Sundance Kid firing his six-shooter.

'Later.'

Dave treated him to a knowing leer. Jason could smell the ale on his breath. 'Popping back to the nest for a quickie, then? Don't blame you, mate. Give my love to Mel, now, don't forget.'

Jason loathed the easy familiarity of that 'Mel'. He turned away, not trusting himself to answer. When he reached home, Melanie was in the front room. She used it as a study and was tapping on the keyboard of her computer. It was half-term, supposed to be a holiday, but she always found plenty to do. As he walked into the room, she glanced over her shoulder.

'You left early this morning.'

'I tried not to disturb you.'

'I heard the van when you set off.'

'Sorry.'

'Doesn't matter. How did it go?'

'Well, you know. The usual.'

He'd never been good with words, not like Melanie. Anyway, how could you describe what he saw, what he felt? Nothing could have prepared him for this. The terror on the face of the beasts, the staring eyes, the hoarse panting, the blood seeping from the wounds where they had in panic crashed through strands of barbed wire.

'Ready for a sandwich? There's cheese in the fridge.'

She turned back to her computer. He wondered if he should go up behind her and kiss her on the neck. At one time, that would have melted her in a moment, but they had been married four years. Four years! Time to start a family, though she had always been reluctant. Weren't teachers supposed to like kids? But she never behaved like all the other girls he'd grown up with. Always, Melanie was different.

'Good morning?'

'Not bad,' she said, still focusing on the text on the screen. 'There's such a lot of work to do with the national curriculum. By the way, I wouldn't mind a sandwich myself.'

In the kitchen, Jason found the bread knife. He hadn't expected marriage to be like this. What had he expected? He wasn't sure, perhaps he'd never thought clearly enough about it before asking Melanie to share his life. Marriage was what people did, but he had assumed that, because Melanie was different, their life together would somehow be different from everyone else's. After all, she was his fairy bride.

He ran his forefinger along the serrated edge of the knife, remembering how young Kevin Nolan had slit the throat of a terrified lamb the previous afternoon. The lamb was healthy, like all the other creatures down Beggarman's Lane, but that was not enough to guarantee survival. Tests on blood and tissue taken from animals at an adjoining farm had proved positive and the rules of contiguous culling meant that their neighbours had to die.

'I wouldn't mind a cup of tea while you're at it,' Melanie called.

She talked like a woman of fifty, he thought, switching on the kettle. Not that she looked a day over twenty. Her face didn't have a single line. Three years older, he'd only been vaguely aware of her existence during her teens. He'd never spoken to her until the night of a dance in the village hall, a couple of weeks after she finished at college. He'd watched her, with her friends, and found himself hypnotised. She seemed delicate and aloof from their chatter, a slim, almost boyish figure in a simple dress lacking all the slits and embellishments favoured by her companions. Something prompted him to talk to her, even though he had watched her reject overtures from a number of the other young men. Including Dave Sharpe.

A couple of months later, when their unlikely romance was turning into something more than a fling, he tried to explain how he admired her, how he loved to watch her when she was watching something or someone else. There was a stillness about her that entranced him, and something more: an air of not belonging that was neither loneliness nor isolation, but a sort of serene uniqueness with which he had fallen hopelessly in love.

Of course, he found it impossible to describe his feelings. At first she had teased him, but when she realised that he meant to be deadly serious, her tone had softened and she had said that she thought she knew what he meant.

'I never wanted to be one of the crowd,' she said, squeezing his hand.

'You're not,' he said. 'You're almost – well, not quite human.'

'Thanks a lot,' she laughed, withdrawing her hand in mock indignation. 'Sort of alien from outer space, am I?'

'No, no,' he said, his voice becoming hoarse with embarrassment. 'But you're not like Dawn and Becky and all the rest. You're not like anyone I ever met before.'

'I'll take that as a compliment, shall I?'

'You better had,' he said. 'I want to marry you.'

To his amazement, she said yes. No play-acting, no messing. He could not believe his good fortune. Why him? In the past, he'd done all right with the girls, even if he would never be in Dave Sharpe's league. At least he was muscular and fit and poor tubby little Hannah Stott had once told him that his hazel eyes were the most beautiful she had ever seen. He was never mean with money and no woman would ever feel the slap of his hand, which was more than you could say for many men, even in this day and age. But Melanie had a brain and wanted to use it. She could make something of herself.

As for Jason, he didn't think he'd ever find a job that truly suited him. Perhaps his old Maths master had been right in branding him as lazy. It went deeper than a visceral loathing of algebra. Above all, Jason admired beauty. He admired it in a landscape, in a summer sunset, in the face and body of a gorgeous woman. How easy to become lost in rapture, to pass the hours in quiet adoration. But there was no beauty in work. Routine bored him and so he moved from job to job. He had been a garage mechanic, a gardener, a farmhand, a butcher's assistant, a slaughterman at an abattoir.

A week before the wedding, he asked Melanie if she'd ever loved anyone else. Idle curiosity, no hidden agenda – but for some reason, his inquisitiveness upset her out of all proportion. She was usually calm, unworldly even, and he was surprised to see her eyes filling with tears.

'Listen,' she said gently as he stammered an apology. 'It doesn't matter. But you must promise me one thing.'

'Anything,' he said. His worst nightmare was that she would pull out of their engagement. Twice already he had dreamed of her failing to show at the church on the day itself and of his mortification as everyone in the congregation stared at him in horrified sympathy.

'You must keep this promise and never break it.' She thought for a moment. 'I don't suppose you ever heard of Melusine?'

He shook his head. She often treated him as a pupil; it amused her to teach him things. He didn't mind; he was content simply to let her words wash over him, not absorbing the lessons, just luxuriating in her company.

'Melusine was a beautiful fairy but she had a terrible secret.' A far-away look came into her eyes. 'One day each week, she became half-woman, half-serpent. A man fell in love with her and she agreed to marry him, on one condition, that he never saw her on a Saturday.'

'What happened?'

'Someone poisoned his mind, and said that was the day Melusine met her lover. When her husband broke his word and found out the truth, he lost everything. Including Melusine.'

'I don't get it.'

'Listen, I'm like Melusine. I ask just one thing of you. You must promise never to be jealous.'

'So you've got a terrible secret?' His tone was jokey, but her flights of fancy baffled him. 'It's not the new vicar, is it? I saw him across the street the other day. Quite a hunk. The church shouldn't allow it.'

She put a finger to her lips. 'Shhh, darling. No, I don't fancy the vicar, but I do want you to trust me. Now, are you going to promise or not?'

'You really want me to?'

She nodded seriously and he realised that he must not get this wrong. Not now, when he was committed to her. Even though he did not know why, he had to make his promise.

'I swear.'

Her face broke into the loveliest smile and within moments he forgot about Melusine. In the years that followed, there was no hint that Melanie might have a terrible secret. She did not smoke, did not drink, and she had to be persuaded into any bedroom games that were not pretty conventional. Even now, he told himself he was crazy to believe that she was deceiving him.

He took the sandwich and cup of tea into her. 'Here you are.'

'Thanks. So when are you going back?'

'Five minutes.'

'I'll have your tea ready by half six.'

'Great.'

'No problem.'

She was still glued to the computer screen. He drank in the sight of her. Her hair was the same rich chestnut shade he had always loved, her skin was as white and unsullied as when they first kissed. Yet something had changed. He was no longer special to her; she had stopped trying to educate him to understand what appealed to her. Nowadays he featured in her life in much the same way as their shabby old furniture or the framed views of Brimham Rocks that hung on the wall of their living room.

'See you later, then.'

'Mmmmm.'

He closed the door quietly. As he rooted in his jacket pocket for the keys to the van, he wondered who had stolen her affections. Dave Sharpe? Checking the map in his glove compartment, he told himself for the hundredth time that life was not so cruel, that the only reason he was obsessed with the fear that Dave was cuckolding him was because such a betrayal would be too hard to bear.

Heading for the next Infected Premises, he couldn't rid his mind of Dave's gloating smile. As lads, they had played rugby together in winter and cricket in the summer. They had so much in common and people regarded them as bosom buddies. Dave was fun and he was generous, but there were moments when the mask of good nature slipped. Taking a short cut along a single-track lane, Jason remembered a game one July when he and Dave had batted in partnership. It was one of those days of which cricketers dream. The ball kept speeding off his bat to the boundary. Even the best bowlers on the other side were helpless in the face of such a sustained attack. When he was one run short of his century, Dave called him for a quick single. The ball was in the hands of the cover point fielder, a farmer with a famously strong arm. Jason hesitated for a second, then put his head down and ran. His stumps were shattered when he was two yards short of the safety of the crease at the far end. In the bar afterwards, Dave had bought the drinks and said he took the blame. Jason argued with him, saying that if he had set off straight away, he would have made his ground. But secretly, he knew that Dave was right. It was a reckless call, his fault. Perhaps he had been too anxious to see Jason achieve his moment of glory. Or perhaps he had wanted to deny it to him forever. Jason had never scored a ton since.

When he arrived at the site, the man from the Ministry came up as he was slipping on his white biohazard overall and rubber boots. 'You took your time.'

Jason's wave took in Kevin Nolan standing by a picket fence, supping Coke from a can and Bob Garrett sitting in the cab of his van, reading *The Sun*. 'Better things to do with my day than spend hours hanging around here, waiting for the word.'

'Look here, you know the score. We have to get the go-ahead from the vet. But if you keep buggering off, we don't know where we are.'

Jason shrugged. He was freelance, and right now the Ministry needed as much help as it could get. Three million animals didn't kill themselves. None of the slaughtermen liked the Ministry blokes. They were pen-pushers, more comfortable in a warm office than on the land. Most of the slaughtermen had learned their trade on farms, they were countrymen. They didn't have to like what they were doing or the people who paid them to do it.

Bob Garrett jumped down from his cab. 'Eh up, pal. Wipe that smirk off your face. We all know you've been off giving your old lady a good seeing-to.'

Garrett's ex-wife lived across the road from Jason. The previous summer, Jason had spotted him eyeing up Melanie when he brought back the kids and she was sunbathing on the lawn. No matter how many times he told himself that other men were jealous of him, it never helped, never made him feel good. What was wrong with him? Why did he feel damaged by the way they lusted after his lovely fairy wife? And things were getting worse. He couldn't shake off the fear that people were laughing at him behind his back. They knew something that he did not.

Kevin Nolan was sniggering, but Jason didn't rise to the bait. 'How many are we doing this afternoon?'

The man from the Ministry consulted his clipboard. 'Eighty five cattle. Not a big job. I just spoke to the vet. We should be set to go in a couple of minutes.'

Jason opened the door of his van and picked up the gun from the passenger seat. 'Better get ready, then.'

Their task did not take long. They were using captive bolt guns rather than rifles. A blank cartridge fired a four inch steel bolt into the animal's skull and a spring retracted the bolt. Once the animal had been stunned in this way, it was pithed, by means of a steel rod being thrust through the hole and into the brain.

As usual, not everything went according to plan. One bull had to be shot and pithed four times. The more he fought for life, the more Jason's temper frayed. What was the point of struggling? The bull wasn't sick, but it had to die anyway. Those were the orders. He wanted it over as quickly as possible and resented the doomed bull for delaying the inevitable. The more time you had to think about what you were doing, the worse it was for everyone.

'Where next?' he asked the man from the Ministry.

'There's a couple of dozen lambs penned up the other side of the barn at the end of the lane. You and Garrett head off there now, I'll catch up once I've had a word with the farmer.'

The farmer had turned up during the killings. He'd stayed over by the fence, watching the destruction of his herd. Jason could tell the man was close to tears. In the early days, he had talked to the farmers whose herds he shot, tried to console them. But what could you say? Most people round here reckoned that it would be enough to vaccinate the animals and claimed the culling was unnecessary. But the powers-that-be in London thought differently, and that was what mattered.

Jason held the lambs while Bob Garrett shot them. He took care not to look at the faces of the creatures, settling his gaze instead on fields in the middle distance. The countryside was full of death, but Nature didn't seem to notice. Ragged robin, elderflowers and foxgloves still bloomed.

'These fellers in the Thatched Tavern were talking last night,' Garrett said. 'They'd killed fifteen hundred sheep and cattle on one farm and then they were told to disinfect round a jackdaw's nest for conservation reasons. Christ, would you bloody believe it?'

Jason grunted. Perhaps all wars were like this; everyone had an anecdote to tell. Live lambs suffocating to death under the corpses of sheep with cut throats. Wagons driven by young squaddies, carrying the carcases to the burial pits and leaking blood all along the country lanes. Each story-teller liked to spin a yarn more absurd or more horrific than the last.

'You all right?' Garrett asked. 'You look – sort of glazed. On a promise for tonight, then?'

Jason felt his chest tightening. He wanted to grab the man, shake him by the neck until he choked, demanding to know why he kept talking about Melanie. What was going on – something that he, the poor old husband, was the last to know?

He strode away, unable to trust himself to speak. Surely he was wrong in suspecting Dave. What about Garrett himself? He was an older man and Jason supposed he was good-looking if you like that sort of thing. Or even Kevin Nolan? Kevin's last year at the school had been Melanie's first as a teacher. Jason remembered her saying that he was a rascal, but somehow she couldn't find it in her heart not to like him. That was the trouble with Melanie. She never saw through people, she was too naive to realise that the men she liked were only interested in one thing.

'Where are you going?' Garrett demanded.

Jason pointed to the heap of bodies on the ground. 'I've had enough of this.'

'If you don't wait for whatsisname to show up and sign you off, there'll be hell to pay.'

Jason shrugged. 'So what?'

He'd walked away from jobs before. Even as he clambered out of his overall and boots, his headache was easing. Garrett give a disgusted shake of the head. Kevin Nolan was grinning. Surely, *surely*, Melanie couldn't have slept with that lad?

Even as he sped back to the village, he told himself that he couldn't confront her. It wasn't so much that he lacked the balls to do it, but he remembered what she had said about Melusine. He dared not demand to know if she had taken a lover. What he needed was reassurance.

It could still be okay, he thought, as he jolted over the disinfectant mat. We can start again. Soon, maybe, she'll be ready to try for a family. That will make all the difference.

'I didn't expect you back so soon,' Melanie said when he opened the door of the study.

'I've jacked it in,' he said. 'The money's good, but I'm sick of the smell and the faces of the animals as I kill them.'

She swallowed. 'What are you going to do?'

'Dunno. I'll find something.'

'But there's no work! Haven't you heard. The countryside is closed. No tourists, no trade, nothing. People are going bankrupt right, left and centre.'

'All right, it might take a while.' He thought for a moment. 'What's up? Don't you want me under your feet all day?'

'It's not that!' Two pink spots appeared in her cheeks. It wasn't like her to be flustered. 'We can't go on like this.'

'Me spending cash we haven't got at the Wheatsheaf, you mean?'

'Don't shout! I know you need to unwind . . .'

'Too right,' he said, and marched out of the house.

Ten minutes later, nursing a pint in the saloon, he was wondering if he'd been too rough with her. They hardly ever argued; neither of them were natural combatants. When Sally asked him if he was okay, he bit her head off.

'Why? Don't I look okay?'

'I only asked,' she said in an injured tone. 'And if you want to know the truth, you look as miserable as sin.'

It dawned on him that he hadn't been happy for a long time. Not since before the coming of the plague, that was for sure. Maybe he should offer Melanie an olive branch. It wasn't a Yorkshireman's habit to say sorry, but he wasn't proud. He would do anything, if it would help to recapture the love they had shared at one time. Maybe even work out his contract with the Ministry. He pulled his mobile out of his pocket and dialled home. He would apologise right now, and then go back and see what else he could do to make amends.

The number was engaged. He tried again a couple of minutes later, with the same result. Her parents were dead and she seldom socialised. The head teacher was on holiday and her two closest colleagues had taken a party of pupils to France. Who could she be talking to?

'Dave not in tonight?' he asked.

Sally shook her head to show that she bore no grudge for his sharp tone earlier. 'He said that he would be busy in the garden until it got dark. He's building a rockery, you know.'

Oh really? Jason's head was swimming and it wasn't just down to the beer. 'Same again, then.'

As darkness fell, Dave showed up. He spotted Jason and gave him a wicked grin. 'What's up, mate? Abandoned your old lady? I dunno, you'd better take care. You know, women are like cars. You've got to keep their engines tuned.'

'You've been looking after Cheryl?' a fat man at the bar demanded.

Dave found this amusing. 'Matter of fact, I've been out in the garden.'

'Oh yeah? Planting a few seeds?'

The fat man and Dave roared with laughter and fell into ribald conversation. Jason sat glowering and monosyllabic for a couple of rounds before summoning up the energy to head for home. If Dave had been with Mel, she would need time to have a bath, make herself decent. He didn't want a confrontation this evening. He had to think things through.

Although he could hold his beer better than most, he was swaying slightly as he walked through his front door. All the lights were out. It wasn't late, but Melanie must be in bed. She would probably say she needed the sleep, after he had woken her so inconsiderately that morning. Perhaps she was already fast asleep; she was bound to be tired.

On tiptoe, he made his way into the study. At night she left her mobile on her desk. He lifted it up and checked the list of recent calls. It was the first time in the marriage that he had ever snooped on her, but he couldn't help it. A familiar set of digits came up at once. His guts lurched. The number belonged to Dave Sharpe.

He started to climb the stairs, wanting to have it out with Melanie, but half-way up he changed his mind and went back down again. Better leave it until morning. He couldn't sleep beside her, though. Not after what she'd done. *Dave Sharpe.* His thoughts were as grid-locked as an urban motorway, but he could still guess what had happened. Dave and Melanie must have had a fling, but he'd two-timed her and got Cheryl pregnant. Perhaps Melanie had been too stingy in bed for him.

Melanie must have lost her heart to Dave. Yes, that explained everything. How she had fallen for Dave's mate on the rebound, her lapses into frigidity, even the story about Melusine. She did have a terrible secret after all.

He spent the night dozing fitfully on the lumpy sofa in their living room. At about four he woke from a nightmare. A dead bullock had risen like a zombie from the pile of carcasses and come towards him, intent upon taking revenge. The room was chilly in the middle of the night, but sweat was sticking his shirt to his chest. His head was pounding and the stale taste of beer lingered in his mouth.

Why had she done this to him? Dave was no fool; he must have picked up a hint that Melanie still held a torch for him. For all Cheryl's famously voracious appetites, he wouldn't have been able to resist the opportunity to be able to turn Jason into a cuckold. Humiliating his old 'friend' at the same time as enjoying the sweet pleasures of Melanie's tender flesh would double the fun.

At ten to seven, he heard the alarm shrilling in the bedroom. Moments later, Melanie came hurrying down the stairs, calling his name. When she saw him, her face turned crimson. In that instant, he knew that she knew he knew.

'What are you doing?' Her voice was croaky, uncertain.

'You should have told me the truth,' he said. 'We never should have got married.'

'What are you talking about?' She was no good at feigning innoc-ence. He thought she was naturally honest. Living a lie must have been a torment, but things had gone too far for him to feel a spurt of sympathy.

'Admit it. You're in love with Dave Sharpe, aren't you? That's always been your secret, hasn't it, *Melusine*? But you never had the bottle to tell me.'

No actress could have faked the horror in her eyes. 'You've got it all wrong.'

'You lied to me,' he said quietly. 'But I found you out in the end.'

'You don't understand!'

'Believe me, I do. You slut.'

Tears were dribbling down her cheeks. For a moment she seemed transfixed and then she gave a little cry and ran out of the room and up the stairs. He heard her locking the door to their bedroom. No problem. He wasn't going after her just now. There was something else – this came to him in a slap of understanding – that he must do first.

He didn't bother to wash or shave; he was past all that. From upstairs came the sound of loud racking sobs, but as he unlocked his van, he felt a strange sense of calm, as if for the whole of his life he'd been wandering aimlessly, but now he'd found a mission.

Where could he find Dave Sharpe? At one time Dave's round had covered the village and its outskirts, but now he was a floater and covered for colleagues who were sick or on holiday, so he moved around the area. He said he preferred this; he liked the variety, but more than that, there was often a chance to meet new women. Countless times he regaled the Wheatsheaf saloon bar with anecdotes of nymphomaniac housewives who asked him in while their husbands were out at work. If only his restless womanising hadn't encompassed Melanie.

As Jason turned on the ignition, he saw the bedroom curtain twitch. His wife, furtively watching him drive out of their marriage. He slammed his foot down on the accelerator and the van shot out into the road, narrowly missing a milk float. His plan was to follow a circular route, heading out west first and then up and around the hillside before returning to the village. Sooner or later, he was sure to come across Dave Sharpe.

It took longer than he expected, but five miles from home he finally spotted his target. Dave was delivering a parcel at an isolated cottage at the end of a short lane. The woman on the doorstep was white-haired and frail, so Dave would not be lingering. The lane was narrow and Jason parked his van across to block it. He watched the woman go back inside her home and Dave climb on to his bicycle. Jason picked up the bolt gun from the passenger's seat. Keeping it behind his back, he shuffled out of the van to face his enemy.

'What . . . oh, it's you! Christ, Jason, what are you playing at?'

Jason said nothing. Dave dismounted and leaned his bike against the hedge. He marched up and stared into Jason's eyes.

'Lost your tongue?'

'I've lost everything,' Jason said.

An odd light came into Dave's eyes. 'Is this about Mel?'

Jason showed him the gun. They were within touching distance of each other. Jason caught a whiff of the other man's after shave. After shave! What sort of a postman doused himself in that muck when he went out on his round of a morning? Only one who wanted to shag any woman stupid enough to give him the glad eye.

Dave's cheeks lost all colour. Hoarsely, he said, 'What are you doing? Put that down.'

Jason lifted the gun and put it to Dave's forehead. 'You think I'm stupid, don't you?'

'I think you're mad. You've lost it, mate, totally lost it.'

Dave tensed. Jason knew that he was going to try to grab the gun. He would only have one chance to do this. As he fired, he tried to close his eyes, but they wouldn't shut. He saw agony in Dave's eyes as well as hearing his scream. Just like my first day at the abattoir, he thought.

The pithing was over so quickly. Even as the old lady opened her door, coming to see who or what had screamed, Jason was back in the van, reversing over the body just to make sure before turning for the village. Some of Dave's blood had splashed over him, but he didn't care. His mind was as empty as the fields as he raced along the narrow winding lanes to his home. What was he going to say to Melanie? Was she truly lost to him forever? Ought she to die as well?

Within minutes he was back. The front door was ajar. Bolt gun in hand, he kicked it wide open and strode inside. He could hear Melanie weeping. Well, now she had something to weep about. He took the stairs two at a time. The bedroom door was shut. If she'd locked it, he meant to kick it down. But when he smashed the gun against the door, it swung on its hinges.

A woman cried out. Then he heard another voice, softly murmuring. As he stepped inside the bedroom, something occurred to him. *This is all wrong*. Melanie was with someone. Yet he had killed Dave Sharpe.

Melanie was in bed. Her eyes were puffy, her cheeks wet. Her companion had wrapped a plump arm around her shoulders. They were naked, both Melanie and Cheryl Sharpe. *Yes, I got it so wrong*.

Helpless as doomed lambs, neither of them able to move or speak, the lovers stared at him.

His hand shaking, he pointed the gun first at his wife and then at Cheryl, before changing his mind and raising it instead to his left temple. The cold steel nuzzled his skin. This, at least, was a necessary death.

Green wounds

NATASHA COOPER

Something was biting into Trish's thigh. She woke. Her feet were tangled up in her briefcase and the cords of the airline's goody bag, and her head lolled near her neighbour's. She muttered an apology. They wouldn't land in Washington for another hour. She felt grimy and fretful. Was she mad, too?

The invitation had arrived long before September 11, and it had been irresistible. What barrister in her position could have refused to give a paper at an important international conference on 'The Problem of Vengeance'? But now the whole world was jittery about flying, and stories of anthrax led every news bulletin. Friends and colleagues had accused her of taking stupid risks for a bit of self-promotion. Only George, her boyfriend, shared her view that to duck out now would be giving in to terror. But even George had clung to her before she left for the airport.

To Trish, the biggest risk was offending her hosts, even though her brief was limited to personal vengeance. She had drafted and redrafted all the parts of her paper that anyone could mistake for a reference to any state's response to terrorist outrages. But she wasn't happy about it.

The captain announced his descent. Trish's neighbour's knuckles were almost bursting out of his skin as he clutched the armrest. The engines roared, the wheels screamed, but the landing was perfect. Like water bursting through a dam, tension poured out of everyone. Even the staff looked relieved.

Outside the terminal, she found astonishing weather. Here they were, in November, with dazzling sunshine lighting up red and orange trees against a bright blue sky. She'd been a fool to bring fleeces and sweaters and boots.

'You never can tell,' the taxi driver said, when she commented on it. 'I've been here only one year, but already I know the weather is very duplicitous. One day freezing, the next like this. Even on New Year's Day it can be hot.'

I want to live in Washington, Trish thought, turning to watch the huge white buildings of the Mall flash past the windows. Up ahead was the Capitol, familiar from a hundred films, and just as magnificent.

The check-in clerk at the hotel handed her a fax when she'd registered, which surprised her. She waited until she was alone in her room before ripping open the envelope to find that George had written:

You'll be a wow! Enjoy it. And don't forget to have some crab-cakes. They're the best in the world. Love, GEORGE.

Typical, she thought, smiling as she went to run a bath. Still, eating local delicacies was one way of learning about a country.

Later, dressed in a new black suit with a soft coral shirt to give her pale face some colour, she went downstairs to meet her host.

'Great to meet you. It's going well so far, but be prepared for strong views in the Q and A session at the end. People really care about this issue.'

'I know.' Trish felt her palms begin to sweat. She knew she'd be fine once she got started. It was only the waiting that was hard.

A burst of polite clapping welcomed them into the auditorium. Trish hardly heard it, concentrating on not tripping up the steps to the stage. She kept an eager smile on her face while she was introduced.

'Now, to explore the arena of personal vengeance, we have Patricia Maguire from London. Patricia is a barrister of fifteen years' experience, mainly in family law. The title of her paper today is: "Vengeance and the Victim Culture".'

Trish had never used her full name and felt unsettled. But she was a pro, so she smiled some more. She had a sheaf of newspaper cuttings with her and laid the first on the overhead projector before she said anything at all.

'Gotcha!' screamed the caption under a grainy photograph of a woman throwing paint over a small man, who cowered between two uniformed police officers.

'That woman,' Trish began, pitching her voice to take account of the size of the place and the muffling effect of all the bodies in it, 'believed the man in the photograph was guilty of the abduction, rape and murder of a three-year-old child.'

With the stage lights shining at her, Trish could see very little of the people in front of her, but she sensed them settling, as though they knew where they were now. Most of them would expect a story of mad vigilantes and mistaken identity.

'He was guilty. What's more, she was not his first victim. He had sexually abused and killed at least eight other children that we know of.' Trish could feel hostility from the audience. 'There are very few people in British prisons serving what we call "a whole life tariff", but he is one. Quite rightly.'

They were still listening, but they didn't like her yet. She could cope with that, use it, work with it.

'The woman in the photograph was not related to any of his victims. Five months later, she was charged with criminal damage for breaking into the flat of a quite different offender. We have to accept the fact that she enjoyed the sensation of outrage. A lot of people do. Which is why it sells newspapers.' Trish removed the cutting.

'It is, however, quite natural to want those who have caused you suffering to suffer in their turn.' Even through the dazzle she could see heads nodding. 'But "natural" does not equal "wholesome". There are many toxic substances that are completely natural.'

She put two other cuttings on the projector. 'Now, these women *are* mothers of his victims. The one on the left is a campaigner for the reintroduction of capital punishment; she is prey for media interviewers whenever anyone wants an angry victim's point of view. The one on the right is a teacher, who has visited her daughter's killer in prison. She has said that while she can never forgive what he did, she has forgiven the man himself.

'One of these women lives with her husband and three children. The other lives alone, after two failed marriages. Who is there in the audience who will guess which is the happy one?'

Trish waited, peering through the dazzle to see several people moving out of their seats towards the central microphone. The first to reach it was a middle-aged woman, narrowly beating a young bearded man.

'The one who forgave, of course.'

'Of course. We all know that, don't we?'

She could feel their support at last. Checking the clock, she saw she had thirty-five minutes to deliver the main part of her paper. They would listen now, even if they didn't all agree. The words began to pour through her throat like honey. Even though she had her whole paper printed out in front of her, in huge type, she barely looked at it, just keeping her place with one finger on each paragraph as she reached it.

'And so I would say to anyone who has been injured, physically or emotionally,' she said, at last: 'whenever you feel that exciting surge of outrage, that instinct to hit back, to take satisfaction from the pain of the person who has hurt you: hold back. Remember what Francis Bacon wrote: "A man that studieth revenge keeps his own wounds green." Let the law deal with the offender, make yourself draw a line, and let your own wounds heal. Thank you very much.'

There was real warmth in the applause, but several of the subsequent questions were hostile. The session leader looked uncomfortable as one man harangued Trish for her stupidity and lack of sympathy for victims. She kept her temper but she knew she'd need time out before she could safely join the champagne reception that was to follow the session. Any provocative remark now and she might snap.

It was wonderful to breathe real air outside the hotel, instead of the reconditioned exhalations of all the other delegates. Trish felt her shoulders easing as she walked round the block. After fifty yards, she stopped mouthing the insults she'd like to have bellowed at the vengeance-freak in the audience. She looked around, wanting to make sure she didn't get lost, although with the comforting sight of the Capitol's dome over the top of the buildings, she couldn't go far wrong.

At the end of the block, she turned right and saw a shabbier street than the one she'd been in. Running footsteps pounded up behind her.

'Oh, Trish, you fool,' she told herself, gripping her file of cuttings more tightly against her chest. They felt like a breastplate, but a pretty flimsy one.

The footsteps were right behind her now. Someone was grunting too. She didn't know whether to turn or not. Some people thought you could frighten off most potential muggers by drawing attention to them; others that any scream or other sign of fear would pump them up to greater violence.

A hand grabbed her shoulder. The heavy breathing was now battering at her ear. She walked on, saying a pathetic 'excuse me' over and over again.

She felt his other hand on her shoulder and then her whole body whirled as he flung her against the wall. Winded, still clutching the cuttings to her chest, she was terrified she might wet her knickers.

The man was young, white and bearded, and his eyes were wild. His breath was hot on her face and smelled of alcohol. His lips were wet and mumbling, and his eyeballs moved frantically. She started to tell him she had no money. He clamped his hand over her mouth. Over his shoulder, Trish searched for any sign of help. But she was alone in the street with this maniac.

'I . . . I . . . I . . . ' he said. 'You . . . you . . . you . . . '

Oh, no, she screamed in silence. Murdered because my mugger can't tell me what he wants.

She remembered the violent and demented clients she'd represented in the past. Some had been nearly as frightened as the people they'd hurt. She put both her hands on his wrist, quite gently, and pulled a little, while trying to make her eyes communicate friendliness.

'You . . . you . . . you . . . '

She nodded, forcing herself to smile through her fear. He wouldn't be able to see that, but he must feel the movement of her mouth and realise what she was doing. And it might make her eyes look softer.

'You . . . you . . . you . . . '

The hardness of the wall behind her was the only thing that gave her any support. His hand moved a little. She kept hers on his wrist, still not gripping or tugging. At last, he let her pull him away from her mouth. Then he seized her neck and gripped hard. She forced herself to keep the smile in place.

'I haven't any money with me; or cards,' she said, choking. 'I just stepped out of the hotel for a moment. People know where I am.'

'I don't w-want money,' he said without much hesitation. His breathing was almost normal now.

'Then what?' Was this another vengeance-freak? She'd known there were raw nerves in the audience, but she'd tried so hard not to scrape any badly enough to provoke anyone. Had he lost a sibling to a paedophile?

'You . . . you . . . you . . . '

Trish closed her eyes again.

'You were r-right in there.'

'What?' She began to hope she might get out of this alive, maybe even unhurt.

'W-what you said. It was right. My brother w-w-wa . . . Shit! He died. My brother died like that. Everybody hates the killer. M-my mom's in hospital. My dad's drunk and mad at me. The killer's on death row. I'm going to write to him now. B-because of what you said.'

Trish felt tears under her eyelids. Her whole body started to shake. He let her go. She leaned forwards against his shoulder.

'I'll t-t-take you back now. You shouldn't walk alone here. It's not s-safe.'

Contre temps

RAFE MCGREGOR

Megan Brown knew she was driving the unmarked Chevy Caprice too fast as she sped towards the airport. She forced herself to slow down and control her emotions. 'Sorry.'

'What?' asked Staff Sergeant Gaffney.

Megan didn't want to tell him, but she knew he wouldn't leave it alone. 'It's just this place.'

'Quebec City?'

'The whole damn province. These Quebeckers really piss me off. Canada is supposed to be a bilingual country, but do you see any signs in English, 'cause I don't? They all speak it better than we do French, but they won't use it. And I bet they'll be out burning the flag again, tonight, just like they did last Canada Day. I mean, who the hell do they think they are?'

'Don't let it bother you,' was Gaffney's terse reply. He was a man of few words.

'I can't help it. Today is the day for all Canadians to be proud of their country. I swear I'm gonna shoot someone tonight. Why don't we let them secede if that's what they want? See how long they last without our subsidies. I make a point of never using any French when I'm here – not that I can remember much from school.'

If Gaffney was listening, he was hiding it well.

'And what about this, Staff? Why's Mills calling us back to HQ when we're in the middle of a surveillance detail? I don't like it.'

Gaffney shrugged, 'Dunno. He wants to see us, so we go an' see him. Just get us there in one piece.'

Megan sighed, but said nothing.

On arrival, they were shown straight into the superintendent's office. He was a thin, humourless man, impeccably dressed and groomed. 'Staff Sergeant Gaffney, Constable Brown? I'm Donald Mills. I'm in charge of C Division Combined Forces, as you probably know.' He glanced at the third man in the room. 'This is Lieutenant Bauche, from the SPVQ. Sit down, please. It's a pleasure to have our Ontario colleagues aboard.'

Now Megan really was worried. Aboard what? Gaffney was supposed to be running an independent surveillance, reporting to his own Combined Forces superiors back in Ontario. It didn't sound good. Out the corner of her eye she noticed the city cop leering at her. She wasn't impressed. Bauche was in his late thirties, with a shaved head, pockmarked cheeks, and teeth like a rodent. And he was a French Canadian.

'I'll tell you right out, Staff, your team has been seconded to me effective immediately. The good news is, it'll probably only be for twenty-four hours.'

Gaffney nodded, 'What about Beam, sir?'

Mills gestured towards Bauche. 'The SPVQ will be taking over until we wrap up Operation Cable Car. That's why I wanted to see Constable Brown as well. I believe you found Beam first?' he asked Megan.

'Yeah, sir. You're familiar with Godasse Monbourquette?'

'The Bandidos' armourer?'

'Yes sir. We were watching him in Toronto. He had a very brief meeting with the man we've identified as John Beam. You can't miss him because of the scar on his face. We followed him down here yesterday. So far all we know is that he entered the country from Ireland on Wednesday. He spent last night at the Hilton. At the moment he's in Battlefield Park, headed for the Citadel. We think he's going to meet someone – soon.'

'Another biker?'

'We don't know, sir.'

Mills nodded. 'Inspector Ames told me your initial work was excellent. He also said you're just waiting out your seven for promotion?'

'I hope so, sir,' she tried to sound modest.

'Glad to hear it.' He addressed Gaffney. 'To maintain continuity, I'm assigning Constable Brown to Lieutenant Bauche's squad.'

Megan started a protest – thought better of it – and shut up.

'*Mademoiselle*, I look forward to our mutual liaison,' said Bauche with a smirk.

Megan curled her lip in response.

'You'll report to Lieutenant Bauche until your team takes over the surveillance again. Thank you, Lieutenant,' said Mills.

'*Merci, monsieur*.' Bauche stood, and held the door open for Megan.

Megan took another look at him, and couldn't contain herself any longer – promotion or not. 'Sir, may I have a word in private?'

'No.'

Megan was still fuming as Bauche drove the Dodge Intrepid onto 9th Airport Street. 'Let's get a couple of things straight, Lieutenant.'

'*Oui*, if you like,' he replied genially.

'First, it's not *mademoiselle*, it's "officer" or "constable". Is that clear?'

'If you wish to remind me of your rank, I might observe that in the *Service de police de la Ville de Québec* constables show more courtesy to their officers than I have yet to see.'

Megan gritted her teeth. The jerk couldn't even speak English properly. 'I don't give a damn about the SPVQ. You've got the highest unsolved homicide rate in the country. That tells me everything I need to know.'

'*No, no –* '

'Secondly, you can drop the Gallic charm, it's wasted on me. Then you can tell me what you know about Beam.'

'I assure you, *madem* – Officer – Brown, I have been fully briefed by your commandant. Even as we chat so amiably, my deputy is taking over from your Sergeant Gaffney's deputy. This man, Beam, he is no longer in the park. He is taking a tour around *La Citadelle*. There is nothing to be concerned about. A dozen of my best men are on this job. You will see, and you will be more respectful.'

Megan doubted it. She curled her lip again, and stared out the window.

Bauche muttered something in French, and shook his head. 'I had hoped for a more cordial *détente*.' He gave Megan another lascivious smile, but she was ignoring him. He took the opportunity to run his eyes over her dark blonde hair – tied back in a ponytail – her strong shoulders, and the curve of her breasts. '*Pièce de résistance*,' he murmured to himself.

Fifteen minutes later they were still en route to the Citadel when Bauche's cell phone rang. He switched it to speaker and responded to the rapid-fire French in kind. After a minute or so he terminated the conversation abruptly.

'Well?' Megan asked.

'It seems you are not bilingual, Officer Brown. That is deplorable in a police agent, but luckily for you my English it is excellent, no?'

'No. Was it Beam?'

'*Oui*. Beam, he has left *La Citadelle*. He is now carrying a bag – a sporting bag – that he had not before.'

'Who gave it to him?'

'It was not seen. He was with a large tour group.'

Megan wasn't surprised. In addition to the city police's poor reputation, the provincial *Sûreté* had recently been rescued by the Mounties after they made a hash of the biker war between the Hell's Angels and the Bandidos. So perhaps she shouldn't have be surprised when, only two hours after she'd last set eyes on Beam, Bauche's squad lost him somewhere in the Port of Quebec. She shouldn't have been surprised, but she was. Surprised and pissed off.

Very pissed off.

Charter skimmed through the dossier a second time, hoping he'd find something to make the job more palatable. He didn't. He'd killed three times before, always with good reason, never like this. He went through it again, but there was still nothing to justify the execution. The target had been selected because he was going to embarrass a government. That was it, nothing more. And it wasn't good enough for Charter. The target was also a cop. Charter didn't kill cops. Even after four years in the Secret Service, he still believed cops were the good guys. Maybe not every single one, but they deserved the benefit of the doubt. And there was no doubt about Jake Rautenbach: all the evidence pointed to a good cop suffering from combat fatigue.

Born, Melmoth, KwaZulu-Natal, 1974. National Service, South African Medical Services, 1992. Selected for élite 7th Medical Battalion Group, 1994. Qualified Operator 5 Special Forces Brigade, 1996. Parents emigrated Canada, 1996. Commissioned, 1999. Resigned 2003, rank lieutenant. Operational deployments: Lesotho, 1998; Burundi, 2000.

There were seven more operational deployments, but no details. They were all classified above Charter's level.

Recruited by Royal Canadian Mounted Police direct for under-cover work, 2003. Rank: constable; unit: Organised Crime Branch Undercover Operations. Operational deployments: infiltration of one of six Quebec chapters of the Hell's Angels; began August 2003, ongoing.

Within three months Rautenbach had begun providing his hand-lers with top-quality intelligence. In January, they'd lost contact with him. In April, he disappeared: missing, presumed dead. Then, twelve days ago, out of the blue he'd phoned the South African Embassy in Ottawa. He'd been on the run for two months and he wanted to come in. He was completely unravelled – a nervous wreck – convinced that the Hell's Angels, the Bandidos, and his handlers all wanted him dead. Isolated and desperate, he'd reached out to the Secret Service intelligence officer that took the call. Cynthia Cele had quickly established a rapport with him and now she was the only person he trusted.

The problem, as far as the South African government was concerned, was that Rautenbach wanted to talk. He was prepared to give evidence in court against the Hell's Angels in exchange for a new identity, but he also wanted to talk to the SABC about his missions in Special Forces. The pressure of the last eight years had finally cracked him and he wanted to come clean about everything. It was a catharsis that was not going to be allowed to happen. There was no way the government was going to allow him to reveal the details of – at least – seven clandestine military operations in public. They'd sooner kill him. If Charter hadn't found his own mission so repellent, he would've laughed at the irony. Rautenbach phoned the South African embassy because he didn't trust the Mounties, and in doing so, he'd sealed his fate. It wasn't the Mounties who wanted him dead, it was the South Africans.

He was coming in tomorrow, the second of July, on Charter's thirty-sixth birthday.

Charter looked down at the sports bag with the MacMillan TTR-50 sniper rifle inside. He opened the curtains in his room at the Holiday Inn Select. The Au Coeur de Saint-Roch church towered above the plaza. Rautenbach would be at the entrance tomorrow at noon. It was fifty metres away, if that. An easy shot.

The scar on his cheek twisted as he scowled.

Megan was exhausted. She'd spent most of the night helping Bauche and his Keystone cops look for Beam. She'd been back on the job before breakfast, and she hadn't left Bauche's side all morning. It was the only way to make sure the dickhead put some effort in. But despite her efforts, and the extra men assigned to the job, Beam was nowhere to be found. Not only was Bauche incompetent and lazy, but he showed a complete lack of remorse or embarrassment. Meanwhile Beam was probably long gone. Probably left Quebec City yesterday.

Lucky for some.

After nearly five fruitless hours with Bauche, she was beginning to enjoy riling him. 'Every single hotel?'

'*Oui*, *oui*! I have heard you the first time, Officer,' he gripped the steering wheel tightly.

Sooner or later he was going to lose his temper. Megan hoped sooner. 'You've showed this photo to every reception in every hotel in this dump?'

'My men have done exactly that. I tell you again, I am in command. I give orders, and they are followed to the letter. I am rapidly tiring of your chastisement. It is irritating in the extreme.'

'What about the one we just passed?' Megan indicated over her shoulder, south on the *rue de la Couronne*.

'*No*, not that one,' said Bauche, before lapsing into French. There was a problem with the traffic up ahead, and everything had ground to a halt.

'Take off! You haven't checked the Holiday Inn?'

'*No*, Officer, I have not, nor will I be checking it.'

'You damn well will! Turn around.'

'You are a most ignorant woman, are you not? All police have been ordered to stay away from Saint-Roch. It is where Operation Cable Car is taking place. How could you not know this?'

'Because I've been too busy trying to find the suspect you lost!'

Bauche smiled, pleased to get a reaction at last. 'I am aware of this. In my position as lieutenant of criminal investigations, I know all that takes place in the *Ville de Québec*. And I know more than you, even though your Combined Forces is responsible for this operation.'

'I don't care about Operation Cable Car, I want to find Beam.'

'Ah, but you should care. Cable Car concerns an agent from your own force,' said Bauche as they inched forward in the traffic queue.

'Fascinating. Now let me out. If you won't check the Holiday Inn, I will.'

'It is not permitted. In a few minutes, your force will secure their agent outside the *Au coeur de Saint-Roch*, *l'église et la rue Saint-Joseph*. The Holiday Inn is situated next to *l'église*. We are not permitted to go there. All uniformed and plain clothes *officiers de police* have been ordered to keep away. This agent is . . . how you say . . . excitable? They do not want him scared away from – '

'I don't care. Just stop. I'll keep a low profile, no one will know.'

'*No*, I will not. This is an operation of international significance. I will not disobey orders, and neither will you. Your colleague,

he is from *Afrique du Sud* and there is an agent from their government working with the Combined Forces. It is all of the utmost
importance.'

'Where did you say he's from?' asked Megan.

Traffic stopped again, and Bauche turned to her. '*Afrique du Sud . . .*
er, Africa South?'

'South Africa. You realise Beam is South African?'

'And what of it?'

'And he's been in contact with Monbourquette. Monbourquette,
the armourer.'

They started moving again. 'I do not see what you are meaning.
The solution, it is simple. My men have contacted the hotel by
telephone. Beam is not there.'

'Does the Holiday Inn overlook this church?'

'*Oui, oui*, it does.'

Megan gripped his arm, 'And it's the only hotel where you haven't
shown this photo?'

'*Oui*, we have already discussed this matter. Let go of me,
woman, I – '

Megan was out the car before he could finish. She heard a loud
'*putain*' from behind as she dodged a couple of cars to reach the
pavement. She weaved her way through the pedestrians and broke
into a jog. The Holiday Inn receptionists needed to see the photo,
and they needed to see it now.

Charter scanned the plaza below. He'd paid for a late check-out,
and had already packed his luggage in the car. All except for the
MacMillan. In addition to its awesome killing range, the rifle was
a semi-automatic with a five-round magazine. If something went
wrong, he might get time for another shot. Might. The silencer
would help, but in all likelihood Rautenbach – nervous wreck or
not – would realise he was under fire and his training would take
over. Not to mention the Mounties. If they were any good they'd
have him covered and away in a matter of seconds. In which case it
would most likely be just the one shot. He would have to make it
count.

He checked his watch: five minutes to go.

No sign of Rautenbach or Cynthia yet. Charter had worked with
Cynthia before, in London. She was an ex-cop from Gauteng, and he
liked her. He doubted she knew anything about the execution or his
mission. He wondered if she would've agreed to meet Rautenbach if

she'd known she was being used to set him up. Probably not. Some
people had managed to keep their integrity intact. Charter's scar
twitched. He had never killed a cop before, and he didn't feel like
starting on his birthday.

Megan ran into the Holiday Inn forecourt, barged her way through
the queue, and flashed her identification card at the receptionist.

'*Bonjour madame. Je peux vous aider?*'

Did any Quebecker speak English? 'I'm looking for this man,' she
waved the photo of Beam, 'Have you seen him?' The receptionist
looked about thirteen beneath his designer stubble. He took the
photo and squinted at it.

Bauche appeared at her elbow, breathing heavily. '*Je suis agent de
police du SPVQ. Vouz avez vu cet homme?*'

Come on, come on.

'*Il est ici à l'hôtel?*'

Yes or no? Either he's been here or he hasn't.

'*Euh . . . oui, monsieur l'agent . . .* '

Yes, what? Was he here?

'*Et où est-il en ce moment?*' asked Bauche.

'*C'est bien Monsieur Charter?*'

Bauche pointed at the photo. 'This is Mr Charter. He is here now!'

Charter? It must be him. No one could mistake that scar. Megan
was thinking quickly: Beam was still in the hotel; the Mountie would
be outside the church . . .

'*Il est dans la chambre six cent huit . . .* '

She charged off. 'Come on, Bauche! He's going to kill him. We've
got to get him before he makes the hit!'

'I will take the stairs, you will take the elevator,' he shouted from
behind.

Another one of Bauche's bright ideas. There were three elevators,
so they'd be better off sticking together. Megan took the first one,
punched number sixteen, and drew her Smith & Wesson. A guest
was about to step in with her, but saw the pistol and changed his
mind. Bauche disappeared off to the right and the lift doors finally
closed. She prayed there would be no stops.

Charter saw Cynthia mount the eleven steps to the semi-circular
daïs outside the church entrance. She stopped outside the first set
of red doors and he took up the MacMillan. He rested it on the
ironing board, the last three inches of the twenty-seven inch barrel

protruding from the neat circular hole he'd cut in the window. He centred the sights on Cynthia. She was hard to miss in an orange skirt-suit that seemed all the brighter for her dark brown skin. An attractive woman, calm and poised, exactly as he remembered her. She walked slowly along the daïs, as if admiring the architecture.

Charter took his eye from the sight: three minutes after twelve.

He used the bolt action to slide the first round into the chamber. The Macmillan used heavy-calibre bullets, half an inch in diameter. The exit wound from a torso shot would be fatal, but Charter would aim for the head. Rautenbach's death might be undeserved, but it would at least be painless. He focused on Cynthia again, relaxed his shoulders and arms, and waited.

Thirty seconds later Rautenbach appeared.

Two, three, four, five . . .

Megan watched the numbers light up as the elevator climbed. How long was it going to take Bauche to run up sixteen floors? What was he thinking? Maybe if you got past the huge nose, bad skin, and buck teeth, he was a finely-tuned athlete. She doubted it.

Six, seven, eight, nine . . .

Chances were, she'd be on her own up there. She cocked a round into the chamber of the nine-mil, a compact model she was comfortable with.

Ten, eleven, twelve, thirteen . . .

She'd drawn her service pistol several times in the past six years, but never fired it in anger. Never shot to kill like her sister had. And her brother. He'd just gone out to Haiti with his regiment. He wouldn't hesitate – would she? She rested her right index finger on the trigger guard. Thanks to Bauche, she might just find out. She swallowed loudly, her mouth suddenly dry.

Fourteen, fifteen, sixteen . . . the elevator bumped to a halt.

Megan took a deep breath, moved her finger to the trigger, and flexed her knees. The door opened. She moved out quickly, weapon held low. *Six cent huit*. Room eight on the sixteenth floor. It was off to the right. She pointed the nine-mil at the door. No sign of Bauche. No time to wait. Could she kill Beam if she had to?

No time for questions.

She moved up to the right-hand side of the door, side-on. Took a last breath. 'Police!' She fired twice at the lock, kicked the door open, and burst in –

It took her less than three seconds to realise she'd screwed up. *Six* was six, not sixteen. Fucking French, why couldn't they speak more slowly? She turned and sprinted for the stairs.

Bauche was on the sixth floor. Slumped against the wall of the stairwell, flailing at a Ka-Bar knife sticking out of his shoulder. His Beretta was lying on the floor next to him. He saw her and shouted something incomprehensible.

'Where is he? Where's Beam?' she bellowed.

Bauche started gabbling again, waving downstairs.

Megan took them three at a time. Down the stairs, into the lobby, out onto the *rue de la Couronne*. But Beam, Charter, or whoever the hell he was, was gone. And he had left a decapitated corpse lying sprawled outside the *Au couer de Saint-Roch, l'église et la rue Saint-Joseph*. Megan stood on the crowded pavement and swore.

Maybe it was time for French lessons.

The perfectionist

PETER LOVESEY

The invitation dropped on the doormat of The Laurels along with a bank statement and a Guide Dogs for the Blind appeal. It was in a cream-coloured envelope made from thick, expensive-looking paper. Duncan left it to open after the others. His custom was to leave the most promising letters while he worked steadily through the others, using a paperknife that cut the envelopes tidily.

Eventually he took out a gold-edged card with his name inscribed in the centre in fine italic script. It read:

The most perfect club in the world
has the good sense to invite

Mr Duncan Driffield

a proven perfectionist

to be an honoured guest at its annual dinner
Friday, January 31st, 7.30 for 8 pm

Contact will be made later

He was wary. This could be an elaborate marketing ploy. He'd been invited to parties in the past by motor dealers and furniture retailers that turned out to be sales pitches, nothing more. Just because no product or company was mentioned, he wasn't going to be taken in. He read it through several times.

It has to be said, he liked the designation 'a proven perfectionist'. Couldn't fault their research. He was a Virgo, born under a birth-sign known for its orderly people, strivers for perfection. To see it written down as if he'd already achieved the ideal, was specially pleasing. And to see his name in such elegant script was another fine touch.

Yet it troubled him that the club was not named, nor was there any address, nor any mention of where the function was to be held. Being a thorough and cautious man, he would normally have looked them up before deciding what to do about the invitation.

The phone call came about eight-thirty the next evening. A voice that didn't need to announce it had been to a very good school spoke his name.

'Yes.'

'You received an invitation to the dinner on January 31st, I trust?'

'Which invitation was that?' Duncan said as if he was used to getting them by every post.

'A gold-edged card naming you as a proven perfectionist. May we take it that you will accept?'

'Who are you, exactly?'

'A group of like-minded people. We know you'll fit in.'

'Is there some mystery about it? I don't wish to join the Free-masons.'

'We're not Freemasons, Mr Driffield.'

'How did you get my name?'

'It was put to the committee. You were the outstanding candidate.'

'Really?' he glowed inwardly before his level-headedness returned. 'Is there any obligation?'

'You mean are we trying to sell something? Absolutely not.'

'I don't have to make a speech?'

'We don't go in for speeches. It isn't like that at all. We'll do every-thing possible to welcome you and make you feel relaxed. Transport is provided.'

'Are you willing to tell me your name?'

'Of course. It's David Hopkins. I do hope you're going to say yes.'

Why not? he thought. 'All right, Mr Hopkins.'

'Excellent. I'm sure if I ask you – as a proven perfectionist – to be ready at six-thirty, you will, to the minute. In case you were wonder-ing, it's a dinner jacket and black tie affair. I'll come for you myself. The drive takes nearly an hour at that time of day, I'm afraid. And it's Dr Hopkins actually, but please call me David.'

After the call, Duncan in his systematic way tried to track down David Hopkins in the phone directory and the Medical Register. He found three people of that name and called them on the phone, but their voices had nothing like the honeyed tone of the David Hopkins he had spoken to.

He wondered who had put his name forward. Someone must have. It would be interesting to see if he recognised David Hopkins.

He did not. Precisely on time, on the last Friday in January, Dr David Hopkins arrived, a slim, dark man in his forties, of average height. They shook hands.

'Is there anything I can bring? A bottle of whisky?'

'No, you're our guest, Duncan.'

He liked the look of David. He knew intuitively one of the special evenings in his life was in prospect.

They walked out to the car, a large black Daimler, chauffeur-driven.

'Luxury.'

'We can enjoy the wine with a clear conscience,' David explained, 'but I would be dishonest if I led you to think that was the only reason.' When they were both inside he leaned across and pulled down a blind. There was one on each window and across the part-ition between the driver and themselves. Duncan couldn't see out at all. 'This is in your interest.'

'Why is that?'

'We ask our guests to be good enough to respect the privacy of the club. If you don't know where we meet, you can't upset anyone.'

'I see. Now that we're alone, and I'm committed to coming, can you tell me some more?'

'A little. We're all of your cast of mind, actually.'

'Perfectionists?'

He smiled. 'That's one of the attributes.'

'I wondered why I was asked. Do I know any of the members?'

'I doubt it.'

'Then how – '

'Your crowning achievement.'

Duncan tried to think which achievement could have come to their notice. He'd had an unremarkable career in the civil service. Sang a bit with a local choir. Once won first prize for his sweet peas in the town flower show, but he'd given up growing them now. He could think of nothing of enough merit to interest this high-powered club.

'How many members are there?'

'Fewer than we would like. Not many meet the criteria.'

'So how many is that?'

'Currently, five.'

'Oh – as few as that?'

'We're small and exclusive.'

'I can't think why you invited me.'

'It will become clear.'

More questions from Duncan elicited little else, except that the club had been established for over a hundred years. He assumed – but had the tact not to ask – that he would be invited to join if the members approved of him this evening. How he wished he was one of those people with a fund of funny stories. He feared he was dull company.

In just under the hour, the car came to a halt and the chauffeur opened the door. Duncan glanced about him as he stepped out, wanting to get some sense of where he was. It was dark at this time, of course, but this was clearly a London square, with street lights and a park in the centre and plane trees at intervals in front of the houses. He couldn't put a name to it. The houses were terraced, and Georgian, just as they are in almost every other London square.

'Straight up the steps,' said David. 'The door is open.'

They went in, through a hallway with mirrors and a crystal chandelier that made him blink after the dim lighting in the car. David took Duncan's coat and handed it to a manservant and then opened a door.

'Gentlemen,' he said. 'May I present our guest, Mr Duncan Driffield.'

It was a smallish ante-room, and four men stood waiting with glasses of wine. Two looked quite elderly, the others about forty, or less. One of the younger pair was wearing a kilt.

The one who was probably the senior member extended a bony hand. 'Joe Franks. I'm president, through a process of elimination.'

There were some smiles at this that David didn't fully understand.

Joe Franks went on to say, 'I qualified as a member as long ago as 1934, when I was only nineteen, but I joined officially after the war.'

David, at Duncan's side, murmured something that made no sense about a body left in a trunk at Brighton railway station.

'And this well set-up fellow on my right,' said Joe Franks, 'is Wally Winthrop, the first private individual to put ricin to profitable use. Wally now owns one of the largest supermarket chains in Europe.'

'Did you say "rice"?' asked Duncan.

'No. "Ricin". A vegetable poison.'

It was difficult to see the connection between a vegetable poison and a supermarket chain. Wally Winthrop grinned and shook Duncan's hand. 'Tell you about it one of these days,' he said.

Joe Franks indicated the man in the kilt. 'Alex McPhee is our youngest member and our most prolific. Is it seven, Alex?'

'So far,' said McPhee, and this caused more amusement.

'His skene-dhu has more than once come to the aid of the club,' added Joe Franks.

Duncan wasn't too familiar with Gaelic, but he had a faint idea that the skene-dhu was the ornamental dagger worn by Highlanders in their stocking. He supposed the club used it in some form of ritual.

'And now meet Michael Pitt-Struthers, who advises the SAS on the martial arts. His knowledge of pressure points is unrivalled. Shake hands very carefully with Michael.'

More smiles, the biggest from Pitt-Struthers, who squeezed Duncan's hand in a way that left no doubt of his expertise.

'And of course you've already met our doctor member, David Hopkins, who knows more about allergy reactions than any man alive.'

With a huge effort to be sociable, Duncan remarked, 'Such a variety of talents. I can't think what you all have in common.'

Joe Franks answered, 'Each of us has committed a perfect murder.'

Duncan heard the statement and played it over in his head. He thought he'd got it right. It had been spoken with some pride. This time no one smiled. More disturbingly, no one disputed it.

'Shall we go into dinner, gentlemen?' Joe Franks suggested.

At a round table in the next room, Duncan tried to come to terms with the sensational claim he had just heard. If it was true, what on earth was he doing sharing a meal with a bunch of killers? And why had they chosen to take him into their confidence? He could shop them to the police and they wouldn't be perfect murderers any longer. Maybe it was wise not to mention this while he was seated between the martial arts expert and the Scot with the skene-dhu tucked into his sock.

The wine glasses were filled with claret by an elderly waiter. 'Hungarian,' Joe Franks confided. 'He understands no English.' He raised his glass. 'At this point, gentlemen, I propose a toast to Thomas de Quincey, author of that brilliant essay *On Murder Considered as One of the Fine Arts*, who esteemed the killing of Sir Edmund Godfrey as "the finest work of the seventeenth century", for the excellent reason that no one knew who had done it.'

'Thomas de Quincey,' said everyone, with Duncan just a half-beat slower than the rest.

'You're probably wondering what brings us together,' said Wally Winthrop across the table. 'You might think we'd be uncomfortable sharing our secrets. In fact, it works the other way. It's a tremendous relief. I don't have to tell you, Duncan, what it's like after you commit your first, living in fear of being found out, waiting for the police siren and the knock on the door. As the months pass, this panicky stage fades and is replaced by a feeling of isolation. You've set yourself apart from others by your action. You can only look forward to keeping your secret bottled up for the rest of your life. It's horrible. We've all been through it. Five years have to pass – five years without being charged with murder – before you're contacted by the club and invited to join us for a meal.'

David Hopkins briskly took up the conversation. 'It's such a break in the clouds, that discovery that you're not alone in the world. To find that what you've done is valued as an achievement and can be openly discussed. Wonderful. After all, there is worth in having committed a perfect murder.'

'How do you know you can trust each other?' Duncan asked, without giving anything away.

'Mutual self-interest. If any one of us betrayed the others, he'd take himself down as well. We're all in the same boat.'

Joe Franks explained, 'It's a safeguard that's worked for over a hundred years. One of our first members was the man better known as Jack the Ripper, who was in fact a pillar of the establishment. If *his* identity could be protected all these years, then the rest of us can breathe easy.'

'That's amazing. You know who the Ripper was?'

'Aye,' said McPhee calmly. 'And no one has ever named the laddie.'

'Can I ask?'

'Not till you join,' said Joe Franks.

Duncan hesitated. He was about to say he had no chance of joining, not having committed a murder, when some inner voice prompted him to shut up. These people were acting as if he was one of them. Maybe, through some ghastly mistake, they'd been told he'd once done away with a fellow human being. And maybe it was in his interest not to disillusion them.

'We have to keep to the rules,' Wally Winthrop was explaining. 'Certain information is only passed on to full members.'

Joe Franks added, 'And we are confident you will want to join. All we ask is that you respect the rules. Not a word must be spoken to anyone else about this evening, or the existence of the club. The ultimate sanction is at our disposal for anyone foolish enough to betray us.'

'The ultimate sanction – what's that?' Duncan huskily enquired.

No one answered, but the Scot beside him grinned in a way Duncan didn't care for.

'The skene-dhu?' said Duncan.

'Or the pressure point,' said Joe Franks, 'or the allergy reaction, or whatever we decide is tidiest. But it won't happen in your case.'

'No chance,' Duncan affirmed. 'My lips are sealed.'

The starters were served, and he was pleased when the conversation shifted to murders in fiction, and some recent crime novels. Faintly he listened as they discussed *The Silence of the Lambs*, but he was trying to think what to say if someone asked about the murder he was supposed to have committed. They were sure to return to him before the evening ended, and then it was essential to sound convincing. If they got the idea he was a mild man who wouldn't hurt a fly he was in real trouble.

Towards the end of the meal, he spoke up. It seemed a good idea to take the initiative. 'This has been a brilliant evening. Is there any chance I could join?'

'You've enjoyed yourself?' said Joe Franks. 'That's excellent. A kindred spirit.'

'It's got to be more than that if you want to be a member,' Winthrop put in. "You've got to provide some evidence that you're one of us.'

Duncan swallowed hard. 'Don't you have that? I wouldn't be here if you hadn't found something out.'

'There's a difference between finding something out and seeing the proof.'

'That won't be easy.'

'It's the rule.'

He tried another tack. 'Can I ask something? How did you get on to me?'

There were smiles all round. Winthrop said, 'You're surprised that we succeeded where the police failed?'

'Experience,' Joe Franks explained. 'We're much better placed than the police to know how it was done.'

Pitt-Struthers, the strong, silent man who trained the SAS, said, 'We know you were at the scene on the evening it happened, and we know no one else had a stronger motive or a better opportunity.'

'But we must have the proof,' insisted Winthrop.

'The weapon,' suggested McPhee.

'I disposed of it,' Duncan improvised. He was not an imaginative man, but this was an extreme situation. 'You would, wouldn't you?'

'No,' said McPhee. 'I just give mine a wee wipe.'

'Well, it's up to you, old boy,' Winthrop told Duncan. 'Only you can furnish the evidence.'

'How long do I have?'

'The next meeting is in July. We'd like to confirm you as a full member then.'

The conversation moved on to other areas, a lengthy discussion about the problems faced by the Crown Prosecution Service.

The evening ended with coffee, cognac and cigars. Soon after, David Hopkins said that the car would be outside.

On the drive back, Duncan, deeply perturbed and trying not to show it, pumped David for information.

'It was an interesting evening, but it's left me with a problem.'

'What's that?'

'I, em, wasn't completely sure which murder of mine they were talking about.'

'Do you mean you're a serial killer?'

Duncan gulped. He hadn't meant that at all. 'I've never thought of myself as one.' Recovering his poise a little, he added, 'A thing like that is all in the mind, I suppose. Which one do they have me down for?'

'The killing of Sir Jacob Drinkwater at the Brighton Civil Service Conference in 1995.'

Drinkwater. He remembered being at the conference and the sensation of the senior civil servant at the Irish Office being found dead in his hotel room on the Sunday morning. 'That was supposed to be a heart attack.'

'Officially, yes,' said David.

'But you heard something else?'

'I happen to know the pathologist who did the autopsy. A privileged source. They didn't want the public knowing how Sir Jacob was killed, and thinking it was a new method employed by the terrorists. How did you introduce the cyanide? Was it in his aftershave?'

'Trade secret,' Duncan answered cleverly.

'Of course the security people in their blinkered way couldn't imagine it was anything but a political assassination. They didn't know you had a grudge against him dating from years back, when he was your boss in the Land Registry.'

Someone had got their wires crossed. It was a man called *Charlie* Drinkwater who'd made Duncan's life a misery and blighted his career. No connection with Sir Jacob. Giving nothing away, he said smoothly, 'And you worked out that I was at the conference?'

'Same floor. Missed the banquet on the Saturday evening, giving you a fine opportunity to break into his room and plant the cyanide. So we have motive, opportunity.'

'And means?' said Duncan.

David laughed. "Your house is called The Laurels, for the bushes all round the garden. It's well known that if you soak laurel leaves and evaporate the liquid, you get a lethal concentration of cyanide. Isn't that how you made the stuff?'

'I'd rather leave you in suspense,' said Duncan. He was thinking hard. 'If I apply to join the club, I may have to give a demonstration.'

'There's no "if" about it. They liked you. You're expected to join.'

'I could decide against it.'

'Why?'

'Private reasons.'

David turned to face him, his face creased in concern. 'They'd take a very grave view of that, Duncan. We invited you along in good faith.'

'But no obligation, I thought.'

'Look at it from the club's point of view. We're vulnerable now. You're dealing with dangerous men, Duncan. I can't urge you strongly enough to co-operate.'

'But if I can't prove that I killed a man – '

'You must think of something. We're willing to be convinced. If you cold-shoulder us, or betray us, I can't answer for the consequences.'

A sobering end to the evening.

For the next three weeks he got little sleep, and when he did drift off he would wake with nightmares of fingers pressing on his arteries or skene-dhus being thrust between his ribs. He faced a classic dilemma. Either admit he hadn't murdered Sir Jacob Drinkwater and was a security risk to the club; or concoct some fake evidence, bluff his way in, and spend the rest of his life hoping they wouldn't catch him out. Faking evidence wouldn't be easy. They were intelligent men.

'*You must think of something,*' David Hopkins had urged.

Being methodical, he went to the British Newspaper Library and spent many hours rotating the microfilm, studying accounts of Sir Jacob's murder. It only depressed him more, reading about the involvement of Special Branch, the Anti-Terrorist Squad and MI5. 'The files remain open' the papers said. Open to whom? With all that high-security involvement how could any ordinary man acquire the evidence the club insisted on seeing?

More months went by.

Duncan weighed the possibility of pointing out to the members that they'd made a mistake. Surely, he thought in rare optimistic moments, they would see that it wasn't his fault.

He was just an ordinary bloke caught up in something out of his league. He could promise to say nothing to anyone, in return for a guarantee of personal safety. Then he remembered the eyes of some of those people around the table, and he knew how unrealistic it was.

One morning in May, out of desperation, he had a brilliant idea. It arose from something David Hopkins had said in the car on the way home from the club. '*Do you mean you're a serial killer?*' At the time it had sounded preposterous. Now, it could be his salvation. Instead of striving to link himself to the murder of Sir Jacob, he would claim another killing – and show them some evidence they couldn't challenge. He'd satisfy the rules of the club and put everyone at their ease.

The brilliant part was this. He didn't need to kill anyone. He would claim to have murdered some poor wretch who had actually committed suicide. All he needed was a piece of evidence from the scene. Then he'd tell the Perfectionists he was a serial killer who dressed up his murders as suicide. They would be forced to agree how clever he was and admit him to the club. After a time, he'd give up going to the meetings and no one would bother him because they'd think their secrets were safe with him.

It was just a matter of waiting. Somebody, surely, would do away with himself before the July meeting of the club. Each day Duncan studied the *Telegraph*, and no suicide – well, no suicide he could claim as a murder – was reported. At the end of June, he found an expensive-looking envelope on his doormat and knew with a sickening certainty who it was from.

The most perfect club in the world
takes pleasure in inviting

Mr Duncan Driffield

a prime candidate for membership

to present his credentials after dinner
on July 19th, 7.30 for 8 pm

Contact will be made later

This time the wording didn't pamper his ego at all. It filled him with dread. In effect it was a sentence of death. His only chance of a reprieve rested on some fellow creature topping himself in the next two weeks.

He took to buying three newspapers instead of one, still with no success.

Mercifully, and in the nick of time, his luck changed. News of a suicide reached him, but not through the press. He was phoned one morning by an old civil service colleague, Harry Hitchman. They'd met occasionally since retiring, but they weren't the closest of buddies, so the call came out of the blue.

'Some rather bad news,' said Harry. 'Remember Billy Fisher?'

'Of course I remember him,' said Duncan. 'We were in the same office for twelve years. What's happened?'

'He jumped off a hotel balcony last night. Killed himself.'

'Billy? I can't believe it!'

'Nor me when I heard. Seems he was being treated for depression.'

'I had no idea. He was always cracking jokes in the office. A bit of a comedian, I always thought.'

'They're the people who crack, aren't they? All that funny stuff is just a front.'

'His wife Sue must be devastated.'

'That's why I'm phoning round. She's with her sister. She understands that everyone will be wanting to offer sympathy and help if they can, but for the present she'd like to be left to come to terms with this herself.'

'OK.' Duncan hesitated. 'This happened only last night, you said?' Already, an idea was forming in his troubled brain.

'Yes. He was staying overnight at some hotel in Mayfair. A reunion of some sort.'

'Do you happen to know which one?'

'Which reunion?'

'No. Which hotel.'

'The Excelsior. Thirteenth floor. People talk about thirteen being unlucky. It was in Billy's case.'

Sad as it was, this *had* to be Duncan's salvation. Billy Fisher was as suitable a 'murder victim' as he could have wished for. Someone he'd actually worked with. He could think of a motive, make up some story of an old feud, later.

For once in his life, he needed to throw caution to the winds and act immediately. The police would have sealed Billy's hotel

room pending some kind of investigation. Surely a proven perfectionist could think of a way to get inside and pick up some
personal item that would pass as evidence that he had murdered his
old colleague.

He took the five-twenty-five to London. At this time most other
travellers were going up to town for an evening's entertainment.
Duncan sat alone, avoiding eye contact and working out his plan.
First he needed to find out which room on the thirteenth floor Billy
had occupied, and then devise a way of getting in there. Through
the two-hour journey he was deep in concentration, applying his
brain to the challenge. By the time they reached Waterloo, he knew
exactly what to do.

A taxi ride brought him to the hotel, a high-rise building near
Shepherd Market. He glanced up, counting each set of windows with
its wrought-iron balcony outside, and thought of Billy's leap from
the thirteenth. Personally, he wouldn't have gone so high. A fall
from the sixth would have killed anyone, and more quickly.

Doing his best to look like one of the guests, he stepped briskly
through the revolving doors into the spacious, carpeted foyer and
over to the lift, which was waiting unoccupied. No one gave him a
second glance. It was a huge relief when the door slid across and he
was alone and rising.

So far, the plan was working beautifully. He got out at the twelfth
level and used the stairs to reach the thirteenth. It was now around
seven-thirty, and he was wary of meeting people on their way out to
dinner. He paused to let a couple ahead of him go through the swing
doors. They didn't turn round. He moved along, looking for a door
marked 'Staff Only' or something similar. There had to be a place
where the chambermaid kept her trolley, and he found it just the
other side of those swing doors.

At this time of day the rooms were made up and the maid had gone
off duty. Duncan found some worksheets attached to a clipboard
hanging from a nail in the wall. All the thirteenth-floor rooms were
listed, with ticks beside some of them showing, presumably, those
that had needed a complete change of linen and towels. On the latest
sheet, number 1307 had been struck out and marked 'not for cleaning'. No other room was so marked. He had found Billy Fisher's
hotel room. Easy as shelling peas.

He took a look at the door of 1307 before returning to the lift.
No policeman was on duty outside. It wasn't as if a man had been
murdered in there.

Down in the foyer, he marched coolly up to the desk and looked at the pigeon hole system where the keys were kept. He'd noticed before how automatically reception staff will hand over keys when asked. The key to 1307 was in place. Deliberately Duncan didn't ask for it. 1305 – the room next door – was also available and he was given it without fuss.

Up on the thirteenth again, he let himself into 1305, taking care not to leave fingerprints. His idea was to get out on the balcony and climb across the short gap to the balcony of 1307. No one would suspect an entry by that route.

The plan had worked brilliantly up to now. The curtains were drawn in 1305. He didn't switch on the light, thinking he could cross to the window and get straight out to the balcony. Unfortunately his foot caught against a suitcase some careless guest had left on the floor. He stumbled, and was horrified to hear a female voice from the bed call out, 'Is that you, Elmer?'

Duncan froze. This wasn't part of the plan. The room should have been unoccupied. He'd collected the key from downstairs.

The voice spoke again. 'Did you get the necessary, honey? Did you have to go out for it?'

Duncan was in turmoil, his heart thumping. The plan hadn't allowed for this.

'Why don't you put on the light, Elmer?' the voice said. 'Now I'm in bed I don't mind. I was only a little shy of being seen undressing.'

What could he do? If he spoke, she would scream. Any minute now, she would reach for the bedside switch. The plan had failed. His one precious opportunity of getting off the hook was gone.

'Elmer?' The voice was suspicious now.

In the civil service, there had been a procedure for everything. Duncan's home life was similar, well-ordered and structured. Now he was floundering, and next he panicked. Take control, something inside him urged. Take control, man. He groped his way to the source of the sound, snatched up a pillow and smothered the woman's voice. There were muffled sounds, and there was struggling, and he pressed harder. And harder. And finally it all stopped.

Silence.

He could think again, thank God, but the realisation of what he had done appalled him.

He'd killed someone. He really *had* killed someone now.

His brain reeled and pulses pounded in his head and he wanted to break down and sob. Some instinct for survival told him to think, think, think.

By now, Elmer must have returned to the hotel to be told the room-key had been collected. They'd be opening the door with a master key any minute.

Must get out, he thought.

The balcony exit was still the safer way to go. He crossed the room to the glass doors, slid them across and looked out.

The gap between this balcony and that of 1307 was about a metre – not impossible to bridge, but daunting when you looked down and thought of Billy Fisher hurtling towards the street below. In his agitated state, Duncan didn't hesitate. He put a foot on the rail and was up and over and across.

Just as he expected, the doors to 1307 were unfastened. He pushed them open and stepped inside. And the light came on.

Room 1307 was full of people. Not policemen, nor hotel staff, but people who looked familiar, all smiling.

One of them said, 'Caught you, Duncan. Caught you good and proper, my old mate.' It was Billy Fisher, alive and grinning all over his fat face.

Duncan said, 'You're . . . ?'

'Dead meat? No. You've been taken for a ride, old chum. Have a glass of bubbly, and I'll tell you all about it.'

A champagne glass was put in his shaking hand. Everyone closed in, watching his reaction – as if it mattered. He *knew* the faces.

'Wondering where you've seen them before?' said Billy. 'They're actors, mostly, earning a little extra between engagements. You know them better as the Perfectionists. They look different out of evening dress, don't they?'

He knew them now: David Hopkins, the doctor; McPhee, the skene-dhu specialist; Joe Franks, the trunk murderer; Wally Winthrop, the poisoner; and Pitt-Struthers, the martial arts man. In jeans and T-shirts and a little shame-faced at their roles in the deception, they looked totally unthreatening.

'You've got to admit it's a brilliant con,' said Billy. 'Retirement is so boring. I needed to turn my organising skills to something creative, so I thought this up. Mind, it had to be good to take you in.'

'Why me?'

'Well, I knew you were up for it from the old days, and Harry Hitchman – where are you, Harry?'

A voice from the background said, 'Over here.'

'I knew Harry wouldn't mind playing along. So I rigged it up. Did the job properly. Civil service training. Got the cards printed nicely. Rented the private car and the room and hired the actors and stood you all a decent dinner. I was the Hungarian waiter, by the way, but you were too preoccupied with the others to spot my false moustache. And when you took it all in, as I knew you would – being such a serious-minded guy – it was worth every penny. I wanted to top it with a wonderful finish, so I dreamed up the suicide, and' – he quivered with laughter – 'you took the bait again.'

'You knew I'd come up here?'

'It was all laid on for your benefit, old sport. You were totally taken in by the perfect murder gag, and you were bound to look for a get-out, so I fabricated one for you. Harry told you I'd jumped off the balcony, but I wasn't the fall-guy.'

'Bastard,' said Duncan.

'Yes, I am,' said Billy without apology. 'It's my second career.'

'And the woman in the room next door – is she an actress, too?'

'Which woman?'

'Oh, come on,' said Duncan. 'You've had your fun.'

Billy was shaking his head. 'We didn't expect you to come through the room next door. Is that how you got on the balcony? Typical Duncan Driffield, going the long way round. Which woman are you talking about?'

From the corridor outside came the sound of hammering on a door. Duncan covered his ears.

'What's up with him?' said Billy.

The Lammergeier vulture

CHRISTINE POULSON

Anne was every inch the Englishwoman abroad: in itself that wasn't a good enough reason to murder her, but it certainly made the task more palatable. Gerald regarded his wife with distaste. Her broad-brimmed straw hat had left a red rim on her forehead and her fair hair was lank and wispy. Her ankles were lumpy with mosquito bites and her cotton shirt was creased.

They were in the shady construction above the throne room at Knossos, where they had taken refuge from the heat and the crowds. The swallows that nested in the corners of the roof darted and wheeled above their heads. Gerald was well aware that Anne was more interested in the birds than she was in the Minoan antiquities. In the past this, too, would have been a source of irritation. But after all it was bird-watching which had persuaded her to come to Crete and bird-watching which would get him out of his fix.

Gerald had planned the accident for the last few days of the holiday, partly because he thought it would look less suspicious, but also because he needed time to work himself up to it. The ten days they had so far spent in Crete had certainly helped. The history of the island was bloody and cruel. The Mycenaeans, the Romans, the Venetians, the Turks, the Germans – they had all invaded and they had all left their mark. Death was everywhere. The museums were stuffed with sarcophagi the size and shape of hip-baths. At one archaeological site there was even evidence of human sacrifice. One more corpse would be neither here nor there, Gerald told himself.

He smiled at his wife. 'All right, darling?'

Anne smiled back. 'Fine. I think I'll sit here a bit longer. I'm enjoying the shade. You go ahead and explore the palace.'

Gerald stepped out into the sun. It was as if a hot and heavy cloak had been dropped on his shoulders. He felt a prickling of sweat on his back and chest. It was always the same: at first the heat seemed intolerable but after a few moments one grew accustomed to it. The glare of sunlight off the stone hurt his eyes and he fumbled for his sunglasses in the leather shoulder bag that he always carried south of the Alps. As he made his way down the steps he was engulfed by a crowd of tourists coming up. He stood still and let them flow round him. It was like being jostled by a herd of cows. When he was at last alone, he walked over to the parapet. There was a fine view of the palace storeroom, open to the sky now, but still containing large earthenware jars for wine and oil. He stopped to admire the pots. Robust yet elegant. Ceramics were something he knew a lot about. In fact they were what had brought him and Anne together in the first place.

His thoughts drifted back to that day five years ago when he had gone to Lavender House to value its contents for insurance. As he sat there with Anne in the elegantly proportioned room, examining her father's fine collection of eighteenth-century English creamware, it dawned on him that he had found the love of his life. Not Anne, no, oh God, no! It was the house. Not very large, or very grand, just a little Regency villa in Greenwich, but it was perfect, inside and out. It was one of Gerald's profoundest beliefs that beautiful things belong by rights to the person who can most appreciate them. And no one appreciated beautiful things more than he did. Oh, Anne was fond of Lavender House, of course she was – it had belonged to her parents and she'd grown up there – but she didn't care for it the way he did. It was really just an accident of birth that she was living there instead of him. Luckily there was a way to rectify that. Anne was lonely. Both her parents had recently died within a few months of each other. She was nearly forty and her job as a biology teacher at a private girl's school in North London didn't provide many opportunities for meeting men. In her spare time she ran a local Girl Guide pack – Gerald suppressed a smile when she told him about that – and went bird-watching. He'd been able to let her make most of the running. Six months after that first meeting they were married.

It was unfortunate that Gerald's job at the auction house had come to an end so soon after that. The old lady had been sharper than she looked, hadn't believed his valuation, and he still felt that the direc- tor been extraordinarily stuffy about what was, after all, just a bit of private enterprise. Anne had been very good about it – of course he hadn't told her everything – and had helped to set him up in the little antique shop in Kensington High Street. And now that had gone wrong, too, and this time he had to answer to Michael. He'd been running at a loss and Michael's proposition had seemed like the answer to a prayer. At first Gerald hadn't really understood. Michael looked and talked like any other prosperous business man, a bit flash maybe with his black Mercedes and heavy gold cuff-links, but nothing out of the ordinary. That was before Michael had explained how recourse to the law wasn't really an option in his line of work. There were, however, other ways of making sure that no-one went back on a deal. And no-one ever had. 'At least . . . I tell a lie,' Michael said. He smiled at Gerald. 'There was someone once. Remember that bloke who was found in a burned out car in Epping Forest last year? Never did identify the body, did they?' Gerald looked at him uncertainly, wondering if this was a joke. He saw that it wasn't. And now Michael was insisting that Gerald had abstracted one of those packets of white powder that he had agreed to bring over from Holland in a shipment of dodgy Delft vases. It was all a mistake, but he was demanding that Gerald pay him double its street value . . .

This was something Anne wouldn't be understanding about.

And yet in the end she herself had solved his problem by suggesting the holiday in Crete. He had jumped at the opportunity: it would at least get him out of the country. As he was flicking listlessly through the guide-book, he had come across the section on flora and fauna, and a more long-term solution had occurred to him. 'The Lammergeier vulture,' he read, 'wing span up to three metres. Habitat: remote mountain ranges. Nests in caves on precipices.' Precipices! Remote! The words seemed to jump off the page. He could see the towering, craggy cliff, hear the sea thundering below. The eager ornithologist, trying to get a glimpse of one of these magnificent creatures, leans out just a little too far and . . . Well, who was to say that it was anything but a tragic accident.

Crete was the perfect place for it. In England there would have been far too close a scrutiny. Not just from the police but from Antony Evans, too. Just his luck that Anne's solicitor should have been married to an old friend of Anne's. Since that friend had died a couple of years ago, Evans had been hanging around far too much for Gerald's liking. Interfering bastard! Gerald was almost sure that if it hadn't been for Evans he could have persuaded Anne to dip deeper into her capital and then all this wouldn't have been necessary.

And now it was almost time to put the plan into action. Gerald had been very careful. He had waited for Anne to suggest the excursion in search of the Lammergeier vulture. He had known that she would. It was one of the rarest birds in Europe.

A hand fell on Gerald's shoulder. He jerked as if he'd been electrocuted. He turned to see a man pointing something grey and metallic at him. For a terrible moment, he thought one of Michael's men had tracked him down. Then he saw the smiling Japanese faces, one male and one female. It was a camera the man was offering to him. Now he was gesturing to himself and his companion. He wanted Gerald to take a photograph of them. Expansive with relief, Gerald gave them his most charming smile, put his bag down, and took charge of the camera. It was a big Nikon with a lot of attachments and it took the man a minute or two of sign language to show Gerald how to use it. Then another group of tourists arrived. It was a while before he could get a clear shot of the honeymooning couple.

At last it was accomplished. They parted with nods and smiles. Gerald picked up his bag and went to look for Anne.

It wasn't until late that evening when they arrived at their hotel on the south-east coast that he realised his passport had been stolen.

The tourist police were adamant. Gerald would have to drive back to Iraklion and get a temporary visa from the British Consul. Otherwise he would not be allowed to leave the country. There was nothing for it, Anne's accident would have to be delayed for a day. It would look strange if he didn't get this problem straightened out right away and anyway he didn't want to find himself stranded in Crete afterwards.

Normally, he would have persuaded Anne to share the driving, but she'd gone down with food-poisoning – those shrimps at lunch probably – and had spent the night throwing up in the bathroom. Gerald was furious with her. If anything further had been needed to harden his heart, this was it: a two and a half hour drive each way to Iraklion – much of it on winding mountain roads. And it wasn't as if he had a decent car. Anne was too mean to hire one of those sporty Suzuki Jeeps and he was stuck with a little Fiat without air-conditioning.

When Gerald got to the Embassy he spent the whole day being shunted from official to official. He didn't even have time for a proper lunch. By the time he arrived back at Makriyiolos at seven o'clock in the evening he felt like a wrung-out rag. His shirt was sticking to his back and he wanted nothing more than a long, cold beer.

Anne wasn't in their room and her handbag had gone, too. He looked around for a note. Nothing. Well, she couldn't have gone far without the car. He washed and changed his shirt. Then he went to reception to see if she'd left a message.

The proprietor explained that Madame Maitland had gone out around two o'clock. She had told the proprietor that she wanted to go bird-watching and had asked about the best place to hire a moped. Had she not returned? The proprietor looked grave. Perhaps Madame had sprained her ankle, or, God forbid, an accident on the road . . . His grandson would help Mr Maitland to search for her. He waved away Gerald's objections. No, no, he must insist. He turned and issued a peremptory command through the bead curtain that led to the family's living quarters. A swarthy youth wearing a white t-shirt with the sleeves cut off appeared.

This, it seemed, was Yiorgos. He spoke just enough English to direct Gerald along the coast road and up into the mountains along a series of hair-pin bends. This suited Gerald just fine. He didn't want to talk. He needed time to think. It hadn't occurred to him for a single moment that the silly bitch would go on her own. Suppose she *had* sprained her ankle. It would scupper all his plans. He wanted to thump the steering wheel in frustration.

Higher and higher they climbed. The little hire car laboured as Gerald nursed it up one in four gradients. He was beginning to feel that he was welded to his seat when Yiorgos gave a grunt and indicated that Gerald was to turn right.

'Up here?' Gerald was incredulous. It was no more than a dirt track.

Yiorgos nodded. Gerald shrugged and turned off the road. They jolted and rattled over the rutted track, the wheels throwing up stones that clanged alarmingly on the underside of the car.

'Madame,' Yiorgos said suddenly.

There by the side of the track stood a white moped. Beyond it a footpath led up among rocky outcrops onto the headland.

Gerald pulled up behind it. Without a word he and Yiorgos got out of the car. It was cooler up here and there was a stiff breeze.

'Anne!' Gerald shouted. 'Anne! Where are you?'

They stood and listened. There was no reply.

They struggled up the path, Gerald calling out Anne's name from time to time, Yiorgos calling 'Madame'.

A spectacular sunset of dusty pink and coral and orange was blossoming in the west. The sky above them had darkened to that wonderful blue that always made Gerald think of Bellini altarpieces. As they got higher a series of headlands, each hazier than the last, revealed itself. The vegetation grew sparser and scrubbier. They were coming to the crest of the headland. The path wound round huge rocks. The cliffs were steeper, sheer in places.

Gerald became aware of a faint whispering sound. It was a few moments before he realised that it was surf breaking on rocks a long way down. They reached the summit. There was a drop of about fifty metres almost straight into the sea. As he stood looking down, Gerald shivered. Even with the thought of Michael to spur him on, could he really have pushed Anne off here? A flash of light caught his eye. The setting sun was glinting on the lenses of a pair of binoculars lying far below on a rock. Gerald had scarcely had time to take in the significance of this, when Yiorgos gave a squeal of alarm and grabbed his arm. Startled, Gerald looked up. With his free hand Yiorgos was crossing himself. He was muttering something in Greek and looking up into the evening sky. Gerald followed his gaze. His stomach lurched. The hairs stood up on the back of his neck. About twenty feet up, floating towards them on motionless wings was the most enormous bird Gerald had ever seen. The creature had a wing-span of at least eight feet. As it drifted over their heads, its shadow fell on their upturned faces. He glimpsed a hooked beak and talons big enough to seize a child.

It was the Lammergeier vulture.

'I am desolated that your trip to our island has ended in this tragic mishap.'

It was not the first time Captain Michaelaki had said this, nor did he suppose that it would be the last. Every year there was at least one fatality. It was hardly surprising given the millions of tourists that visited Crete. Usually it was some young idiot without a helmet speeding around a mountain bend on a Vespa, occasionally an accident in the water. A fall from a cliff was rarer . . .

Behind him the ancient air-conditioning unit clattered and whirred. He looked thoughtfully across his mahogany desk at Gerald. The unfortunate lady's binoculars on the rocks, her straw hat caught in a bush half-way down the cliff, *A Field-Guide to the Birds of Europe* wedged in a crevice: the story they told could not be clearer. And what better alibi could Mr Maitland have? At the very moment his wife had been setting out on her moped, he had been sitting in the office of the vice-consul in the British Embassy in Iraklion. There were no gaps in his story and the hotel proprietor's grandson had accompanied him to the scene of the accident. And yet. . . and yet . . . why was the man so calm? The English were of course noted for their – what was the word? – yes, sang froid. But still . . . he thought of other British holiday makers to whom he had broken bad news, the crumpled clothes, the faces bewildered and red from sun-burn and tears. He noted Gerald's tailored shorts, the white linen shirt with the sleeves turned up to reveal tanned forearms, the expensive leather shoulder bag. He had met many middle-aged men like Gerald: Italian or French, or even, it had to be admitted, Greek: a little too dapper, a little too trim. There was probably another woman somewhere. But after all, why not . . . family was family, sex was, well, sex was something else. His thoughts strayed to a certain young widow in a flat near the harbour at Sitia . . .

With an effort Captain Michaelaki brought his thoughts back to the present. Gerald was looking expectantly at him.

The Captain cleared his throat. 'I am hopeful, but not, you understand, confident that we shall recover the poor lady's body.' He prided himself on the elegance and correctness of his English, better than many a native speaker he had often been told. 'Hopeful, but not confident,' he repeated. 'The currents – it could be days or . . . ' He frowned and shrugged his shoulders to indicate that the body might never be recovered.

'How long must I stay?' Gerald asked. 'There will be so much to sort out at home.'

Captain Michaelaki spread his hands. 'I see no need to detain you at present.'

'But won't you need me to identify the . . . to identify my wife.'

'The manager of the hotel has kindly offered to do to that. If it should be necessary.' Or possible, he thought, after the fish had done their work. But in truth identification wasn't likely to be much of a problem. There wouldn't be more than one blonde, middle-aged woman washed up on the beach or found tangled in a fishing-net.

'It only remains for me to extend my heart-felt condolences. Here is my card.' He pushed it across the desk. 'Please feel free to contact me at any time.'

As Gerald got to his feet, he said. 'If you should find her . . .'

Captain Michaelaki knew what he was going to say. 'We will of course co-operate fully with British Consul in arranging for the dear lady's remains to be sent home.'

The Captain opened the door for Gerald and watched him walk down the corridor. Something about the set of his shoulders revived his earlier suspicions. He felt a crazy impulse to call him back. All his instincts told him that there was something wrong here. But what exactly? He watched as Gerald became a dark shape against the light from the door onto the street, and then disappeared altogether. A formal report would be forwarded to the British authorities – that

was always the case with the death of a holidaying British national –
and they would hold an inquest. It might be worth having a quiet
word with the vice-consul the next time they met for a glass of
brandy and a game of backgammon . . .

Gerald paid off the taxi at the top of Croom's Hill so that he could
walk the rest of the way and savour the anticipation of taking possession for just a little longer. During the winter the view from here
took in the loop of river round the Isle of Dogs and you could see for
miles across north London. Today the leaves obscured that view but
through a gap in the trees he caught a glimpse of Canary Wharf
looking surprisingly close in the afternoon sun.

Gerald took a firmer grip on his case and set off down the hill. On
this warm Saturday in July Greenwich had a festive air. A silver Rolls
Royce with ribbons on the bonnet was parked outside the Catholic
Church of Our Ladye Star of the Sea. In Greenwich Park people
were strolling with their children and lovers lay entwined on the
grass. Somewhere nearby a wood-pigeon was cooing. Was it Henry
James or Edith Wharton who said that 'summer afternoon' were the
most beautiful words in the English language? How right they had
been. Gerald felt a sense of well-being that was inseparable from the
warmth of the sun.

Really things couldn't have worked out better. He was well aware
that the Captain suspected him of murdering his wife. How ridiculous the man had been with his pedantically formal English! All
the same there had been a shrewdness about him that would have
made Gerald uneasy if he really had murdered his wife. And that was
the delicious irony of it. He was completely in the clear. Good old
Anne had done his dirty work for him.

A bend in the road and Lavender House came into view. His
footsteps quickened. The house was set back a little and a laurel
hedge screened it from the road. The late afternoon sun had transformed the upper windows into sheets of gold. He turned into the
little circular drive and stood there just drinking it all in: the little
portico with its fluted columns and cobweb fanlight, the glistening
ivy clinging to the walls, the delicious contrast between red brick
and white paint.

He frowned. Right in the middle of the little front lawn was a
child's tricycle. Those brats from next door must have been making free with the garden again. The yellow and blue plastic jarred
horribly. It was a small thing, but it had broken his mood. Anne had

been too easy-going about lost balls and so on. That would have to change. He picked up his case and stepped briskly towards the house.

As he lifted his key to the lock he felt a thrill that was almost erotic. At last he was taking possession. He fumbled for a moment or two. The key wouldn't go in. He looked harder at the lock. It was a Banham. His key was a Yale.

He stepped back and looked up at the house. Something else was wrong. Now that the sun had left the windows the house had a blind, pained look. He saw that the chinoiserie curtains in the first floor drawing room had gone. In their place were the kind of curtains he thought of as tart's knickers, great drooping festoons of some ghastly chintz. He stepped over to the window of the little study on the left of the front door and cupped his hands around his eyes against the light. He saw polished floor-boards, a small black leather sofa. Where were the little escritoire, the Persian rug?

He went back to the front door and leant on the door bell. Deep inside the house a child begin to bawl. Footsteps approached. There was the rattle of the safety chain being slotted into place. The door was opened and a woman of about thirty with abundant frizzy dark hair looked out. He had never seen her before in his life.

He heard himself stammer: 'Who are you? How long, how, that is, when you did you . . .?'

'We moved in yesterday.'

A wave of dizziness swept over him. He put out a hand to the door jamb to support himself. The woman misinterpreted the gesture. A look of alarm appeared on her face and she began to close the door.

'Please,' Gerald said. 'It's all right. It's just that . . . I live here . . . I mean, used to . . .'

Something in the woman's face changed.

'Are you Mr Maitland?'

He nodded.

'Wait a minute.' She closed the door.

He heard her shoes clack-clacking away on the polished floor boards. A few moments later they returned. She opened the door and thrust a brown envelope through the gap.

'The solicitor left this for you.'

She closed the door.

Gerald's knees were trembling. He only just made it back to the pavement. He sat down with his feet in the gutter and looked at the envelope. It was A5 size and stiff. The flap was stuck down with sellotape. He fumbled with it for a moment or two, then tore it open.

A passport slithered out and flopped onto the pavement. He opened it, and saw his own face staring back up at him. He felt inside the envelope and brought out a single sheet of paper.

DEAR GERALD,

Did you really think I had no idea of what you've been up to? Long before you were so keen to go bird-watching with me, I decided it was time to hatch a plot of my own. A clean break is always best, don't you agree? By the time you read this Lavender House will have been sold, the furniture and ceramics auctioned off, and Antony and I will have started our new life together. It wouldn't be so very difficult for you to find us but I wouldn't bother if I were you. I think the police would be very interested in an account of your recent activities and in a sample of what I found under the spare bed. Both are lodged somewhere safe.

I never did get to see the Lammergeier vulture. But you can't have everything, can you?

Gerald was half aware of a car drawing up at the kerb. A shadow fell across the page. He felt a chill before he even looked up. Just for a second he thought it was the police.

When he saw who was standing over him, he wished that it was.

Lost

RUSSELL JAMES

The first they heard of it in the Deptford Arms was fifteen minutes before he arrived. Vinnie Dirkin had stumbled in, a wide grin across that smashed face of his, and he'd produced the photo from his trouser pocket. It had a creased and damaged look like Dirkin's face, and he flattened it out on the low counter.

'Have you seen her?' he asked. 'There could be money in it.'

Chippy Naylor was at the counter getting the drinks. 'Where's the snap from, Vinnie – her mummy's photo album?'

Dirkin leant back. 'There's a detective trying to find her.'

'Detective? You're not turning nark on us, Dirkin?'

The man was outraged. 'I never narked no one in my life. This is private – a private eye.'

'Get off! In Deptford?'

'Honest. Geezer's trailing round the boozers, carrying a wad of these little snaps.'

Naylor picked it up. 'You say there's money in it?' He studied the photo blankly. 'I'll ask me mates.'

'Give us the photo back,' said Dirkin.

Naylor had paid for his round by now, and when he carried the tray of drinks to a side table, he kept the photo. The boys glanced at it and asked Vinnie, 'What do *you* get out of it?'

'Nothing. The man's just handing out the photos.'

'A cop?'

'No way.'

'Who's the girl then?' Clyde asked. 'A runaway?'

The boys squinted at the crumpled photograph, not because they really thought they might recognise the girl but because the idea of a detective – a private one – in Deptford was extraordinary, and quite flattering in a way.

Vinnie said, 'There's an advert about her in the *Mercury*. He's carrying that around with him too.'

Clyde held the photo to the light as if it might have been a counterfeit. 'So this detective will pay money for a lead on her?'

'No, careful – they tried that on him in the Erin. When he *finds* her is what he said.'

Naylor grinned at him. 'What you doin' up the Irish pub, Vinnie – feeling brave?'

'Business,' replied Vinnie grandly. 'Anyway, one of the paddies tried to give the tec the runaround.'

'And?'

'He's a big feller.'

'That don't stop paddies.'

'Hey,' Clyde said. 'D'you hear about those two paddies saw a notice – Tree Fellers Wanted. "That's a shame," says Paddy. "*Tree* fellers – and there's only two of us." '

Chippy cackled.

'Anyway,' said Vinnie, 'I think they knew him.'

'Oh, he's Irish? You didn't say.'

'No, not Irish, but there was something. Someone knew him.'

'He's a cop. I told you.'

'That wasn't it. Can I have my photo back?'

Clyde was curling it between his fingers. 'So if he's private, looking for a teenager, then her parents must be paying his fee. And you reckon they put an advert in the paper? Yeah, you're right, there could be money in it.'

Chippy said, 'Nah, that's just a schoolgirl no one ever saw. Give it back to him.'

'All in good time.' Clyde shielded the photo like a playing card, taking a peek at it on his own. 'She ain't a school girl. Looks about eighteen.'

'Don't get excited,' Naylor said. 'She's one of four million birds in London.'

'Anyway,' Clyde continued, still studying the photo, 'she might be eighteen *here*, when the snap was taken, but you know how it is: she leaves school and this is the last picture her family's got.'

Chippy Naylor turned to Dirkin dithering by his side. 'I think Clyde's fallen for her. He'll pin the photo up by his bed.'

'I'll pin his nose against his face.'

Which brought a grin or two around the table – a fight was entertainment. Clyde sneered, then flicked the photo across the table as if throwing in a poker hand. 'I wouldn't steal your woman, Vinnie. Dunno where she's been.'

Vinnie started forward but banged his knee against the corner of the table. Chippy placed a hand on Vinnie's chest. 'You want us all thrown out? Ignore him. Show your photo to someone else.'

Vinnie scrabbled for it on the table. 'You wanna meet me, Clyde? Just name the time.'

From the other side of the table Clyde sneered again. 'Look at the fuss you've caused. It's only a photograph.'

*   *   *

The pub had been quiet for about ten minutes when Joe Venables finally walked in. He was a large gentle-looking man with curly iron-grey hair, and was wearing black. Something about the way he approached the bar suggested he had not come in to buy a drink. He muttered quietly to the landlord.

By this time Vinnie was in the rear with a bunch of kids, but at Chippy Naylor's table they didn't need Vinnie to tell them who this was. They watched Venables approach a young couple at the bar and show the photo. They watched him continue to a table near the door. By the time he reached them they had each rehearsed what they would say.

Clyde and Lucky Lennox leapt in at once. Clyde was saying, 'Hey, I've seen that babe before,' and Lennox: 'Didn't she used to hang around the Duchess?'

Joe Venables smiled at them. 'Now there's a thing,' he said. 'All night, not a single sniff of her, and now suddenly two people at the same table both recognise her immediately. And you, sir – ' he was looking at Clyde ' – you must be six feet from my photograph.'

'I don't forget a face.'

'But maybe you saw her picture in the *Mercury*?' Joe turned to Lennox: 'And where might you have seen her?'

'At the Duchess,' replied Lennox promptly.

'I can't believe my luck,' Joe said, sitting down. 'As you may have read in the *Mercury*, there is a reward if you help me find her, but – ' he paused, ' – a smack in the face if I get the runaround. Now, the Duchess, you said – '

'It's a little night club over – '

'I know where the Duchess is.'

Lennox paused. 'I didn't realise you was local.'

Joe shrugged. 'There are no border guards in Deptford.'

Lennox glanced at this amiable but heavy man. 'Well, you could *try* the Duchess. Look, if you do find something, do – um – I mean, how does someone get their hands on this reward?'

'Let me have your name.'

When Lennox hesitated Venables smiled. 'If your information is genuine I'm sure you'll want to give me your name. How about you, son?' This was aimed at Clyde.

'I ain't sure. She looks familiar, you know?'

Venables made a gesture with his hand, palm uppermost, asking for more.

Chippy intervened. 'The thing is, we seen the photo earlier, so we had time to think about it.'

'You mean that fellow in the back room – he showed it to you?'

'Oh.'

'I noticed him when I came in. Never caught his name.'

'He's Vinnie Dirkin,' Lennox said.

Joe started to stand up. 'I'll leave a photo. My number's on the back.'

The men's eyes fastened on the snap as if it were a ten pound note. 'There *is* a reward then?' Clyde asked again.

'If I find her.'

'When a girl goes missing,' Chippy remarked, 'you should check the Albert.'

'The black pub?'

Naylor nodded. 'You know it?'

'That's my job,' Joe told them. 'But I'll finish here first.'

*   *   *

The Royal Albert was so loud that Venables abandoned conversation; he simply thrust his way through the crowded pub and held the photo to people's faces. The music here had the deadening beat of an amplified heart. Lights were minimal. The air was full of smoke – some of it tobacco – and when men saw what Venables was engaged in they swayed aside to let him through. He was hot, his eyes were itching, and he understood why so many in the darkened hall wore shades. He saw a little guy dancing before him, grinning like a puppet, and when Joe tried to speak to him the man made as if either he could not understand English or the music was too loud for him to hear Joe's words.

The man mimed that the two of them should step outside.

On the cold pavement the music was so loud that Joe wanted to go back inside to turn it down. But the little guy brought his mouth close to Joe's ear: 'Right, I've seen her, don't know her name.'

'Recently?'

The man shrugged. 'Not for several weeks. She went away.'

'You know where?'

'No.' The man brought his head back so he could gaze at Joe's face, then he leant forward again. 'But I have seen her. She used to be around. You put her in the paper, didn't you? Are you her father?'

'No.'

'And you're not a cop?'

'No. I'm looking for her.'

'Relation?'

'If you help me find her, there'll be money in it.'

'Are you managing her?'

'Her family has asked me to help. I'm a private detective.'

The man leant back again, studied him, then let his face loosen in a smile. 'No kidding – a private eye?'

'That's right.'

'In Deptford? Shit.' He shook his head at the incongruity.

Joe asked, 'Well?'

'You're not her Daddy, then?'

'We've been through that.'

The man was nodding his head to the music. 'And you're not – well, no, you're not the kiddy's dad, either, right?'

'I told you – wait, which kiddy do you mean?'

'*Hers*, man. I mean, you knew she was pregnant, right?'

Joe's eyes gleamed. 'It didn't say that in the *Mercury*.'

'Ah shit, man, does this news bring you grief? I'm sorry, right?'

'You knew she was pregnant?'

They were shouting this conversation in the street. The man took a step away. 'Well, I ain't seen her recently, man. Expect she's had the kid by now.'

'Hey, hey.' Joe didn't want to lose him. 'How did you know that she was pregnant?'

'Shit, man, she was enormous. She probably dropped the thing by now.'

Venables fumbled in his pocket. 'It was definitely this girl here?'

The man took another step away. 'I don't know. She looked like her. This was weeks ago. Hey, I'm through here, man. OK?'

'Where can I find her?'

'You're the detective.' He saw Joe's face. 'Look man, don't waste time hassling *me*. Try the Duke of Edinburgh.'

*   *   *

Squashed in halfway down a road lined with terraced houses, the Duke of Edinburgh looked to be a quiet pub. Compared to the Albert it was quiet, despite the upright piano and the old boy with his hat angled at the back of his head, pounding out the favourites – East End music hall. A huddle of locals enthusiastically joined in the refrains. An old lady with a throbbing accent sang out the verse:

> The ballroom was a-filled with-a fashion's throng,
> It shone with a fousand lights.
> And there was a woman 'oo passed along,
> The fairest of all the sights.

And the ragged chorus, helped by the surprisingly resonant voice of Joe Venables, joined in:

> She's only a bird in a gilded cage,
> A be-eautiful sight to see.
> You may fink she is happy and free from care –
> She is not, though she seems to be.

Joe moved closer to a table beneath the dartboard where some youngsters seemed self-conscious about joining in. Perhaps they didn't know the words.

> It's sad when you fink of her wasted life,
> For yoof cannot mate with age.
> And her beauty was sold for an old man's gold,
> She's a bird in a gilded cage.'

As the song ended, Joe laid his glass on their table. 'I'm looking for a young woman.'

'You'll be lucky 'ere!'

'Pauline – Pauline Estobel. D'you know her?'

'Sorry.'

He produced a photo. They shook their heads. He said, 'She drinks in here.' They shrugged. He said, 'She's pregnant.'

One of the girls at the table looked at him carefully. 'You her Dad, then?'

'Friend of the family. She's not in trouble. If you do see her, my phone number's on the back. There's fifty quid for anyone helps me find her.'

'Well, if she's pregnant she wouldn't come in here.'

Joe smiled encouragingly. 'Oh, but she did. She lived nearby.'

'Where?'

'She moved away.'

'Then she could be anywhere by now, couldn't she?'

Joe nodded again. He looked tired, human, the sort of man that you would like to help. 'I just need a start to help me find her. Her mother is frantic – you can imagine – she even placed an advert in the paper. You might have seen it? Look, I'll leave the photo with you. Ring any time, no questions asked.'

He was disappointed. Most of the pubs had simply been places to tick off his list but that little fellow outside the Albert had told him the Duke of Edinburgh was where she drank. And it was less than five minutes away from Endwell Road, where Pauline had lived. No forwarding address, of course, just a suggestion that she had gone up west. But from Deptford most places *were* up west.

It was a pity that Miss Estobel had not left a forwarding address. She had paid off her rent and disappeared as if she had always intended to vanish away. According to the landlord in Endwell Road she had returned from hospital while he was out and had immediately cleared her flat and left. The landlord said that Pauline had told him previously that she would be living with the kiddy's father, but her tale did not accord with the fact that no man ever showed up at the house. No one helped her collect her things. Joe had checked with the hospital but, unfortunately, they had no record of a Pauline Estobel. He got lucky at the local ante-natal centre where they *had* heard of her and, yes, they did have her home address. It was the room in Endwell Street.

* * *

Two days later Joe called at Mrs Estobel's house to tell her that the trail was cold. In Deptford, one or two people had remembered Pauline but no one had seen her for about three months. None of her older friends from school days had heard a word. 'The best we can hope,' Joe said, ' – and it's the likeliest explanation – is that after the trouble she caused at home she is making a new life for herself elsewhere. I could continue looking, of course, but with little to go on it will be expensive. But once she has settled down with the baby there's a pretty good chance she'll be in touch. I know this is difficult to accept, Mrs Estobel, but you may have to be patient and sit and wait.'

* * *

That was what he had meant to say. But Mrs Estobel was not easily deflected. She sat in her pastel drawing room, opposite a thirty-inch embroidered *commedia dell'arte* clown in a wicker nursery chair, and she allowed him to get half-way through his speech – to the word 'expensive', which seemed a good place to interrupt – before she raised her hand and said, 'Father Venables, you're not suggesting we should give up? It would be the death of me.'

'I think it's wiser,' Joe said. 'And I'm not a Father now, as you know.'

'A man like you is ordained for life.'

Mrs Estobel had attractive eyes – sad sorrowful eyes on the brink of tears – eyes that would appeal to many men.

'I have a new vocation,' Joe said, and smiled. 'I think Pauline is bound to settle soon, and after that there's every chance – '

'She's had long enough. No, Father, my fear is that she's in desperate straits. She could be too frightened or ashamed to return home.'

'Frightened?'

'Too proud, perhaps. It's silly, because *we* were the ones in the wrong. Patrick was upset, of course, which is why he reacted the way he did – when she told us she was pregnant. He was always . . . Patrick saw things in black and white.'

'Well, perhaps – '

'I wish *you'd* buried him, Father. You were always . . . The man who came after you is too young, too insubstantial. He has no gravitas.'

'Perhaps the job suits someone less substantial.' Joe smiled and patted his thickening waist.

Pauline's mother sighed. She was a small, compact woman, burdened with what appeared a permanent sadness. She had lost her daughter, then her husband, yet her determination not to give up aroused Joe's sympathy. He wanted to help before he left.

She blinked. 'Look, Father, I – '

'Joe.'

'What?'

'Joe. Or Mr Venables, if you'd prefer.'

She closed her eyes briefly and shook her head. 'It does not come naturally, I'm afraid. You're still a priest, as far as I'm concerned. I'd like you to continue trying to trace my Pauline. She's all that's left to me.'

'Mrs Estobel, my advice – '

'No, don't.' She waved a tired hand. 'No sensible advice. I'm her mother. Since Patrick died I live in an empty house.'

'I've explored all the obvious avenues – '

'The *obvious* ones.'

'Her friends and school mates, the room she rented.' He took her tiny hand into his familiarly comforting clasp. 'Mrs Estobel, don't you think – '

'No.'

'We've done all we can.'

'*You* have.' Her face was pinched.

'Yes.'

She crumpled slightly. 'I didn't mean that. We must go on search-ing, looking under every – '

'I've looked. Sometimes we – ' He saw her head jerk. 'Sometimes we have to face the fact that someone we love has left us, and has chosen to make their way alone.'

'I want her back.'

Joe nodded. 'Of course. And I'm sure she'll come back eventually. But for now – '

'Don't say that. Please, Father   Mr Venables – don't refuse to help. I'll pay you for your time.'

'You've paid enough. I'll bill you for my time to date, but that will be my final account. I'm sorry.'

She said, '*I* shall not stop looking.'

*   *   *

She held out the photo. 'This is my daughter. I'm trying to find her.'

The two men seated at the pub table shook their heads. She said, 'She used to come here.'

'Never seen her,' one of them mumbled.

The man behind the bar called, 'Hey, missis! What you selling?'

Mrs Estobel looked strained as she proffered the photo. 'I am trying to find my daughter. Perhaps you remember her?'

He glanced at the photo. 'Oh, her.'

'You've seen her?'

'I've seen her photo. Had a bloke in a couple of days back. You had that advert in the paper.'

'That's right. I believe my daughter used to come to this pub. Perhaps she still does?'

'Nah.'

'But she used to. Can't you remember? Please try.'

He shrugged helplessly. 'We get lots through here. A girl comes in once or twice – well, it don't register, you see?'

'My daughter was pregnant. Do you remember that?'

'Ah.' He reached across the bar for the photo, gazed at it and shook his head. 'Still don't register. You sure it was this pub?'

His tone was sympathetic, and the customers in the small pub listened silently. An old man said, 'Better let us see it. You never know.'

But she could tell from their faces that no one expected to recognise the girl. She added, 'There's a reward for anyone who helps me find her.'

The old man gazed at the snap with little hope. 'Pretty girl. Yes. She run away?'

Mrs Estobel took a breath. 'Yes.'

The old man passed the photo to a thin girl who had moved across to stand close to them. He said, 'Yes, they do that sometimes, run off and hide. A shame. I suppose you'd like to see her little baby?'

Mrs Estobel nodded, watching as the thin girl passed the photo on. 'I'd like to see the baby *and* my daughter – she has nothing to fear.' This last was to the room at large.

The thin girl eased herself onto a stool beside her as Mrs Estobel announced in a trembling voice: 'I've put my phone number on the back. Please phone – in absolute confidence. If anyone does know where she is . . . please tell her I only want to help.'

*   *   *

Mrs Estobel had not realised how many pubs there were in Deptford. Outside some she hesitated, feeling that these were not ones her daughter would have entered, but she gathered her courage and plunged inside. And in one of the larger, more terrifyingly noisy places someone gave a glimmer of recognition – nothing definite, it didn't lead anywhere, but was enough to encourage her to go on. The larger the pub, she thought, the more people; and the more people, the more chance somebody might recognise Pauline. Mrs Estobel had handed out dozens of photos, and occasionally as she placed a photo in someone's warm hand she felt an unaccountable shiver of expectation, and she peered into that person's face looking for a sign. She would think, this is the one. But it wasn't. Outside in the cold night air she realised that the shiver of hope was no different to that felt by people buying their weekly lottery ticket: there's something about the numbers this week . . .

The High Street was quiet. The Deptford Arms was dead, and the little corner pub, The Windsor Castle, did not look promising. But she went inside. Here, the few customers were older, less likely to have known Pauline, but she still showed the photo. At one table, drinking alone, was a girl who seemed faintly familiar – a thin girl – a school friend perhaps? Or she might have been in a previous pub.

She smiled cautiously at Mrs Estobel. 'Not much luck then?'

Mrs Estobel was tired. 'No, but I have to keep trying.'

'You can sit here if you like. Take the weight off.'

'Once I sit I won't be able to stand up again.'

'Yes, you look like you need a rest.'

The girl was urging her to sit down – and finally she did. The girl said, 'I'd offer you a drink, but I'm skint.'

Mrs Estobel ignored that. 'I'll buy something in a moment.'

'You don't have to buy anything in here. They don't mind if you just sit.'

There was something waif-like about the girl that reminded Mrs Estobel of the sad child pictured in the posters for *Les Misérables*. She sat with her shoulders hunched as if she was cold.

'You'd think someone would remember her,' said Mrs Estobel. 'But I suppose people are wary of speaking to me?' She watched the girl. 'There's no need.'

The girl met her eye for a brief moment. 'No questions asked?'

'None. And there'd be some money . . . discreetly.'

The girl was glancing around the pub. Mrs Estobel asked quietly, 'Would you like to go somewhere more private?'

The girl pushed her glass aside as if Mrs Estobel had accused her of trying to pocket it. 'Oh, I don't know. What for?'

Mrs Estobel kept her voice low. 'So we could talk.'

Nervously, the girl shook her head.

'Did you know my daughter?'

*   *   *

Mrs Estobel felt that the girl was rather too melodramatic. Though if something had happened to Pauline that required this caution – and if no one but the thin girl would admit to even recognising her – then perhaps her worst fears might be justified. If her daughter had become involved with some south London gang . . . But that was ridiculous – Pauline was an ordinary middle-class girl who had fallen pregnant and run away from home. It was odd that she should have chosen this unsavoury area, but for Pauline to mix with unwholesome characters was stretching likelihood too far. Yet this furtive, thin girl had asked Mrs Estobel to go out of the pub on her own and to walk to the burger bar along the High Street and wait for her there. Mrs Estobel had chosen a table away from the window, where the girl would see her only after she came in. *If* she came in. She had seemed so nervous she might easily bolt.

Mrs Estobel sagged in the plastic chair. She was weary after trudging round noisy bars and now, in this brightly lit, aromatic fast-food café, she felt small and alone. When the waitress appeared with notebook and smile, Mrs Estobel said, 'Just a coffee for the moment. I'm waiting for a friend.'

'Cappuccino, Espresso, Speciality?' The waitress pointed to the laminated menu.

'Just ordinary, if I may.'

'Standard or extra large?'

'Standard. We'll order when my friend arrives.'

While waiting for coffee and the thin girl Mrs Estobel continued to brood about her daughter. Pauline had definitely lived in Deptford when she first moved away because Father Venables had found the room she had rented in Endwell Road. Earlier today Mrs Estobel had called there herself, but the landlord could tell her no more than that Pauline had moved out once her child had been born. She hadn't left any forwarding address. She hadn't any visitors, no friends. Could it really have been like that? It was horrible to think of her own daughter living alone in this hard unfriendly area, waiting for her baby to arrive. What had happened afterwards? All anyone could tell her was that Pauline had quit her rented room, had given birth and disappeared. As if she'd done it deliberately. For the several months she had lived in Deptford she had been noticed by almost no one, and once she left, no one remembered her.

When the waitress arrived with her coffee Mrs Estobel thanked her and glanced to the door. 'I'll order in a moment, if you don't mind.'

Perhaps it was not surprising no one remembered Pauline. As her pregnancy had progressed she would have become increasingly housebound, and despite her parting words to the landlord Pauline did not appear to have had a boy friend. She would have had to cope with the child alone.

Earlier that day Mrs Estobel had retraced the same path as Joe Venables: the few local shops, the Well Woman Clinic, the neighbouring houses made into flats. People responded to her queries warily. Some had already been approached by Joe Venables, others were simply suspicious of anyone asking questions. One woman refused to believe that she was really Pauline's mother. Tomorrow, she decided, she would bring a second photo of Pauline and herself together.

She glanced up to see the thin girl slip in through the door.

* * *

As the girl wolfed down her food Mrs Estobel grew impatient. The girl was visibly ravenous. Presumably she had suggested they meet in here so she would be bought a meal. She sat opposite Mrs Estobel, spearing chips and sausages with stooped concentration, cramming them into her mouth so she could not speak. Though it was late – ten o'clock at night – she had asked for the Giant All Day Breakfast. 'You can eat burgers any time.'

Mrs Estobel tried to extract answers before the girl finished her food. All she had learned so far was the thin girl's name. 'Now Charlotte, where can I find Pauline?'

The girl stabbed the last piece of sausage and gulped it down. 'I dunno where she's living *now*. I didn't say I knew that, did I?'

'You haven't said anything much.'

Charlotte took a large bite from her soft granary bap. 'I dunno if she'd want me to tell you.'

'When did you last see her?'

Charlotte swallowed some bread. 'Must've been . . . oh, two weeks ago.'

'Where?'

Charlotte glanced around as if someone might have been listening. 'At my place. She came to see me.'

Mrs Estobel leant forwards. 'You're a friend of hers?'

Charlotte shrugged. 'So-so. Are you having a pudding?'

Mrs Estobel gazed at her steadily. 'I think you should tell me something first.'

'You're not trying to bribe me with a pudding?'

'You could earn more than a pudding, Charlotte.'

'Yeah, it said that in the paper.'

'You saw my advertisement?'

Charlotte licked her lips. 'Well, I knew it was her immediately.'

Mrs Estobel remained unsure whether to believe the girl or not. 'Her name was in the advert.'

'Right – but I always called her Polly. That's what she called herself – Polly, not Pauline.'

'Polly?' Mrs Estobel frowned. If that was trial shot from Charlotte it hadn't worked: her daughter had *never* been a Polly. 'You said she came to see you a couple of weeks ago. Why?'

Charlotte shrugged. 'Friends. You know.'

'Do you think she'll come again?'

'I expect.'

'Will you give her a message from me?'

'Of course – *if* I see her.' Charlotte stared at her. 'Can I have a pudding – please?'

Mrs Estobel nodded impatiently. 'Tell her, when you see her, that . . . Tell her that her Daddy died suddenly in an accident. That's important, you see – she doesn't know he's dead. Tell her that I want to see her again, very much.'

Charlotte glanced away then back. 'And her baby – you want to see it?'

'Yes, I – Have *you* seen . . . the baby? I don't even know if it's a boy or a girl.'

'Oh, it's – ' Charlotte smiled. 'It's a boy. He's very nice.' She waved the menu to attract the waitress. 'Death By Chocolate, with cream and ice cream.' She glanced across at Mrs Estobel. 'Anything for you?'

She shook her head. 'Another coffee, please.'

When the waitress had left them, Charlotte asked, 'Did she tell you who was the baby's father?'

Mrs Estobel paused. 'No, she wouldn't. That made it all so much worse.'

'You must have . . . made a guess?'

'Pauline kept herself to herself. Perhaps you found her to be like that?'

Charlotte shrugged. Then Mrs Estobel suddenly asked, 'Tell me, then, about the baby – what's his name?'

'Jamie.'

Mrs Estobel repeated the name softly. 'What is he like?'

Charlotte grinned. '*Like* – you mean, is he black or white? No, you don't have to worry – he's white, all right. D'you think he wouldn't be?'

Mrs Estobel did not answer, so Charlotte pressed further: 'Did Polly ever have a black boy friend?'

'No.'

'Well, then. Don't look like that. The baby's white, healthy – well, quite healthy – brown hair, blue eyes . . . I *think* they're blue.'

'What d'you mean, *quite* healthy – is something wrong with him?'

The waitress arrived with the Death By Chocolate and another coffee. Charlotte took her first mouthful of sticky dessert before saying, 'Well, he had a bit of a cold last time I seen him.' She took a second mouthful. 'He did seem a bit run down, but Polly looks after him as best she can.' A third mouthful was poised upon her spoon. 'Is Jamie your first grandson?'

'Pauline was our only daughter.' Mrs Estobel blinked. 'I mean, she *is* our – she's *my* only . . . ' She raised her napkin to her lips.

'Yeah. Sorry about your husband.' To cover any embarrassment, Charlotte scooped some more chocolate fudge into her mouth. When she had swallowed it she said, 'Still, at least now you can try to get in touch with her again. Wouldn't he let you?'

Mrs Estobel sat upright in her chair. 'Is that what Pauline told you?'

'She seemed a bit . . . You know how uptight she could be.' Charlotte filled her mouth again.

Mrs Estobel sighed. 'I suppose she told you that it was Daddy who turned her out?'

Charlotte nodded sagely.

'He was ridiculously old-fashioned about . . . her predicament – partly because she wouldn't tell us who the father was, and partly because, well, Patrick was a deeply religious man. Afterwards, of course, he was most awfully upset.'

'Even so, he wouldn't have her back?'

'He was very proud. Strong-minded.'

Charlotte scraped the last chocolate smears from her glass dish. 'You never thought it might be *his* baby?'

Mrs Estobel jerked back from the table. 'What a terrible thing to say! Pauline surely didn't tell you that?'

'It's not unusual. I mean, him throwing Pauline out – didn't it make you think?'

Mrs Estobel exhaled. 'That's quite enough of that. There is no question of it.'

'All right, all right. I didn't know, you see. No need to get all shirty. I'd better go.'

As she stood up from the table, Mrs Estobel rose too. 'No, don't go. Can't you tell me where Pauline is?'

Charlotte glanced towards the door. 'I don't know. She'll probably be in touch.'

'And you *will* tell her?'

'Oh, sure. D'you want me to give her anything?'

'Money, you mean? No, I – '

'You don't trust me, do you? Well, I've got your phone number. So long.'

She began to leave.

'Look, Charlotte, please – '

'D'you want to see the baby – shall I tell her that?'

'Of course.'

Charlotte paused. 'Right. Thanks for a lovely supper.'

She was gone.

*   *   *

On the evening of the third day of plodding around Deptford, Mrs Estobel sat alone in her drawing room, tired feet propped on the pale camel stool, television chattering in the corner, a smeared tumbler at her side – gin and tonic finished, wet slice of lemon lifeless at the base – when the telephone rang. She reached slowly for the handset. A week ago, when the advertisement had first appeared in the *Mercury*, she had had twenty calls a night, but now they had diminished to one or two. Some held promise, most were instantly dismissible, none told her what she wanted to hear.

'Mrs Estobel? I said I'd ring.'

'Who's that?'

'You know, when I heard from her again.'

'Who am I speaking to?'

'Charlotte. You know, we met in Deptford?'

'Charlotte.'

'In the Windsor. We had a meal.'

'I remember. Have you seen Pauline?'

'Well, not exactly.'

'Oh.'

'I've sort of seen her. You haven't seen her yourself, Mrs Estobel?'

'No. Why – did she tell you she'd get in touch with me?'

'Well, no.'

'I see. What d'you mean – you've *sort* of seen her?'

'Well, it's awkward.'

'Awkward?'

'You know, speaking on the phone. Um, could I see you?'

'Of course. Where had you in mind?'

'You could come to my place. I can't get out, you see?'

'To your flat?'

'Yeah, you know, any time – well, no, some time soon.'

'Tomorrow?'

They arranged to meet the following morning. Evidently the girl had no job. She gave an address – hesitantly – but would say no more about what she wanted to talk about. At least she didn't want to meet in a restaurant.

*   *   *

The flat comprised two meagrely decorated rooms separated by a plain panel door. A corner of the front room had been crudely modified to form a kitchenette, and the furniture included a general-purpose dining table and several chairs. Only the television set looked new.

Charlotte sat Mrs Estobel in a repellent soft armchair and placed herself in a wooden chair opposite. The door to the second room remained closed.

'No luck then?' began Charlotte.

'Not yet.'

'I've put the kettle on.'

'Fine.' Mrs Estobel had decided not to ask questions; the girl had brought her here to reveal something and would be better at her own speed. For a few moments they stared at each other. Then Charlotte glanced over her shoulder to the kitchenette.

'It's nearly done,' she said. 'Coffee or tea?'

'Coffee,' replied Mrs Estobel. 'One sugar. Black.' She doubted the freshness of Charlotte's milk.

As the girl tinkered with the cups they rattled on their saucers. 'Polly says she's sorry, you know? She couldn't come.'

'Why not?'

Charlotte sniffed. 'Doesn't want to face you, I suppose. It must be awful for you. I mean, you're the grandmother.'

'Yes.'

'And you've never even seen your grandson.'

'No.'

She wanted to ask when Charlotte had last seen them, but she made herself stay quiet.

'Well, I dare say you'll be seeing him soon,' Charlotte said. 'It's boiling now. No sugar, right?'

'*One* sugar.'

'Oh yes, you said.'

Charlotte poured hot water into the cups. When she lifted them in trembling hands some coffee slopped into the saucers. Charlotte glanced from one rattling cup to the other like a nervous actress on first night. 'I'll bring them one by one.'

She put down the cup with most coffee in its saucer and approached Mrs Estobel with the other clutched in both hands. Half way towards her she was halted by a sound from the other room – the reedy, waking cry of a baby. Mrs Estobel did not turn round, but gazed instead at Charlotte's face. The girl stood motionless, her thin shoulders hunched over the coffee cup, an abject expression on her face. The baby cried again, more vigorously.

Mrs Estobel stood up. 'Give me the coffee, Charlotte, while you go and see to the baby.'

'No, it's all – '

Mrs Estobel took the cup. 'Once they start they don't give up.'

Charlotte dithered another moment, then scuttled past to the other room. Mrs Estobel came behind to peep inside. It was a bedroom in semi-darkness – the mother's single bed, the tiny baby in a cheap carry-cot. Charlotte leant over, scolded softly, then picked it up. There was no one else in the darkened room.

Mrs Estobel sipped her coffee. 'So you've got a baby too, Charlotte? Let me have a look.'

She couldn't see the baby properly because it had its back to her, its face buried in Charlotte's neck. The girl stared wide-eyed as if Mrs Estobel might want to take it from her. 'He'll be all right. He's just woken up.'

Mrs Estobel remained patiently a few feet from her, and spoke in a calm voice: 'He wants his breakfast, I suppose. Do you breastfeed?'

The thin girl hugged the child more closely. 'I can manage. I know what to do.'

She showed no sign of it.

'Well, don't stand on ceremony,' urged Mrs Estobel. 'Put his milk on the stove to warm and we'll talk later.'

'He's my baby.'

Mrs Estobel looked at Charlotte sharply. 'What's his name?'

Charlotte busied herself with the baby, and seemed reluctant to leave the bedroom. Mrs Estobel sensed that she had not been brought here by chance. Neither perhaps had the baby. Of course, it was possible that the baby did belong to Charlotte and that the girl was behaving oddly because she was ashamed of her own fatherless child. Perhaps she really had not meant Mrs Estobel to know of it. Anything was possible. Mrs Estobel went back into the living room and sat on a wooden dining chair. The armchair had had a musty smell.

Charlotte emerged. 'I'll make the milk then.'

'That's right.'

Holding the baby in one arm, Charlotte crossed to her kitchenette. Mrs Estobel stood up. 'Let me hold him while you warm it.'

'No, stay away. The baby's mine.'

Mrs Estobel did not say anything. She watched as Charlotte used her one free hand to run water into a saucepan and place it on the electric ring. From the shabby fridge she took a pre-filled bottle and slipped it into the water so it could warm.

Mrs Estobel sniffed pointedly. 'I suppose you'd better change his nappy.'

'Afterwards.'

'Don't you change it first?'

'No.' Charlotte peered into the water.

'I always liked my baby to be clean before it ate. Clean nappy, clean botty, then some food. That's what I did with Pauline.'

'No point,' muttered Charlotte. 'Put him in a clean one, he messes that. He might as well do everything in one.'

'Fashions change,' said Mrs Estobel. 'But I didn't like to hold Pauline smelling of poo. It didn't seem right while she was eating.'

'I know what I'm doing. I'm a good mother.' Charlotte lifted the bottle from the water and tested it against the back of her hand. The baby whimpered.

'You *are* his mother, then?'

Charlotte dropped the bottle in the water. 'What d'you mean? Course I'm his mother. I'm – Oh, you . . . '

Her face crumpled, became small and pinched. For a moment she stood quivering in the kitchenette, then with a small cry she rushed to the armchair and sat the baby in it. He immediately began to cry.

Charlotte shouted, 'You want to take him away from me – I know you do!'

'Why should I?'

'Because you – Well, you can't have him. He belongs to me.'

Mrs Estobel felt strangely calm. 'Is that Pauline's baby?'

'I didn't steal him.'

Charlotte grabbed the baby and held him close.

'That's why you invited me here, isn't it?'

'I didn't steal him.'

'Oh, Charlotte.'

'She gave him to me.'

'Gave?'

'She did, she did. She *left* him here.'

'Pauline left my grandson here?'

Charlotte collapsed into the armchair and the baby gave a startled scream.

'Oh, feed him, for God's sake, Charlotte – feed the poor little thing.'

*   *   *

The following morning, when Mrs Estobel arrived carrying baby blankets, two cardigans, bright coloured hoops on a plastic ring, she half hoped to find her daughter with Charlotte in the flat. After a surprisingly good night's sleep Mrs Estobel still could not believe what Charlotte had finally told her the day before – that Pauline had never bonded with the baby, had resented her, had constantly found fault, and had then abandoned her to her friend. It did not seem credible. Pauline could not behave like that – no mother could. Perhaps she was using Charlotte to re-establish contact – had *lent* her the baby, as it were, to give her mother a chance to see the child. Last night, as Mrs Estobel had journeyed home alone, she had imagined Pauline returning to the flat to hear from Charlotte how she had been. Perhaps Pauline had seen the advertisement in the *Mercury*. It must have been a shock for her to read that the parents she had walked away from, who had thrown her out, were now advertising to bring her back.

'Polly hasn't been here,' Charlotte insisted. 'She never comes.'

Mrs Estobel smiled and shook her head. 'Of course she comes – don't start that again.'

'She doesn't.'

'I'm not stupid, Charlotte, I understand.'

'Huh!'

'Was it because she saw my advertisement?'

'I don't know.' Charlotte was jigging the baby on her knee. His face was wet. In one pink and wrinkled hand Jamie held a ring of plastic discs which he was trying to slide into his mouth.

Mrs Estobel tossed back her head. 'Yes, she must have seen it.'

Charlotte shrugged.

'Did you tell her that – her father is dead?'

Charlotte shrugged again.

'Well, you must.'

'I never see her now.'

Mrs Estobel frowned. Charlotte was being tiresome. 'No, Charlotte, you saw her this morning – when she left the baby with you again.'

The child was stroking its face with the plastic toy. Charlotte said, 'I don't think she's still in London.'

'Oh, really – why do you say that?'

'I haven't seen Polly for weeks. All it is, well, there was a couple of times a parcel arrived. They was just left here – for the baby.'

'A parcel – nothing else?'

'No.'

Charlotte adjusted the baby on her knee. Though he still clutched the plastic rings, they seemed to have lost their appeal and he was concentrating on something else. 'She never left me no address. I reckon she used to wait till I went out.'

'I don't believe you, Charlotte.'

'It's true. Because of Jamie – she didn't want to see him. It was easier for her, you know?'

'Oh, come on.'

'You never saw her in those last weeks, Mrs Estobel. She wasn't right inside her head. She blamed the baby for – oh, I don't know. I expect she'll come to her senses one of these days.'

'And then she'll want her baby back?'

'No!' Charlotte glared at her. 'Anyway, she don't even send parcels any more.'

'You mean she has disappeared?'

'Pretty well. But a couple of weeks ago she posted me some money in an envelope.'

'So she's still . . . '

'But she didn't write. I don't suppose she knows what she wants to say.'

'Was there a card?'

'No.'

'Then how did you know it came from her?'

'Who else could it have come from? Anyway, it wasn't much.'

Charlotte dipped her head and rested it alongside the baby's. 'That means you're mine now, you little darling. Ain't that right?'

* * *

Mrs Estobel could not stay away. On each of the next three days she deliberately arrived at different times, hoping she might catch Pauline on a secret call. It seemed that Charlotte, in her slovenly way, was at least *trying* to be a mother, although she had a regrettable habit of silencing Jamie's whimpering by filling his mouth with something else.

'I have to,' she explained. 'Or I'll get complaints. I don't want the landlord to turn me out.'

Mrs Estobel could not – would not – accustom herself to the idea of her grandson being raised, temporarily, she hoped, by an amiable slattern in a rented basement. She began to wonder if she could snaffle the child away. In one of her fantasies she took Jamie for a walk, called a taxi and disappeared. She had as much right to him as Charlotte had – more. Jamie was her flesh and blood. He was her heir, her link to Pauline. Though even so, mused Mrs Estobel, did she really want him for her own – *without* Pauline? Did she want to *rear* the child? She was approaching fifty now. To regain her daughter would be a glory, but to bring Jamie up could not be contemplated. She could hire a nanny, of course, but if somebody else were to look after the child, as seemed inevitable, then why shouldn't that somebody be Charlotte?

Mrs Estobel studied the thin lank-haired girl. Today, with Jamie asleep in the other room, Charlotte seemed at a loss to know what to do. She sat awkwardly, picking at her fingernails in her lap.

'Perhaps you should look for a better flat. This is hardly an ideal place to bring up a baby.'

Charlotte suddenly grinned. 'Well, at least he can't fall off a balcony.' She scratched her head. 'I've got to leave here anyway. I can't pay the rent.' She sniffed. 'You see, 'cos of Jamie I had to chuck my job.'

'What are you living on?'

'Nothing much – you know how it is. If you chuck your job you don't get Social.'

'But surely, with a little baby – '

'He's not *my* kid, is he? I mean, I *love* him like he's my own, but what am I supposed to tell them down the Social – I'm looking after him for a friend? No, I'll have to take the kid and do a bunk.'

'You *can't*. Where would you go?'

'Who knows? Get away from here. Somewhere else, you know, some other town where no one would know me. Then I could tell them Jamie was *my* kid.'

'That would never work.'

'What else am I going to do? Don't worry, once we've settled – well, *if* we get settled – I'll send you a card one day with our address. Maybe I'll send a photo when he gets older.'

'You *must* stay here, Charlotte. It's the only address Pauline knows. And I need you here at this address to help me find her.' Mrs Estobel paused. 'But I suppose you don't really want to find her?'

'And lose the kid, you mean? Oh, she wouldn't want him back.' Charlotte smiled a strangely empty smile. 'No, Jamie's got to stay with me. It's like I'm his mother now.' She snorted and shook her head. 'Like I've become your daughter.'

Mrs Estobel closed her eyes. 'I want my Pauline.'

'Well, I'd like to help, of course. But I'm afraid I can't.'

* * *

A week later, at eleven in the morning when the doorbell rang, Mrs Estobel rose from her pale pink armchair and entered the hall. She opened her front door to a tremulously sunny day, and was surprised to find Joe Venables standing politely on her step.

'I've come to make a final report, if that's all right.'

She ushered him in to her pastel sitting room, still uncertain how to address him: first he had preached to her from a pulpit; now he had returned to her as a tradesman. On her hearthrug they waited for each other to sit.

Joe said, 'I found the clinic where she had the baby.'

'Mr Venables, would you like some tea?'

He seemed surprised to be diverted: 'No. No, thank you. I had tried the general hospital – '

'The case is closed, I'm afraid.'

Joe stared at her. Then she threw her head back and explained, 'I have found the baby.'

Joe nodded. 'I know you met Miss Morrissey.'

'Who?'

'Charlotte Morrissey.'

Mrs Estobel was nonplussed. 'Have you spoken to her too?'

He nodded again and licked his full red lips. 'When Pauline ran away from home she tried to arrange an abortion. Did you know?'

Mrs Estobel did not answer him directly. 'She may have tried to, perhaps, but she did not go through with it, I'm glad to say.'

'Her pregnancy was too far advanced.'

The corners of Joe's mouth sagged, and for a moment she could see the priest again. He said, 'She was given lots of sensible advice – the kind I might once have approved of.'

'Once?'

He looked tired again. 'Nowadays I am not so sure. Am I telling you anything you don't already know?'

He leant forward, and for a moment she expected Father Venables to lay a comforting hand upon her knee. But he only smiled at her. 'Pauline carried her baby to full term under an arrangement in which the baby would be immediately adopted. Once it had issued its first cry it was whisked away. She never saw the child again.'

'No.'

'They recommend immediate separation, you see? It helps ensure that the mother doesn't form a bond. They say it's the most humane course in the longer term.'

'That is not what happened.'

Joe sighed. 'It isn't what Charlotte Morrissey told you, but it *is* what happened. When a girl goes to that kind of agency, the procedure is invariably the same. She is persuaded to deliver the child – literally to deliver it, to be relieved of it – then she is free to go. Once the mother has rested, she gets out of bed, gets dressed and leaves. Puts the whole thing behind her. Hopefully she will learn from the salutary experience. That's the idea. Some people would say that the whole experience should *be* a punishment to that kind of mother. If only you hadn't got into this mess in the first place, they would say.'

'Pauline didn't have the baby adopted, Mr Venables. Perhaps she ought to have done, but – '

'The worst thing about my job is that I don't always bring people what they want. The baby that you saw in the flat was Charlotte Morrissey's. She was conning you – extracting money from you.'

'Not at all.'

'You have paid the rent.'

'Well, yes – '

'Three months in advance. And you paid money towards the housekeeping.'

'Charlotte has no job – '

'But she draws her money from the state – not a lot, but it does include a child and rent allowance. I hear you offered to help her find a better flat?'

'She resisted that.'

'Then let you "overcome" her brave resistance. She is not a professional grifter, Mrs Estobel, but she played her cards quite well. Had the game continued, she might have taken you for quite a haul.'

'It isn't the money.'

'No.'

For a short while they remained silent. Then she asked, 'Was Pauline part of this?'

'No, Charlotte never knew her. You were just someone she overheard in a pub.'

'But . . . ' Mrs Estobel was silent for a moment.

Joe said, 'It was nothing personal.'

She took a deep breath and looked him in the eye. 'Do you know where Pauline is now?'

'No.'

Joe sighed.

'Isn't there anything I can do?'

'Not now, I'm afraid. It is too late.'

'But I'm alone here,' she cried. 'This whole house – empty. You must help me, Mr Venables. I'll pay anything.'

Joe seemed to withdraw inside himself before he replied. 'I'm afraid I can't do that. There are some things that when you lose them you can't buy back.'

His voice was faint and distant, and it sounded to Mrs Estobel as if it had been drawn from a soul in torment. They stood in her blush-pink room and stared bleakly at the carpet.

The obstacle

DAVID STUART DAVIES

It's funny how some men's minds work, especially men like Steve Calthrop. Steve was a serial adulterer with a track record going back more than fifteen years and yet when he began to have suspicions that Angela, his patient doormat of a wife, might have found some action of her own, he was beside himself with indignation.

Steve had broad, obvious good looks, a floppy mess of hair that women went for and a fine line in sharp suits. He was also the possessor of a winning smile when the occasion required it – usually when an attractive woman walked in the room. He really had no trouble in pulling the ladies and charming them into some hotel bedroom with him. It was only after they discovered that his sexual performance did not quite live up to the expectations generated by his smouldering glances and groping digits that his conquests eventually realised they were having an affair with a fairly empty vessel – in more ways than one. And so they quickly extricated themselves from his loins and went back to their boyfriends or husbands with a renewed enthusiasm that surprised both parties.

Steve was too self-centred to realise that he was forever being given the frigid elbow by these women because by the time he received the 'I don't think we should do this any more' phone call, his eyes had wandered on to his next victim.

Meanwhile, Angela – stoical, loyal, much-cheated-upon Angela – turned a blind eye and carried on cooking his meals, ironing his crusty pyjamas, cleaning up after him and granting him his conjugal rights on the rare occasions that he demanded them.

It was an ideal arrangement – for Steve.

So it was with some dismay and a sense of hurt pride that Steve Calthrop began to suspect that Angela was playing him at his own game – was playing away, in fact. At first there were just a few subtle signs of her transgression: the new, sharper haircut, brighter lipstick, jazzier earrings, and somehow the hems on her dresses seemed shorter.

He could see above her knees again. Then there was the sudden switching off of her mobile when he entered the room followed by the embarrassed furtive, shy smile. All doubt was swept aside when he discovered a Valentine card in the cutlery drawer: it featured a fluffy emetic teddy bear hugging a crimson heart. He would never send a card like that. He would never send one at all.

Surely here was evidence that he had been right in his suspicions: Angela was having an affair. He was crushed. He felt his manhood shrivelling. How could she do this to him after sixteen years of marriage? Hadn't he loved, cared and provided for her through sickness and health, including that dodgy period when she had developed hives and was virtually mute during orgasm? He was cast into a well of despair. His sharp suits sagged and his hair failed to flop seductively.

In the end he confided in Bob Matthews, a colleague from work. One night they lingered over lager at the Boar's Head, the company local. As they reached the chemical dregs of the second pint, Steve let loose. Bob, who had met Angela at various corporate functions, was flabbergasted. He tugged his blonde forelock in an expression of his amazement.

'Angela?' he exclaimed as though discovering the secret of alchemy. 'You are having me on. Angela! Come on. Steve. Her world revolves around you.'

'I know. I know. Or rather I thought I did. But apparently now there's a new bastard in orbit!'

Bob shook his head in disbelief, again. 'You've been working too hard. You've been overdoing it, I reckon. This is your tired imagination at play, conjuring up weird scenarios.'

Steve was not buying this. He grimaced and stared down at his empty glass. 'It's not my imagination, Bob, because, you see, deep down, I know. I know.'

'But do you have proof?'

Proof! Well, no he hadn't.

As the third pint arrived, Steve realised that Bob had a point. All he had at present were a collection of suspicions, surmises and a tatty unsigned Valentine card. He could – would dearly love – to be wrong. He realised, perhaps too late, that Angela was his rock, his harbour, his haven. Without her, he would be adrift on the cruel sea of life with only his fading looks, his empty charm and his instant libido. He really was nothing without Angela.

As he drained his glass and the cold lager sloshed around in his gut, all he could think of was that it was likely that he, Steve Calthrop, was a cuckold, a patsy with a randy wife. Proof, yes by God, he had to have proof.

But how to get it?

He could follow her. But Bob shook his head. 'Too crass,' he said. 'Get a private detective to do it for you.'

'What?'

'A private detective. You can hire 'em. They'll do your dirty work without you leaving your armchair. My sister used one when her husband had an affair with his bank manager. Discreet chap – the detective, I mean. Monkton I think was his name.'

Steve shook his head. 'It all seems so sordid.'

'Well, I suppose it is. But you want to be certain, don't you?'

Steve stared into the middle distance with a three pints of lager blur. 'I'm not sure. I'm not sure, yet.'

The subject was dropped and only raised its head nearly a week later when Bob popped into Steve's office. He slammed the door behind him and leaned with his back against it. His face was taut and drained of colour. Steve looked up from the computer screen with some annoyance at being disturbed, but one glance at Bob's countenance told him that something was up.

'Angela went out last night, didn't she?' Bob said breathily.

Steve nodded. 'It's her Weight Watchers' night.'

'Well I don't know the name of the man whose weight she was watching but she was certainly interested in parts of his body which are situated below the belt.'

'What the hell do you mean?'

'I saw her coming out of The Lion's Share, that new place on the ring road, north of Bradford near to the big Sainsbury's . . . '

'That's twenty miles away.'

'Well, if you're playing away . . . you're playing away. Don't dirty your own doorstep, eh?'

'What did he look like . . . this man?'

'Difficult to say. She was all over him. Tall, darkish, thinning on top.'

'A bald git!'

Bob shrugged, the colour returning to his face. 'I was in traffic. I didn't get too long to see – but it was Angela all right. I'll swear to that.'

Steve bit his lip. He hadn't done that since he was a child. 'What was the name of that detective?'

That night as Angela served him his evening meal, Steve studied her every move, her every expression for signs that would betray her guilty secret. She behaved as though there was nothing wrong, that she had no secret life. But he saw her for what she was: a dissembling bitch. It was then that Steve Calthrop decided to kill his wife. He was going to murder her – to have done with the hussy. He stabbed his meat with a deliberate ferocity in the pleasure of his decision.

'Isn't it cooked enough?' asked Angela, in her innocence.

Bob was as good as his word. He told Steve that he had set Monkton on the case and he felt sure he would come up with the requisite information within a week. Information was what Steve wanted but he was not concerned about proof now. He didn't have to see Angela with this balding Romeo – he knew.

Monkton was efficient. Within five days he had produced a report which Bob passed on to Steve. Angela was indeed having an affair. It was with a certain Alberto Costello, a waiter at La Traviata, an Italian restaurant in Bradford, land of the balti and the curry house. Typical, thought Steve, for Angela to plump for a fucking oddball, an Italian in a city full of Asians. In his self-centred and increasingly obsessed mind, Steve failed to see the irony of this assessment, for Angela had originally chosen him, too.

According to Monkton, on the nights when Angela had told Steve she was going to Weight Watchers or to help paint the scenery for the Walton Players' latest farce (their productions were always farces, even when they attempted Ibsen or Pinter), she had been meeting Signor Alberto in The Red Rooster or The Lion's Share – they seemed to alternate – before repairing to the said waiter's town house on the Heaton estate, west of the city. What they did there, Monkton stated in his dry, failed copper prose, he could not be sure, but it required the bedroom light to be switched on and the curtains drawn. Steve read the report twice. Now his plan had changed. He would kill them both. Why should the greasy Italian live if he was going to kill the love of his life?

That night as Angela set off for her Weight Watchers' meeting, Steve appeared to be more attentive than usual. He gave her a big kiss, sloppy and unappetising, and told her to 'look after herself'. Within half an hour of her departure, he left the house himself carrying a briefcase that contained just one item, a fully loaded pistol. It's amazing what one can get off the internet with the right kind of searches.

The Heaton estate, like so many rabbit-hutch housing developments, was a maze of identical ticky-tacky houses with the occasional cul-de-sac thrown in for bad measure. Steve felt like a rat in one of those experiments, trying to find his way to the food. His goal was the inappropriately named Pleasant Crescent, just off Sunshine Rise. After a few wrong turns and many expletives he found it, and more importantly he found Bella Vista, home of wife-stealer Alberto Costello.

Steve parked some fifty yards away and after transferring the pistol from the briefcase to his coat pocket he made his way to the house. Bella Vista was in darkness apart from a lighted room upstairs: the bedroom. 'The bastard,' he hissed, anger growing inside him. He hadn't actually planned what he was going to do once he had reached this stage of his mission. He reckoned he would play it as he had played the many seductions he had carried out over the years: by ear.

Surprisingly, he found the front door unlocked. He stepped inside the house and stood in the darkened hallway and listened. At first he heard no sound at all and then there seemed to be a rustling noise from the living room to his right. Gun in hand, he moved into the room which was illuminated faintly by the amber glow of the street-lamp outside. He thought he could make out a figure sitting on the sofa. As he peered in the semi-darkness, the lights clicked on, splashing the room in a garish, unflattering light. There on the sofa was his wife, Angela, dressed only in black bra and panties. She was staring at him without expression.

Suddenly he felt a sharp blow to the hand and his gun flew from his grasp and landed at Angela's feet. She picked it up calmly and aimed it at her husband.

Steve turned quickly to face his assailant and looked into the face of the man he had trusted, Bob Matthews.

'What the hell's going on here?' he asked, feebly.

'It's what's known as a trap, Steve. You went for it like a tart on heat. You see, there is no Alberto or Monkton, just Angela and me. And we want to be together for the rest of our lives. I know it sounds corny, but we love each other. Something that you couldn't possibly understand. Now, the only obstacle that's in our way is you. And you know what one has to do with obstacles, don't you?'

'Remove them,' said Angela, standing and cocking the pistol.

'I couldn't agree more, my love,' said Bob. 'I couldn't agree more.'

Slaughter in the Strand

KEITH MILES

Herbert Syme had never travelled in a first-class carriage before but nothing else would suffice. It was, in a sense, the most important day of his life and it deserved to be marked by the unaccustomed display of extravagance. Impecunious librarians like Herbert were never allowed to pose as first-class passengers on a train to London. Indeed, they could hardly afford to travel by rail at all on a regular basis. Herbert always rode the six miles to work on his ancient bicycle, weaving past the countless potholes, cursing his way up steep hills, hoping that the rain would hold off and that no fierce dogs would give chase. Today, it was different. Instead of arriving at the library breathless, soaked to the skin and, not infrequently, with the legs of his trousers expertly shredded by canine teeth, he was sitting in a luxurious compartment among the élite of society.

The fact that he was an outsider made it even more exhilarating. Habitual denizens of the privileged area were less than welcoming. They saw Herbert Syme for what he really was, a tall, slim, stooping man in his forties with a shabby suit and a self-effacing manner. The whiff of failure was unmistakable. What was this interloper doing in their midst? Murmurs of resentment buzzed in Herbert's ears. The rustling of newspapers was another audible display of class warfare. They were professional men and he was trespassing on their territory. They wanted him out. The elderly lady in the compartment was more vocal in her criticism. After repeatedly clicking her tongue in disapproval, she had the temerity to ask Herbert if he possessed the appropriate ticket.

The librarian withstood it all without a tremor. While his companions took refuge behind their copies of *The Times*, Herbert took out the letter that had transformed his dull existence. It was short and businesslike, but that did not lessen its impact. He read the words again, fired anew by their implication.

Dear Mr Syme

Thank you for submitting your novel to us. It has found favour with all who have read the book. Subject to certain changes, we will consider publishing it. To that end, we request that you come to this office on Wednesday, May 16 at 3 p.m. precisely to discuss the matter with Mr Roehampton. Please confirm that you are able to attend at this time.

Yours sincerely,

Miss Lavinia Finch (Secretary)

There it was – his passport to fame and fortune. Other passengers might be going on routine visits to the capital, but Herbert Syme was most certainly not. Thanks to the letter from Roehampton and Buckley Ltd., he was in transit between misery and joy. Long years of toil and derision lay behind him. Success had at last beckoned. Putting the magical missive into his pocket, he reflected on its contents. His novel had found favour at a prestigious publishing house. Instead of spending his days stacking the work of other writers on the shelves of his branch library, he would take his place alongside them as an equal. Herbert Syme would be read, admired and envied. Everyone's perception of him would alter dramatically. Publication was truly a form of rebirth.

'May I see your ticket, please, sir?'

'What?' Herbert came out of his reverie to find the uniformed ticket inspector standing over him. 'Oh, yes. Of course.'

Newspapers were lowered and each pair of eyes was trained on Herbert as he extracted his ticket and offered it to the inspector. Everyone in the compartment wanted him to be forcibly ejected. They longed for his humiliation. To their utter disgust, the inspector clipped the ticket and handed it back politely to its owner.

'Thank you, sir,' he said.

Herbert was elated by the man's deference. It was something to which he would swiftly adjust. From now on, it would be a case of first-class all the way.

The sheer size, noise and bustle of London were overwhelming at first. Herbert had never seen so many people or so much traffic. Garish advertisements competed for his attention on walls, passing vehicles and in shop windows. It was bewildering. Crossing the Strand was an ordeal in itself, the long thoroughfare positively swarming with automobiles, omnibuses, lorries, horses and carts, mounted policemen, rattling handcarts, stray dogs, hurtling cyclists and darting pedestrians. When he eventually got to the correct side of the road, Herbert took a deep breath to compose himself. He needed to be at his most assured for the critical interview with Edmund T. Roehampton. The fact that he would be dealing with one of the partners in the firm, and not with a mere underling, augured well. His novel would finally see the light of day – *subject to a certain changes*. Whatever those changes might be, Herbert vowed that he would willingly agree to them. A publisher was entitled to make minor adjustments and add refinements.

When he located the premises of Roehampton and Buckley, Ltd., he met with his first disappointment. Such a leading publishing house, he assumed, would have palatial offices that signalled its lofty position. Instead, it appeared to operate out of three rooms above a shoe shop. Mindful of the request for punctuality, Herbert checked his pocket watch, cleared his throat, rehearsed his greeting to Mr Roehampton and climbed the stairs. When he entered the outer office, he heard Big Ben booming in the distance. A second disappointment awaited.

The middle-aged woman seated at the desk looked over her pince-nez at him.

'May I help you, sir?' she said.

'Er, yes,' he replied, finding that his collar was suddenly too tight for him. 'I have an appointment with Mr Roehampton at three o'clock.'

'What name might that be, sir?'

'Syme. Herbert Syme.' His confidence returned. 'I'm an author.'

'Ah, yes,' she said, her tone softening. 'Mr Syme. I remember now. I'm Miss Finch. It was I who wrote to you to arrange the appointment. Welcome to London, Mr Syme. Mr Roehampton will deal with you as soon as he returns from his luncheon.'

'Luncheon?'

'He and Mr Buckley always eat at their club on a Wednesday.'

'I see.'

'Do take a seat. Mr Roehampton will be back within the hour.'

Within the hour! So much for punctuality. It had taken Herbert all morning simply to reach London. To arrive in the Strand at the stipulated time had required a huge effort on the part of the provincial author. During the wayward journey from the station to the offices of Roehampton and Buckley, Ltd., his provincialism had been cruelly exposed. His instincts were blunted, his accent jarred, his lack of sophistication was excruciating. He was made to feel like a country mouse in a metropolitan jungle. All that would soon vanish, he reminded himself. He was going to be a published author. As he sank down on the chair beside the door, he consoled himself with the fact that that he had made it to the top of Mount Olympus, albeit situated above a shoe shop in the Strand. It was only right that a mortal should await the arrival of Zeus from his luncheon.

Miss Lavinia Finch offered little decorative interest to the observer. A spare, severe woman of almost exotic ugliness, she busied herself at her typewriter, striking the keys with a random brutality that made the machine groan in pain. She ignored the visitor completely. Herbert did not mind. His gaze was fixed on the oak bookcase that ran from floor to ceiling behind the secretary. The firm's output was stacked with a neatness that gladdened the heart of a librarian. He feasted his eyes on the impressive array of volumes, thrilled that he would be joining them in time and deciding that he, too, when funds permitted, would acquire just such a bookcase in which to exhibit his work. Herbert was so caught up in his contemplation of literature that he did not notice how swiftly an hour passed. The chimes of Big Ben were still reverberating when Edmund T. Roehampton breezed in through the door.

A third disappointment jerked Herbert to his feet. Expecting the Zeus of the publishing world to be a huge man with a commanding presence, he was surprised to see a dapper figure strutting into the room. Roehampton was a self-appointed dandy, but the fashionable attire, the dazzling waistcoat and the gleaming shoes could not disguise the fact that he was a small man with a large paunch and a face like a whiskered donkey. Seeing his visitor, he doffed his top hat, pulled the cigar from between his teeth and manufactured a cold smile.

'Ah!' he declared. 'You must be Syme.'

'That's right, sir. Herbert Syme. The author of – '

'Well, don't just stand there, man,' continued Roehampton, interrupting him. 'Come into my office. We must talk. Crucial decisions have to be made.' He opened the door to his inner sanctum and paused. 'Any calls, Miss Finch?'

'None, Mr Roehampton,' she said.

'Good.'

'But you do have an appointment at four-thirty with Mr Agnew.'

'Syme and I will be through by then.'

He went into his office and Herbert followed him, uncertain whether to be reassured or alarmed by the news that a bare half-an-hour had been allotted to him. Had he come so far to be given such short shrift? Roehampton waved him to a seat, put his top hat on a peg, then took the leather-backed chair behind the desk. Raised up on a daïs, it made him seem much bigger than he was. Herbert relaxed. The office was much more like the place he had envisaged. Large and well appointed, it had serried ranks of books on display as well as framed sepia photographs of the firm's major authors. Herbert wondered how long it would be before his own portrait graced the William Morris wallpaper.

Roehampton drew on his cigar and studied Herbert carefully.

'How is Yorkshire?' he asked abruptly.

Herbert was thrown. 'Yorkshire, sir?'

'That's where you come from, isn't it?'

'No, Mr Roehampton. Derbyshire. I come from Derbyshire.'

'I knew it up was up there somewhere,' said the other dismissively, opening a drawer to take out a manuscript. He slapped it down on the desk. 'Well, Syme, here it is. Your novel.'

'I'm so grateful that you are prepared to publish it, Mr Roehampton.'

'Subject to a certain changes.'

'Yes, yes. Of course,' agreed Herbert. 'Anything you say.'

'Then let's get down to brass tacks,' said the publisher, exhaling a cloud of acrid smoke. 'Interesting plot. Well drawn characters. Good dialogue. A novel with pace.' He gave a complimentary nod. 'You're a born writer, Syme.'

Herbert swelled with pride. 'Thank you, sir.'

'But you still need to be weaned.'

'I await your suggestions, Mr Roehampton.'

'Oh, they're not suggestions,' warned the other. 'They're essential improvements. Mr Buckley and I could never put our names on a book with which we were not entirely and unreservedly satisfied.'

'And what does Mr Buckley think of *Murder in Matlock*?' wondered Herbert. 'Your letter said that it had found favour with all who had read it.'

'Yes. With Miss Finch and with myself. We are your audience.' He heaved a sigh. 'Mr Buckley, alas, is not a reader. The perusal of the luncheon menu at our club is all that he can manage in the way of sustained reading. What he brings to the firm is money and business acumen. What I bring,' he added, thrusting a thumb into his waistcoat pocket, 'is true literary expertise and a knack of un-earthing new talent.'

'I'm delighted to be included in that new talent, Mr Roehampton.'

'We shall see, Syme. We shall see. Now, to business.' He consulted the notes written on the title page of the manuscript. 'Omissions,' he announced. 'Let us first deal with your omissions.'

Herbert was baffled. 'I was not aware that I'd omitted anything.'

'Yours, sir, is a novel of sensation.'

'I see it more as a searching exploration of the nature of evil.'

'It amounts to the same thing, man. *Murder in Matlock* inhabits the world of crime and that imposes certain demands upon an author.'

'Such as?'

'To begin with, you must have a Sinister Oriental. A murder story is untrue to its nature if it does not have at least one – and preferably more than one – Sinister Oriental.'

'But there are no orientals, sinister or otherwise, in Matlock.'

'Invent some, man,' said Roehampton with exasperation. 'Import some. Bring in a Chinese army of occupation, if need be.'

'That would upset the balance of the narrative.'

'It will help to sell the book and that is all that concerns me.'

Herbert was deflated. 'If you say so, Mr Roehampton.'

'As to your villain, his name must be changed.'

'Why? What's wrong with Lionel Jagg?'

'Far too English,' explained the publisher. 'We need a wicked foreigner. Do you know why Wilkie Collins chose to christen the villain of *The Woman in White* with an Italian name? It was because he felt no Englishman capable of the skullduggery to which Count Fosco sank. I applaud the thinking behind that decision, Syme. Follow suit. Lionel Jagg commits crimes far too horrible for any true-born Englishman even to contemplate. Henceforth, he will be Count Orsini.'

'An Italian count in Matlock?' wailed Herbert. 'It's unheard of.'

'Anything can happen in Yorkshire.'

'Derbyshire, Mr Roehampton. Derbyshire.'

'Yorkshire or Derbyshire. Both are equally barbarous places.'

'That's unjust.'

'Let us move on. Criminals must be exposed early on to the reader. Lionel Jagg concealed his villainy too well. Count Orsini must be more blatant. Equip him with a limp and one eye. They are clear indications of villainy. A hare lip is also useful in this context. And he needs an accomplice, just as evil as himself.'

'Not another Sinister Oriental, surely?'

'No, no. Don't overplay that hand. A Wily Pathan will fit the bill here.'

Herbert was aghast. 'Wily Pathans in *Derbyshire?*'

'Metaphorically speaking, they are everywhere. They are the bane of the British Empire and we must remind our readers of that fact. Now, sir, to the most frightful omission of all. A hero. Your novel must have a Great Detective.'

'But it has one, Mr Roehampton. Inspector Ned Lubbock.'

'Wrong name, wrong character, wrong nationality,' insisted the publisher, stubbing out his cigar in the ashtray with decisive force. 'Lubbock is nothing but a country bumpkin from Derbyshire.'

'Yorkshire,' corrected the other.

'There – I *knew* the novel was set in Yorkshire!'

'In Derbyshire. Inspector Lubbock is a Yorkshireman, working in Matlock. I thought I made that abundantly clear.

'What's abundantly clear to me, Syme, is that you need to be more aware of the market you are hoping to reach. The common reader docs not want a bumbling detective from a remote northern fastness. He expects style, charm and intellectual brilliance, In short, sir, the Great Detective must be French.'

'Why?' groaned Herbert.

'Because there is a tradition to maintain,' asserted the other. 'Vidocq, Eugène Sue, Gaboriau. They all had French detectives, and not simply because they themselves hailed from France. Consider the case of Edgar Allan Poe, the American author. What is the name of his sleuth? Chevalier Auguste Dupin. It's inconceivable that someone called Ned Lubbock should solve *The Murders in the Rue Morgue*.'

'It's just as ludicrous to have a French detective hailing from Yorkshire.'

'Change his birthplace to Paris.'

Herbert descended to sarcasm. 'The Rue Morgue, perhaps?'

'And give the fellow more substance,' said Roehampton, sweeping his protest aside. 'This is the age of the Scientific Detective, the man with a supreme intelligence. Think of Sherlock Holmes. Think of Monsieur Lecoq. Think of The Thinking Machine.'

All that Herbert Syme had thought about for years was publication. Elevation to the ranks of those he idolised most would solve everything. It would rescue him from a humdrum life in a small provincial library where he was mocked, undervalued and taken for granted. Five years had gone into the creation of the novel that would be his salvation. In that time, he had grown to love Inspector Ned Lubbock, to marvel at his invention of the dastardly Lionel

Jagg, and to take a special delight in the meticulous evocation of his native Derbyshire. His hopes were dashed. Edmund T. Roehampton was mangling his novel out of all recognition. He felt the grief of a mother whose only child is being slowly strangled in front of her. Anger began to take root.

'Inspector Jacques Legrand,' decreed Roehampton. 'That name has more of a ring to it. He uses scientific methods of detection and outwits the villains with his superior brainpower. Needless to say – and I must repair another omission of yours – he must be a Master of Disguise. Just like Hamilton Cleek – the Man of the Forty Faces.'

Herbert struck back. 'And what does this preposterous French detective disguise himself *as*?' he asked, his Derbyshire vowels thickening in the process. 'An Italian Count or a Wily Pathan? Or maybe he can pretend to be the commander of an invading Chinese army. And where do his changes of apparel come from? I should warn you that there are no costume hire shops in the Peak District.'

'I'm glad that you mentioned that, Syme.'

'Does that mean I've got *something* right at last?'

'Far from it. Your location is a disaster.'

'You're going to take Derbyshire away from me as well?' cried Herbert.

'I have to, man. Shift the story to London and we enlarge its possibilities.'

Heavier sarcasm. 'In which part of the capital is Matlock to be found?'

'Nowhere, fortunately,' said Roehampton with a complacent chuckle. 'Unlike your home town, we do have more than our share of Sinister Orientals here so that's one problem solved. My shirts are washed at a Chinese laundry and they are obsequiously polite to me but there's still something ineradicably *sinister* about them.'

'They're foreigners, that's all, In Peking, you would appear sinister to them.'

'That's beside the point. Your novel is not set in China.'

'No,' said Herbert, desperation taking hold. 'It's firmly rooted in Derbyshire. How can a book called *Murder in Matlock* be set in the city of London?'

'By a simple slash of the pen. Here,' said the publisher grandly, indicating the title page of the manuscript. 'I crossed out your effort and inserted my own. I venture to suggest that it will have more purchase on the reader's curiosity.'

Herbert was shaking with fury. 'You've stolen my title as well?'

'Improved upon it, Syme. That is all.'

'In what way?'

'See for yourself,' advised the other, pushing the manuscript across to him. 'Ignore the blots. My pen always leaks. Just imagine those words emblazoned across the title-page of your novel. *Slaughter in the Strand*.'

'But there's no mention of the Strand in the book.'

'There is now, Syme. I've also included some other elements you failed to include. As well as being a killer, Count Orsini must be a Prince of Thieves just like Arsène Lupin. You see?' he said, eyes glinting. 'The Franco-Italian touch once more. Inspector Legrand must solve the crime by playing with a piece of string while sitting in the corner of a restaurant. Notice the hint of Baroness Orczy there? The Old Man in the Corner. It adds to the international flavour of the novel. On which subject, I must point out another fatal omission.'

Herbert gritted his teeth. 'Go on,' he growled.

'There are no German spies in the book. We must have spies for the Kaiser. Remember le Queux, a true English patriot as well as a brilliant writer. He's warned us time and again about the menace of the Prussian eagle. Yes, Syme,' he concluded, sitting back with a grin, 'those are the few changes I require. Make them and your book may stand a chance in a busy marketplace.'

'Except that it won't be *my* book,' snarled Herbert.

'What do you mean?'

'I mean, Mr Roehampton, that you have been hurling names at me that I neither like nor strive to emulate. Vidocq, Sue, Gaboriau, Baroness Orczy, William le Queux. They merely skate on the surface of crime. I tried to deal with the subject in depth,' argued Herbert, rising to his feet. 'If you want an international flavour, listen to the names of those who inspired me to write *Murder in Matlock*. Dostoevsky gave me my villain. Balzac supplied me with my insight into the lower depths of society. Maupassant taught me subtlety. Goethe schooled my style. You wave Wilkie Collins at me, but a far greater English writer suggested the infanticide with which my novel begins – George Eliot, the author of *Adam Bede*. My debt to them is there for all to see. I'll not have it obliterated.'

Roehampton blinked. 'Am I to understand that you reject my emendations?'

'I refuse to put my name to the rubbish you've concocted.'

'Ah, yes,' said the publisher, rubbing his hands. 'That brings me to my final point. Whatever form the novel finally takes, we cannot possibly put your name on it.'

'Why not?'

'Be realistic, man. Syme rhymes with Slime. The critics would seize on that like vultures. Herbert Syme sounds like, well, what, in all honesty, you are, a struggling librarian from a Yorkshire backwater.'

'Derbyshire!' roared Herbert. 'Matlock is in Derbyshire!'

'That point is immaterial in a novel called *Slaughter in the Strand.*'

'I loathe the title.'

'It will grow on you in time,' said Roehampton persuasively. 'So will your new pseudonym. Out goes Herbert Syme and in comes – wait for it – Marcus van Dorn. It has a bewitching sense of mystery about it. Marcus van Dorn. Come now. Isn't that a name to sow excitement in the breast of every reader?'

Herbert exloded. 'But it's not *my* name!'

'It is now, Syme.'

'You can't do this to me, Mr Roehampton.'

'I'm a publisher. I can do anything.'

It was horribly true. Herbert's great expectations withered before his eyes. He was not, after all, going to be an author. If this was how publishers behaved, he was doomed. Life would become intolerable. All the people to whom he had boasted of his success would ridicule him unmercifully. He would have to return to the library with his tail between his legs. Every time he put one of Roehampton and Buckley's books on a shelf, the wound would be reopened. It was galling. Publication was not rebirth at all. It was akin to the infanticide with which his novel had so sensitively dealt.

The villain of the piece was none other than a man whom he had revered from afar. Edmund T. Roehampton had not only hacked his book to pieces, he had altered its title and deprived the author of his identity. It was the ultimate blow to Herbert's pride. His gaze fell on his precious manuscript, disfigured by ink blots and scribbled notes, then it shifted slowly to the gleaming paper knife. A wild thought came into his mind.

'Well,' said Roehampton, 'do you want the book published or not?'

'Only if it's my novel.'

'Make the changes I want or it will never get into print.'

Herbert stood firm. 'I'll not alter a single word.'

'Then take this useless manuscript and go back to Yorkshire.'

'Derbyshire!'

It was the final insult. As Roehampton reached for the manuscript, Herbert grabbed the paper knife and stabbed his hand. The publisher yelled in pain but there was worse to come. Pushed to the limit, Herbert dived across the desk and stabbed him repeatedly in the chest, avenging the murder of his novel with a vigour he did not know he possessed. Alerted by her employer's yell, Miss Finch came bustling into the office. When she saw the blood gushing down Roehampton's flashy waistcoat, she had a fit of hysteria and screamed madly. Herbert was on her within seconds. Lavinia Finch was an accomplice. She had not only typed out the guileful letter to him, she had read the finest novel ever to come out of Matlock and pretended to admire it. She had deceived Herbert just as much as her employer and deserved to die beside him. He stabbed away until her screams turned to a hideous gurgling. Both victims were soon dead.

Herbert Syme had travelled in a first-class carriage on the most significant journey of his life, but his return ticket would not be used. A horse-drawn police van was his mode of transport now. As he sat in handcuffs behind bars, he reflected that he had, after all, achieved one ambition. His name would certainly be seen in print now. Every newspaper in Britain would carry the banner headline – *Slaughter in the Strand*. A treacherous publisher may have provided that title but its author would not be Marcus van Dorn. It would be Herbert Syme, the most notorious criminal ever to come out of Matlock in Derbyshire. He liked that. It was a form of poetic justice.

The masquerade

SARAH RAYNE

I seldom attend parties unless I think they might be of use in my career, so it was all the more remarkable to find myself attending this one. This is not due to shyness, you understand, nor to a lack of self-confidence – I value myself and my attainments rather highly. But I have always shunned larger gatherings – the chattering, lovely-to-see-you, how-are-you-my-dear, type of event. Loud music, brittle conversation, ladies air-kissing one another and then shredding each other's reputations in corners. Not for me. My wife, however, has always enjoyed all and any parties with shrieking glee, telling people I am an old sobersides, and saying with a laugh that she makes up for my quietness.

But here I was, approaching the door of this house whose owners I did not know, and whose reasons for giving this party I could not, for the moment, recall.

It was rather a grand-looking house – there was an air of quiet elegance about it which pleased me. One is not a snob, but there are certain standards. I admit that my own house, bought a few years ago, is – well – modest, but I named it 'Lodge House' which I always felt conveyed an air of subdued grandeur. The edge of a former baronial estate, perhaps? That kind of thing, anyway. My wife, of course, never saw the point, and insisted on telling people that it was Number 78, halfway down the street, with a tube station just round the corner. I promise you, many is the time I have *winced* on hearing her say that.

This house did not appear to have a name or a number, or to need one. There was even a doorman who beckoned me in; he seemed so delighted to see me I felt it would be discourteous to retreat.

'Dear me,' I said, pausing on the threshold. I do not swear, and I do not approve of the modern habit of swearing, with teenagers effing and blinding as if it were a nervous tic, and even television programme-makers not deeming it necessary to use the censoring bleep. So I said, 'Dear me, I hadn't realised this was a fancy-dress party. I am not really dressed for it – ' You might think, you who read this, that someone could have mentioned that aspect to me, but no one had.

'Oh, the costume isn't important,' said the doorman at once. 'People come as they are. You'll do very nicely.'

He was right, of course. Dressed as I was, I should have done very nicely anywhere. I am fastidious about my appearance, although my wife says I am pernickety. Downright vain, she says: everyone laughs at you for your old-fashioned finicking. I was wearing evening clothes – one of the modern dress shirts the young men affect, with one of those narrow bow ties that give a rather 1920s look, and I was pleased with my appearance. Even the slightly thin patch on the top of my head would not be noticeable in this light.

Once inside, the house was far bigger than I had realised; huge rooms opened one out of another, and the concept put me in mind of something, although I could not quite pin down the memory. Some literary allusion, perhaps? It would be nice to think I had some arcane poet or philosopher in mind, but actually I believe I was thinking of Dr Who's Tardis. (Pretentious, that's what you are, my wife always says. We all have a good laugh at your pretensions behind your back.)

There were drinks and a buffet, all excellent, and the service – well, you have perhaps been to those exclusive, expensive restaurants in your time? Or to one of the palatial gentlemen's clubs that can still be found in London if one knows where to look? Then you will have encountered that discreet deference. Food seemed almost to materialise at one's hand. I was given a glass of wine and a plate of smoked salmon sandwiches straight away and I retired with them to a corner, in order to observe the guests, hoping to see someone I knew.

The term 'fancy-dress' was not quite accurate after all, although a more bizarre collection of outfits would be hard to find anywhere. There was every imaginable garb, and every creed, colour, race, ethnic mix – every walk of society, every profession and calling. Try as I might I could see no familiar faces, and this may have been why, at that stage, I was diffident about approaching anyone. It was not due to my inherent reticence, you understand: in the right surroundings I can be as convivial as the next man. This was more a feeling of exclusion. In the end, I moved to a bay window to observe, and to drink my wine – it was a vintage I should not have minded having in my own cellars. Well, I say *cellars*, but actually it's an under-stairs cupboard containing several wine-racks bought at our local DIY centre. It is not necessary to tell people this, however, and I always remonstrated with my wife when she did.

By an odd coincidence, the wine seemed to be the one I had poured for my wife quite recently, although I have to say good wine was always a bit of a waste on her because she never had any discrimination; she enjoys sugary pink concoctions with paper umbrellas and frosted rims to the glass. Actually, she once even attended some sort of all-female party dressed as a Piña Colada: the memory of that still makes me shudder and I shall refrain from describing the outfit. (But I found out afterwards that Piña Colada translates, near enough, as strained pineapple, which seems to me very appropriate.)

But on that evening we had been preparing to depart for my office Christmas dinner, so I was hoping there would be no jazzily-coloured skirts or ridiculous head-dresses. It's a black tie affair, the office Christmas dinner, but when my wife came downstairs I was sorry to see that although she was more or less conventionally dressed, her outfit was cut extremely low and showed up the extra pounds she had accumulated. To be truthful, I would have preferred to go to the dinner without her, because she would drink too much and then *flaunt* herself at my colleagues all evening; they would leer and nudge one another and I should be curdled with anger and embarrassment. Those of you who have never actually walked through a big office and heard people whispering, 'He's the one with the slutty wife', can have no idea of the humiliation I have suffered. I remember attending a small cocktail party for the celebration of a colleague's retirement. Forty-three years he had been with the firm, and I had been asked to make the presentation. A silver serving-dish had been bought for him – I had chosen it myself and it was really a very nice thing indeed and a change from the usual clock. I had written a few words, touching on the man's long and honourable service, drawing subtle attention to my own involvement in his department.

You will perhaps understand my feelings when, on reaching the hotel, my wife removed her coat to display a scarlet dress that made her look – this is no exaggeration – like a Piccadilly tart. I was mortified, but there was nothing to be done other than make the best of things.

After my speech, I lost sight of her for a couple of hours, and when I next saw her, she was fawning (there is no other word for it) on the Chairman, her eyes glazed, her conversation gin-slurred. When she thanked him for the hospitality she had to make three attempts to pronounce the word, and by way of finale she recounted to four of the directors a joke in which the words *cock* and *tail* figured as part of the punch line.

The really infuriating thing is that until that night I had known – absolutely and surely *known*! – that I was in line to step up into the shoes of my retiring colleague. I had been passed over quite a number of times in the past (I make this statement without the least shred of resentment, but people in offices can be very manipulative and the place was as full of intrigue as a Tudor court), but this time the word had definitely gone out that I was in line for his job. Departmental head, no less!

And what happened? After my wife's shameless display at the retirement cocktail party they announced the vacancy was to be given to a jumped-up young upstart, a pipsqueak of a boy barely out of his twenties! I think I am entitled to have been upset about it. I think anyone would have been upset. *Upset*, did I say? Dammit, I was racked with fury, and a black and bitter bile scalded through my entire body. I thought – you lost that promotion for me, you bitch, but one day, my fine madam, one day . . .

Nevertheless, I still looked forward to that year's Christmas party. I had always counted the evening as something of a special event, so before we left, I poured two glasses of the claret I kept for our modest festivities, setting hers down on the low table by her chair. She did not drink it at once – that was unusual in itself and it should have alerted me, but it did not. I remember she got up to find my woollen scarf at my request, and then, having brought it for me, asked me to go upstairs for her evening bag. She knows I hate entering her over-scented, pink-flounced bedroom, but she sometimes tries to tempt me into it. I have learned to foil her over the years: the room makes my skin crawl, and her physical importunities on those occasions make me feel positively ill. It was not always so, you understand. I fancy I have been as gallant as any man in my time.

So, the evening bag collected as hastily as possible, I sat down with my wine, although it was not as good as it should be. There was a slight bitter taste – it reminded me of the almond icing on the Christmas cake in its tin – and I remember thinking I must certainly complain to the wine shop. I set down the glass, and then there was confusion – a dreadful wrenching pain and the feeling of plummeting down in a fast-moving lift . . . Bright lights and a long tunnel . . .

And then, you see, I found myself here, outside the big elegant mansion with the doorman inviting me in . . .

It was instantly obvious what had happened. The sly bitch had switched the glasses while I was getting her evening bag. She realised what I was doing – perhaps she saw me stir the prussic acid into her glass while she pretended to find my scarf, or perhaps she had simply decided to be rid of me anyway. But whichever it was, I drank from her glass and I died instead. The cheating, double-faced vixen actually killed me!

It seems this house is some sort of judgement place, for the doorman came back into the room a few moments ago and said, 'Murderers' judgements', very loudly, exactly as if he was the lift-man at a department store saying, 'Ladies' underwear'.

Are these oddly-assorted people all murderers then? That saintly-looking old gentleman in the good suit, that kitten-faced girl who might have posed for a pre-Raphaelite painting? That middle-aged female who looks as if she would not have an interest beyond baking and knitting patterns . . . ?

Having listened to fragments of their talk, I fear they are.

' . . . and, do you know, if it had not been for the wretched office junior coming in at just that moment, I would have got away with it . . . But the stupid girl must go screaming off to Mr Bunstable in Accounts, and I ended up being convicted on the evidence of a seventeen-year-old child and the bought-ledger clerk . . . Twenty years I was given . . . '

'Twenty years is nothing, old chap. I got Life – and that was in the days when Life meant Life . . . '

' . . . *entirely* the auditor's own fault to my way of thinking – if he hadn't pried into that *very* small discrepancy in the clients' account, I shouldn't have needed to put the rat poison in his afternoon tea to shut him up . . . '

' . . . I always made it a rule to use good old-fashioned Lysol or Jeyes' Fluid to get all the blood off the knitting needle and they never got me, never even suspected . . . But that man over there by the door, he very stupidly cut costs: a cheap, supermarket-brand cleaner was what he used, and of course it simply wasn't thorough enough and he ended his days in Wandsworth . . . '

' . . . my dear, you should *never* have used your own kitchen knife, they were bound to trace it back to you . . . An axe, that's what I always used, on the premise that you can put the killing down to a passing homicidal maniac – What? oh, nonsense, there's always a homicidal maniac somewhere – I've counted six of them here tonight as it happens – matter of fact I've just had a glass of wine with a couple of them . . . Charming fellows . . . '

Well, whatever they may be, these people, charming or not, *I'm* not one of them. *I'm* not a murderer. This is all a colossal mistake, and I have absolutely no business being here because I did *not* kill my wife. I suppose a purist might argue that I had the *intention* to kill her, but as far as I know, no one has yet been punished for that, although I believe the Roman Catholic Church regards the intention as almost tantamount to the actual deed –

And that's another grievance! I may not actually have attended church service absolutely every Sunday, but I never missed Easter or Christmas. As a matter of fact, I rather enjoy the music one gets in a church. (Once I said this to my wife – hoping it might promote an interesting discussion, you know – but she only shrieked with laughter, asked if I was taking to religion, and recounted a coarse story about a vicar.)

But I have been a lifelong member of the Church of England and I should have thought as such I would have been taken to a more select division. However, there may be chance to point this out later. Presumably there will be some kind of overseer here.

It's unfortunate that for the moment I seem to be shut up with these people – with whom I have absolutely nothing in common. And all the while that bitch is alive in the world, flaunting her body, drinking sickly pink rubbish from champagne flutes. Taking lovers by the dozen, I shouldn't wonder, and living high on the hog from the insurance policies . . . Yes, that last one's a very painful thorn in the flesh, although I hadn't better use that expression when they come to talk to me, since any mention of thorns in the flesh may be considered something of a *bêtise* here. They'll have long memories, I daresay.

But I shall explain it all presently, of course. There's bound to be some kind of procedure for mistakes. I shall stand no nonsense from anyone, either. I did not kill my wife, and I'm damned if I'm going to be branded as a murderer.

I'm *damned* if I am . . .

Symptoms of loss

JERRY SYKES

When I was a kid it seemed like every radio in the country was tuned to the same station.

Walking home from school on summer afternoons, I would often catch the loose fragments of a song as they drifted through a stream of open windows and rolled into another three-minute twist of sound and emotion. It was as if each radio was a tiny speaker connected to an invisible jukebox loaded with all the hits from down the years, the music that had become as much a part of the atmosphere as the air we breathed.

Like most people, I remember many of the songs from my child-hood, although very few of them hold any special significance. It is only later, in adolescence, that we begin to attach certain records to defining moments in our lives, the heartfelt playlist invariably dis-playing symptoms of loss. As a child music is still very much in the background, a soundtrack to our eddying emotions.

The radio in our house sat on the kitchen windowsill, and one of the abiding images of my childhood is of my mother, hands plunged deep into suds and staring out across the rumpled back garden, providing whispered harmonies to the songs that stirred her heart.

She had been a professional singer back in the early sixties, nothing fancy, just one of a stable of backing singers contracted to one of the major record labels, but she had sung on a number of top thirty hits. Photographs of her at the time show that she had mastered the look, all solid hair and panda eyes, but she was destined never to make it out of the chorus.

My mother first met Greg Price, a skinny kid with dreams of stardom who would practise his Elvis swivel in the mirror until his legs ached, in September 1961 when they shared backing vocal duties on a Christmas record for some starch-hipped crooner. By the time the single hit number five the week before Christmas, my mother was pregnant and they were living together in a cold and damp fourth-floor bedsit in Hornsey. They were married on the first Saturday of the New Year.

In May 1962 my father was killed in a hit-and-run accident on the Seven Sisters Road as he walked home from a late night recording session. His body was found slumped against a streetlight early the following morning by a man out walking his dog, the dog walking in lazy circles around my father and barking in his face.

My mother never remarried, although she was only seventeen when I was born in July that year. I remember a number of boyfriends, but none of them seemed to be around for more than a couple of months. Not that she was lonely – she had a wide circle of friends and my Aunt Celia would often come and stay with us for long periods, usually following a break-up with her most recent husband (four at the last count).

My mother loved the sweet soul music of Philadelphia and Motown, Curtis Mayfield and The Isleys, and I would often lie awake at night listening to her singing along with the radio in her tobacco-deep voice. I would imagine her standing in a pool of warm moonlight, hips moving in rhythm with the music, and my heart would trip with joy.

A few days before she died, I sat at her bedside holding her hand and listened as she told me that the vicar had agreed for a song to be played at her funeral. She would not tell me the name of the song, and in the days immediately following her death I hid from grief in trying to figure out what it might be. She had a black sense of humour and I soon narrowed it down to a shortlist of three: the first two on the list – Harold Melvin's *If You Don't Know Me By Now* and The Chi-Lites' *Have You Seen Her* – were a bit too obvious, and in the end I settled on Marvin Gaye's *Abraham, Martin and John*, with its poignant and telling refrain ' . . . only the good die young'.

But nothing could have prepared me for that moment when the vicar pressed the play button and the cool morning air was filled with the hiss of the small tape recorder giving way to a galloping drumbeat that roared across the small church like a parade of wild horses.

It took me a while to place the song, but after a couple of bars I recognised it as The Tornados' *Telstar*, an instrumental from the early sixties that had been Number One on both sides of the Atlantic. There is no doubt that my mother would have known the song, but as to why she had chosen it to be played at her funeral . . .

I glanced around to check the faces of the other mourners. At my mother's request it was a small crowd, mainly friends she had known for a long time, people I had grown up with, crossing paths every couple of years. But I saw no trace of recognition as the tape poured out the remains of the song, or even surprise. Most of the faces just seemed to stare straight ahead, heads gently tilted back to stop the tears from falling, mouths tight in concentration.

Except for my Aunt Celia.

She held her face up to the ceiling and I saw a knowing smile grace her lips, crinkling the corners of her eyes. I stared at her, willing her to look over, and after a moment or so I was rewarded as her eyes flickered in my direction. Her smile seemed to jump out at me and I found myself smiling back at her.

It had been four years since I had last seen Celia, since my mother had moved out to Kent, in fact, and I had only managed to speak to her briefly before the service, but as I turned to face the front again the years slipped away and I caught a glimpse of myself in grey flannel shorts and knotted hair, always knotted hair.

Telstar faded to the rumbling of the turntable (my mother had made the tape herself, not even the vicar had been allowed a preview) and the vicar pushed the stop button on the tape recorder. After the service I thanked him for his kind words and for carrying out my mother's last wish and invited him back to the house for a drink.

*   *   *

A couple of days later I drove into London to visit my mother's solicitor.

It was a cold March day and the grey sky was filled with rolling clouds as I drove through the City and up into Islington. I left the car in Sainsbury's car park and walked through to Upper Street where the office was located over a remainder bookstore.

The stairwell smelled of turpentine and paint from the DIY store next door, and as I reached the first floor landing I felt a little light-headed and my vision briefly rippled in and out of focus. I pushed the door to the outer office open and entered a small reception area. A heavy-set woman of around forty lifted herself from behind an old wooden desk and smiled, running her hands over her hips.

'So sorry to hear about your mother, Mr Price. You must forgive me for not coming to the funeral, but we only heard the news yesterday when Mr Rhodes got back from holiday.' She came around the desk with both arms extended and for a moment I thought she was going to hug me.

'That's all right, it was only a small affair,' I said, holding up my hands in a calming gesture to keep her at arms' length. 'I'm sorry, Mrs . . . ' I pursed my lips, slowly shook my head.

'James,' she said, stopping so close to me I could smell her perfume, or maybe the paint fumes had penetrated this room as well. 'Audrey James. I knew your mother quite well, although of course we didn't see each other much since she moved out to the country.'

'No, she seemed to lose touch with a lot of her friends.'

'Anyway, Mr Rhodes is expecting you,' she continued. 'You can go straight through.' She gestured to a door to the rear of her desk. 'Can I get you anything?'

I nodded, still feeling the effects of the paint fumes. 'Just a glass of water, please.'

'A glass of water,' she repeated, committing it to memory, before heading through the outer door.

Despite the invitation to go straight through, I knocked on Rhodes's door before walking into his office.

He was standing at the window looking down at the traffic on Upper Street but turned as he heard me enter the room. He was a tall man, over six-six, and uncomfortable in his frame. To compensate, he had developed a stoop, his head hanging low as if his neck stuck out horizontally instead of vertically from his torso. A navy pinstripe suit hung from bony shoulders and his long fingers looked like fleshy links of chain protruding from the cuffs.

'Ah, Jeff,' he said. 'How are you doing? Bearing up?'

I shrugged. 'Fine, I suppose. As good as can be expected.'

'Good, good.' He swept his left arm out in front of him. 'Take a seat, make yourself comfortable.'

I lowered myself into the dark green leather sofa set to the side of his desk.

Rhodes placed his hands on his hips and arched his back, popping a few vertebrae, before settling again behind the dark mahogany desk. He began riffling through some papers, slipping them back into blue folders. 'If you'll just bear with me . . . How's Nancy?'

'Fine.'

'Kids?'

'They're okay. A bit young to understand, you know, although I do feel I should try and explain . . . heaven and hell and all that.'

'Heaven and hell, yes, good,' he mumbled, distracted. 'Ah, here it is.' He pulled a file from the stack at the side of his desk, read the label. 'Oh no, not that one. Sorry . . . '

Rhodes continued to look through the files.

My mind drifted back to the day of the funeral. 'Presumably you've looked over my mother's file since . . . since her death,' I said. He peered up at me through twisted eyebrows, nodded imperceptibly. 'I don't suppose you came across anything about *Telstar* – you know, the record from the sixties?'

Rhodes leaned back in his chair, a grin spreading across his face. His huge hands grasped the edge of the desk. 'She told you?' he said.

I shook my head, puzzled. 'It was played at the funeral, she asked the vicar . . . '

He frowned, the lines in his forehead forming a deep V. 'So she didn't tell you?'

I didn't understand and raised my hands in submission, shook my head again. 'Tell me what? She told me she'd asked the vicar to play a song at the funeral, a tape she'd made. *Telstar*. I never heard her mention it before.'

Rhodes hunched over his desk, threaded his long fingers together. He looked like a vulture sitting on a rock. 'In her will your mother left you just short of a million pounds in performing royalties from the recording of *Telstar*.'

I looked at him blankly, trying to get a hold on the information he had just imparted. I searched for a betrayal of the words in his eyes, but all I could see was true pleasure at the delivery of the surprise.

'Performing royalties? I don't understand. My mother, ah, performed on *Telstar*? She was a singer, a backing singer. *Telstar*'s an instrumental.'

'Well, as far as I am led to believe – and all that I have to go on is a letter from your mother – it was in fact your father who performed on the recording. And therefore, quite naturally, upon his death the royalties transferred to your mother, his wife.'

Although we had never been poor, my mother and I had never had the sort of lifestyle that a million pounds could bring. 'So where has the money been all this time?'

'A trust fund was set up in your name. To be realised upon your mother's death.'

'And you didn't know anything . . . '

Rhodes cut me off with a shake of his head. 'The first I knew of this was when I opened the letter yesterday morning.'

'Did she mention anything else about my father?'

'No, nothing. She never talked about your father.'

We sat in silence for a few moments, absorbing the news. Rhodes eventually began detailing the remainder of the will, but I had wandered into the shadows and alleys of my childhood and his words broke apart and disappeared before reaching my ears.

I knew very little about my father and had often wondered about him, but every time I thought about asking my mother I would be overcome with a terrible guilt, as if the very act of asking about him was to admit to my mother that her love was not enough. I had not even seen a photograph and over the years my image of him had developed into one featuring a blond Elvis pompadour dripping over a handsome face twisted and scarred by the elusive bittersweet taste of success.

The revelations about *Telstar* brought the image a little more into focus and with it a new determination to find out more about him.

* * *

Just north of Holloway Road station, I pulled over behind a dark green VW van and climbed out of the car. I waited for a break in the traffic, and then ran across the busy road. I stood on the edge of the pavement to avoid the crowds of people shuffling through the morning, and took in the building before me.

The ground floor formed part of a bicycle shop that sported a huge yellow sign running the length of three storefronts. Rows and rows of different types of bikes were lined up outside the shop, and neon coloured shirts filled the windows.

The circular blue plaque fixed to the wall between the windows on the first floor read:

JOE MEEK

RECORD PRODUCER

'THE TELSTAR MAN'

1929–1967

PIONEER OF SOUND

RECORDING TECHNOLOGY

LIVED, WORKED AND

DIED HERE

There are perhaps a couple of hundred similar plaques scattered throughout London, each commemorating the life and work of people who have lived in the capital, and located on the buildings most famously associated with them. Because of a twenty-year-dead rule, the majority were for people of whom I had never heard and in whom I had little interest. I had seen the plaque in Holloway Road on many occasions and it didn't tell me anything about Meek that I didn't already know.

An independent record producer before the term was invented (he had often been dubbed the British Phil Spector), he had created a number of hits in the late fifties and early sixties before the worldwide success of the Tornados' *Telstar* (named after the first communications satellite) in 1962 had made him a household name. A promiscuous homosexual, the more famous he became, the more terrified he became of being involved in a scandal that would jeopardise his career. The terror had eventually led to his suicide in 1967, ironically the year in which homosexuality had ceased to be illegal.

I ran back across the street and pointed the car in the direction of the Central Library.

* * *

A huge Victorian slab of weathered stone, the inside of the library looked more like a video rental store but I managed to locate a couple of books that touched on Meek and *Telstar*.

I could find no mention of my father, although I did come across a listing of the musicians who had played on *Telstar* – guitar, bass, keyboards, drums – so unless my father was working under a pseudonym then something strange was happening. And while it was true that many singers at the time had their names changed to conjure up images of hot and rugged masculinity, the same could not be said for the backing musicians. That was certainly the case with *Telstar*.

As for Meek himself, there were a couple of interesting facts concerning his extra-curricular activities. In 1963 he was arrested and charged with importuning in a public place, an event that served only to fuel his paranoia and lay him open to threats of blackmail. Even more interesting was the fact that prior to his suicide, Meek had shot and killed his landlady in a tormented rage over the possibility of being questioned by the police over the murder of a teenage boy. There was no suggestion that Meek himself had been involved in the murder in any way, but this time the fear had obviously been enough to push him over the edge.

Perhaps the most telling item of all, and certainly from my perspective, was that in the early sixties musicians (including those in successful groups) were simply hired hands and as such were paid a flat Musicians' Union rate for any recording sessions they played on, regardless of the outcome, demo or record, hit or no hit. The record company or, as in Meek's case, the independent producer, would re-tain all the rights to and subsequent royalties from the performances.

I left the library and wandered up to Highbury Fields where I sat on a bench and watched two men in suits kicking a football around, their red faces bubbling with perspiration. I thought about the million pounds and tried to retrace its route back to my father, but which-ever way I turned it was an immediate dead end.

On the way home I drove through Camden Town and stopped in at Virgin Records. As I expected, there was nothing under Meek or the Tornados but there was a whole pile of sixties compilations, mainly from '63 and the Beatles onwards, and I managed to find one that contained *Telstar*.

As I listened to the track over and over again, I began to hear a kind of wailing sound hiding behind the drums as the song faded into darkness. The sound was not quite human, but it was the closest thing to a vocal on the record and I wondered if it was in fact the sound of my father's million-pound performance. And then again, maybe it was just the sound of the silent scream of frustration in my head.

*   *   *

The following day the girls began asking questions about their grandmother. Since she had fallen ill and moved down to Kent a few years earlier they had spent a lot of time in each others' com-pany and now, a week after her death, the girls were beginning to sense that something was wrong. Nancy could see I was still a little shaky and offered to break the news to them for me. I gratefully accepted and left her to it.

I drove over to my mother's house with the intention of sorting through her belongings. We had put the house on the market and the place needed to be cleared. Most of the stuff would be going straight to the charity shop but I wanted to sort through everything first to see if there was anything personal that I wanted to hold on to.

My mother had moved from a cramped two-bedroom flat into a spacious three-bedroom house and as she had never been a hoarder, her belongings rattled around the cold house.

I spent a couple of hours moving all the items intended for charity into the front room. All personal items I stacked into a cardboard box on the kitchen table to be taken home and sorted through later. As I worked I had a feeling that I was being watched, as if someone was looking over my shoulder, a sense of being temporarily haunted.

I left the bedroom until last, believing that that would be the place where I was most likely to come across anything concerning my father. But my mother had never been one for sentiment and the only thing of interest I found was an old shoebox containing twenty mint copies of *Landing Lights*, the first record she had sung on, a stack of ten-by-eight promotional photos turning brown and curling at the edges, and a reel of tape from an old reel-to-reel tape recorder. I put the shoebox in the cardboard box on the kitchen table and then carried the box out to the car.

* * *

Celia Drake emerged from the patio doors carrying two cold cans of beer. She handed one to me and pulled the tab on the other, pouring the beer into a long glass before settling on the wooden bench and tucking her feet up under her thighs.

She offered me a cigarette and when I shook my head, she lit one for herself, tossing the match into a glass ashtray on the table between us. Her green eyes were violently alive in the sunlight.

I popped the tab on the beer and took a long swallow.

'You never met my father, did you?'

Celia shook her head. 'No, that was before my time. I didn't meet Meg until, oh, sixty-four, I think. Sixty-four, sixty-five, some time around then.'

'My mum ever talk about him?'

A frown creased her face. 'Not really. Maybe in the abstract, as if he was an interesting place she'd once visited or something.' She fixed me with a stare. 'Why, you keen to find out about him now?'

'Yeah, well, I always felt a little awkward before, you know. But I thought that now mum's dead . . . ' I shrugged. 'Besides, I always got the feeling she was making it up as she went along when she spoke about him.'

She lifted her face to the sun and smiled. 'I know what you mean.'

My mother would often make up stories about my father, romanticising him, bedevilling him, weaving him into tales that I myself had read in the Sunday papers or seen on TV.

Celia pulled on the cigarette and blew a streamer of blue smoke into the air over her head. She looked at me with a directness I had never seen before and said, 'You're going to find out sooner or later so you might as well hear it from me. Your mother and father were never married.'

For some reason this did not shock me as much as I thought it would. Or Celia. She saw the lack of response in my eyes and said, 'You don't seem surprised.'

'No. I guess I never really thought of my mum as having been married. I mean, it was all over before I was born, and . . . well, I've never even seen a wedding photo or anything like that.'

'Your father was just a kid who only ever wanted one thing in his life. To be a pop star. So what's he gonna do when he finds out your mum got herself knocked up? Put on a suit and go out and get himself a regular job? Besides, the way I understand it, Meg was not the only one to fall for his charms.'

'But she still used his name.'

Celia shrugged her shoulders. 'It was 1962. They were still locking up single mothers in mental hospitals back then, you know.'

I took a sip of beer and looked out across the lawn. Purple and yellow crocuses poked through the faded grass. I had not mentioned my inheritance to Celia, I wanted to piece together the story of my father without any prompts or false leads.

'You remember how he died?'

'Sure, he was hit by a car when he came out of The Rainbow one night. He'd been to see Billy Fury or one of those other guys he always wanted to be and stepped right out in front of a car. I heard he was a little drunk.'

'Did anyone see it happen? Anyone with him?'

Celia shook her head. 'I don't know. Meg never really talked about it.'

'Would he have made it, do you think?'

'As a singer? Well, she always said he had a good voice and I think he did have some sort of deal with Joe Meek lined up when he had the accident. You know, the *Telstar* guy.'

I nodded, a loose smile of recognition playing on my lips.

She pointed at me with her glass. 'Bill Jackson, that's who you want to talk to. Shared a flat with Greg round about the time he was killed.' She leaned forward and added, 'Knew your mum, too. She had an affair with him right after you were born. Didn't last long but they were pretty close and stayed friends afterwards.'

'So he's still alive?'

'Had a card from him just last Christmas. He lives down your way on the coast somewhere near Deal.' She gently tapped me on the arm. 'I'll go get the address for you,' she said and lowered her feet to the ground and walked into the house.

The thought of my mother being in love filled me with an unbear-able feeling of sadness and when I moved to hug Celia before I left I felt a tear squeeze from my eye and my heart swell with warmth and pride at my mother's selfless devotion. I knew that she had had boyfriends, but how could my young heart have known if she had truly been in love and had put that love aside to care for me?

*   *   *

Deal was one of those old seaside towns that had died with the ad-vent of cheap package holidays in the mid-sixties. It seemed appropriate that a musician whose career had been all but over when the Beatles were still in Hamburg should have chosen to retire there. As I drove through the outskirts of the town I tried to imagine what the place must have been like in its heyday, but none of the images that flickered in my head had any connection to the sad grey buildings and sad grey people that slumped along the side of the road.

I drove along the seafront past the pier. A number of people braved the cold wind blowing off the sea and a café at the end appeared to be open, but the whole place had the feeling of having been abandoned: a commuter town where everyone had forgotten to go back home again.

I headed out towards Kingsdown and as I moved into the country-side colour began to bleed back into the landscape. I found the village without much trouble and, after stopping to ask directions in the village store, followed a narrow lane down to the coast road. Between the road and the sea a dozen or so wooden chalets kept watch across the channel.

I left the car on the road and walked up the narrow pathway to the sky blue chalet in the centre of the row and knocked on the door. The chalets appeared to consist of a single room and I wondered how safe they would be in a storm. Only fifty feet of pebbled beach separated them from the sea. The pastel paintwork only added to the sense of fragility.

Jackson was home and after I introduced myself he ushered me through the front door. I scanned the room: partitions in the two far corners isolated what I took to be a bedroom and a bathroom. A kitchen crept into the living area from the wall directly to my right. A battered acoustic guitar was the only sign of his past.

Jackson was a wiry man with his hair brushed back in a threadbare DA, drainpipe jeans, and a fisherman's smock. His eyes still held a boyish light and I wondered what had brought him to this isolated corner of the country. He made a pot of coffee and settled into an old armchair below the rear window. I pulled out a chair from the small dining table and sat facing him.

I started to ask him about my father but he held up his hand and stopped me. A dark sadness befell his eyes and he took a deep breath. 'Joe Meek didn't used to write songs, he used to hear the completed record in his head and then try and capture that sound on tape. His flat, his studio, was always full of musicians: there'd be the rhythm section in the living room, guitar and vocals in the bedroom, keyboard in the loo, strings out in the hall and the brass section lined up down the staircase. Joe would be in the kitchen with his equipment pulling it all together. And if he didn't hear the sound he wanted, well, he'd try something else. I once saw him stamping on the bathroom floor to get just the right drum sound he wanted. He wasn't afraid to take risks and try something new. It was that same 'outthereness' that pushed him to take risks in his private life and leave him open to predators.

'Your father wanted to be a star. He thought Billy Fury was the greatest singer he had ever seen, *Halfway to Paradise* the greatest song he had ever heard. He was like that, Greg, everything was big, he had no time for anything less. Fury was greater than Elvis, greater than Buddy Holly, and Greg Price was going to be bigger than all of them.

'He had some kind of deal with Meek to record a couple of songs with the Tornados – Greg liked the idea that they'd originally been Fury's band, as if he'd stolen them from him or something. But then Meek changed his mind. He had the idea for *Telstar* and wanted the band to become some sort of keyboard-led Shadows – the Shadows were incredibly popular at the time and Meek wanted a piece of the action. Greg was furious. He tried to blackmail Meek about his homosexuality, but Meek was already being leaned on by a bunch of goons and when they got to hear about it . . . ' He drew a finger theatrically across his throat.

I stared at the man, incredulous. 'Are you saying my father was murdered?'

'Well, it's more of a gut feeling, I don't have any proof.'

I nodded for him to go on. I could feel my heart beat against my ribcage and my face felt numb. Suddenly a man who had been killed before I was born was the most real person in my life.

His shoulders had slumped and he stared out of the window. A watery redness had seeped into his eyes. 'I remember him telling me that he'd been threatened by a couple of thugs one night, guys he'd seen hanging round the café near Meek's flat. I just thought it was another one of his stories, even after he was killed. There was nothing to suggest that the accident had been anything but an accident.

'But then a year or so later, when I'd been seeing Meg for a couple of months, Meek's assistant Johnny Wood asked me why I was still working, why didn't I just get hitched to your mum and retire. When I asked him what he meant, he said something about Greg having been sacrificed for her benefit.'

' "Sacrificed for her benefit." You know what he meant by that?' Jackson shook his head.

'Did you ask my mother what he may have meant?'

He shook his head again. 'She wouldn't talk about it.'

'Did my father play on *Telstar*? Is that what this guy Wood meant, do you think?'

Jackson looked at me with a puzzled expression on his face. 'Your father was killed before *Telstar* was recorded,' he said.

'Yes, of course,' I said, the words drifting away from me.

My head was beginning to feel a little foggy and I suggested we take a walk along the beach, and for a couple of hours he chatted about the early days of the British pop scene. Time had dulled his memory and there was only real feeling in his voice when he spoke of his old friends.

I could smell salt on the air and the rhythm of the surf breaking on the pebble beach had a calming and refreshing effect on me. I felt at ease for the first time since my mother's death.

As we walked back along the pathway and stopped in front of his chalet, Jackson said, 'Greg was a ruthless man and a great user of people. He used your mother, dumped her the minute he heard she was pregnant. But he didn't deserve to die.' He looked out across the flat grey expanse of the sea, his face heavy with a sadness that had been buried for a long time. 'He was a good friend to me.'

I drove home with the feeling that at last my father was becoming a real person, with flesh and blood and hopes and ambitions and a mean streak as wide as it was long.

I was still no closer to finding the truth about *Telstar*, but Jackson had told me that Johnny Wood still lived at the flat in Holloway Road.

*   *   *

The following morning I stood outside the bike shop looking up at the windows on either side of the blue plaque. It was almost eleven and the blinds were still drawn. I rang the bell and waited.

The features on Wood's large face were bunched close together and large patches of tired skin reflected the dull light emanating from the naked bulb hanging from the ceiling of the hallway. Strands of brittle grey hair covered his scalp.

He closed his eyes and nodded as I introduced myself, as if he had been expecting me. He turned and I followed him up the stairs.

I refused the offer of a drink and sat on the edge of the sofa and waited for him to speak.

'I first met your father back in January '61,' he began, a new energy in his eyes. 'He was just a kid – nineteen, twenty – and like every other kid who came around he wanted to be a star. Joe used to let some of 'em hang around, helping out, running errands, that sort of thing. Good-looking kids, Joe always had good-looking kids hanging around, especially if they didn't mind staying over.' He raised his eyebrows and looked at me knowingly. 'Greg could sing a little, he even played on a couple of records, I think. He was never gonna be a star, but he kept on pestering Joe to let him make a record.

'One morning, right out of the blue, Joe tells me he's gonna let Greg do *Walk Her Home* with the Tornados backing him. I think Greg must've stayed over the night before . . .' Wood paused to light a cigarette and let the full meaning of his words sink in. I let his words hang in the air. 'Told me to call in the guys, we were gonna do it that afternoon. Anyhow, a couple of hours later, Joe changed his mind, told me to scrap it.'

'Greg was furious. He came around late that night smashed out of his head. It was around ten and I was in the kitchen recording some overdubs with Joe, who was in the living room. The two of them got into this huge argument, a fight – I could hear it all through the speakers in the kitchen – and Joe hit him over the head with a guitar. I heard this awful scream and ran into the living room, but Greg was already dead, just lying there with his head in this pool of blood. Joe was standing over him with the guitar still in his hand. Next thing I knew Meg was in the room – she'd been staying with Mrs Harvey downstairs since Greg had walked out on her – pushing everyone around. She sent me out to the kitchen and told me to sit tight and I just sat there shaking, I was shaking so much I could hardly light a cigarette.

'When I turned up the next morning Joe was sitting in the living room just staring at the spot where Greg had fallen. He'd been up all night and his eyes were sunk deep in his face. He told me that they'd bundled Greg into the boot of his car and gone and dumped him in the road up behind the Rainbow some place. Made it look like an accident.' He pulled on the cigarette. 'And then your mother asked me for a copy of the tape.'

'The tape?' I said.

'Yeah, the tape. I'd left the machine running and got the whole thing down on tape.'

I remembered the tape I had found in my mother's house. 'You still have a copy?'

He shook his head, no.

It now seemed pointless asking whether or not my father had played on *Telstar*, the royalties had obviously been the pay-off. 'You know what happened after that?'

'Joe never mentioned it again. I think he went to the funeral, though.'

'And you have no doubt that she was blackmailing him?'

'Joe was always getting blackmailed, he said it was the curse of the famous queer. I think he just dealt with it the same way he did any other threat – he paid up and hoped that she wouldn't come back for more.'

A pained expression of satisfaction came over Wood's face and I had the feeling that he had been waiting in the flat for nearly forty years to tell me the story.

Over the next few days I tried desperately to hold on to the image I had of my mother. But it seemed that the more I learned about my father, the closer I came to knowing him, the further she slipped away, drifted into an alien darkness. The rasping angel of my childhood had become a dark and vengeful siren.

I had no intention of going to the police and I had no problem in reconciling myself to the money. Theoretically, it belonged to my father and whatever reservations I may have harboured about it being blood money soon dissolved when I told myself that because my mother had taken herself out of the loop (by creating the trust fund) it was a legitimate inheritance.

My acceptance of the money was also the acceptance of my father the star and his posthumous number one.

The beautiful irony of this did not strike me until a couple of months later. Nancy and I had stolen an early summer break from the kids and were enjoying a weekend in Brighton. Browsing among the junk shops in the Lanes on the Sunday morning, I came across an old tape recorder and I immediately thought of the reel of tape that I had found in my mother's house. After my meeting with Johnny

Wood I had tried to forget about the tape but a primal curiosity got the better of me and I put down two crisp five pound notes on the glass counter and walked out of the shop with the tape recorder under my arm.

As soon as I got home I dug the shoebox containing the reel of tape out of the attic and set up the equipment. The tape had faded over the years and there was a persistent background hiss but it was still possible to make out what was happening.

I listened with calm detachment as the sound of two men arguing broke into violence, with cries of pain riding a backbeat of flesh being struck. And then there it was, the final heart-wrenching scream of my father as the killing blow of the guitar connected with his head.

But it was the realisation that the cry was exactly the same cry that rode the fadeout of *Telstar* that brought the cold smile to my lips.

Big end blues

MARGARET MURPHY

The moment I clapped eyes on her I knew she was trouble. So what did I do? You guessed it – I took a few steps back, broke into a run, and did a flying leap into her arms. That's me all over: always hitching my cart to the wrong pony. Thing is, she's got style, has Norma. They say imitation's the sincerest form of flattery – well, with us it wasn't so much imitation as coordination. Fact is, we wanted to make an impact and since Norma's eye for colour and texture is more refined than mine, I went along with her choice. I mean in *every* detail. Skirt, blouse, jacket, shoes – even those little extras fashion shops call 'accessories'. If Norma bought it, so did I. We shuffled the colours around a bit – you don't want to look ridiculous, do you? But in all essentials we were identical.

It was Norma came up with our showbiz name. We were in a shop. Hers was a black denim jacket, red skirt, white scooped neck T-shirt. Mine was red jacket, black skirt – the tops were the same, as I recall. She looked at us, a glory of patchwork side by side in the mirror, and said it straight off: 'The Harlequin Twins'. It was a joke of course. You had to see us to get it. I sometimes wonder what folk make of us, her a tall, willowy blonde and me, a short, well-stacked brunette.

She has a good length of stride, does Norma – pretty impressive in stilettos. If you've ever worn them, you'll know what I mean. She glides, I wobble, but only a bit, and very fetchingly, I'm told.

We do a double act – on and off stage. Country and Western mostly – and when the mood takes her Norma can work the Mississippi Delta into her everyday chat like she was born to it.

We were having a bad day. A grey December afternoon in the north of England is depressing enough, but our transport was well and truly knackered, and it looked like we'd have to cancel our gig because we didn't have the wherewithal to pay for repairs. A grey

December afternoon in the north of England with no escape route –
that's death on wheels – except our wheels weren't rolling.

'Big end's gone,' the mechanic said, slamming the bonnet and wiping
his hands on a filthy towel.

'Why, thank you, honey,' Norma said, fluttering her eyelids and
twanging all over the place. 'All that dieting's been worth the
while.' She slid her hands over her perfectly toned buttocks just
to hammer home the point, but he wasn't having it. She was wearing the white denim skirt – thigh length (just) – and the fringed
nubuck jacket in red. Shoes to match the jacket and morals to
match the skirt – at least that's the gist of what she was trying to put
over to him.

He just narrowed his eyes and carried on wiping his hands. Must've
been a poof. It's worked before: she gets the job done on the promise
she'll make it up to him after we've got the van back – well, she can't
very well have him handling the goods with those grimy palms, can
she? Of course, by the time he arrives at The Dog and Duck, all
spruced up in his best jeans and trainers, we're halfway down the M6,
twenty minutes from our next gig.

We were set up for a theme pub in Birmingham. All the staff dress
up as cowboys and cowgirls. Four slots over two nights. The pay's all
right, if you can manage your money, but Norma's got a hunger for
shopping and we wouldn't be the Harlequin Twins if I didn't keep
up, now, would we? Besides, on the road, you've got other expenses,
like food and drink, make-up, equipment, but Mike the mechanic
wasn't playing, and it looked like our motor problem would be the
big end of a beautiful partnership.

We decided to think about it.

When Norma needs to think, she walks. So we walked. Every
few steps I had to run a bit just to keep up. We fetched up a couple
of miles away, near the docks. Empty warehouses on one side of
the road, a flattened plot on the other. Someone had put up a
billboard: 'Industrial land with outline planning permission'. Some
hope.

Norma stopped at the bus shelter and wiped the seat with a paper
tissue, parking her bum carefully on the edge of the narrow yellow
strip of plastic. Which made me think.

'Plastic,' I said, sitting next to her.

'No.' Norma has a rule – kind of a code of honour – never upset
your credit-card companies. Why? Because they pay for your clothes.

We were already up to our limit on account of the Birmingham gig demanding a new outfit each. 'No plastic,' she said.

I shrugged. They would probably have checked our creditworthiness anyhow.

Just then, a big, wheezy old removals van pulled up at the kerb, throbbing with pent-up bass rhythms. A bloke got out – well, I say 'bloke'. He was more simian than *Sapiens*. Bloody huge, fat and all, but enough muscle so you wouldn't be tempted to call him names. He opened the cab door and the music boomed out, loud enough to rattle your teeth loose. He jumped down with a wrench of some sort in his hand. Big wide thing it was, with handles both ends, like a plane propeller – a device with wings, to avoid embarrassing slippage – only for men.

Norma looked over at him and said, 'Hey, love, you couldn't turn that shit down could you?' No offence in it, just a polite request.

He growled – no, seriously – he really *growled*, like a dog, only bigger and meaner. And twice as dangerous. He started towards us with that bloody great wrench in his hand and I think, *there's nobody between us and the river*. This bloke could do whatever he wanted and we wouldn't able to raise a minor quibble, never mind an objection.

We ran. God knows where we thought we were running *to* but when someone as ugly as that looks at you like that, you don't think, you just run – anywhere, so long as it's *away*. He lobbed the wrench and I got it between the shoulder blades. I went down hard, about halfway across the road.

I'm winded and crying. I see this shadow over me like in some horror flick and I roll over, so at least I can see what's coming. He bends down and lifts me by the front of my jacket and I think *I'm dead*. Then I hear Norma, like her voice is coming from far off, but it's clear.

'Pooky,' she says, 'Now don't you be a grizzly old bear. You know we didn't mean no harm.' Where she got Pooky from, I don't know. She's always coming up with names like that – she thinks they sound authentic Southern USA.

The big bastard drops me, and I fall on my back, whooping, trying to get my breath. Norma's standing the other side of me, smiling, swinging that shiny wrench back and forth between her legs. Her image doubles, quadruples, on and on, like a thousand tiny images in a glitter-ball and I think, *Oh, God no – Norma don't* . . .

* * *

She pays the mechanic in cash, not wasting a smile on him this time, just completes the transaction and leaves. I'm driving. The van's never sounded so good. We motor for a while with the radio turned down low.

'All right?' she asks.

I'm not, but I nod anyway, gripping the wheel tight to stop my hands shaking.

She sorted everything. Got him off the road, over to his lorry. I helped her drag him on a piece of tarp we found in the back. It was empty aside from that one piece of ratty tarp. I said a prayer he had finished for the day, that someone wasn't waiting on a doorstep, checking the time, anxious for the removals man to arrive. We draped him over the engine and closed the bonnet over him. He looked like one of those joke dummies you sometimes see, half way up a wall – Santa with a sackful of goodies, that kind of thing.

'It won't fool anyone, you know,' I say.

'Correction,' she says. 'It won't fool anyone *for long*.' Just long enough for us to get away, she meant. I suppose she thinks I'm being ungrateful. 'In the meantime . . . ' She digs into her handbag and fans a handful of cash. 'Enough to be going on with.'

I nibble my lip and she sighs. 'Denise, honey, I'm gonna say this one more time.' She doesn't often turn the Southern charm on for me. My stomach lurches – because when she does, it means trouble. 'But this is the *very* last time.' She checks off the points on her fingers. 'Nobody saw us. We left no fingerprints. Not one bitsy clue. And it's not like he knew us. Who's going to suspect two sweet little ladies like you'n'me?' She bats her eyelashes and looks at me all innocent.

She's making me nervous, but I've got to admit she'd been thorough. Insisted on walking back into the city centre, rather than get a taxi, despite my bad back. She wore a disguise, so when she tried the numbers he had considerately written on a scrap of paper alongside his credit cards in his wallet, she was unrecognisable. I wouldn't have known her – her own *mother* wouldn't have known her in that get-up. Dark glasses, I would have expected, but she also wore a woolly hat – not a strand of hair showing – she even bought some cotton wool balls and stuffed in her mouth to fatten her cheeks. I was impressed. Norma is vain: she doesn't make herself look plain without a damn good reason.

'They take pictures at cash-tills these days you know,' she told me. Proud of herself.

I'm proud of her, too. Me – I'd've walked in to the nearest cop shop and made a tearful confession. Ruined the rest of my life. Not Norma. Still I *am* nervous – kind of in awe of her.

'Pull over.'

I do as I'm told. A quick glance around and then she drops Pooky's wallet down a drain at the side of the road.

'Untraceable, see? And that's the end of it.'

I want to believe her, honest I do. But she's got that look on her, like the day she gave us our stage name, and I know that this is only the start. For Norma and Denise read *Thelma and Louise*. It's only a matter of time.

Murder in the air

YVONNE EVE WALUS

Belinda smoothed down her flight attendant's uniform, served dinner to the first-class passengers, administered poison to the man in the front row, switched off the cabin lights and entered the galley. She washed her hands twice, scrubbing between the fingers and under the fingernails. With a disposable tissue, she wiped a small sachet (in case the porous paper managed to retain fingerprints), and threw it into the trash bin in the galley. Everything was going according to plan.

Then she hesitated. Slowly, ever so slowly, she bent down to retrieve the sachet. Yes. It made a lot more sense to change the plan and dispose of the sachet in the passengers' WC. Why hadn't she realised it before?

'Belinda, are you all right?'

Belinda flinched, but she kept her on-the-job smile on as she turned to face one of the other girls. 'Sure, Cathy. Why do you ask?'

'You look flushed, darling. Does it have anything to do with that passenger you are seeing? You know, the one who travels first-class with us from Bangkok every week?'

'I'm not seeing anybody,' Belinda could feel the heat in her cheeks. 'I'm engaged, remember?' She held up her hand so that Cathy could look at her ring. If you didn't know, you might think the diamond was real. 'Whatever made you think – '

'Don't worry, Bel. I won't tell a soul.'

'Won't tell what?'

'That I saw the two of you together yesterday. In the centre of the Patpong red light district? Whispering like a pair of lovers – '

'Someone's calling you,' interrupted Belinda. She felt dizzy. Damn Cathy all the way to hell! What was she doing in that part of town, anyway? There was nothing but sleaze in Patpong: no jewellery shops, no interesting temples.

Think, Belinda, think. Cathy might promise not to tell now, but what will she say to the police tomorrow when the passenger in the front row is found dead in his seat?

*   *   *

It was purely by accident that Belinda became an air hostess. At school, she hadn't thought further than the next party. When someone asked what she wanted to be when she grew up, Belinda would say the first thing that came to mind. 'A doctor,' she had said on her tenth birthday. 'A secretary,' she announced five years later. 'An air hostess,' she said when she turned eighteen. By then, she knew better than to expect the job to be a string of exciting trips to foreign countries. But it didn't matter one bit, because she wasn't serious about becoming an air hostess anyway.

Not until Jerry twisted his lips into a crooked grin and fired, 'An air hostess? Fancy that. I thought they only employed *beautiful* girls.'

Jerry. Belinda smiled. Jerry. To impress him, she had applied for a position with a major airline, sailed through the interview, which involved being measured and weighed, and visited Jerry wearing a triumphant smile and a pretty sapphire uniform.

'I hope you realise you'll simply be a glamorised waitress,' he'd said, his fingers stroking the fabric of her skirt. 'Serving dinner, cleaning up and disposing of nausea-bags filled with sick. Single male passengers will hit on you and turn nasty if you don't play along. You will earn next to nothing and there won't be any tips. And in no time at all, you'll be twenty-five and your career will be over. There will be others, years younger than you, queuing up for your job. Whatever will you do then?'

Belinda never let herself forget that question.

*   *   *

The aeroplane toilet for the first-class crowd was almost as tiny as the cattle-class cubicle, but the disposable towels were thicker, there were hand cream jars and aftershave lotions on the shelf, and the soap smelled of almond. Almond . . . Belinda pursed her lips and crumpled up the paper sachet. Fingerprints? She smoothed out the wrinkles with a tissue and wiped vigorously.

Then she froze. DNA tests! How could she have not thought of it before?

Was she brave enough to dispose of the sachet by eating it, knowing what it had contained? Belinda shivered. Her knowledge of poisons and lethal doses was sound, thanks to hours of research in anonymous internet cafés, and yet she couldn't bring herself to swallow the sachet that had contained the deadly powder.

She let hot water run over the sachet. The paper began to disintegrate. Belinda rubbed it between her palms. When the paper pulped, she threw it in the bin. If anybody questioned her fingerprints on it, why, what more natural for an air hostess than to pick up a piece of rubbish and throw it out?

Satisfied at last, she pushed the hatch of the disposal bin. All done. Now she could catch some sleep.

Slipping out of the toilet cubicle, she suddenly became aware of a shadow on the wall. With a sense of foreboding, she watched Cathy's shoulders disappear down the stairs to the main cabin. What was Cathy doing upstairs, in the first-class part of the plane, when business class was her usual area?

I have to do something about Cathy, Belinda thought.

*　　*　　*

She'd been planning it for months. Reading about arsenic and strychnine, learning that even ordinary aspirin can be poisonous, albeit not lethally so. But knowing all the time that it would be cyanide. Jerry used it to kill butterflies for his collection. Ether would have achieved the same end, but Jerry insisted on cyanide. It made him feel important, 'For goodness' sake, whatever you do, don't open the cupboard in my study,' he would warn his guests. He'd pause, then grin: 'I store my cyanide there!'

So cyanide it would be. A present for Jerry, from the prettiest butterfly in his collection.

*　　*　　*

Belinda was about to sit down in her crew chair when the service light flickered. She sighed. Some people. They'd pay a fortune for the first-class ticket, the equivalent of her own quarterly earnings (the *regular* ones, that is), but instead of enjoying the comfort, they would toss and turn all night, requesting champagne, a snack, another magazine . . .

Soon, Belinda promised herself, soon she would be just like them. Thanks to the passenger in the front row by the window. She avoided looking in that direction.

'Ms Rogers?' she whispered, bending over the plump elderly woman and switching off the service light. That was part of the job, knowing the rich passengers by name and remembering which ones of the regulars take lemon in their tea and who prefers milk. 'How can I help you, ma'am?'

Soon, she would have enough money to buy first-class tickets and sprawl in one of the deep armchairs. But would she want to travel? Or would she simply go shopping in designer stores by day, and dance with Jerry in luxurious hotels at night?

'Another brandy to help you sleep, ma'am? Oh, something sweeter? Amaretto . . . of course, Ms Rogers, right away.'

Amaretto. The smell of almonds invaded Belinda's nostrils again as she poured the amber liquid. The passenger in the front row had had a cold. How fortunate. He hadn't smelled a thing.

*   *   *

Cyanide prevents the body's red blood cells from absorbing oxygen, Belinda recalled, as she put away the bottle of amaretto, *causing immediate unconsciousness, convulsions and death*.

That could have presented a problem. Had Mr Fisher begun gasping for breath, he could have alerted the other passengers. Fortunately, Mr Fisher had been in the habit of taking sleeping pills. 'I can't sleep in anything that moves, my dear,' he always told her as he requested tea after his three-course first-class dinner. He would wash down his caviar and two blue capsules with a full cup of disgustingly weak milky brew.

Last night, of course, his tea emitted a faint aroma of bitter almond. Thoughtfully, Belinda had included an almond biscotto to go with his tea, to account for the smell. Mr Fisher had accepted it with a confident 'thank you', and curled his short fat fingers around her long slim ones for a second.

Even now, Belinda shook off the feeling of distaste as she remembered the touch of his rubbery skin on hers.

'Your amaretto, Ms Rogers. I hope you enjoy it. Please let me know if there is anything else you might need to make your journey more comfortable.'

'Thank you, love. You're a good kid.'

Guilt hit Belinda right in the hollow of her stomach. I'm not a good kid, she thought. I did what I did because I want a break, a chance to set myself up in life, a retirement fund for when crow's feet make me unfit to do this job. I know what I want, and I went for it.

And the cost? The life of another human being, a despicable human being, to be sure, but a human being nonetheless.

His life for mine, she thought.

It made her feel even worse.

* * *

Pouring cyanide into a sachet in Jerry's bathroom had been easy, just one firm flick of a wrist. She even remembered to wipe the jar and replace it in the cupboard exactly as she had found it.

'Happy birthday, Belinda,' Jerry had said when she returned to the lounge. There was a loud pop and the murmur of sparkling wine on glass. 'Thought I'd forgotten your twenty-fourth, didn't you?'

'Oh, Jerry!' She raised her glass, tasted the cheap bubbles. Suddenly, she froze as she noticed something at the bottom of the glass, something round and golden and very glittery.

'I can't ask you to marry me, girl,' Jerry smiled his sorrowful lop-sided smile. 'I didn't even have money for a real diamond. But I was hoping you'd say yes anyway, and then, perhaps, one day – '

Sooner than you imagine, Belinda had thought, patting the sachet full of cyanide hidden safely in her pocket.

* * *

The plane struck an air pocket and jolted. Belinda opened her eyes and consulted her watch. Almost time to prepare breakfast. She rubbed her eyes. Then she remembered.

The guilt was even worse the morning after. It took all of Belinda's strength to perform her morning routine.

'Good morning, Ms Rogers. Did you manage to get any sleep in the end? What would you like for breakfast? Certainly, ma'am. Good morning, Dr Lake. Your usual? Coming right up. The weather is going to be lovely, the captain says. Good morning, Mr Fisher. Mr Fisher?'

Assuming a concerned expression, Belinda shook the stiff shoulder. She had planned to faint and let somebody else deal with Mr Fisher's untimely demise. But that might have caused panic among the passengers. Years of professional behaviour took over against her will.

'Certainly, sir,' she smiled at the dead man. 'I'll wake you just as soon as we land in Johannesburg. Let me just take that pillow from you. I know they make your neck stiff.'

She stowed away the pillow, turned around and headed for the cockpit.

It was only with the cockpit door firmly shut behind her, that she said: 'Captain, we have a problem.'

And then she closed her eyes and slid carefully to the floor. The cockpit was not big enough to lie down in, but she made the best of the space available.

I wonder what Mr Fisher was doing with a pillow, she thought as she waited for somebody else to deal with the situation.

*   *   *

'It's probably all my fault,' Belinda sobbed in the airport rest room. She was glad that she could hide her face on Cathy's shoulder, because that meant that she didn't have to bother with her mimicry. 'He looked a bit off when I saw him last night, but I didn't think anything of it. Perhaps he was feeling unwell? I should have asked him whether he was up to flying. I should have checked up on him after lights out.'

'Don't upset yourself, Bel. You just did your job. You did everything you were supposed to do.'

And then some, Belinda thought.

'Oh, Cathy, the police will never believe I'm innocent! Not when they find out that I knew him! Not when they find out I was the one who served him his meal last night.'

'I won't tell the police about your being friendly with him, darling. I promise. But I hope you can help me in return?'

Belinda raised her eyebrows in a silent question.

'It's just that, you see, I'm so terribly broke at the moment. It's temporary, of course, and I'll pay you back just as soon as my luck changes at the roulette table, but in the meantime, could you lend me a few grand?'

*   *   *

The policeman seemed friendly enough, polite in that slightly patronising and slightly chauvinist manner that belonged to the older generation. He introduced himself as Detective Inspector Walsh.

'Just tell me in your own words what happened, Miss,' he said.

Belinda did, starting at helping Mr Fisher to his seat and ending with finding him dead. She omitted a few crucial details.

'So you were the only person serving him last night? The champagne and macadamia nuts on boarding the aircraft, the Perrier, the dinner with the wine, the tea?'

'Yes.' Belinda's left thumb found her cheap engagement ring and twisted it round and round on her finger. 'Unless he ate something in the VIP lounge, before boarding.'

Did that come across too eager to lay the blame elsewhere? The detective looked at her, without saying a word, his face devoid of expression. He simply waited for her to continue. Belinda fought the urge to fill the silence with unnecessary words, words that might incriminate her.

Her patience was eventually rewarded.

'Did you know Mr Fisher well, Miss?' asked DI Walsh.

Belinda had prepared for the question. 'He was a regular passenger. He travelled on that Friday flight from Bangkok several times a month. I knew him as well as I do any regular first-class passenger.'

'But how well did you know him outside of the aeroplane?'

Belinda felt her hands go clammy. 'What do you mean?'

The detective's expression was still blank. 'We have reason to believe you knew Mr Fisher in your private capacity.'

Belinda took a tiny handkerchief out of her jacket's pocket and pressed it to her lips. Hard. The pain did the trick. Her eyes started to sting. She continued the pressure on the tender spot until a large tear rolled down her cheek. She knew she looked pretty and vulnerable.

'I'm sorry,' she whispered, not bothering to wipe away the tear. 'This is all so very difficult.'

The detective nodded encouragingly.

'We're not supposed to get friendly with the customers of our airline,' Belinda began. 'I could lose my job over this.'

That was a clever trick, she thought, to pretend to worry about the job at this point.

Walsh hastened to promise discretion if what she'd said had nothing to do with the case. That gave Belinda a chance to fabricate her new lie.

'It's only that, you see, Mr Fisher felt bored in Bangkok. On a few occasions, he asked me to accompany him on sightseeing tours. We went to see the Emerald Buddha and explored the city together.'

'So you knew him pretty well then?'

'Not really. He didn't say much during those trips. We'd meet up and stroll together or share a taxi if the weather was too hot. I talked mostly about my fiancé,' Belinda glanced pointedly at her engagement ring, 'and Mr Fisher listened.'

'That's not quite how I have it,' said Walsh.

Belinda pulled a shocked face. 'Sometimes people invent gossip where there is none,' she murmured.

'And did you get, ahem, financially rewarded for these sightseeing trips?'

Belinda didn't have to act the flush that flooded her cheeks.

'I most certainly did not!'

At the end of the interview the standard question came. Had she noticed anything unusual, a small detail that had been off, even if it seemed totally irrelevant to the investigation . . . .

Belinda wondered whether it was safe to mention how tired Mr Fisher had acted.

*   *   *

When they'd met in Patpong that Wednesday, Mr Fisher had given her the dealer's address.

'I'm too busy to deliver the goods myself this time, Doll,' he'd said. He always called her Doll, and he always put his hand on her thigh whenever the opportunity presented itself, his fat fingers crawling under her short skirt. He said 'too busy', but his grey face and lacklustre eyes looked drained. 'Soon I might have to stop this particular enterprise altogether.'

With the address of the dealer, Mr Fisher had given her a larger than usual consignment. That's when Belinda had known she had to put her plan into action on the very next flight.

*   *   *

'Miss,' said DI Walsh. 'Did you notice anything unusual ?'

'No, I'm sorry,' replied Belinda. 'Nothing that I can think of.'

She pocketed the business card with Detective Walsh's contact details and promised to be in touch should she remember anything.

*   *   *

'A nice rack,' said Walsh. 'Much better than the previous one.'

'And did you see those cheeks?' his partner made fondling gestures in the air. 'I'd love to book her just to have an opportunity to help her sweet bottom up into the van. Hey, can we do that? She was the last person to see the dead man alive. And she served him his food.'

'Hold your horses. We don't know the M.O. yet.'

'Still. I would book her. Or at least follow her.'

'You mean, have her followed,' grinned Walsh.

'Nah. Why give anybody else the pleasure?'

*   *   *

Belinda waited a whole week before she felt secure enough to recover the parcel she had hidden in the airport's crew rest room the day after the murder. She went into one of the booths and opened the water reservoir. She breathed a sigh of relief. It was still there, taped to the underside of the lid, a sealed plastic bag containing a more than a kilogram of the highest quality cocaine.

It had belonged to Mr Fisher. Like many before it.

But this time Belinda would do more than carry it through customs taped to her bare skin under her pretty uniform. This time, she would sell it herself and pocket the full amount.

And then what, Belinda mused. Would she become Jerry's wife, the crown of his butterfly collection? Odd, the more she thought about the marriage, the less she desired it.

And the more she blamed Jerry for what she had done.

If only he hadn't mocked her into becoming an air hostess. If only he were able to make more money. If only he didn't keep cyanide in his cupboard . . .

* * *

'We finally have the autopsy results,' said Walsh to his partner.

'What took them so long?'

'Talcum powder.'

'Huh?'

Walsh enjoyed the effect of his news. 'Talcum powder, you know, like what ladies put between their boobies? They found a substantial quantity in his stomach, taken around the time he'd had his dinner on the plane.'

'Is talcum powder poisonous?'

'Nope. Mr Fisher died of asphyxiation. The doctor's best guess is, smothered with a blanket or a pillow. But it took them a while to figure out what the powder in his stomach was.'

'So why did he eat talcum powder? Licked it off his girlfriend, you think?'

'You are sick, you know that, Smith?'

'Yeah.'

* * *

It was difficult to find the dealer's address in the poshest suburb of London, but eventually Belinda reached the correct house. Before she could ring the bell at the gate, the front door opened, revealing a familiar silhouette. Belinda had just enough time to hide in the hedge.

From the safety of her hiding place, Belinda watched Cathy and the drug dealer come out the house. He didn't look like a drug dealer at all, more like a successful businessman or a politician. He and Cathy shook hands. Cathy's smile was as wide as her jaw.

My-my, thought Belinda. Mr Fisher's enterprise must have been larger than I'd ever imagined.

Then another thought struck her: if Cathy had also been Mr Fisher's carrier, she would have had just as good a motive for killing him. Belinda thought back to the night of the murder. Fact one: Cathy had been upstairs in the first-class cabin where she had no reason to be. Fact two: the pillow on the dead man's armchair even though he never used them. Fact three: Cathy needed money.

Belinda fingered through the contents of her purse until she found Walsh's card with his number on it. She wanted to call him straight away, but she daren't see him as she was, loaded with the cocaine.

She waited for Cathy's car to disappear around the corner, before she herself rang the bell.

She was just stepping into the garden when somebody grabbed her elbow. From the corner of her eye, she noticed that the arm holding her was clad in police uniform.

'I want to speak to Detective Inspector Walsh,' she said.

'I'm sure you will in good time,' replied his partner. 'You have the right to remain silent. Anything you say can and will be used against you in a court of law.'

Homework

PHIL LOVESEY

English homework
Judy Harris – Year 10
'In your opinion, is Hamlet merely faking his madness, or is he really
insane?'

This term we have been studying *Hamlet,* a play written ages ago
by William Shakespeare. It's quite good, though the words are all
strange for modern people to really understand. There's lots of stuff
that is really, really old, and that Sir needed to try and explain to us
before it made any sense, not that most of the class seemed bothered,
goofing around as usual.

Most of us thought that the film was better than the book, but that
Mel Gibson bloke still used all the old words, so that when there
wasn't much going on except him talking in that way, I noticed that
quite a few of the class were either mucking about, or texting. I even
told Sir about this after one lesson, but all he did was sort of smile at
me, then tell me that Shakespeare wasn't for everyone, and maybe it
was better for me if the class didn't think I was telling tales, which
seemed quite harsh, as I was only trying to help him.

The story of *Hamlet* sort of goes like this; there's this prince
(Hamlet) who lives in another country a long time ago. His dad dies,
and his mum marries Hamlet's uncle, so Hamlet doesn't get to
become the king. He gets real mad about this, and reckons his mum's
a bit of a whore for marrying his uncle, especially when the ghost of
his dad comes back and tells Hamlet that the pair of them were an
item before he died, and that his brother even dripped poison into
his ear and murdered him, just so he could get off with Hamlet's
mum and become king.

This was quite a spooky bit in the film, the ghost thing, and most
of the class were watching, except Cheryl Bassington, who was still
texting her boyfriend under the desk. He's an apprentice plumber

who lives down our road, and I often see him pick her up on his crappy little motorbike thing. She reckons they've done it lots of times, which I think is lame at her age, as I reckon you should save yourself for someone who really loves you.

Hamlet has a woman who loves him. Her name's Ophelia, and she sort of hangs around the palace, pining for him. It's that Helena Bonham Carter in the film, and all the lads in the class were right crude about her in her nightie. Steve Norris made a sort of 'joke' about boning-Bonham-Carter which even Sir sniggered at, but I just thought was sick. I think Ophelia's really sad, because she really does love Hamlet, but when he starts acting a bit mental, she gets really upset. He tells her that he never loved her, and that she should go away and become a nun. Even Polonius (her own dad!) uses her to test if Hamlet really is mad, which seems well odd – but then Polonius gets stabbed behind a curtain anyway, which serves him right for being such a bad dad in the first place. My Dad wouldn't ever do such a thing to me, regardless of what the papers said about him at the time of the robbery.

It seems that in *Hamlet*, everyone's only after power, and that they're prepared to do anything to get it, even if it means killing their family, marrying incestuously, using their kids, or faking madness that really hurts people. I think that's very bad of them all. Ophelia is so cut up about Hamlet being horrible to her that she goes and drowns herself, and even Hamlet doesn't seem that bothered. Neither did the boys in the class, who asked for that bit to be shown again, as they reckoned you could see Helena Bonham Carter's tits through the wet nightie. Thank goodness someone tells her brother what a schemer Hamlet is, so that he comes back really angry and tries to kill Hamlet in a duel.

We all thought that the ending was right crap, because nearly everyone dies. Hamlet, his Uncle, his Mum, Ophelia's brother; they all end up dead in this big hall, either poisoned or stabbed with poison-tipped swords. Dave Coles reckoned that the *Macbeth* we did for SATS in Year 9 was better because there were real nude women to perv over, and hangings and beheadings and stuff. When I told him I'd hated that film, loads of people laughed at me, and I felt right stupid, especially as Sir didn't tell them off for being so cruel.

Maybe that was when I decided to do what I've done to you, Sir. Maybe that was the moment that it all made a sort of sense. Like I've written, maybe some people simply want power, and don't really care about other people's feelings. Like you, then. Just two terms in the school, obviously wanting to be the trendy young teacher, join-ing in with them, laughing at me, not stopping it like other teachers would have done. Perhaps it was just another tiny, all too quickly forgotten moment for you, but believe me, Sir, it went well deep with me. Well deep.

That night, I told my Mum about what had happened in your class. She was cooking – well, I say cooking, putting a ready-meal in the microwave for Uncle Tony for his tea, more like. Because she has to have it on the table for him when he gets in, or there's trouble. He rings on his mobile from *The Wellington Arms*, tells her to have it ready in five minutes, then suddenly she's all action, heaves herself up from the sofa, sends me up to my room as she gets it done.

Once, his meal wasn't ready. I heard the result, upstairs in my room. Lots of shouting, then a scream. Mum's scream. Then what sounded like moaning. I didn't come down until the door slammed half an hour later, and I saw Uncle Tony walking away from the house from my bedroom window. Mum wouldn't look at me, sort of flinched when I tried to put my arm round her. She was trying to stick a torn-up photograph of her and Dad back together, but her hands were shaking too much, and she was trying not to cry. I asked if I could help. It was a nice photo – her and Dad on honeymoon in Greece, both of them looking right young and happy on a beach in front of all these white hotels. She swore at me and told me to get back upstairs to my room.

Hamlet used to love his dad as well. Then he went away to some college somewhere, and when he came back his dad was dead, and his uncle had married his mum. The problem is that his dad is now a ghost, and tells him that he was murdered, so that makes Hamlet really angry. He also doesn't know if it's just his mind being tricky with him, so he decides to set a trap to see if his uncle is really guilty or not. Hamlet gets these actors to do a play which is sort of like his uncle killing his dad, and watches his uncle's reaction. He wants to 'prick his conscience'.

Dave Coles went 'wheeey!' when Mel Gibson said the word 'prick' – which everyone but me thought was real funny. I thought it was a good plan of Hamlet's. He wasn't saying 'prick' like a penis; he was saying it like a needle, pricking his uncle's brain to see if he was guilty. I think I'm cleverer than most of them in the class because I read more and understand these things, that words can have more than just the obvious meaning. I think it's because I'm not allowed to use the computer at home (Uncle Tony's on it most of the time he's in), so I don't have any M.S.N. or anything. Or a mobile phone. Just books, really. A bit of telly sometimes, downstairs, when Mum's finished watching the soaps. But mostly I'm in my room, thinking and reading.

I write to Dad a lot. Tell him about school. Mum says I can't talk about some of the stuff that goes on in the house, as it would only upset him. She says that even though Uncle Tony isn't my real uncle; he's doing us a massive favour by staying with us when Dad's away. They used to be good mates, Dad and Uncle Tony, working at the warehouse together, going down the pub, but when it all went wrong, and the Police came for Dad, they sort of fell out.

What's really great is that Dad's letters are getting longer each time he writes back to me. Just a page in the beginning, now it's often three or four. His spelling's really coming on too, because of all the classes he's been taking. He's been well behaved, so they've allowed him more time to study. He says he's taking his GCSEs too! Strange, isn't it, Sir? There I am, in your class, studying *Hamlet* for my English GCSE Shakespeare coursework, and my Dad's doing exactly the same thing. At thirty-eight, too. He reckons once he's done his English, Maths and Science, he'll do loads more subjects after that. He says one bloke further down the wing he knows has got 19 GCSEs! See, Sir? They tell you all this stuff about people in prison being right thick and scummy, but there's some of them really trying to improve themselves. Dad's got another two years left, so I reckon he'll have more qualifications than me when he gets out. How weird will that be, eh?

In Dad's last letter, he talked about Uncle Tony, and said that even though they weren't best friends any more, it was good that he had agreed to lodge at ours, and help pay the rent and stuff. He said it was the least Uncle Tony could do, because really, he owed Dad big time. He also said that the years would fly by, and when he finally got released, he'd got a surprise that would keep me, Mum and him happy and rich for years. When I showed Mum the letter, she screwed it up and chucked it, said my Dad was talking nonsense, told me never to mention it again. I'm not sure, but I think it was to do with the robbery at the warehouse. Thing is, although the Police had CCTV film of Dad loading stuff into a van when he shouldn't have been, the actual stuff was never found. The local newspaper said it was worth over £100,000 – though you can't believe everything they say, *can you*, Sir?

Dad doesn't like me to visit, see him where he is, so every other Saturday, when Mum and Uncle Tony go to Norwich, I go to the reference library in town. It's nice there, warm. I don't use the internet stuff, prefer to look through the books and old newspapers they have on this stuff called micro-film. Honestly, Sir, it's amazing. Thousands and thousands of newspapers from all over the place going back years and years. All catalogued to make searches easier. People think that the internet is the way to find out stuff, but I reckon searching through the old newspapers in the reference library is better. There's loads of interesting stuff in those papers, articles people can't be bothered to upload onto the web, because I guess it would simply take too long. Can be frustrating, though, and you have to have a little bit of luck and patience. Yeah, luck. I guess that's how I managed to find you. Sir. Luck and patience. And, of course, a bloody good reason. And you made sure you gave me plenty of those, didn't you, Sir? Calling me a sneak, not helping me when the others laughed at me. I began to wonder why you did that, Sir. Why you wouldn't help me. And then I noticed, figured out why. Just one of those chance things that no-one else saw, but I did.

It was a Wednesday, the last lesson before lunch, and we were all in your classroom as Mel Gibson was waffling on about whether or not to kill himself (*To be or not to be*; remember, Sir, you made us watch the bloody thing ten times that lesson?), and true to form I could see Cheryl Bassington texting away in the darkness on her mobile under the desk. Except it wasn't her plumber boyfriend she was texting, was it, Sir? Because when she pressed 'send' – the next thing that happened was you got your phone out from your jacket and read the screen as discreetly as possible. I saw you, Sir. Watched it happen. You, Sir. Someone who should be trusted to educate us; getting secret texts from a fifteen-year-old girl. Well, naturally my conscience was 'pricked', as Shakespeare might have said . . . .

I began wondering what Hamlet would do in my situation. You know, needing to find stuff out, but not wanting to be caught doing it. So I did what he did – pretended to be a loony for a bit. That lunchtime, I went and sat right next to Cheryl Bassington and started eating a bit weirdly, mixing my pudding into my pizza and making stupid noises and giggling. Very Hamlet, Sir, you'd have been proud. Anyway, I could see my plan was working, and that Cheryl and her mates couldn't wait to get up and leave. The next bit was so easy – just as they were going and calling me all sorts of names, I suddenly leant over and clung on to Cheryl, slipping a hand into her coat pocket and grabbing the mobile as she yelped and tried to hit me to get away. Mr Price came over and began shouting at us to behave, but Cheryl and her mates just swore at him and ran off. He asked me if I was all right, and I said I was fine, then went straight to the toilet block, locked my self in and went through the phone.

They're really quite easy to figure out, these mobile things. There's a kind of main menu with all sorts of helpful symbols to direct you to all the stuff stored on the phone. I found myself looking at Cheryl's pictures first, and let me tell you, Sir, there's some right rude stuff on there. Not just of bits of the plumber, either, but stuff of you, as well. And not like shots taken in class when you weren't watching, but photos of you smiling right at the camera, in bed, with her . . . .well, you were there, you know the rest . . .

I couldn't believe how bloody stupid you'd been, what a crazy risk you were taking. If Cheryl showed any of this stuff to the wrong person – you'd be out of a job, wouldn't you, Sir? They'd probably stick you in prison, too, wouldn't they? And my Dad tells me what they do to people like you in prison, Sir. Really horrible things that even the wardens (he calls them 'screws') turn a blind eye to. Really, really stupid of you, Sir.

Next, I went into the text-menu, and found loads and loads. From you, to her; from her back to you. Some of them went back as far as six weeks, which, considering you've only been teaching here for just over two terms kind of makes you a very fast worker, I guess. They have names for people like you, Sir.

Anyway, the most recent series of texts between the two of you were about meeting up on Saturday night. At the usual place, apparently, wherever that was. You'd suggested half-eight, and Cheryl had simply replied with one of those really lame smiley-face things. Sad. And sick.

But, seeing as no-one had complained, no rumours had started, I had to assume that no-one else knew about you and her. Except me, of course. Which really made me think about things for a while.

Strange life you've led, Sir. Like I say, the reference library comes up with all sorts of stuff. One of the main reasons I went there was to find out more about what had happened to my Dad. It even made one or two of the national papers, because I guess it was what those newspaper people refer to as a 'slow news week'. Seems one of the main things about it was the fact that the police reckoned Dad had to have had someone helping him that night. There were two CCTV cameras that covered the warehouse, but only one was trained where it was supposed to be, on the loading yard. The other one was pointing across the road at (and here, I'm going to use a quotation, just like you told me to) *'the entrance to a nearby youth-club, where a group of under-age girls could be seen to be drinking and cavorting with young lads'*.

See what I'm saying, Sir? If someone had been helping Dad (and he's never admitted as much, even to me) then the camera wasn't pointing the right way to catch them. It was watching young girls instead. Maybe it was looking for trouble from them, but then again, you know better than that, don't you, Sir? For guess what I found when I researched our town's CCTV company a little further? That's right, a picture of you, stood with the two other operators on the launch of the company five years ago. You – unmistakeably. Your name on the caption thing, everything. A big photo of all three of you, smiling in front of loads of little television screens, the article telling people how you could remotely direct and move all these little cameras around the town to catch criminals and keep us safer. Sort of like you playing *Big Brother*, wasn't it, Sir? Only, not the crappy programme on the telly – the book by George Orwell. Like I say – I read a lot, I really do.

And once I found out about your 'preferences' from Cheryl's mobile, things started to drop into place. I began piecing it together as I sat in those toilets on that Wednesday lunchtime. Just over a year, you've been teaching. Eighteen months my Dad's been inside. According to the papers, at Dad's trial, the CCTV company admitted they'd received a resignation from one of their operators for 'failing to comply with company policy whilst monitoring the immediate area around the warehouse'. That was you, wasn't it, Sir?

I reckoned you left the job, took a quick teacher-training course somewhere, then got the job here. But, like I say, it was only a theory. I could have been wildly wrong. So I decided to do what Hamlet does, and devise a test (another conscience-pricker) to see if I was right. Here's what I did . . .

Firstly, I texted you back on Cheryl's phone. You remember that one, Sir? The one where she asked to meet you that night, at *The Wellington Arms*? That was me, not her. But less than a minute later, the phone buzzed in my hands with your reply, something about having to be really careful, it was quite a public place.

And I was giggling now, as I replied, insisting we must meet, that I was worried, had something to 'tell you' that I might need to see a doctor about. I remember having to stop myself from laughing when I pressed 'Send'.

Next, I deleted the messages and dropped the phone down the toilet. Now, even if Cheryl and her mates did find it, the thing wouldn't work. You wouldn't be able to secretly text her before the 'meeting' in *The Wellington*. You were most likely going to show up, and she had no idea about it. Quite a scheme, eh? I think even Hamlet would have been proud of me, don't you, Sir?

It's a good play, *Hamlet*, and has been interpreted in many different ways. It seems to me that the central question – does he fake his madness to get revenge on those who've betrayed him? – is almost impossible to answer. Perhaps Shakespeare was trying to say that all revenge is a form of madness, as it can consume our minds as we go for it.

I think Dad's the sanest man I know. Yes, he did a stupid thing and got caught, and now he's being punished for it. But he's never talked of revenge – even though I reckon he'd probably want to get that CCTV operator who spent too long looking at young girls getting drunk, rather than also catching his accomplice on the night of the robbery. The Police never found any fingerprints or anything, but the fact is that Dad *couldn't* have done it on his own. Someone else must have helped him, been inside the warehouse, handing him the boxes of stuff to load into the van, just out of shot of the properly sighted camera. But when the Police went through the tapes, Dad was the only person on them. Doesn't seem very fair, does it, Sir? My Dad in prison, and the other man going free because you didn't do your job properly?

Chances are, Sir, you never made the connection between me and Dad. Judy Harris, I mean, it's not as if it's a very uncommon surname, is it? Sort of invisible to you, aren't I? The swotty kid who complains about the others, tells tales on them; the easy one to ridicule. The plain one, the one that doesn't wear make-up, giggle at you as you pass by on the corridor. Just invisible old Judy Harris, gives in her work on time, does all the homework, tries her best. Strange how life can turn out, isn't it, Sir?

Back to my conscience-pricker. Having arranged for you to be in the *Wellington*, I decided that Mum and Uncle Tony needed a little more culture in their lives. I went to the precinct on the way home, bought myself a copy of the *Hamlet* DVD, told them both that after tea, I thought it would be a really nice idea if we all sat down and watched it together. Well, of course, Uncle Tony – already a little drunk at this point – raised a few objections, said he didn't mind watching Mel Gibson stuff, *Mad Max* and the like, but he was buggered if he was going to sit down and watch a 'load of Shake-speare shite all night'. (See, another quotation, that's two so far; doing right well, aren't I, Sir?).

Anyway, I made a bit of a fuss, and eventually Mum decided to smooth things over and asked Uncle Tony really nicely if he'd do this one thing. I said it'd make us all feel more like a proper family, and Uncle Tony sort of made a throaty noise, shrugged and gave way, saying he'd give it half an hour, and if it was bollocks, then he'd leave it.

So, Sir, just after half-seven that night, I put *Hamlet* on our DVD player. Imagine that – a bit of real culture in our grotty house. Amazing, eh? And then I did what Hamlet does, watched my mother and my uncle real close as the story unravelled . . .

It didn't take long, say twenty minutes at the most, and that's even with all the old language to cope with. Mum and Uncle Tony soon got the gist of it – the betrayal of Hamlet's father – and began sort of shifting uncomfortably and giving these sideways looks at each other. Honestly, Sir, it worked a treat.

Uncle Tony started coming out with all this stuff about Mel Gib-son going 'poofy', and that he was much better in *Braveheart* and the *Lethal Weapon* films, so I just knew he was begging for an excuse to leave what was becoming more and more embarrassing for him. So at that point I decided to tell him about you, Sir. Not the Cheryl Bassington stuff, or even the way you were so mean to me; no, instead I told him about the other stuff.

Yeah, I know, I lied. But just a white one, really. And Hamlet himself does that, doesn't he, when he tells poor Ophelia that he doesn't really love her any more? I told Uncle Tony that when I was in town buying the DVD that a strange bloke had come up to me asking me my name and where I lived, and that when I told him, he asked me if Tony Watts lived with us. When I said he did, I said that the man wanted to speak to him about 'the favour' he'd done my Uncle Tony with the security cameras, and that as far as he was concerned he thought that Tony Watts owed him, big-style, and that he'd be waiting in the *Wellington* at 8:30 to 'sort it all out'.

Well, my Uncle Tony being the sort of bloke he is, you don't have to try too hard to imagine his reaction. He was well angry, and began swearing and cursing, telling me I should have told him much earlier, asking for a description of you, then grabbing his coat and storming off, slamming the front door behind him so loudly that the walls shook. Mum looked right ashen, turned the DVD off, and told me to get straight upstairs to my room, and that she thought I'd caused enough upset for one night. Uncle Tony didn't come home that night.

That was two weeks ago, and you've been off school since, haven't you, Sir? At Thursday morning's full-school assembly, the head told us that you'd been attacked the previous night, and were staying away to recover. Two broken ribs and a fractured jaw, the local paper said, with a couple of witnesses saying you'd been beaten up by a Tony Watts (unemployed) in the car-park of *The Wellington Arms*. Police, apparently, are still trying to find a motive, but I'm sure with a little 'help' they'll have a clearer picture of why he did that cruel thing to you.

Uncle Tony's on remand, as we can't afford the bail, so he'll be inside till the court-case, which should be really interesting. The police have already interviewed my Mum about Uncle Tony, but they haven't got to me yet. I'm not sure whether to tell them what I know, or to keep quiet about it. I'll write to Dad and ask him what he thinks I should do.

Our supply-teacher isn't very good, but she's told us to finish these assignments, and the school will send them to you to mark while you recover. I'm sure that when you read this, Sir, you'll realise why you were attacked that night, together with how much I know about you that you'd rather other people didn't.

In conclusion, I say that whether Hamlet was faking his madness is irrelevant. How sane are any of us, anyway? And isn't the very idea of faking madness a bit mad in the first place? Maybe you should know, Sir, the amount of faking you've done in the last few years.

I look forward to receiving my A* for this essay. After all, I really did my homework on you.

Special delivery

ADRIAN MAGSON

184, Cedar Point Road stood in about two isolated acres on a narrow, winding road leading into the hills of North Carolina's southern Appalachians. In front of a set of steel gates was a mailbox on a pole, the kind with a little flag so you can see if anything has been delivered. The box had a bullet-sized hole in it. Call me a worry-wart, but I found that ominous.

I thumbed the entry-phone on one of the stone pillars and waited while the insects and heat and silence settled around me like an itchy blanket.

'Yeah?' A reedy voice came from the entry-phone.

'Jake Crompton to see Mr Krasky,' I announced, and wondered if they had a fishpond I could throw myself into for a day or two.

'Who?'

'Jake Crompton – '

'No. Who're you after?' The voice sounded testy, as if I'd spoiled an afternoon nap with my damn-fool question.

'Mr Krasky. Gus Krasky?'

'Oh. *Gus*. Why didn't you say so? Are you the guy from England?'

'Yes.'

'C'mon in.' There was a buzz and the gates began to trundle open on their tracks.

I drove up a curving drive and stopped in front of an impressive plantation-style house with a clapboard front. Twin pillars stood either side of a gleaming black door mounted with a scroll-shaped brass knocker. The windows of the house were blanked off by heavy curtains, lending the place a deserted, slightly desolate air.

As I stepped out of the car a man appeared at the side of the house. He was carrying a pair of shears and wore leather gardening gloves. Under his weathered baseball cap he was burned a deep tan and looked about ninety.

'Hey-up, young fella,' he greeted me, and beckoned me to follow him. 'Gus said you was comin'.' His voice was as reedy in the flesh as it had been over the entry-phone. 'He's out seein' some people 'n said to wait. I'm Frank.'

I told him that was fine, and on the way round the side of the house asked him about the mail-box.

'Ain't nuthin', he replied shortly. 'Dumb kids with a squirrel gun.' He gave me a knowing look. 'I guess that don't happen much where you come from.'

'No,' I told him, thinking about south London. 'Our kids use Semtex.'

We arrived on a terrace bordering a fifty-foot swimming pool. It was overlooked by a double set of French doors beneath a large balcony. It looked like the set of *High Society*, where Grace fenced with Frank before opting for Bing.

Upholstered loungers were scattered around the terrace. Off to one side was a barbecue bay big enough to roast a small elephant. In the background, the garden extended into a thick carpet of trees which ran up a slope for half a mile before meeting the sky.

'There's drink 'n stuff,' said Frank, indicating a table in the shade. 'You fancy a swim, go right ahead – there's towels there, too. Won't cost you nuthin'.' He smiled genially, face creasing like old, soft leather. 'Don't go in the house, though, y'hear?'

This last sounded like he meant it, so I nodded. He pottered away, leaving me with the hum of the pool pump and the trickle of a small fountain at the far end of the terrace.

I dropped my bag by the table and poured some chilled orange juice. I slugged it back, feeling the coldness seeping outwards as it went down. It felt so good I topped it up and went for a stroll round the pool.

Out in the open the sun bounced off the water's surface like liquid fire. I hadn't brought a costume, but suddenly it seemed too good an opportunity to waste. I stripped off and fell into the water, feeling the freshness soaking right into my pores. I hadn't been skinny-dipping since I was ten years old.

I kicked my way to the far end, counting tiles on the bottom. It had been a while since I'd done any swimming, period, and I had to stop for the occasional cough when I breathed in at the wrong moment. After a couple of lengths I rolled on my back, squinting against the sun. When I looked towards the house, to check I hadn't gathered an audience of old ladies from the local church harmony group, my heart bounced off my rib cage.

My clothing had disappeared. Along with my bag.

The bag contained the envelope from Alvin Culzac. It was my sole reason for being here. Without it, I might as well consign myself to a life-long exile somewhere so remote even God wouldn't find me.

I came out of the water like a floundering walrus. When I rubbed the water from my eyes, I saw my bag over by the table.

'For a second, there, I thought I was going to have to come in and rescue you.'

The voice was soft and languid and came from the shadows near the table. I squinted through the glare of the sun and saw a long, bare leg swinging back and forth, a stylish sandal hanging from five elegantly-painted toes.

The owner of the voice appeared, holding my shirt. As she shook the creases out, a faint jangling came from a clutch of bracelets on her wrist.

That's when I remembered I was naked. Before I had to choose between going back in the pool or sucking in my stomach and smiling bravely, she handed me my shirt and turned away.

'I moved your things to save them getting creased,' she said. Her voice a slow, Bacall-type drawl. 'Down here everything wilts in the humidity, y'know?' She glanced back with a raised eyebrow and the barest hint of a smile.

'I'm sorry.' I retrieved my trousers and grabbed a large towel. 'The gardener . . . Frank? – he said it was okay to take a dip. I didn't have a costume . . . '

'Costume? Oh, you mean swim-shorts. You're from England, aren't you?'

While she obligingly turned her gaze away I towelled myself dry, studying her profile. She was tall and slim, with auburn-tinted, glossy hair. I'd already seen clear, dark eyes which seemed full of humour and a mouth which curled at the edges, and one eyebrow was slightly cocked as though she found the world permanently puzzling. She wore a thin cotton sun dress with brown polka-dots on a cream background which set off her tanned skin to perfection. I put her age at somewhere in the late thirties.

She stepped closer, bringing with her a delicate trace of lemons. She tilted her head sideways. 'I'm Lilly-Mae Breadon. How 'bout we go for a walk? Gus'll be along soon.' As she walked away round the end of the pool, I couldn't help but admire the movement of muscle down the back of her thighs under the sun dress. Well, it would have been impolite not to.

'In case you're wondering,' she said conversationally, 'I only work for Gus.' She turned her head and gave me a grave look, and I realised she'd dropped the country drawl. 'No more, no less. Other people think otherwise, but I don't care.' The smile had gone, signifying she probably cared more than she pretended. 'How about you, Jake? What do you do?'

'I carry things,' I explained.

'Things?'

'Small packages mostly – usually documents but increasingly electronic storage devices. To anyone, anywhere.' It sounded lame, but it pays well and suits my way of life. A lot of my work comes from the agency run by Culzac.

'Is it legal?'

That's something I often wonder, but I live with the thought that it's best not to ask. Before I could reply, a car roared up to front of the house, followed by doors slamming and the sound of footsteps. Lilly-Mae looked past me and muttered, 'Shoot.' Then her face assumed a welcoming smile and she waved her fingers in greeting. 'Hi, Gus, darlin' . . . guess who I've got here?' The drawl, I noticed, was back in place.

'I know who you've got there, Lil,' a deep voice replied sourly. 'Just where'n hell were you taking him, is what I want to know.'

The muscles in my back flinched at the accusation in the man's voice. I turned to see a bear of a figure standing by the pool. Gus Krasky was dressed in work jeans and a check shirt, and two other large men hovered behind him, both wearing suits and look-alike faces. Their stance gave them the look of a wrestling tag team, but they were nowhere near as worrying as their boss.

He was holding a rifle pointed right at my chest.

Krasky wore the aura of a bad-tempered construction foreman, as if the entire world was there solely to annoy him. His hair was cut in a military-style brush-cut, and I guessed his age at fifty-plus but it was hard to tell. I knew we weren't going to become best buddies even without the cold look he gave Lilly-Mae, as if we'd been caught red-handed in the bushes.

He looked pointedly at my feet. I'd forgotten to put my shoes back on. 'You some kinda nature freak?' he muttered. Then he turned and went inside, leaving me to follow. The wrestler twins watched me go, their dull expressions no doubt the result of too much inbreeding.

Inside, Krasky jerked his head at Lilly-Mae, who went round opening the curtains and revealing a scattering of armchairs and coffee tables and, in one corner, a desk bearing a telephone, a small lamp and a laptop computer. When she was finished he said, 'You got things you gotta be doing.' It wasn't a question. She flushed slightly, then walked to the door, a faint frown on her face.

'Nice to meet you,' she drawled in that low voice, 'Mr Crompton.'

'Umm . . . you, too,' I said neutrally.

Krasky scowled and finally put the rifle down by the desk. I dropped the envelope in front of him and made for the door. I could do without the alpha male display.

'Where are you going?' he snapped.

'The package is delivered,' I said. 'I'm booked on a flight from Charlotte.'

'Uh-uh. Take a seat.' He pointed at a chair across the desk.

'Pardon?'

'Relax,' he growled. 'I have a delivery for you. It's what you do, isn't it – deliveries?'

'Yes. But I work for Mr Culzac.'

'I know that. I already checked with him, and he said it was okay. Now, you want to earn some easy money or just go back to London with what you've got?'

Actually, I was in no hurry to get back just yet, but I had no idea what Krasky wanted me to do for him. And why didn't he use his own people, of whom at least three were within snarling distance?

'All right,' I said. 'But no drugs.'

He gave me a hard look. 'What is it with you Brits? You think everyone over here's a crack-dealer?' He reached in one of the desk drawers and pulled out a bulky envelope which he tossed across to me. 'Your fee. In advance. I got an envelope to go to Palm Springs. It'll be ready for you in the morning, with an address. And no, I can't spare any of my own people. Any questions?'

'Only one. Is there a hotel near here?'

He nodded. 'Ask Frank on the way out.'

I found Frank waiting for me, idly ripping the heads off some flowers. He looked sour but gave me directions to the hotel. As I drove back down the drive, I looked back and noticed Lilly-Mae at an upstairs window. She was still frowning.

By eight next morning I was back at the Krasky gates leaning on the bell. It was probably earlier than planned, but I was hoping it would get me away from here sooner rather than later. While waiting I stepped over to the wounded mailbox for a closer look. The flap hung open like a drunk's mouth and I poked my forefinger through the hole and felt the sharp edges on the inside. On the other side of the box was an identical hole. Some squirrel gun.

I went back and pressed the entry button again, then noticed the iron gates were already off the latch. I pushed them back and drove up to the house.

The door-knocker brought reverberations inside the house but no response. After a few heartbeats I walked around the side of the house towards the pool.

That's where I found Frank. Only he wasn't doing any gardening.

He was floating in the shallow end, head down as if he was searching for something on the bottom. A widening ribbon of red was coming from a large hole in his back.

I stared at him for a few seconds, as if he might suddenly flip over and ask me if I wanted some juice and by the way, why not take a swim while you're waiting? Then reaction kicked in. I ran and grabbed a long-poled skimmer for collecting debris from the surface of the water. I slid it under his body, taking care not to let him sink. I dragged him to the edge; the last thing I needed was to have to go in and fish him off the bottom. As he bumped against the side, he turned with a slow-motion roll and stared up at me with a look of surprise on his weathered face.

Have you seen those films where the hero finds a floater in the pool and drags it out single-handed for mouth-to-mouth resuscitation? Hah. One tug at Frank's body told me there was no way I could lift him out. Dry and alive, he was lightweight; dead and wet, it was like lifting a small family car. And he was leaking.

I decided to leave him where he was.

Using the buoyancy of the water I flipped him over again and studied the hole in his back. There were scorch marks around the wound. No wonder he looked surprised.

Since he wasn't going anywhere, I let him drift away, then went over to the house. I tried the French doors, but they were locked. Same with the windows. I eventually arrived back at the front door and tried the handle.

It's the one thing cinema audiences always expect the hero to do, but he rarely does. Mainly because it's more fun to take out a gun and blow holes in the woodwork. All very useful if you have a large gun to hand. I didn't.

As I touched it, the door swung open, emitting a wave of cool air.

'Hello?' I called out, feeling desperately English. If I were Hugh Grant I'd be holding a tennis racquet and wearing flannels and pumps. What should I do next – announce the bad news about how they'd got a dead gardener floating in the pool? I just hoped his replacement could tell a camellia from a giant redwood.

Across a large foyer was the living room where I'd had my chat with Krasky. It looked the same, even down to the laptop, its power light winking at me.

The kitchen was empty and clean. No notes, no open drawers, no ransacking. I was halfway up the stairs when a little voice of caution kicked me in the ear and shouted at me. '*What the hell are you doing? Frank didn't commit suicide – the killer could be up here waiting to blow your stupid head off!*'

In rapid succession I found two bathrooms, a dressing room and four bedrooms, all yielding a deserted, opulent – if slightly garish – interior and no signs of anyone with a grudge against inept gardeners. One of the front bedrooms held a familiar lemony aroma and an array of clothing scattered carelessly across the bed. No bodies in the bathroom, just a whole load of jars and bottles. That Lilly-Mae was a messy bird.

Whoever had shot Frank hadn't come inside and gunned down the rest of the household, but where were they? Then another thought occurred; what if Frank's assailant had come *from* the house rather than to it? Had Gus finally got fed up with Frank's attempts at horticulture and taken up his gun in a fit of rage? Had Lilly-Mae – ?

Ridiculous. That kind of thing doesn't happen. I should call the police. What was the number Americans dialled in the movies? 555 or 911? On the other hand, what would I tell them? That I'd come to pick up a package to take to Palm Springs – and no, officer, I had no idea what was in it nor who it was for – and found Frank the gardener trying to drink the pool dry? I'd seen programmes about how gun-toting law officers in LA dealt with suspects – even innocent ones. They beat the crap out of them.

I ran down the stairs and was about to open the front door when I saw a dark, broken line on the tiles leading through to the kitchen. Somehow I'd missed it on my way in.

It was a line of blood.

I stopped, breathing heavily. This was getting worse. I stepped over to the front door and pulled it open . . . and found myself face to face with a gawky youth in jeans and a T-shirt bearing a company logo. Behind him was a bright red van with the same logo down the side.

'Hi,' he greeted me with a cheery wave. 'Should I go on round back?'

Don't let him do that! the inner voice screamed, and I managed to shake my head, quickly pulling the door to behind me so he couldn't see the blood on the floor. Somehow I didn't think blood and bodies were what pool cleaners usually found when doing their job.

He looked at me. 'Is there a problem?'

'Sorry,' I gabbled. 'Heavy night last night. Can you come back later?'

He grinned in understanding. There's nothing another man can relate to more than an obvious hangover and the need for absolute silence. 'Hey – sure thing,' he chuckled. 'I got plenty of other stuff to do.'

I nodded and waved a hand to avoid the need to talk further. He probably wouldn't recognise my accent but I didn't want to risk it. With my luck he'd studied at Oxford for three years and could spot a UK regional accent at a hundred paces.

I closed the door and leaned against it, breathing slowly to lower my pounding heart rate. That had been way too close. I waited until he'd gone, counted to fifty, then stepped outside and closed the door after me.

The gates were still open. I paused at the road, about to drive away, when something caught my eye. It was the mail-box; balanced carefully on top was a small, brown envelope.

I jumped out and picked it up. It was one of those with a padded interior. Through the padding I could feel a familiar outline. Attached to the front of the envelope was a Post-it note bearing the words: *D. Selecca – Hyatt Regency Palm Springs. Leave at front desk.*

It must be the package Gus had wanted me to deliver. Instinct told me to leave it where it was and beat a retreat. But he'd already paid me. So why wasn't he here? And where were his two goons, the In-bred Twins? And Lilly-Mae?

Two minutes later I had my answer. Less than a mile down the road I spotted a small, dark Toyota. Lilly-Mae was standing by the driver's door.

As I pulled over she detached herself from the car and walked on shaky legs towards me. She looked sick, like all the buzz of yesterday had been sucked out of her.

'Are you okay to drive?' I said. She nodded dumbly. 'Okay, follow me.' I wasn't sure where to go, but anywhere away from here seemed a good idea. Once I was sure she was following, I headed towards Charlotte and civilisation. On the way I prayed we didn't meet a testosterone-charged SWAT team coming the other way. Somehow '*English tourist dies in police shoot-out on lonely mountain road*' wasn't quite the obituary I'd been planning.

At the first shopping mall I pulled in and Lilly-Mae followed. We found a fast-food joint with two bored waitresses and no customers. I ordered coffees and sat her down across from me. She looked worse up close.

'What the hell happened back there?' I asked. Call me Mr Delicate, but I hate puzzles.

'Did you find Frank?' Her voice was barely a whisper.

I felt a chill down my back. I'd been hoping she hadn't seen that much. 'Yes. You?'

She nodded. 'I knew something had happened, but not what or how. It was all a blur, y'know.' She shivered and sipped her coffee, dribbling a little down the side of the cup. By the way her hands were shaking, events of the last few hours were catching up with her.

'So what did happen?' I asked softly. Uncle Jake the psychologist. A problem shared is a problem pushed onto someone else, according to my mother.

'Ab . . . about two this morning, I heard Gus and Frank shouting at each other downstairs. Frank sounded really mad. He was accusing Gus of being a snake and saying how he'd get us all killed. I thought I heard your name mentioned and the police. Gus told him to watch his mouth or he'd regret it. There was a lot more shouting then a shot, followed by a splash from out back. I figured someone fell in the pool but I couldn't see because my room's at the front. Next thing, Gus yells up to say I should grab my things and get out.'

'What about the twins?'

'Jesse and Dino? I didn't see them.'

'Where is Gus now?'

She shrugged, her eyes filling up. 'I don't know. When I got downstairs he was gone. There was some . . . blood on the floor. It looked real bad. I couldn't see him anywhere.'

'You went looking?'

'Sure . . . why not? I didn't think he'd do me any harm. I wasn't thinking straight. That's when I saw Frank in the water.' She sniffed and wiped her nose on a paper napkin. 'I didn't know what to do. He was dead, so I figured I'd best get away from there. I didn't know who to trust, so I drove to a quiet spot I know and slept in the car. Then this morning I rang your hotel but you'd already checked out. I came back to see if you were here. Or if Gus was.'

'To do what?'

She looked totally lost. 'I don't know. Something. To make sure it wasn't a bad dream, I guess. It's my home, too . . . sort of. I also wanted to stop you getting caught up in . . . whatever it was.' She stared back at me. 'You seemed a nice guy. Besides, I thought you might be able to help me.'

'Had they ever argued before?'

'A few times. Quite a lot recently. Frank was a straight-talking guy, even though he worked for Gus. He openly disapproved of Gus's business deals, but I never figured it would come to this.' She shook her head. 'Gus has been acting strange for weeks. He can be such an asshole sometimes.'

She was right; it takes an asshole to shoot an employee. Yet there had to be more to it than a simple divergence of views. 'What kind of business is he in?'

She gave me an odd look. 'You don't know?'

'Why should I?'

She sighed and pulled a face. 'He's supposed to be in construction – he has a site just outside Charlotte. That's the work I do for him, although it's not much. But that's just a sideline now. You want something that doesn't come from Wal-Mart, Gus can get it.'

'You mean stolen goods?'

'I guess,' she said quietly. 'He sells weapons.'

'What – pistols? Rifles?' I figured somebody had to.

She winced at the tone in my voice. 'Mostly bigger than that.'

'Machine guns or mortars?' I was actually joking, but Lilly-Mae jumped in her seat.

'Mortars.' She stabbed the air with a decisive finger. 'I've heard him say mortars once. And rocket launchers.'

Holy Moses. Mortars and rocket launchers were used in theatres of war. No wonder Frank hadn't liked it. Suddenly I was squarely in the frame with an arms dealer. I pulled the envelope out of my pocket and studied the Post-it note.

'What about this D. Selecca?' I asked. He'd probably be into aircraft carriers and intergalactic star ships. I wasn't far wrong.

'The same,' confirmed Lilly-Mae. 'Only bigger.' She shivered as if someone had walked over her grave. 'I met him once. He gave me the creeps. He calls himself Dwight, but Gus said his real name is Diego. He pretends he's American, but he comes from down south. Colombia, I think.'

Colombia. Colombia meant coffee. And drugs.

'What are you going to do with that?' she continued.

I fingered the envelope again. We needed to get away from here. But I needed to do the job I'd been paid for.

'D'you have to?' said Lilly-Mae, reading my thoughts. 'I don't think anyone would hold you to it.'

She was right, of course. But maybe I'm old-fashioned. I stood up. 'Let's go to the airport.'

We took a shuttle flight to Palm Springs. I hadn't got a definite plan, but was coasting on instinct to see where it led. All I knew was, I couldn't simply leave and go back to England without finding out what had happened. Don't ask.

When we cleared arrivals I rang the Krasky house. If anyone had found Frank by now, the place would be teeming with murder squad detectives bawling at each other to get results from the lab like yesterday and did anyone bring coffee and bagels? Well, that's how they do it on *Columbo*, anyway. There was no answer.

We took a cab into Palm Springs which, with its lush green lawns, broad, tidy streets and low-rise, stylish buildings, was slumped gracefully in the sun like a dozing salamander. The Hyatt Regency was on North Palm Canyon Drive in the downtown area. I paid off the cab, and while Lilly-Mae found somewhere to wait nearby, I walked into the cool interior.

'May I help you, sir?' the receptionist turned away from chatting to a man in a suit and gave me a full-wattage smile.

'I've a delivery for Mr Selecca,' I said. I was betting on Selecca being a man. For some reason I couldn't imagine Krasky keen on doing business with a woman.

To my surprise she turned to the man in the suit. He wore Clark Kent spectacles and had a build to match, and looked at me with a faint air of suspicion. The girl faded into the background.

'There's no name on it,' he said, taking the envelope and turning it over.

'There was,' I replied. 'Look, I have to go – '

But he stepped aside and gestured for me to go towards the stairs. 'What's your hurry?'

There didn't seem any point in arguing, so I walked ahead of him until we reached the first floor. He indicated a door and led the way inside.

Sitting by the window was a neat, compact man in golf slacks and a sports shirt. He was wearing an unbelievably bad toupee. I wondered if he realised it looked like a piece of road-kill.

'Who's this?' he breathed harshly, staring at me with coal-black eyes and licking his lips like a lizard.

They say that in the presence of real danger you can feel a change in temperature, as if the spirits are warning the unworldly of impending doom. All I got was a click of metal. When I turned my head, Mr Muscles was holding a very large automatic pistol pointing vaguely in my direction, like he wanted to use it but was reluctant in case he made a mess of the carpet. With his free hand he handed Selecca the envelope.

'He brought this.'

'Sorry about Paulie,' said Selecca, flapping a vague hand. 'He watches too many bad movies. You want a drink?'

After seeing the size of Paulie's cannon, what I needed was a pee. But I decided to go for a hasty withdrawal instead.

'No, thanks,' I said politely. 'If I can see some ID, though, I'll be on my way.'

'Oh. Okay.' He looked mildly surprised, but reached into his back pocket and produced some credit cards all in the name of D. Selecca. One was an Amex.

'That will do nicely,' I said. Before I could move, he had the envelope opened and slid a data stick into his palm. It was two inches long by half an inch wide. He turned it over a couple of times like he'd never seen one before. Then he peered into the envelope as if expecting to find something else. In the distance I heard the whoop-whoop of a police car. The atmosphere in the room was very still.

'What's this?' he asked, looking at me with those cold, dark eyes.

'It's what I was given to bring here,' I said, 'by Gus Krasky.'

The police siren came closer, the noise beginning to overlay Selecca's breathing and the rustle of the envelope.

'Krasky? Krasky said bring it here? To me? Why?'

'That's right,' I replied carefully. 'I don't know why.'

Selecca flicked the stick to Paulie and pointed to a laptop on a side table. 'Check it.'

Paulie inserted the stick with his free hand and tapped the keys while keeping the gun pointed at me. 'It's a bunch of letters,' he said finally. 'Letters from you to Jean-François Aboullah.'

Selecca's eyes bulged as if he'd swallowed snake bile. Then the phone jangled, making us all jump. I hoped Paulie's finger wasn't curled too tightly around the trigger. Accidental discharges can kill you.

Selecca snatched up the phone. 'Yeah?' He looked at me. 'Sure – he's here. Who is this?' Then he handed me the phone with an irate snarl. 'What's this – a family business? You got your sister keepin' tabs on you? We ain't finished, you and me.' He flicked the torn envelope away from him and stomped across to the window.

I wondered if I was in a bad dream and any minute I'd wake up in bed at home, safe from all this. *I don't have a sister.*

'Jake . . . get out of there!' It was Lilly-Mae. There was a background clutter of traffic noise and a man's voice issuing orders. 'You've got less than two minutes!'

'Wha-who . . . ?' The phone went dead. Suddenly I didn't want to be here. Call me sensitive.

'My sister – Emma,' I said, snatching for a name. 'She's a worrier . . . says we have to catch a flight out in the next hour. I'd better go.' I started towards the door and found Paulie in my way, his gun at head height. Then a police siren gave a whoop right outside before being choked off in mid-stream. Instantly Paulie jumped towards the window and looked down. He cursed and looked at Selecca.

'There're cops everywhere!'

It was all the opportunity I was going to get. I was across to the door and through it before they could stop me, and running along the corridor towards the stairs. I had no idea what the police activity was about, but after Lilly-Mae's warning I didn't want to stay and find out.

Halfway down the corridor was an ice machine. I grabbed a plastic ice bucket and filled it with cubes just as the door at the end opened and two men in suits appeared. Behind them was a uniformed cop. They didn't even spare me a glance, but hurried by, the uniform holding the door for me. Whoever they were here for, it evidently didn't include guests bearing ice buckets.

Downstairs another cop was blocking the fire door to the outside. This one didn't look like he would let me go by so easily, so I veered towards the reception area and wandered through as casually as possible, keeping as far from the desk as possible. Then someone grabbed my arm, nearly upsetting my ice-bucket all over the floor.

It was Lilly-Mae.

'Keep walking,' she hissed, and steered me towards the front door, chatting away excitedly about what a wonderful time we'd have on the aerial tramway and how we could take a hot-air balloon out over the desert or maybe drive out to the Indian Canyons. By the time we reached the outside and I ditched the ice-bucket, she almost had me believing we were newly-weds.

Five minutes later we were in a Tex-Mex restaurant a few blocks away, facing each other over margaritas with a good view of the street.

'We should head for the airport,' I suggested. First rule of not being caught: run away quickly.

'Uh-uh.' Lilly-Mae shook her head. She looked wonderful, as if she'd been relaxing on a beach all day instead of rescuing inept Englishmen from the clutches of Mafia-type gunmen. 'We're safe enough.'

'We are?'

'Sure. Selecca won't set the police on you . . . he'll be too busy trying to worm his way out of trouble. With his record, that won't be easy.'

'Having a man with a gun in his room won't help.'

'That's Paulie.'

It reminded me that she probably knew a lot about people like Selecca and Paulie. I felt depressed. Why couldn't I meet someone normal?

'You phoned just in time,' I said. 'Thanks.'

She gave me a no-problem look. 'What did Selecca say?'

'He wasn't expecting the package.' I told her about his reaction to the contents of the data stick. 'He was about to quiz me when you rang. Then the siren went off.' I paused as a knowing smile spread across her face. 'Was that you, too?'

'Yup. Lil' old me.'

'And the police?'

She looked puzled about that. 'No. They were already on their way. But I guessed where they were going and was worried you'd get picked up with Selecca.'

'Quick thinking.'

'Thank you. After I spoke to you, I thought maybe I should start a diversion. I saw this police cruiser out back with nobody in it, so I let it whoop.' She rolled her eyes and flapped her hand as if she had been shocked breathless. 'Gosh, loud, huh?'

I didn't ask how she knew where to find the siren button in a police car.

'Good job you did. Paulie was about to shoot me. You saved my life.'

She made a face, dropping into a cornball drawl. 'Aw shucks, really? Where I come from, that means I own you. Gee, I ain't never owned nobody before.'

I couldn't help but laugh. There was something about Lilly-Mae which veered erratically from sophisticated and elegant to plain screw-ball. Whichever was real and which was the put-on I couldn't tell, but right now it didn't matter. Still, there was something bothering me about the envelope. 'I'm still confused,' I said, looking Lilly-Mae straight in the eye, 'about the envelope being on the mailbox. It wasn't there when I arrived.'

Lilly-Mae looked blank. 'You didn't see anyone in the area?'

'Only the pool man. At least, that's what he said he was.' When I described him, Lilly-Mae nodded.

'That's Billy. He's the pool man, all right.'

'Well, someone must have dropped off the envelope after I'd gone to the house. But why leave it there? What if I'd taken one look at Frank and run for the airport and home?'

'Unless . . . ' She chewed her lip. 'Unless you got there earlier than expected.'

We let that one settle between us for a while. She was right: I'd been hoping for an early departure. 'So whoever left it there didn't know I was already inside, but counted on me seeing the envelope when I arrived and automatically bringing it to Palm Springs, seeing as I'd already been paid.'

Lilly-Mac's eyes went wide. 'But that could only have been – '

I nodded. 'Gus Krasky.' I wondered if it was Gus who set the police on Selecca.

'If we could look at the computer,' suggested Lilly-Mae, 'we might see what was downloaded to the data stick. We could go back to the house tomorrow.'

Great. This was turning into *Mission: Impossible*. 'You're kidding.' What had been exciting at first was wearing off like the coating on a cheap Singapore watch. Anyway, I already knew what was on the stick.

'But I have a key,' Lilly-Mae insisted, before I could explain. 'And I know a back way in through the woods.'

See, this is what comes of raising girls on Nancy Drew mysteries. They forget quilting and want to conquer the world instead.

'Two things,' I said. 'First, the stick held copies of letters from Selecca. So we don't need to look any closer. Second, I want to try something.' I led her over to a phone and dialled the number. While it rang, Lilly-Mae crowded in on me so she could listen. She smelled fresh and soapy, and I remembered what she had looked like in that backless sun dress. Then someone picked up the phone.

I waited for them to speak, but all I could hear was wheezy breathing and the mouthpiece rasping against stubble. Definitely not a cleaning lady. Lilly-Mae pressed closer, eyes like dark liquid pools and her arm sliding round my waist.

'Gus?' I said finally.

'Who is this?' It was a man's voice. In the background came a burst of radio static. I felt the hairs move on the back of my neck. *Cops*. I put the phone down. I could see Lilly-Mae had reached the same conclusion. 'They must have found Frank.'

'And now they've got Selecca – and the stick.' Lilly-Mae chewed her lip.

Back at our table, I said, 'Have you ever heard of a Jean-François Aboullah?'

She shook her head. 'I don't think so. Why?'

'Because the letters on the stick were from Selecca to Aboullah. If it's the same Jean-François Aboullah I'm thinking of, Selecca's been corresponding with a man who tops probably every Western government's list of people not to talk to. He's an African war-lord.'

'Oh, gosh,' said Lilly-Mae, her voice suddenly tiny.

'What?'

'I know Gus wasn't happy with Selecca,' she said. 'They used to be really thick, always cooking up deals together. But a few days ago I heard Gus telling Frank about having evidence that would put Selecca out of the picture, if he needed it.'

'What sort of evidence?'

Her eyes were like liquid pools. 'Stuff about arms deals. He mentioned Africa, and something about a State Department blacklist. Is that serious?'

'If it's an official one, yes,' I said. 'And there's Gus.'

'Huh?'

'Across the street.' I pointed through the window to where the In-bred Twins, Jesse and Dino, were lumbering by on the other side. They were followed at a discreet distance by a casual and surprisingly chipper-looking Gus Krasky.

I grabbed Lilly-Mae in time to stop her going after him. 'Wait.'

'But what's he doing here?'

'What else? He's come to make sure his plan goes right.'

'Plan?'

'Think about it. He pays me to drop off a package for Selecca. The same night he has an argument with Frank about something that could "get us all killed", and Frank mentions the police and me. Frank gets shot. Gus can't let me near the house, so he leaves the envelope at the gate, knowing I'll see it, knowing it will end up with Selecca, because it's what I do. I deliver stuff. And he wants Selecca out of the way.'

'You mean it was him who called the police? But that could implicate him, too – especially if you'd been arrested.'

'Not necessarily. The instructions were for me to leave the envelope at reception. It was just bad luck that Paulie was standing there when I arrived. He didn't give me a chance to walk out.' I went over to the phone and re-dialled Gus's number. The same husky voice answered.

'In the main room,' I said softly, 'there's a desk with a laptop.'

'What? Who is this?' The man sounded annoyed, like a cop with a headache.

'Just tell me and I'll explain. The laptop.'

'Laptop? There's no laptop here. Wha – '

'How about the blood in the hall?'

'Blood?' He sounded really irate now. 'What blood? Look, fella, we had a call about an intruder, but the place is empty. And clean. Who are you – ?'

I cut him off and looked at Lilly-Mae. Gus had cleaned the place up. 'There's no laptop and no blood. I bet there's no Frank in the pool, either.' I stared up at the ceiling, thinking about all the land around the house. Lots of places to bury a body. If the letters were genuine – and I guessed they were – they were bad news for Selecca. He'd have a hard time explaining them to the Federal agencies. Somehow Krasky must have obtained copies. All he had to do was sit tight and feign ignorance, no matter what Selecca tried to throw at him in exchange for a deal. None of it could be traced back to Gus. As for me, I was a complete unknown who'd happened to walk conveniently into the middle of a take-over bid. Clever.

Lilly-Mae looked sick. 'He used us,' she said, her voice faint. 'He killed Frank; he lied and ran out on me, and he nearly got you shot or arrested with Selecca. And all for what?'

'It's called competition. Get rid of Selecca and he'd pick up all of the business going. It must have been worth his while. But risky, as

Frank tried to tell him.' Frank must have threatened him with the police and paid the price.

Thirty minutes later we were at the airport waiting for a flight out. Lilly-Mae had been very quiet since leaving Palm Springs. She turned to me. 'Are you married?'

'Why?'

She shrugged. 'Just making conversation. I was wondering if there was a Mrs Jake waiting at home, that's all.'

'There was, once,' I said truthfully. 'But she moved on. How about you?'

'Me, too. He was in the navy. It didn't work out.'

'So how did you come to be with Gus?'

'Living in his house, you mean?' She stared absently across the lounge. 'When my husband and I split up a year ago I was living on the coast and needed a job. Someone who knew Gus told me he was looking for help. He had contacts in the San Diego Navy yard and was buying ex-military stuff pre-public auction. He needed someone to deal with paperwork on the construction side, so I applied.' I didn't say anything, and she looked at me with a hint of fire in her eye. 'Gus was my boss, period. I lived at his place, but I had my own room.'

'I know,' I said smugly. 'I've seen it.' I explained about searching the house.

'So what are you going to do now?' she asked.

'Go home, I suppose. You?'

She shrugged. 'Head back to the coast. Start again. I've done it before. I need to get my stuff from Gus's place, though.'

The indicator board showed my flight number. There must be something about airports that appeals to the romantic in me. Either that or I need my bumps examining. 'You mean clothes?'

She thought for a while, then shrugged again. 'I guess. Mostly. But I can always buy more. And I could stay with Mom for a while.' She gave a half smile and seemed to brighten up at the idea. 'I've done that before, too.'

I took out the envelope Gus had given me and looked inside. I was half expecting it to be full of plain paper. But it wasn't. Whatever else Gus Krasky might be, he believed in paying well.

'Do you have your passport with you?'

'Sure,' she said. 'It was a habit my dad got me into. Why?'

'No reason,' I said, my pulse beginning to beat a little faster. 'I just wondered if you'd like to take a holiday. On Gus's account.'

'With you?' She gave a flash of her old smile and looked at me as if I might suddenly pop and disappear. As the smile blossomed into an excited grin, I stood up and took her arm.

'Why don't we,' I suggested, 'go out and buy ourselves some swimming costumes, and look for somewhere hot and quiet to hide away for a while?'

She laughed in a way that made my spirits soar. '*Costumes*? Did you say *costumes*? That's *so* cute.'

'Tomayto, tomarto,' I responded easily. 'You'll get used to it . . .'

A darkness discovered
[*a John Dakin mystery*]

MATTHEW BOOTH

I

I stared down at the body. 'I don't know him.'

Cox bunched his fists into his coat pockets. 'Look closely.'

I didn't need to look any closer. I'd noted the details already. The man was not much older than me, late thirties, dark hair, not yet streaked with grey. Maybe he'd had an easy life. He wore an expensive suit and his shoes were caked with mud. I wondered if he had been dragged along the canal bank. And he'd had the back of his head knocked in by something hard and blunt.

'I don't know him,' I said again, moving a small distance away.

'He must have known you,' said Cox, reaching into his coat pocket and pulling out a forensic bag. I stared at it, aiming for casual interest, probably managing cautious panic. I had already recognised one of my own business cards lying in the corner of the bag. Cox folded the bag around the card, handing it over to me. He read the words on the card as he did so. ' "John H. Dakin: Private Investigations". You doing much business, by the way, Dakin?'

I shrugged, putting my hands in my jacket pockets. I wasn't taking the card from Cox for all the business in the world. 'I'm getting by.'

'So how come he ended up with your card on him?' Cox asked, nodding his head towards the body. He toyed with the card in the bag as he waited for an answer.

'I leave my cards anywhere and everywhere. That's part of the deal of being on your own.' I cocked my head to one side. 'Makes it easier to meet people. Like speed dating. Ever been speed dating, Cox?'

The inspector didn't reply. Above us, a tram rumbled its sad way along the tracks. We were standing under the line at Cornbrook, midway between the centre of Manchester and the Old Trafford football stadium. It was a suburban No Man's Land, neither one thing nor the other, in many respects. What a man in a fairly well made suit would be doing lying there with the back of his head missing was anybody's guess.

Cox had phoned me at my office half an hour earlier, asking me to meet him, giving me just enough information to make it clear I was expected to turn up, but not enough for me to concoct any sort of alibi, story, or excuse. We had that sort of relationship. I think he liked me more than he cared to admit. Up until that call, I had been sitting at my desk doing what private detectives do when they are not detecting, and I was doing it with the air of a man with nothing to do and all the time in the world to do it in.

It had been the second call of the morning. The first had been something which I had taken as routine, fairly unimportant, barely exciting. As it turned out, that first call was the prelude to the entire darkness which followed.

The voice was precise, almost clinical in its exactness. Its age was difficult to determine, but there was something about it which demanded attention, so I doubted it was a man anywhere under fifty. Maybe that is a prejudice I never knew I had until that moment.

'Mr Dakin?' he asked. I confirmed it. 'My name is Heller. My employer wishes to engage your services and requests that you meet him at two o'clock this afternoon at his address. Would that be convenient?'

'I don't know, Mr Heller,' I replied. 'I'm not sure what my commitments are for today.'

'If your time is filled, Mr Dakin, I shall not trouble you further.'

'Whatever you prefer, Mr Heller,' I cut in. 'It's just that I don't like to make any decisions until I know what's being asked of me. So, if it's all the same to you, I'd prefer it if we skipped the starter and got to the main course. What exactly can I do for you?'

Heller clicked his tongue against his teeth. 'I am not at liberty to give any details of the matter myself, Mr Dakin, other than to confirm to you that it is a matter of extreme personal importance to my employer. You will forgive me for my discretion, which is to some extent imposed upon me.'

'We all have our crosses to bear,' I said. 'If you give me your employer's name, I'll consider us friends.'

There was a slight pause. I rolled a pencil along my fingers, and I waited. I had all the time in world. Nothing had changed.

'I work for Ernest Pemberton,' said Heller. 'You will know the name, no doubt.'

I did. Ernest Pemberton was one of those names which most people knew. He was primarily a property developer, in this country and on the continent. Manchester was finding itself unable to get through a month without producing at least three new blocks of luxury apartments, hotels, or office sites. It was my guess that Pemberton Properties were heavily into these. But Pemberton didn't restrict himself to property. He had shares in companies reaching across the country, and he had investments in enterprises worldwide. I've never had a head for business, but even I knew Pemberton was a name to respect.

'So, how can I help?' I asked.

'Mr Pemberton is extremely ill. His doctor holds out very little hope for anything beyond perhaps six months. Before that time elapses, Mr Pemberton requires a service from you. Please be at the following address at two.'

I made a note of the address, confirmed my attendance, and replaced the receiver. I spent an hour trying to find out what I could about Pemberton Properties and its director, but there was very little which I thought might be of use. Sometimes things go like that. It's not always easy to know what it is you need when the whole purpose of your engagement has been kept from you. I'd just decided to give up the game and roll my pencil across my fingers again, when Cox phoned.

And now, Cox and I stood on the canal bank with a dead man lying between us like a dirty secret. 'Any idea of a weapon?' I enquired.

Cox gave a shrug. 'Nothing definite. Something heavy, blunt, probably round in shape.'

I was toeing some mud on the canal bank. 'A large stone or rock maybe.'

'Could have been.'

'What're you thinking, Dakin?'

I shrugged. 'If you plan to kill a man, you take something with you. Knife, gun, lead pipe, candlestick, spanner: something. If you use a rock on a canal bank, you're using the first thing which comes to hand.' I shrugged. 'That's the way I see it.'

'So . . . ' urged Cox.

I resisted the temptation to roll my eyes. 'So it suggests to me that maybe the murder wasn't planned. Which means the killer came here to meet this poor sod for a totally different reason.'

He was nodding. 'What reason?' he asked.

'When we find that out, we can all go home,' I replied. 'How long has he been dead?'

'Forensics say about four or five hours. We'll know better after the autopsy.'

'And he was discovered at about eight this morning?'

'Making the time of death in the early hours.'

'Say three a.m.,' I said.

Cox ran a hand through his blonde hair. 'Where were you, Dakin?'

I couldn't help but smile. 'In bed, Cox, like most of the population. Where were you?'

He didn't give me an answer, other than to shrug his shoulders. 'I suppose this man, whoever he was, was on the point of hiring you. That's why he had your card. Question is, what did he want you to do?'

I shook my head. 'We won't know any of that until we know who he was. And we need to know why whoever killed him left my card on him.'

'We found the card in his suit pocket: the left outside one. Having taken the wallet from the inside pocket and checked the trouser pockets, maybe the killer thought he'd been thorough.'

I told Cox to keep me posted on developments. I was as anxious as anybody to know what the dead man had wanted with me, and why someone had made sure that he didn't get in touch. For now, I had an appointment with some money; but I had no idea how dirty the business involved with that money was about to get, nor how dark the blackness which was descending would be.

2

The address Heller had given me was in Wilmslow, half an hour's drive or so from my office on Deansgate. The house was large, standing proud at the end of a long driveway, lined on either side by furze bushes which bordered vast lawns exceptional in their meticulousness. The house itself, rising to three floors, wouldn't have looked out of place in a period drama. The walls were whitewashed, the windows latticed, the entrance framed by two stone pillars; the overall effect was one of ostentation.

I was admitted into a large hallway, all polished floors and oak-panelled walls, with a large spiralling staircase winding its way from the centre. Standing in front of me was a tall, thin man, with neatly cropped hair, a light grey suit, and a wine-red tie. His hand was outstretched, his smile fixed in place, and an air of cool efficiency emanated from him.

'Mr Dakin,' he said, shaking my hand with the strength and assurance I would have expected. 'I am grateful to you for being so punctual.'

'Mr Heller,' I said. I hoped it sounded more of a statement than a question.

'Indeed, I am Patrick Heller. I am Mr Pemberton's office manager,' he added, by way of an introduction. I nodded without smiling at his avoidance of the term secretary. I assumed we both knew that it was his true job description.

He took me into a large room, furnished like a study, with three of the four walls lined with bookcases. The books on the shelves were protected by glass doors, and I stared at my reflection within them. I was probably the cheapest thing in the room. Sitting at a leather-topped writing desk was a man of about sixty. He was staring at me with cobalt blue eyes. His expression was fixed, almost stern, but it came as no surprise to me. Self-made men are often hardened by experience, and it frequently shows in their faces; they have to be to survive, and to succeed. Heller introduced me and left the room, closing the door behind him without a sound.

'I asked Heller to find me a private detective of a respectable nature,' said the man. 'Has he?'

I shrugged. 'That would have to be for you to decide.'

He studied me for a moment, a long moment, before he broke into a smile. 'A good answer. I've seen all sorts of men, dealt with every type, and I can tell in a moment which have the balls to deal with me and which do not. Do I scare you, Mr Dakin?'

'I doubt you get up early enough to come close to scaring me, Mr Pemberton.'

He slammed the desk with a laugh. 'Help yourself to a drink, and be good enough to pour me one. With ice. But it has to be our secret. Doctor's orders.'

I poured two whiskies, put ice in one, and handed it to him. He sniffed it deeply, and sipped it, like a man who isn't able to indulge his pleasure too often. I felt sorry for him because of it.

'You know who I am?' he asked at last.

'By reputation.'

'I'm a simple man, Mr Dakin. I like honesty, hard work, and no bullshit. It's how I got all this.' He waved his glass around the room, signifying the entire estate. 'How do you stand on hard work and honesty?'

'They're preferable to bullshit.'

He cocked a smile at me. 'You'll do for me, Mr Dakin. I need your help with something which I can't put right myself. It concerns my nephew, Maxwell. My late brother's son.'

'He's got himself into some sort of trouble?'

'Not recently, not that I am aware of. 'But five years ago, he had some . . . ' He searched for the words. 'Perhaps we should simply say difficulties. You remember the Kilgate shooting?'

I shifted in my seat. Kilgate: a name from the recent past, and one which had often drifted in and out of my conscience. It was ten years or so since it happened, but somehow the resonance of the single gunshot fired late one night in the library of a house called Kilgate in a wealthy suburb of Manchester still reverberated across the decade. It was one of those cases: just as the shockwaves seemed to die down, something happened to drag the whole thing back into life. Maybe it was something to do with the fact it was never solved.

'I remember it,' was all I said.

'Perhaps you could give me a summary,' murmured Pemberton.

'Do you need one?'

He gave me a slight smile. 'Humour me. I'm paying for your time.'

Fair point. 'Kilgate, an estate in Bowdon, maybe twenty minutes from here. Makes this place look like a bedsit. Belonged to a man called Owen Faldene.' I took a sip of whisky. 'I say owned because about ten years ago someone blew Faldene's brains out in his own library. From the angle of entry it looked as though the weapon had been fired by a left-handed person: that the back left hand side of Faldene's head was missing suggested as much. There was a sister but all she did was sob. Despite a number of leads, and some extensive enquiries, nothing was ever proved. There was talk of a suspect, but nothing ever came of it.'

Pemberton shifted uneasily in his chair. He rocked his drink in the glass, as though he was trying to make it feel as uncomfortable as he was. 'What do you know of this suspect?'

'Very little. I didn't work the case myself, even though I was a DI at the time. A friend of mine handled it.' My gaze lost its focus for a moment. 'He's dead now, unfortunately.'

Pemberton didn't seem interested in my friend's death.

'Go on, Mr Dakin.'

I drained my glass, helped myself to another. Pemberton didn't mind, but he declined the offer of a second, holding his glass up in support of his refusal. I spoke as I poured.

'There was some talk of a burglary gone wrong, but no one could find any sign of a break-in. Anyway, even ten years ago, Kilgate had a security system second only to Fort Knox. Owen Faldene, as well as being one of the richest men in the country from his investment banking business, was a known cocaine user, so obviously drugs became a lead. Nothing much came of it. He had a string of lovers, and one in particular came under suspicion. Her name was Kenyon – Julie, I think – but she had an alibi. Then there was the suspect who was in the frame for a while. It went back to the coke use. From what I remember, he was Faldene's supplier.'

Pemberton was nodding. 'You have a good memory for a man who was not involved in the investigation.'

'Force of habit.'

'You will remember,' went on the old man, 'that the man was never charged. He too had an alibi, though I suspect it was treated with some suspicion, given the narcotics connection.'

'It wouldn't be the first time.' Sad, but true. It was part of what we like to call the British justice system.

'Nevertheless, the alibi held, which meant the police could do little about it. But the man remained the prime suspect.'

'On what grounds?' I asked.

'Primarily, the drugs connection,' he replied. 'There was a suggestion that a witness had seen someone matching the suspect's description fleeing Kilgate just after the murder.'

'After midnight?' I shook my head. 'Not the best testimony. Dark night, badly lit and isolated area'.

'Precisely. And the alibi was of course in place. There was also the fact that Faldene and the suspect were known friends, but that proved nothing.'

'Six degrees of separation,' I said. 'Anyone can be linked to anyone somehow or other. It means nothing.'

'Which is why there were no charges brought against the man,' replied Pemberton. 'But mud sticks, Mr Dakin, as I am sure you know.'

I knew, only too well. 'What's the connection between me sitting here and the Kilgate murder?'

Pemberton leaned back in his chair. It looked like I had just asked the £1,000,000 question, and my client had no friend to phone. 'The suspect's name was Maxwell Pemberton,' he said.

The nephew with the . . . 'difficulties'.

'Were you his alibi?'

He brushed his fingers along the hair at his temples. His expression answered my question before his voice did, and it did so more directly. 'You are a sharp man, Mr Dakin. Heller made a good choice.'

I wasn't one for compliments. 'Why did you protect him?'

'He is family. Family is an important part of life for a lonely man.'

I didn't question whether it was the uncle or the nephew who was lonely. 'And you thought he needed the alibi.'

'I wanted to help my nephew.' The voice had an edge to it, like a blade flashing in the moonlight.

'But deep down, you believed he was guilty, didn't you? I need your honesty as much as you need mine, Mr Pemberton.'

He sat quietly for a long time and when he finally spoke, Pemberton's voice was little more than a whisper.

'I feared he may have been,' he hissed. 'I thought I was acting for the best.'

'By covering up the truth?'

Pemberton slammed his fist against the desk. 'That is precisely my point, Mr Dakin. I do not know it was the truth. I have thought about it time and time again. Maxwell has promised me faithfully that he was not responsible for the murder, and that he has no knowledge of what happened that night. That he was not even there on the night, for Heaven's sake!'

I let that go. It didn't matter whether I believed it or not.

'I am a dying man,' he went on. 'I have little more than six months left. The fact is that I have nothing to lose now. A death sentence makes a man more philosophical than he might otherwise be. My affairs are in order. My estate, what remains of my family, and my reputation are well provided for. But I have one thing which troubles me, and which I fear may prevent me from resting in peace.'

'That being?'

'Maxwell. Nobody wants to go to eternity with uncertainty on their shoulders. I want to know whether he was involved or not, and if he was then to what extent.'

'He assures you that he wasn't,' I said. John Dakin: Devil's Advocate.

Pemberton heaved his shoulders. 'I gave him an alibi five years ago because I wasn't sure what the truth was. If I am truthful, I still don't know. Maxwell has never been what you might call assured when it comes to integrity. If he was involved, if he was guilty, I will deal with it. If he was innocent, I will do likewise. But I need to know, Mr Dakin. Before it is too late for me to deal with anything.'

Something about his tone, his earnest pleading, made me feel sorry for him. He was a powerful man, a man who had been tough for too long and was used to being on top. For him to talk with such emotional honesty to a man he didn't know somehow forced me to respect him. 'If I find out the truth for you,' I said, 'you may not like it. It might be best to leave it buried.'

'The truth is easier to handle than uncertainty,' was his reply. It sounded as though he was trying to convince himself more than anyone else. Maybe he was, but in doing it, he'd convinced me too. I wondered if it was something to do with his determination, or the look in his eye of a man who had nothing left to achieve. Either way, I was there for him.

'I'll need Maxwell's address,' I said.

'I anticipated as much.' He leaned forward, opened a drawer in the desk. He took out a sheet of paper, on which he wrote an address. He handed it over. 'He can be found there.'

I read the address on the paper. I knew it vaguely. A city centre postcode, a luxury apartment, the smell of money hanging around every keyhole.

'Does Maxwell live alone?' I asked.

Pemberton examined a fingernail. 'Officially, yes. In truth, hardly. I doubt she pays him any rent or expenses.'

A girl-friend.

'Does she have a name?' I asked.

He said the name with a sneer. 'Girling. Amanda, I think is the first name. She's a solicitor, of all things.'

'Do you know which firm she works for?'

He fumbled around in the desk again. He handed me a business card. It was for Amanda Girling, Associate Solicitor, in the firm of Kardin & Weston. There was a mobile number, and a direct office number.

'Has Maxwell been seeing her long?' I asked.

'Does it matter?' snapped the old man.

'Maybe not.' And it probably didn't. I pocketed Maxwell's address. 'I'll pay him a visit, see what I can find out from him. I might need a picture of Maxwell, if you've got one.'

He leaned across the desk and handed me a photo of a young man. 'It was taken two years ago.'

I looked down at the photograph. It had been taken somewhere where the sun shines on the darkest deed, where the ocean appears too clear to hide any secrets. The man in the photo was wearing a striped short-sleeved shirt, and was holding a pint of what was probably ice-cold beer, with a head which was too frothy for my liking. He was smiling broadly. I held the photo in my hands, but I said nothing.

Maxwell Pemberton may have been smiling broadly two years ago, but he wouldn't smile again. I knew that for a fact, because I had seen him before. The difference was that last time I saw him, he was staring sightlessly at me on the canal bank, with the back of his head smashed in.

3

Now the nature of his commission changed. I gave Pemberton details of Maxwell's death and he received it with the granite stoicism I should have expected from him. Without a word, he wrote a cheque for double the agreed fee, and told me the position was clear. The original instructions from him stood, but there was an addition. It was no stretch to wonder what it was.

'I'll do my best to find out who killed him,' I said, 'but you don't need to pay me any more money to do it.'

'Take the cheque,' he hissed. 'Bank it.'

'The police will need to be told about Maxwell, but I'll try to keep you and our business out of it.'

He fixed me with the eyes of the old business cobra he must once have been. 'Then give it to them.'

'When they get it, it won't take them long to latch onto Kilgate. After that, I don't know how long it'll be before they come knocking at your door.'

He gave a gentle shrug. 'So be it.'

I had one last question: was there a reason why Maxwell would have had my business card on his body, as far as Pemberton could tell? He had no idea. No, he had not known whether Maxwell was looking to hire a detective. Yes, his hiring of me and Maxwell's subsequent apparent interest in me was a coincidence. He looked forward to hearing from me with developments.

I made my way back to town, heading for Maxwell Pemberton's flat. It was one of those new, exclusive blocks of apartments which stood behind Deansgate, overlooking the canal. Years ago, there had been nothing there of any use to anybody. Now, any lawyer or doctor worth his salt was bidding for space there, fighting off competition from accountants, surveyors, and small businessmen overreaching themselves. It was the place to be, if you were a certain type. It was the changing nature of Manchester in an estate agent's nutshell: what was once hidden away in shame was now coveted and exclusive.

I wandered around the exterior of the building for a while, thinking hard about things. I had seen enough places like this to know that there was an interrogation from a concierge on the front desk, usually a retired military type who hadn't realised that the Army had discharged him some time ago. Even if I was lucky enough to get one who didn't care who went into the labyrinth of the interior corridors, there was no way I was getting into the flat itself on my own.

I pulled out my mobile and dialled a familiar number.

'Cox, it's me,' I said. 'Listen, I've discovered something about the body.'

'Tell me.'

'His name was Maxwell Pemberton. Nephew of Ernest Pemberton.'

'The property man?' There was a brief silence as it sunk in. 'How do you know?'

'I'm doing a job for the old man,' I replied. 'I can't say what, you know that. But I thought you should have the name.' With that I terminated the call.

Following the paved forecourt around the apartment building, I found myself staring over the murky depths of the canal. Behind me, there was a small row of more drinking establishments and restaurants, seemingly annexed to the apartments where Maxwell Pemberton lived.

I wandered into one of the bars, ordered a pint of Stella, and made another call.

'Amanda Girling.' Her voice was striking in its authority. I could imagine it giving some Hell in Court.

'Miss Girling, my name is John Dakin. I wonder if you could spare me half an hour.'

'If you want an appointment, please contact my secretary.'

'I'm afraid it's fairly urgent.'

'If you phone the office, someone will be able to arrange an appointment.' It sounded tried and tested. I didn't have time for it. And less inclination.

'I'm not a potential client, Miss Girling,' I said. I hoped my voice demonstrated as much influence as hers. 'I'm a private detective. I need to speak to you.'

It had the usual effect: silence. She was probably wondering if I was wearing a grubby overcoat and battered hat. 'A private detective? What's this all about?'

'It's not something I can discuss on the phone,' I replied.

'Does it concern Max?'

I wasn't sure how to handle the question. I aimed for noncommittal. 'Partly. I'm in the bar beneath his flat. Do you know it?'

'The flat or the bar?'

Typical lawyer.

'I know it,' she said.

'How soon can you get here?' I asked.

'Half an hour,' she replied. There was a splitting of a second. 'Is something wrong, Mr Dakin?'

'I'm afraid so.'

'Fifteen minutes.'

She was as good as her word. She walked into the bar with a confident stride, but with each step somehow haunted by a sense of anxiety. She had long, auburn hair, with a delicate but natural curl to it. She was attractive, her eyebrows arched in an oddly sensual expression of enquiry, her thin lips pursed. It was a case of being striking rather than beautiful. I surmised that she was in her midthirties, but she seemed possessed with the energy of a woman ten years younger. She wore a dark trouser suit, and heeled boots which promised a hint of sexual allure amid the cool efficiency of her profession. She was eye-catching; the problem was that the city was full of people who looked exactly like her.

With her was a man. He was tall, handsome, with the self-assurance of someone who has nothing to maintain but his arrogance. He walked close behind her, his hands clasped before him. I wasn't sure if he was trying to hide the fact that they were a couple, or whether he was trying to give the impression that he didn't care whether they were or not. They sat down next to each other, opposite me, both of them staring as though I had infringed on their privacy.

'He beat me to it then,' she said.

I had no option of a reply. 'To what?'

'Hiring someone.'

The man leaned back in his chair with a shake of his head. 'The bloody fool.'

Amanda Girling shook her head. 'We can hardly blame him, Nick. If I wasn't wrapped up in the Lomas case, I'd have done it by now.'

Nick, whoever he was, sighed. 'I know that, but . . . Jesus, I don't know. It just seems so final.'

I was beginning to think I was invisible. I almost forgot it was my meeting, and I felt the need to reassert my authority. For what it was worth.

'Listen, I don't know what either of you are talking about,' I said. 'That's point number one. Second, my understanding was always that three was a crowd.' This said with a nod at Nick Nobody.

'Sorry, this has started badly,' she said. 'Put it down to the shock of it all. This is Nicholas Burdon. A close friend.'

'Of yours?'

Burdon was quick with his reply. 'Of both of them actually. But it has only ever been friends. Despite what Max may have told you.'

It was an easy guess what the whole sorry story was from then. 'Right, I get it. He thought you two were closer than you should be, and you thought he was closer than he should be with someone else. That it?'

The girl nodded.

'You thought Max had beaten you to hiring someone, and you thought he'd suggested to me that you two were more than friends.'

It was Amanda who replied. 'I don't suppose you think Max and I are much of a couple.'

'It's none of my business what sort of couple you are. He hasn't hired me to investigate you two, and nor has anyone else.'

She held her hands out, the palms facing me in what she maybe thought was a gesture of pleading. 'So what is all this about?'

I told her; pretty much the way I had told Pemberton. Like him, she bore it well. With anybody else I might have seen something suspicious in it, but as with Pemberton, Amanda Girling gave the impression of being a woman who dealt with trauma the way she might deal with a professional dispute. She fixed me with a stare which seemed to highlight in turn a sense of disbelief, confusion, shock, and ultimately detachment. The only betrayal of any emotional involvement in the news was a flicker of her eyelids, and a vague attempt to make some words form on her lips. For his part, Burdon simply stared at her, his hand itching to move to her arm in comfort, but thinking better of it.

'Who . . . ?' she stuttered. 'I mean, why would anyone do that? '

'I don't know,' I replied. 'Not yet.'

'Why are the police not here?' asked Burdon. 'I mean, why's it you sitting here telling us this?'

'The police'll be here soon enough, Mr Burdon. For now, I need to ask Miss Girling some questions.'

'Nick, can you get another round of drinks please. Same again.' Amanda played with the watch on her right wrist. I watched the fingers dance over the dial, wondering what good they might do dancing on my spine.

Not looking too happy but taking the hint, my new friend Nick left us alone.

'Any idea who it might have done it?' she asked.

I shook my head. 'Not yet. Listen, I'm sorry. The shock – must be hard.'

She nodded, almost imperceptibly. 'He was perhaps the only man who was ever nice to me. Truly kind. My father died when I was three, so I never knew him, not that I remember. My brother was . . . '

The words never came, so I prompted them. 'Your brother was . . . ?'

Fire flashed behind her eyes. 'He has nothing to do with you.'

Fair point. 'Tell me about you and Max.'

'Things hadn't been good recently, but still . . . ' She looked up at me, almost begging me to ask the question. I obliged.

'What made you think he was seeing someone else?'

There was a flicker of a smile across her lips. 'And for that matter, what made him think I was?'

I looked across at Burdon, struggling with the three drinks to make a triangle in his hands. 'I can probably guess why he thought it.'

'Nick and I are just friends.'

'He creates the impression of being more than that. Or at least wanting to be.'

'His problem, not mine.'

'He's a dangerous sort.' She looked at me quizzically. 'He looks like he'd jump off a balcony if you told him to.'

'He can be protective,' she said. I wasn't sure if it was with a smile or a grimace.

'I've always found men like that dangerous. Loyalty is fine, but misplaced loyalty is sometimes dodgy.'

She nodded. 'I've had some of them in my time. But Nick is different.' She couldn't help but glance over her shoulder. 'He doesn't exactly set off my fireworks.'

I smiled. It was hard not to. 'Probably takes a lot to set off your fireworks.'

'Some find it easier than others.' Her turn to smile.

I looked over at her. 'Like Maxwell.'

'At first, maybe. But recently, he'd changed. Hard to explain how.'

'Lost interest in you?' I said it quietly. It didn't sound a nice thing to say. She nodded quickly; not a nice thing to hear either. 'Because he'd found someone else?'

Burdon returned, placing the drinks on the table. He spilled a trickle of my beer down the side of the glass. 'That's what we thought,' he said.

I looked back over to Amanda. 'Why?'

'He stopped calling me,' she said. 'When I phoned him, more often than not he wouldn't answer. When he did, he was abusive. Said I was checking up on him, that I didn't own him, that he could have a life outside' – she mimed quotation marks with her fingers – 'us'. What does that suggest to you?'

'Any idea who this woman might have been?'

Burdon again: 'Probably a tart he met on a night out. Had a lot of nights out recently.'

Amanda sighed, rubbing her forehead. For the first time, she looked tired, lacking composure. 'For God's sake, Nick . . . '

'But no idea who she might have been?' I asked.

'None,' said Amanda. 'But then he was hardly going to tell me, was he?'

'No-one you suspected?'

Burdon clicked his tongue. 'Hasn't she just said that?'

I gave him a look. 'You've got a lot to say, mate, so start saying something useful. These nights out – where were they exactly? Any ideas?'

Burdon had taken my advice to heart. 'Cavalcanti's,' he said. 'Max told me he had a good time in Cavalcanti's.'

'Where?' Amanda asked.

I was a step ahead of the reply. It was a nightspot, a place of strobe lights, chromium tables, relentless bass lines, and expensive drinks. It catered for the young downstairs, the refined upstairs, and never the twain met. I couldn't see Maxwell Pemberton mingling with the student base on a dance floor to music that he wouldn't recognise; that meant he frequented upstairs, a modern equivalent of a Victorian gentleman's club. But there was a difference. Victorian clubs meant leather seats, cigars, whisky and soda, chat about the Empire. Cavalcanti's was owned by Doyle Cullearn, who ran the city from his leather seat, and whose chat about empire meant controlling his own, be it the drugs, the protection and enforcement, the human traffic, and possibly worse. I had a flash image in my head of Maxwell Pemberton in Cavalcanti's one minute, and the back of his head in pieces the next. It seemed a natural progression.

'Where were you both last night?' I asked.

'Are we suspects?' asked Burdon.

'Not to me,' I replied. 'But I'd still like to know.'

He shrugged. 'I've nothing to hide.'

Amanda cut in. 'We had dinner together.'

I stood up. 'One more thing. Does the name Kilgate mean anything to either of you?'

Amanda Girling stared at me, her brows furrowing, as though I had asked something totally irrelevant. To her, maybe I had. 'What is it? A place?'

'Max never mentioned it?'

She shook her head. 'Not that I remember. I don't know anything about his past troubles. I never wanted to.'

I looked over to Burdon. He was staring at the table, as though I had asked him what his name was, and he thought it was a trick question.

4

Cullearn smiled broadly. 'It's been a long time, Dakin.'

'Would it be a cliché if I said it hadn't been long enough?'

He laughed: a terrible, racking cough of a laugh. 'Probably, but no need to change the habit of a lifetime.'

His office, in the highest echelons of a building in the centre of Manchester's business world, was modern, minimalist in its efficient decor, as slick as the man who owned it and had as much soul as the man himself. I was reminded of Ernest Pemberton: a man who had reached the pinnacle of his power, but aimed higher than he might imagine he could scale. But with Pemberton, the ambition was legitimate, not ruled on intimidation, and didn't cost people their lives.

Cullearn sipped a glass of mineral water. His flabby cheeks rippled as he swallowed. He dabbed his lips with a pocket handkerchief. His hair looked dyed. A bully's constant weakness: vanity masking social deficiency.

'Maxwell Pemberton, you say?' he drawled, making the question sound as though it were nothing more than a waste of his time.

'He was a member of Cavalcanti's. I think you knew him.'

'And if I did,' whispered Cullearn, his voice like a dying asthmatic's last hope for breath. It was something to do with the bulk of weight he carried around. 'If I did, how does it help you?'

'He's dead.' Cullearn shifted in his chair. 'He was spending a lot of time in your clubs.'

'So do lots of people, Dakin. You think I kill them all?'

'I want to know how often you saw him.'

Cullearn lit a cigar, drawing on it as deeply as he did on wandering lives. 'Look, I owe you a favour, Dakin, we both know that. So, I'll be kind: pay off a bit of that goodwill.'

It bristled, and it was meant to. A simple story, but complexly told. In short, he was the reason I left the police, and he saw that reason as a debt to be paid. For myself, I saw nothing to bind us together.

'Yes, I knew Max,' said Cullearn. 'Not best friends, but well enough to welcome him to my social gatherings.'

'I'm sure they're always a storm,' I said.

He smiled. 'Max was a fairly new addition to our scene. You know how it is in this city. One man knows another, who knows another, and who in turn knows somebody else. Everything's connected.'

'And everyone pays a debt?' I suggested. 'You ever heard of Owen Faldene?'

He had been playing with his glass up until that point, but now he fixed me with a stare which was hitch-hiking between interest and defence. 'Ancient history, Dakin. You reading up on the Greeks, too?'

'History repeats itself,' I said. 'One of life's problems. What about Faldene?'

'Names get around.'

'He was shot dead in his house. There was talk that Max Pemberton was his coke supplier. I don't suppose in turn you were Max's supplier? As you say, someone knows everyone . . . '

'No proof.' The voice was like a gunshot. I waited for him to say something else. It didn't take him long. 'And I was never even questioned.'

I couldn't help but smile. I ticked the points off on my fingers. 'Max Pemberton selling coke to Faldene, you selling coke to Max Pemberton; Pemberton being a member of one of your clubs, and Pemberton getting his head pulped. No connection, Cullearn?' I lowered my voice; I was aiming for intimidation. 'You were there that night.'

He toyed with my intimidation. 'Based on what? Guesswork?'

'Tell me the truth. You owe me.'

The effect was startling. He leaned back in his chair, with a look of satisfaction on his face. The debt, such as it was, had always been on his side; but now, I was complicit in a bargain which I had never wanted to acknowledge. I didn't want to say any more, so I waited for him to speak. He killed the cigar with pleasure.

'I didn't see the killing,' he said. 'Blood and business don't mix. But I won't deny I knew the family.'

'Was it a drugs deal?' I prompted.

'Partly,' he replied. 'But the world does not revolve around drugs the way it once did. There are other commodities open for sale in the current market.'

'Arms?'

Cullearn heaved his massive shoulders and allowed me a brief smile. 'The minutiae need not matter. What seems to matter to you, Dakin, is whether I shot a man and bludgeoned another. You know the answers already.'

By which he meant management control: no-one in power has the need to do what is necessary if they can get someone else to do it. I knew that better than anyone. But he had been there, two years previously.

'What did you see, Cullearn?' I asked. 'What happened at Kilgate?'

He spread his palm like a prophet. 'The answer's in the past, Dakin. All I saw was a man fall to the floor with his conscience spilling out onto the carpet.'

'Pemberton shot him?' I asked. Things seemed to be starting to make sense, but something in my bones told me everything about the picture I was forming was wrong. 'Or was it you?'

'I have no blood on my hands, Dakin,' he replied. Maybe he was right: no direct blood at any rate. 'And Pemberton was a petty supplier. He hadn't got ambitions above money. He wouldn't have been able to shoot a rabbit if he were starving.'

'So who else was there?' I pressed. 'Tell me.'

He closed his eyes. 'I've told you everything I can. Don't ask much more.'

'You've told me nothing, Cullearn.'

'You should listen harder. Pay attention in class.' He gave me a little smile.

'Hard to believe you ever went to school.' I walked over to the door, opened it with a cold flourish.

He called my name, urging me to turn round. 'My favourite subject has always been history. Modern history though.' He pointed an unlit cigar at me. 'You like ancient history, and I like recent history. Much more enlightening.'

I nodded at him, and closed the door. Business concluded.

5

I spent the next day or so in routine enquiries. It was all about legwork. I looked into Max's business life, trying to find any concrete connection I could between him and Cullearn. I only had conjecture and instinct to tell me that he was Faldene's drugs lead, and I needed something definite. I found it in one of the lowest alleys in Manchester. Max had been supplying drugs of all classes for as long as anyone could remember. He had started small, but like any successful business, dedication to his cause had resulted in rapid growth. His connection with Cullearn was still indistinct, almost unearthly; I had expected nothing less.

What wasn't unearthly was the fact that Max Pemberton had run out of money.

Initially, I couldn't see how it might come about. Drug dealers aren't known for their poverty, and there was no suggestion that Max had lost his means to capital. But gradually, I scooped out the truth, the legwork paid off, and like a malignant cell in the blood, Doyle Cullearn was at the centre of it. He had systematically eradicated, overtaken, or undercut Max's contacts. Net result: Max had nothing to trade with, and by definition no one to supply to. I wasn't surprised. Cullearn was never going to permit someone he had not personally recruited to walk across his land for long without a retaliation. The coldness of the calculating takeover was somehow more unsettling to me than a direct kill. The ruthlessness of it surprised me less than the motivation. It was Cullearn all over.

Bludgeoning a rival across his head, though, was not.

There was someone else . . .

I phoned Cox as soon as I had the information about the drugs. He seemed preoccupied.

'Busy day,' he said. 'I'm starting to think a job in Sainsbury's might be more in my line. Less hassle.'

'I doubt it's in you somehow,' I replied. 'How's your case going?'

'As you'd expect.' He paused. 'Listen, I need to go and speak to Ernest Pemberton.'

Cox was either fishing, or else he was asking whether he would be standing on any toes. He had a job to do, and I wasn't able to prevent him from doing it. It was the necessary evil of our positions. All he was doing was playing fair. All most of us can do is play fair.

'You've got to do it sometime,' I said. 'I'm not sure he'll have much to say. I don't think he and his nephew were very close.'

'Someone killed one of his family, Dakin,' said Cox. 'You know what they say about blood and water. Maybe it's true.'

'Like every other cliché,' I smiled. 'Let me know how it goes.'

I hung up. I made another call straight away; I thought it was the least I could do.

'It's Dakin,' I said when he had answered. 'I thought you should know; the police are coming to see you.'

'I see,' he replied. He sounded tired. 'I suppose I expected them sooner rather than later. Have you told them anything which you have discovered?'

'No.' Come to that, I hadn't told him. I gave him a brief idea of what I knew. It wasn't easy, but I left nothing out, including the drugs. He bore the news with stoicism.

'I suppose I am not surprised,' he said. 'Does that surprise you?'

'You don't pay me to be surprised,' I replied. 'I need to ask you something – about your illness.'

I heard him exhale deeply. I guessed it was a subject he disliked talking about. 'Does it have any bearing on Max's death?'

'Perhaps. It depends if he knew the severity of your condition.'

The answer was like lightning. 'Absolutely not. I may not have respected my nephew – as you may have inferred – but it doesn't mean I wanted to panic him, or upset him unnecessarily.'

Shielding him from the illness, just as he'd shielded him with an alibi for Kilgate. Maybe the lack of respect was not so straightforward.

More importantly, Maxwell Pemberton had no idea that his uncle was waiting for death and that in six months he might well inherit a fortune. That raised a question: what exactly would a disconnected narcotics dealer do to get money? I wondered for a moment about boundless expectations on the point, then terminated the call.

I thought back over the meeting with Cullearn. He had been trying to tell me something; I knew him well enough to recognise that. The question was what; and whatever it was, had I missed it? You should listen harder. Pay attention in class . . .

History. Not my kind, he had said – meaning, not ancient. Modern history had been his favourite subject. That hadn't been autobiographical – it had meant something. And there was something about blood and business. Cox had mentioned blood too. Thicker than water.

Family. Business. Recent history.

It felt as though someone had lifted a burkah from my face, my vision clearing. For a split second, every colour from the grey of the tarmac to the vibrant and enticing lights of city centre bars seemed brighter, more vivid than I had ever recalled them. Seeing the truth, or even a glimmer of it, does that to your perception. I thought back over the last few days, dragging my memory from its big sleep.

I had it all. I just needed proof. For that, I needed Cullearn's modern history. He had known all along what had happened at Kilgate, and from that he probably knew who murdered Maxwell Pemberton. Now I knew that too, but the difference between Cullearn and me was that I needed to see something done about it. To him, it was literally none of his business. It was simply a family matter between siblings. Not a business concern of Cullearn's.

Because blood and business don't mix. That is what he had meant.

After perhaps three hours of research, I found the proof. Cullearn's modern history: meaning contemporary newspaper reports of the Kilgate shooting. On-line newspaper archives were the source, gained for me by a journalist friend of mine called Carl Bonner. He was the sort of man who thought more about his stories than his style. I liked him. He was a fellow pariah in social terms, but his conscience was as wide as his waistline. I met him in a pub which had seen better days, overshadowed by the exhibition centre which used to be a railway station. He handed me an envelope filled with printed web pages, which I scanned briefly. I was looking for a photograph, something tangible.

'Something new on the Kilgate case, I should know about it,' slurred Bonner.

I pushed his pint further to him. 'Enjoy that. There'll be a story, and you'll get your chance to pick on the bones.'

'Yeah, right, Dakin,' he replied. 'And your job's all sugar and spice.'

I had hardly heard him. Maybe he didn't even say it. I can't remember. At the time, I was staring hard at the face of Owen Faldene's murderer. In turn, that meant I was looking at the face of Maxwell Pemberton's killer as well.

I drove in silence to the address he had given me when I called. I barely noticed what sort of house it was, other than that it was sandstone, with an arched porch entrance. The drive was predictably long and gravelled. What I took to be his car was in the drive, a sleek black extension of his own inadequacies. But he had not been inadequate in one sense. Not at all.

He greeted me calmly, and for a moment I wondered whether he had any idea why I was there at all. He led me through to the sitting room. I declined the invitation to sit down, but I accepted his offer of a drink.

'Whisky?' asked Nicholas Burdon.

'No ice.' There was enough of that inside me already.

He handed me the drink as she entered the room. She was dressed casually, but it made her look no less than the controlled sophisticated personality she was. She gave me a brief smile and leaned against the window sill. Burdon poured her a vodka.

'I'm here about Owen Faldene; and about Max,' I said before adding, 'although the two really go together.'

'What are you talking about?' snapped Burdon. 'We had nothing to do with any of it.'

'You've got everything to do with it, Miss Girling. Except your maiden name isn't Girling, is it? You were born Faldene, and you had one brother. Called Owen.'

She made no reply, other than to fix me with her cold stare. I held out the envelope Bonner had given me. 'In here are duplicates of several documents, printouts of various other items; some might interest you, some might not. But your whole history is in here.'

'Not all of it, I'm sure,' she said.

'Three years ago you married an older man called Girling. He was a solicitor too, got you higher up the ladder than you probably deserved. But a year into the marriage, he died and left you a small fortune.' I waved the envelope at her. 'In here is the certificate. Being a widow probably didn't appeal to you. Not a good career prospect. But more importantly, retaining the name Girling hid your connection with the Kilgate shooting.'

'Why would she want to do that?' asked Burdon, rattling his ice in his glass.

He needed it spelling out to him, so I obliged. 'To distance herself from the fact that ten years ago, she put a bullet in her brother's brain. When I asked you about the Kilgate shooting, you said you knew nothing about Max's past. You couldn't have known he was connected to the Kilgate shooting unless that was a lie.'

Burdon snorted. 'You're insane. What proof is there?'

I kept my eyes on her. 'You hinted to me yourself, Mrs Girling,' – she shifted her position at that; she was supposed to – 'that Owen had been evil. Given your determination to succeed and the emotional armour you wear, it's not hard to speculate what that meant.'

She spoke calmly, but with enough acid to scar the air. 'Owen was an emotional deviant.'

There it was. 'He abused you. To him, you were nothing but an attractive girl. Family ties meant nothing to him.'

She gave me a cold smile. 'Deviant.'

'You heard the deal going on downstairs,' I said. 'Cullearn, your brother, and Max. Arms, drugs, dead souls, whatever it was. It didn't matter to you, and maybe it won't matter to anyone now. But hearing your brother making money, trading on lives and knowing what he had in store for you to celebrate his success tipped you over the edge. You shot him down in front of his associates.'

'I barely saw them,' she said. 'I don't know what that says about me.'

'The post-mortem on Owen Faldene suggested that the shot had been fired by a left-handed person. When we met in the bar at Max's flat, Mrs Girling, I noticed that you wear your watch on your right wrist. A common trait in left-handed people.'

Burdon slammed his glass down. 'That is your proof?'

'It was an indication of her guilt, Mr Burdon,' I replied. 'Nothing more. There are photos of the grieving sister in these printouts too. A new haircut and a change in makeup aren't always enough.'

'The press swarmed around us. It was horrible. There were times when I felt like dealing with myself as I had with Owen.'

The rest was easy. 'From the minute it happened, Maxwell Pemberton sheltered you from the crime. Over time, you fell in love with him. Or at least thought you did.'

'Guilt doesn't necessarily cheapen your emotions,' she murmured.

'Fair enough. But you had no idea he was still dealing in drugs. You had no notion that his connection with Doyle Cullearn from five years ago was still raging strongly. Their relationship, just as yours, soured. Suddenly, Max found himself with no money.'

'The bastard manipulated me,' she hissed. 'He was no better than Owen had been. Cruel, insensitive, predatory. The hypocrite had no more guts than Owen had!'

'He blackmailed you about Owen's murder. Given your career prospects and your ambition, everything seemed in danger of collapse. And all because of Max.'

I was watching her knuckles whiten, her grip securing itself around the glass like a martyr to his faith. I wondered whether I should prepare myself for it coming towards me; but it never came.

'There had been an attraction between you and Mr Burdon here,' I continued; 'Max was aware of it. Despite your denials, his concerns were well founded and he was about to hire me to provide the proof. He needed to protect either his pride at losing you to another man, or his investment about Kilgate. However, before he could phone me, you battered his brains in. But you didn't clear his pockets out properly. You left my card behind. It might have been your biggest mistake.'

Burdon stepped in. 'You're wrong, Dakin. Amanda didn't kill Pemberton.'

I turned on him. ' Well, we both know that you'd do anything for her . . . like providing an alibi. But it won't wash, I'm afraid.' I was back in her face. 'Tell me I'm wrong, Amanda! Tell me you didn't do it.'

Burdon was behind me quicker than I might have credited. He spun me round and clasped my chin in a tight grip, his eyes blazing with passion. 'You're right about one thing. I'd do anything for her. Anything!'

Suddenly, I saw how wrong I had been. Not about everything, only about the end. It was like looking at an abstract painting and not seeing the image until you shifted your gaze. The image now was clear. It had been Burdon who battered Max to death, who failed to clear out the pockets of the dead man, and who felt a raging desire to conceal the past. I slowly bent his fingers away from my throat. He put up no resistance.

'I arranged to meet him,' he said. 'At the canal. I wanted him to . . . ' He lost his words for a moment. 'I . . . I just wanted him to leave her alone. I went to meet him to bargain with him, I suppose. Try to convince him to leave Amanda in peace.'

'He didn't listen,' I said.

His gaze was off-centre, recalling the violent details of his crime. 'He taunted me about it. About Amanda and me, about how she would probably knife me at the first failed sexual encounter. You've no idea how revolting that man could be.'

I think I did, but I didn't voice any of it. Instead, I recalled my initial thought about the Pemberton murder. 'It wasn't premeditated. You picked up the first thing to hand: a large rock.'

'I just wanted him to be silenced,' Burdon whispered, his face taut with emotion. I looked back to Amanda Girling, but she was making no move to comfort him. Instead, she stared as though he had revealed himself to be nothing more than a disappointment after all.

'I need to make a phone call,' I said.

Amanda stepped forward. 'Can't you understand? We just wanted to find some sense of peace.'

I gave a small shrug. 'I don't understand anything about you. And all you've found is a lifetime of darkness.'

Burdon sank back into his chair and we stood for a long moment in silence.

In the end, I phoned Cox and told him where I was. He and his men arrived within quarter of an hour, and I left him to do what he had to.

I went back to my office, intending to call Ernest Pemberton, to let him know the outcome of his commission. I got as far as picking up the phone. Maybe it was the anxiety of explaining that his nephew had been involved in the shooting all along, even if he were not guilty of murder. Maybe it was the sour taste the whole thing had left in me. Whatever it was, I replaced the receiver.

For the moment at least.

I thought about Girling and Burdon, about what had happened between them and what was about to happen to them. I felt as though it meant nothing to me, as though it had nothing to do with me. Blood was not business; not for me.

I stood up from my desk, grabbed my jacket, and walked out of the door and into the heart of the city.